Charles Firecat Burnell

W9-DGW-468

AIMLESS

Memoirs of a Life in Transition

outskirts
press

DEDICATION

This is dedicated to my father, for always accepting me, even when I couldn't see it, to my dear sweet Kelly, who will always rest gently in my heart, and to my children. Thank you for giving me the opportunity to be a mother, a father, and an imperfect human being.

A special dedication also to all those who struggle with defining their sexual and gender identity. Remember to live authentically. You are beautiful human beings and a blessing in this universe.

PROLOGUE

A young man leaned back in his chair. He took a deep breath and ran his fingers through his dark wavy hair. Staring at the phone, he rehearsed the words. "I need a counselor for my 6 year old daughter. Do you work with children? You come highly recommended. Do you have evening appointments? When can you get us in?"

He wondered why this was so hard. He asked the empty room why it had to be this way, but nobody answered. The man did not believe in God. The man did not believe in fate. He believed in facts and data. "The fact is, I am now a single parent, a divorcee, with a troubled child, and I can do this. It doesn't mean I've done something wrong. It's just one of those things, part of being a parent, part of being an adult." His words hit the pale yellow wall, falling flat in the warm stale room.

The man struggled with the task at hand, trying to convince himself that he was not a failure. A few minutes passed in silence before he got up from the kitchen table. Walking softly down the hall, he tried to peek into his daughter's room without alerting her attention.

Firecat had worked hard to remove all the blankets and sheets from the bed. Sitting inside her magic fort, she whispered. The shadow nestled tightly in magic castle and listened intently as she wove ribbons of fantasy with her words. Suddenly she stopped telling her story and froze.

"Ssh. The scary daddy-man is coming."

The young father peeked into his daughters room to find her sitting in the middle of her bedroom. The precocious little girl had dragged all the bedding into a heaping pile of fabric. "Firecat? You doing okay kid?" He inquired, without stepping over the threshold.

The mound of fabric moved slightly and responded, "Yes Daddy. I am a Wizard and this is my magic castle!"

The man chuckled. "Okay. I was just checking on you." He marveled at how much fabric she had managed to locate. He identified towels, curtains, blankets and sheets that he'd not seen in years. "I'm just going to go out in the yard for a little while. You're going to be okay, right? You know how to find me if you need me, okay?"

"Yes Daddy. I'm fine. I'm just playing." The pile shifted slightly revealing his bathrobe in the mound. He started to speak, but thought better of it. He headed back down the hall toward the kitchen, stopping briefly at the linen closet. Opening the doors quickly revealed the answer to the mystery of the fabric castle. He looked up and chuckled again, noticing how pristine the upper shelves appeared compared to the rest of the closet.

Arriving back in the kitchen, the man immediately went back to the table. He sat down, picked up the phone, dialed the number, and waited for the ring tone. He focused on arranging a pencil and notepad in front of him while the phone rang. Soon a pleasant voice responded on the other end of the line. The soothing voice calmed the man's anxiety just enough to help him get through the phone call. Feeling accomplished, he hung up the receiver, took another deep breath, and got up from the kitchen table. In his mind a secretary checked off a box on a task list.

Leaving the kitchen table once more, the man opened

the sliding glass doors onto the back porch. He stepped into the back yard and reached into his breast pocket for a crumpled pack of Camels. Lighting a cigarette, he inhaled, exhaled, and began surveying his yard. In the back office of his mind, the secretary added a Tuesday evening appointment to his calendar for the next 24 months. Another task had been accomplished.

⸺⊸«◉»⊷⸺

The following week, Cat sat on soft brown carpet, playing with a plastic castle. Dad had decided that his daughter would benefit from meeting with a counselor. His peers had insisted that it was 'what any responsible parent would do.'

Cat didn't understand exactly why she was there, but she was pretty sure it had something to do with divorce. She remained silent for at least ten minutes into the first meeting. *If he thinks that this is going to make up for him making my mom leave, he's stupid. But I don't care because there are cool toys here. How come he never buys me cool toys like this?* A woman sat in a comfortable chair, chatting at the little girl about various toys and where they were stored in the room. *Is this what a counselor looks like?*

At first Cat was overwhelmed with the many choices of toys. There were big cardboard blocks, like at her Uncle's house. There were dolls, dress up clothes, a little kitchen, and best of all, there was the plastic castle set. Each time she worked on it, she was able to build it a little more. The counselor let her put it away without taking apart her progress, encouraging her to keep working on building it slowly because it was 'good to have goals that we work toward'.

A few weeks passed and the child began to feel comfortable with the counseling sessions. The counselor sensed that a bond had begun to form and began asking a little more direct questions. *Why does she want to know this stuff? Its kind of weird.* Cat was a little uncomfortable when the counselor asked silly questions sometimes, but it was nice to have someone actually care about her. *Mama used to listen to me. Maybe this woman cares about me?* The counselor sensed a shift in the child.

"It's going to be summer soon." The counselor began. "Are you excited?"

"I don't know. I like the warm weather. I wonder if I will get to see my mom this summer?" The child responded, examining the inside seam of a cow puppet.

"What did you do last summer?" The counselor asked, closely watching the way the child moved in the chair as she responded.

"I was in a Summer Camp last Summer." Cat answered, shifting in her seat. A creeping tingle moved slowly from her foot up the back of her calf. "It was okay I guess." She seemed to forget what she was saying and began vigorously rubbing her feet, dropping the puppet on the floor.

"You want to tell me about it?" The counselor responded, scribbling something into the notebook on her lap.

"I had a friend. He was really nice to me. But then he went away." The little girl responded, getting up, picking up the puppet, and walking to the toy chest. She dropped the puppet into the chest, and began digging through the deep wooden box for something new. "Everyone was mean to me. I didn't like summer camp. Nobody else was nice to me. He was my special friend, but then he went away.

Cat stopped talking. She took a deep breath, closed her eyes, and thrust her hand into the chest to grab a random toy. *I don't like this conversation. Let's talk about something else.*

The counselor frowned. "I'm sorry the girls were mean to you."

Cat exhaled and turned around holding a plastic cow figurine. "Oh the girls weren't mean to me. But they were kind of boring."

The counselor looked confused. "Who was mean to you?"

Cat explained that the girls were boring because they didn't want to play in the dirt, or climb trees, or do anything fun. The girls didn't want to play fun games and the boys wouldn't play with her because she was a girl. "It doesn't make any sense! I'm just like them! My mom says we're all the same and we are all special and there aren't 'boy games' and 'girl games,' there's just 'kid games' and 'grown-up games.'" She threw the cow into the toy chest.

The counselor made a note in her book before tucking it neatly away. "Well, your mom is right. But,its not exactly like that." She looked at the wide-eyed girl who'd stopped at her feet.

Cat shared a story about how the big boy at Summer Camp had kissed her. She told the counselor how she felt 'like magic butterflies were lifting her up' when she kissed the older boy. The counselor told Cat that the boy was bad, for kissing her. "But don't worry honey. That doesn't make you a bad girl."

The woman was concerned. The little girl posed a strange challenge. She made notes in a small notebook, tucking it away in the chair as quickly as she had produced it. She tried to explain to the little girl that liking boys was normal. She wanted to help her to understand that it was a 'grown-up feeling' that would make more sense when she was older. "Do you want me to help you understand?" The little girl nodded, as tiny tears hid behind a small barricade of dirty blond bangs.

Cat shared stories about trying to play with boys at school. The boys at school made fun of her because of her name. The boys in her neighborhood made fun of her for being a girl. The girls made fun of her for not being a real girl. "I don't understand. Why does there have to be a difference? Even the neighbor boy won't play with me now because we don't have the same private parts. Its just stupid." She was mad at the whole world and her counselor seemed to be the only person that truly cared.

The counselor pulled an over-sized hardbound book off the shelf above her desk. "Would you like me to help you understand the difference between boys and girls?" The counselor asked the teary child. "Maybe this book can help us. Come on. Let's sit down on the pillows and go through it together." She moved from her chair to the floor pillows.

The little girl looked at the large book quizzically. "It's a picture book about grown-up girls and boys, of men and women." the counselor responded, as she motioned for Cat to sit down on the floor pillows at her side. As she turned the pages, Cat's eyes widened to observe black and white frames of naked people, displayed on the pages of the big book. "This is what you will grow up to look like." The counselor pointed at a woman lying on the page without clothes, plump breasts and soft curves turned a key inside Cat's tummy and she felt a strange discomfort and pleasure.

Weeks turned into months and Cat looked forward to her Tuesday evenings with the counselor. At first she looked forward to the evenings because of the toys. By summer time, she had lost interest in most of the toys. She was more interested in going to visit with her grown-up counselor friend.

She still didn't understand exactly why she was there, but it was nice to have someone to talk with about the things that really bothered her, and she found it strangely thrilling to go through the big book of nakedness every week while they talked.

The counselor assured Cat that she would start to feel more like a girl when her body started changing from a kid to a grown-up. She said that in the meantime, it was perfectly fine to do all the 'boy' things. "Just don't be surprised when you find yourself caring what boys think."

Cat responded smartly, "I don't care what anybody thinks. I'm just like them. And if they don't know it, they're just stupid."

The counselor corrected the child, "Well, no honey. You are not just like them. You don't have a penis like this, see?" She pointed to picture in the book. She turned the pages, settling on a photograph that showed a clear picture of a woman's genitals. "This is what your private parts will look like when you grow up. See, no penis." But its okay, its supposed to be this way."

AUTHOR'S INTRODUCTION

Memoirs. Where do you begin? I think most biogra-phies start at birth, or shortly before. I really don't remember that far. Certainly not enough to write about it. This is not an attempt at a biography anyway. What I am sharing with you is a story woven from my memories and reflections of the experiences that I have been blessed to have been conscious for. No matter how uncomfortable a memory may be, recalling these experiences has helped my transition, as an artist, as a man, and as a human being.

Everything that I recall really happened, or more accu-rately, I really perceived as happening. Perception and reali-ty walk a fine tightrope with each other. Each one take turns being the rope and the walker, with an occasional umbrella thrown in for balance from time to time. Rather than chang-ing all the names, I have chosen to not include last names, as some names are very common. I have changed names al-together in some instances. I have left my names true to my life as my name has had a direct impact on my experiences and changing it would change the story too much.

If you have crossed my path and find yourself in the sto-ry, consider it a compliment. Our interaction contributed to my transition. Thank you for being in my life. I should also point out that I am not sharing all of the personal details of my relationships with other people. I don't want to give away a story that is somebody else's to tell. There are so many memories that have had a direct impact on the way I have learned to better understand myself, I found it necessary not to include all the details.

The years I spent living with my father provided a solid foundation of structure. He tried to teach his daughter many basic life skills about living as an adult in American society. Economics, the stock market, the voting system, following the law and the repercussions of not doing so, I learned how to do my own dishes and the importance of wiping down the counter in the kitchen and how to do your own laundry. I even learned how to darn my own socks from my dad!

The memories may be blurry and at times more of a conglomerate mess of feelings. Still they have proven to be monumentally important to me, when defining myself as a man and a father. Growing past the adolescent years, and becoming a parent catapulted me forward into a stage of repression and growth very different than what the previous decade had been for me. As a parent I have recalled many memories of my childhood, and have found amusement in the discovery of how much I learned from my father.

Middle School was yet another kind of transition. As is customary in our modern American society, the human species must be thrown together in a virtual cage and forced to interact under the strictest circumstances. The idea is as follows: being a vital time of brain growth, it is the prime time to perform ritual data-dumps in the computers that are the brains of the captive teens. This is promoted as an effective way to systematically program all the teens. They must be prepared for their roles as adults in a manner that supports the economic and social structure of the American culture, or they won't be able to survive.

It is arrogant to believe that instructors can effectively

block the confusing sexuality and gender role identity issues that are being aroused by the mix of bad media programming and raised hormone levels in an enclosed classroom. It would have been much more effective if they had actually taken the time to help us understand what was going on and how to navigate it in a healthy way. This is a natural time for the human to be continually distracted by the rage of pubescent hormones. Why is it considered perfectly acceptable to force the male and female species together in a cage for several hours per day?

My adolescence is an important point of reference for me. This stage represents a line of memory. My adolescent rebellion really started when I realized that moving in with my mother might actually be able to happen. When I became a teenager reality sort of tilted sideways a little. I couldn't trust anyone. Yet, I wanted to be able to trust everyone. Everything was a contradiction. Everything felt like I was watching someone else's life happening in front of me every day. It feels like drawing from a past life when I recall events from my childhood and being a young mother. Whereas when I recall memories from adolescence, it feels like I'm remembering a movie of someone else's experiences altogether.

Born in an apparently female body, July 12, 1974, I was given the name Firecat Starr Burnell. That really doesn't feel like the beginning. When I began consciously and intentionally transitioning from female to male really feels more like the beginning. But truly, there is no beginning and there is no end. We have so many starting points within our cycles. Unique pivotal points frame our life experiences. Some of our stories are so drastically different from other parts of our lives that they seem to take on their own identities.

The process of transitioning forced me to re-examine

my life one memory at a time. As pieces fell together, they slowly began forming the picture that I now look at when I view all that has been my life. So far.

Part One

Part One

Chapter 1

SUBURBAN LIFE

The family finally moved into their first nice house. It was the first time her Dad was ever able to buy a house. *We can paint the walls and put up pictures because it isn't a rental!* They moved into the house on Third Street during the Fourth Grade Winter Break. Starting a new school mid-year was awkward. Dad had made a point to announce, upon their arrival, that this was a time for 'New Beginnings' and that we could all just 'put our past behind us.' Cat couldn't remember much before fourth grade. Living in Sonoma had been so long ago it felt like a dream, and living in Oakland had been a nightmare. She welcomed the opportunity for a fresh start and was inspired by her father's enthusiasm.

Cat was shy, but persistent. Thankful the opportunity for the chance to make new friends, she pushed her comfort zone, reaching out to kids riding their bikes on her block. For a little while, she thought she was making a couple of friends in the neighborhood, but was disappointed when friendships didn't continue onto the school grounds. Within six months, most of the neighborhood kids regularly avoided her, or pretended she didn't exist.

Cat felt awkward and angry. She tried to make friends

with boys and they pushed her away. Girls tried to make friends with her and she pushed them away. Her erratic behavior fueled the adolescent fury, encouraging classmates to make fun of her. Peer exclusion, and her confused reactions to it, provided perfect conditions to covertly brew a storm of depression that remained hidden beyond the horizon. In the evening, when the sun set, and her Dad had not yet returned home, the storm hovered over their house, raining silent misery in her bedroom.

Cat loved their new home, but she hated the town. *All these suburban kids are mean. I don't belong here. But where do I belong?* Springtime felt like it moved slowly and yet, passed in the blink of an eye. The days seemed to Cat a long string of the same day repeating itself. Like Chinese Water Torture, the days were a slow constant tapping on the inside of her skull, that in times provided a melancholy sort of comfort. But most of the time, it distracted her just enough to ensure that nothing really made much sense. Finally, the end of the school year arrived.

⸺⸺«◊»⸺⸺

It was a huge relief when June arrived. The last day of school would be coming soon! Cat lived for the Summer Break. She loved laying in the sun, letting the warm light soak into her skin. She got to visit her mother more during Summer. She got to sleep more. Best of all, this Summer, Dad agreed to sign her up for a Summer program. She would have to take two buses to reach the program in this new town. She reveled in the idea that she would have the freedom to roam on the public bus system. Still, more alone time meant that she spent more time wishing she had more friends. Carrie was the only friendship she had made that continued past the school yard. *But she has lots of friends. She'll probably be too busy to hang out with me anyway.*

Cat had been excited about choosing her classes. She liked the idea of being able to have the opportunity to learn, without the stress of a looming report card, but when it came down to choosing classes, few choices had interested her. Sitting at the dining room table, she reviewed her summer schedule. Registration had been submitted in April. Now in June, she was pleased to see that she had gotten all her first picks. She was most excited about the class entitled 'Bugs and Botany'.

Dad had suggested that she should sign up for a home economics class. He reminded her, "If you want to be able to cook, you have to learn how to do it properly." *Yeah. But what you don't know is that I already know how to cook. I cook all the time. I just clean it up before you get home. Hah!* In an effort to gain official access to the kitchen at home, Cat agreed.

A drawing class made three, and her program was full. Classes met Tuesday, Wednesday, and Thursday every week for six weeks, skipping the week of Independence Day. The drawing class was easy. She would get to be creative!

The first day, Cat entered the Home Economics class, she replayed her father's words in her head. *Remember, if my Dad's girlfriend, Margaret, is ever going to let me make something other than salad, I have to take this class.* The classroom full of girls made her nervous. None of them approached her. Feeling anxious, she located a comfortable chair in the corner to sit by herself. Pulling a book out of her backpack, she accepted her exclusion with relief and silence.

Each morning the instructor would quietly invite Cat to

engage in the activity of the day. Cat would hover in the back of the group briefly, and then retreat to the safety of her book. The instructor, busy with the bubbling girls, quickly forgot the silent student, while Isaac Asimov led Cat into a daydream of possible futures.

Next she went into the art class, where she was able to participate without anxiety. She could do no wrong. Everything was acceptable. Everyone enjoyed themselves so much, they never took the time to make fun of her, or bother her. She didn't make any friends, but she felt accepted. Then her third class was Bugs and Botany.

Bugs and Botany was the highlight of Cat's Summer program. When she arrived the first day, she noticed right away that she was the only girl in the class. *They don't know what they're missing! Science is so cool!* The boys in the class teased her at first. She brushed their comments off easily, with casual jokes and rowdy behavior. By the second week of the program, the whole class had accepted Cat as one of them.

After the morning classes let out, Cat had six hours before Dad was expected home from work and eight hours before it got dark. She spent the afternoons riding different bus lines, just to kill time. Sitting in the back of the bus, she watched people come and go. Eventually, she would get hungry and need to go to the bathroom. Getting on the bus that would take her back home, her head leaned against the window as her thoughts floated above and behind. Somewhere above the moving cityscape, her sadness and daydreams wrestled to form rain clouds that boldly insisted on ushering in yet another new school year

Cat barreled through fifth grade in nervous anticipation of what social challenges Middle School was bound to present. Some of the girls in school were starting to get breasts, and wear make-up. Cat mostly ignored her own breasts, except during the most private discussions when visiting Carrie. When she was at home on the weekend, Cat stayed locked away in her room, safe from all the stress of prying questions and confusing expectations.

The scratchy sound of Anne Murray's voice rose from the small record player, spinning next to Cat, on the brown shag carpet. The floor was littered with recycled paper, covered with her repeated attempts to perfect the most romantic handwriting she could imagine. Clear distinct paths had been cleared, leading to the center where she sat. As the pencil moved across the paper, curves began to take shape. A girl smiled back at the young artist.

The walls around Cat's daydream were shattered. Knocking on her bedroom door brought her attention to the sound of the needle scratching the end of the record. "Be out in a minute!"She responded, tossing the pad and pencil onto a pile of loose papers. She removed the needle from the 45, removed the record from the center pin and searched for it's sleeve. She quickly gave up, leaving it nestled on a pile of loftily signed paper. She unplugged and closed the suitcase turntable and set it carefully next to the records. *Now I won't step on it.*

Cat entered the dining room in her pajamas to find Dad sitting at the table with coffee and a look of determination. She readied herself for a list of complaints and subsequent chores. *I'm sure Margaret has said something bad about me again. I knew I should have gotten dressed early and left before he got up.* "Good morning." She greeted him as she sat down, and then remained silent.

"Have you eaten?" He asked, in response.

"No. I mean, I had a bowl of cereal." She waved her left hand in the air as she spoke. "But that was hours ago. I could totally eat again."

"Okay. Good." Dad's look softened slightly. "Go get dressed, and we can go out to eat." He paused, as she got up. Then, as she started down the hall toward the bedroom, he added. "And then, we'll go Bra shopping." Cat stopped and spun around to look at her father.

"Why?" Flushed and shaking, she tried to hide her fear. She took a deep breath before beginning to protest. "I don't need one Dad." Her protest was met firmly with the brick wall that was her father. Something about his stoic silence frightened her. She never knew what to expect, and therefore there was no way to prepare for it.

She turned back around in defeat and stomped down the hall to the bedroom. Slamming the door behind her, she dismissed the record player and instead opted for the radio. Spinning the dial until she found the perfect song, she turned up the music and proceeded to rant about how unfair life was while digging through her clothes. By the next song, the ranting had subsided and she was singing along. By the end of the third song, she had put on her shoes, and was turning the radio off.

Dad tried to talk to Cat while they drove to breakfast at Lyons. Cat was uncomfortable with Dad taking her shopping for her first bra. *Shouldn't this be a thing Mom does with me?* She didn't know what to say, so she opted for silence. Dad was matter-of-fact about the whole thing, which irritated her more. *It's not so simple. You just don't understand. I don't even want to have breasts. This is all just stupid.*

At breakfast, Cat had a hard time choosing from the menu. At first, going to breakfast had sounded great, but now nothing sounded good. Dad began to show irritation, though he tried to be patient. Finally, she settled on French Toast and the waitress took their menus with a smile. Before she left the table, Dad added, "I think the young lady would also like a Hot Chocolate." He looked at Cat with a smile and a nod. "With all the whipped cream, right?" Cat nodded in agreement without looking up from the table.

"I know you don't like this." Dad began again, after the waitress had departed. "But the fact of the matter is, you're going to need one eventually. A training bra is really just so you can get used to wearing one." He paused. "For when it really matters."

Cat drew circles on the table with her finger. *But I don't want it to happen eventually. I'm not pretty like the other girls. I just want to be invisible.* Dad's voice continued, but the child wasn't listening. Instead, her thoughts were in Carrie's bathroom. The two girls, were standing in front of the mirror, comparing their chests. The waitress returned to the table and Cat looked up to see a small mountain of whipped cream sitting at eye level in front of her.

Once the food arrived, Dad stopped talking. After they finished eating and left the restaurant, he did not pick up his lecture. At a loss for words, he could tell that his daughter was struggling. Hiding his frustration, he showed his support by purchasing not one, but three bras for Cat. She started by picking the smallest, plainest sports bra she could locate. He insisted that she ought to have a few. "You don't want to have to do laundry every day, do you?" Glad when the event was over, Cat was quick to retreat to her bedroom and hide the evidence.

Bothered by how much more Cat began to notice girls, she battled the confusion by trying to mimic the boys she wanted to befriend. She tried harder to engage with the boys on the playground during recess. *It all seems entirely too complicated! What's worse? Now the boys are acting weird around me!* Before, she had been mainly interested in playing boy games, like chase and ball, climbing trees and having wars. She'd gotten irritated when they were distracted by girls. Now, she too was getting distracted and she couldn't explain it. She tried to assert her self control by getting rowdy at school, urging the boys to wrestle and fight with her. It became a running joke among her classmates, that she was just "a boy that looked like a girl", and any "real guy" should be able to fight her.

There was a really cute guy that seemed to make his way through the year by dating most of the popular girls in fifth grade. Cat secretly had a crush on him, which irritated her. They were not friends outside of school, and he had absolutely no interest in dating her. All the other boys stood in his shadow, and she pushed him harder than she pushed the other boys. He responded positively, treating her the same as he treated the other boys. She joked with him about her gender status, and playfully, he affirmed her. With his help, she developed the reputation of being a "girl shaped boy".

While Dad could see that Cat was getting older, and didn't really need 'childcare' any more, he also didn't want her to have enough free time to get into trouble. He insisted that she sign up for Summer School again. This time around,

---

she wasn't interested in any of the class choices, completing her registration by mindlessly checking off choices with little intention of actually going.

She skipped class once the first week, opting to hang out in the park with Carrie. She found out quickly that, although there were no reports cards, attendance was still mandatory. The corresponding lecture from Dad brewed a cloud that followed Cat to class for the duration of the program. She refused to pay attention in class, and instead sat in the back row making jokes.

Soon after starting the summer program, she recognized a guy from her fifth grade classroom. *There's JR! He always refused to acknowledge me as a guy!* She remembered him saying, "gentlemen don't hit ladies". That had totally irritated her. *I am not a lady. I don't feel like a lady. I don't even feel like a girl. What am I supposed to feel like?* Wrapped in self-judgment, the sight of JR chiseled away at what little self-esteem she had built up. She resented him for not acknowledging her, for reminding Cat of her femaleness. She had grown to hate him.

When JR appeared in Summer School, she decided this would give her the perfect opportunity to get him to fight her. Since it wasn't on school grounds Cat wouldn't get in trouble. She devised a plan. *Premeditated humiliation. He humiliated me by refusing to fight me in front of everybody in our class.* She planned all the details of his revenge. *Now I get to humiliate him by making him go home and tell his parents that he got beat by a girl.*

Cat openly challenged him in the mornings. Rushing out at the end of class every day, she hung around the front lawn, watching for JR. Determined she was going to beat him up, she scanned the crowd of kids as they poured out and got picked up or wandered down to the bus stop.

Somehow, he always seemed to escape her. After everyone was gone, she would retreat to the bus stop, defeated.

Weekdays Cat spent roaming all over the Central County with the freedom of a Summer Bus Pass. She hung out with her best friend Carrie, spending nights at her place often. They spent long nights dreaming out loud about what their futures would hold, playing penny poker, sneaking beers, and talking in the dark. Cat would share stories about all the things she would see and do when visiting her mom in Berkeley on the weekends.

⸺ ⸺ ((◉)) ⸺ ⸺

By the end of July, Summer School was over and Cat went to spend August with her mom. Immersed in the counterculture that revolved in and out of her mother's home and life, August was like a Disneyland vacation on drugs in flashback paradise with hippies, freaks, school buses, and motorbikes. Cat began to believe that if she could somehow move in with her mom, it would be like this forever.

Grateful Dead Tour brought tons of Dead Heads to Berkeley. When the Grateful Dead played in Berkeley, Telegraph Ave filled up with hippies and freaks. It was like a circus had come to town. Cat aspired to run off and join them. She was nervous talking with them, and excited when she got to hang out with them at Mom's house. The flamboyant behavior and philosophical attitudes merged to create an appealing discord.

Late in August, Mom loaded Cat up into the back of a truck with a bunch of sleeping bags and backpacks. They drove for hours and hours. She liked riding in the back of the truck. It was really windy so she couldn't sit up without her hair flying wildly about in her eyes. She spent a while sitting up, hair firmly tucked into a hooded sweatshirt, buried under the piles of bedding. It was fun to peek out and watch the world fly behind them.

It didn't take her long to fall asleep. Whenever she woke up they were in a different place. Eventually, they arrived. She didn't completely understand where they were going or what the day would include. The adventure of the unknown was a little overwhelming in her sleepy and disoriented state. Bustling cars and crowds of people that blurred in and out of her perception, soon began to take form.

Saturday, August 24th, 1985, Boreal Ridge felt like the hottest place on earth. Making their way through the crowds, Mom and her friends, loaded with bags and blankets, dragged Cat up the bright hillside. *There are so many people!* What felt like hours passed as they tried to find an empty space for their group to set up. Eventually, they stopped and laid out their blankets. She immediately began taking food out. Her logic said it was picnic time. Mom didn't seem to mind. She unpacked snacks, colored pencils and paper, and soft blankets, positioning herself in the middle of it all.

People came and went. Drums were played. People were nice to each other in every direction around the child. The more she sat and sleepily soaked up her surroundings, the more euphoric they became. Cat moved in and out of her body, floating above the crowd. She watched as time seemed to take a break in the shadows of the woods on either side of the great crowd of people.

The day passed extraordinarily slow. Music played. People danced. Cat danced too. They were all together weaving in and out and around each other. Children and adults. Nobody judged anyone. Everyone was happy, blissful, exuding love. She slipped in and out of reality as the day progressed. By the time the sun set behind the stage at the bottom of the hill, Cat felt like she had been on an adventure a lifetime long, and all she wanted to do was find a cozy place to go to sleep.

Leaving the concert, was a sleepy, grumpy, muddled journey through thick crowds of other sleepy people. Excited, dancing, and half dreaming, they poured down the hill into the parking lot. Once back at the truck, Cat found herself buried back under the blankets again. Asleep before the truck made it out of the parking lot, the world of noisy cars and dusty roads disappeared. When she awoke, they were turning around in the middle of nowhere. She heard someone say "We're lost" and "There's supposed to be a campground." Tucking herself back under a sleeping bag, the voices quickly faded.

Waking up, Cat found herself in a tent by a beautiful river. The early morning was misty and quiet. A stark contrast to the loud dusty river of people gurgling through the ebb and flow of the previous evening's concert, the Yuba River was seemingly silent. Quietly, she made her way down a path that led to a great slab of cement. The slab appeared alien in the otherwise untouched landscape. It sat at the edge of the river, offering a wide, flat area from which one could peer down into the water almost a third of the way across.

Cat crouched down to listen to the water and dip her fingers in the current. Fish moved downstream so naturally, meeting no resistance from the outside world. The fish and the water, the smooth rocks covered with algae beneath the surface, were all exactly where they should be. The only thing unnatural was the great cement slab.

Traveling up the path following the river, Cat found more

great cement slabs. *They looked so out of place.* Wondering how they got there, she recognized these as strange and different in the landscape. She was reminded of how much she did not want to go back to the reality of suburbia. *I don't want to go back to Dad's house. I want to stay here in this magical paradise forever.* Sure that Middle School would be a terrifying experience of judgment and peer rejection, she tried to soak up every second. Breathing in deeply she thought for a moment, if she believed hard enough, she just might be able to stop time.

Slowly other people in the group began to wake up. The smell of campfire and smoky coffee always gave her a good feeling. *The smells and sounds of happy people enjoying themselves in paradise feels wonderful. Why can't I feel this carefree when I'm with Dad?* As more people emerged from tents, she became aware of the presence of more people than had traveled in the truck, where she'd fallen asleep the evening before. Cat recognized many of them as her mom's friends, but she didn't see Mom. *Maybe I fell asleep in somebody else's truck? I'm on a great adventure! No longer being tracked by my parents!*

Cat crept carefully up the path toward the tent from which she had first emerged. Keeping her eyes toward the ground, she took interest in bugs and plants along the path, making sure not to brush against any poison oak. When she reached the tent, her mother appeared nearby.

———⟫⟨⟪———

People were not getting dressed. Cat suddenly felt very uncomfortable and awkward. *How did I not notice this before?* Everyone was naked, or only partly clothed. They seemed only to be concerned about comfort. The rules of the outside world did not apply here in this place. *Time does not seem to have any effect on this world. Beautiful.* She looked down, was ashamed of her own body. *They look so happy. What am I doing wrong?*

The silent child observed, searching for clues to some undefined secret. *How can they sit comfortably, being openly naked? Where is their shame?* She watched people free of shame, free of the guilt of non-conforming. She wanted to feel that freedom. She wanted to absorb their self assurance. She wanted to feel good about herself.

The last big weekend trip before Cat's return to Dad's house for the new school year, she tasted every last breath, as if it were her last breath. Every drop of water, she expected to be the last drop she would ever feel on her parched skin in the destitute lifescape that reality was inevitably bound to throw at her. The last thing she wanted to do was go back to public school. She watched the shameless people playing on the rocks, in and out of the water. *What do they know that I don't? Am I missing something? I'm uncomfortable and afraid. None of them look like they are uncomfortable with themselves. I feel like an alien in my own skin. I don't understand why.*

Mom could see that her daughter was anxious. She tried to assure the child, "Cat, you can wear as few or as many clothes as you like. It's completely up to you." Cat hugged her mother.

"Thank you for bringing me on this trip, Mama. Its really beautiful here." Cat walked to a nearby picnic bench and sat down. *She's trying to be supportive in her own way, but she doesn't get it either.* "So what's there to eat?" Mom responded by dipping into a nearby tent and emerging with a brown grocery sack. Mom placed the sack on the picnic table and began pulling out a loaf of french bread. "Wait-" Cat got up, putting her hands in the air in front of her. "We need to put a cloth on the table first!"

Mother and child covered the picnic table with an old sheet that had been tie-dyed years ago. Pulling the contents out of the sack, they spread out an assortment of fruit, bread, and cheese. Once Cat had gotten settled down eating, her mother wandered up the path to a neighboring camp. When she returned, she carried a steaming hot cup of tea. "It took some searching, but I found hot water. They have coffee if you want some." She said, pointing up a path illuminated by small patches of morning sun.

Cat nodded and went back to picking at the grapes in front of her. Clenching her fingernails together tightly, she pulled the tiny tendrils of grape skin off the end of the stem. *She means well. But she doesn't understand. She wouldn't get it. I don't even understand. I'm just confused.* The child sought some point of reference, but all Mom had given was an open answer.

In an effort to have fun like the people around her, Cat opted for partial clothes. They came and went throughout the day as her anxiety waxed and waned. Cat explored different pools, and kept herself just far enough from the group to isolate herself. Being able to observe, without feeling like she had to interact felt safe. And lonely. She memorized the texture of every moss covered rock. There were so many shades of green and gray and brown. Afraid the fish would nip at her legs, she took special precautions to keep from swimming with the fish.

Cat spent the late afternoon watching wistfully as the men and women frolicked like children in the sun and water. The slabs of cement peppered along the riverbed helped to create a series of pools. Some pools were deeper and cooler, some were shallow and warm. Waterfalls connected the pools. Various sizes and lengths broke up the visage like puzzle pieces. She watched the pieces move around and back again, her view scrambling itself as she moved in and out of her body.

In that moment, in that place, Firecat felt safe and could see so much more from the air. Cat perched on rocks overlooking sun splashed windows into their world. *Fish have no shame. They are in their own element. I want to find a place where I can feel that natural. I want to be somewhere I feel at home, comfortable, and in my own environment.* She left her body lying in the sun on the rocks while she floated above the scene. She felt secure in the freedom that came with floating above everyone, unseen, untouchable.

Chapter 2

CARRIE

The only lasting friendship that survived Elementary School was Carrie. Unfortunately, Carrie would not be going to school with Cat any longer. Without the security of having her best friend by her side, she tried to focus on the positive opportunity of a new school. Middle School offered a fresh start, an opportunity to make new friends with people that didn't have preconceived notions about her. *Maybe I can make new friends with people that will like me with all my weirdness.* She decided that she would reinvent herself.

The first day of middle school Cat showed up wearing a denim mini skirt and a bow in her hair. She had been watching MTV for a couple of years. She had been trying to figure out what was cool and what was not. She saw Madonna, and thought the performer was super cool. *She looks like she makes her own outfits from stuff at the thrift store the way Mom always does. Only Madonna is younger and famous. Of course she's cool! Everyone likes her!* Cat tried to copy her style, hoping it would make people like her. It didn't work. She got made fun of for being a "faker". She was pretending to be something she was not, and it showed terribly.

The first two new friends were Jennifer and Marie. The three girls gravitated toward each other. Finding camaraderie in their misery, they hung out in the grass during the lunch hour. Sometimes they walked around. Gradually, others joined them. *I wonder if I'm an odd friend to have. I'm so manic. My memories are hazy and sort of mixed together. It's really hard for me to remember much of anything but confusion and loneliness. I really want to run away from everything, especially myself. I have no idea why, and it's so frustrating. What do they see in me?*

Jennifer was tall and beautiful with long straight hair. She hid her striking features behind her awkwardness and her very large glasses. She was smart, always did her homework, and got straight 'A's. Cat liked that Jennifer didn't show off how smart she was. *I could get good grades if I really try, but I get so bored! There are too many distractions. Can't I just run away and join the hippie circus?* But when other kids teased Jennifer for being so smart, Cat stood up to them and protected her.

Marie was a bigger girl, also with very large glasses. She got poor grades and had a more difficult time with academics. Jennifer never judged Marie for their differences. Cat didn't talk about boys much with Jennifer and Marie. They talked about bands they liked and especially Duran Duran.

Marie was totally in love with Nick Rhodes. She wore a cool hat just like him and a big trench coat. They mostly joked about surface things. Cat was supportive when Marie bared her misery. Still, she remained guarded, hesitant to really open up. When they asked her random questions, she always had an answer that made her friends feel better. Despite the fact that her new friends seemed pleased by her help, Cat couldn't see any value in herself.

Jennifer was in some of Cat's classes. They studied

together after school sometimes. They were even assigned as partners for class projects. She was uncomfortable and amazed at how nice Jennifer was to her. For the first time ever, Cat felt like she had more than one friend.

———※《◉》※———

Cat stayed friends with Carrie, despite the fact that their parents had enrolled them in different Middle Schools. Dad had chosen to put Cat in a new Middle School. It was supposed to be better because it was next to the High School and across the street from the Community College. It was a longer bus ride. There was always a crowd of dropouts and drug dealers hanging out near campus.

Cat saw Carrie sometimes after school, but mostly just on the weekends when she wasn't visiting her mom. The change in social life felt different for her, almost like a loss. In elementary school, the two of them had spent almost every day together. They had included one another in all of their plans. Now they were each making friends with other people from their separate schools. Often when Cat would call Carrie, she'd be hanging out with other girls. Cat would leave a message, and not get a call back all weekend, to find out later Carrie had just been 'so busy' hanging out with other girls that she never got around to calling back.

Cat felt like she had lost her first love. Carrie was the only person she felt comfortable talking openly with. They had met the first school day after Cat's family moved to Walnut Creek. The two had become pretty close friends in fourth and fifth grade. They rode bikes together and played outside. They got dirty and played like boys. They played with dolls and stuffed animals like girls. They played poker with pennies. They played dress up. It didn't matter who Cat was, no matter what, Carrie was her friend. She had developed a huge crush on Carrie. They were the best of friends for a while.

—— ❧ ——

Sometime in fifth grade I realized I had a crush on Carrie. I wanted so badly to ask her to be my girlfriend, but I didn't know how to say it. If I was a boy, I could tell her that I like-like her, but then she probably wouldn't be hanging out with me then, because she's better than any boy. She was my best friend. I felt terrible about myself and still I could be myself around her and she still liked me. She made me feel really good. I wasn't brave enough to bring up that conversation. I was terrified she would never speak to me again and I didn't want that. I would feel so lonely if she wasn't my friend.

So instead, I asked her, with shuffling feet, if she would still be my friend if I didn't just like guys. She laughed at me and said "Of course, you goofball! I will always be your friend." That was all I had. I got that far and couldn't ask any more. At least we're still friends. That was the closest I could get to telling her that I loved her.

—— ❧ ——

Cat was jealous of the other girls that got more of Carrie's time and attention. She was jealous of the boys that

Carrie dated, when that happened. Always critical of them in her mind, sometimes she'd say things like, "That guy is an asshole. I'd make a better boyfriend than that!" or "What do you see in him?" She didn't like the company Carrie kept and worried her new friends would be bad news.

The two would talk on the phone more than they saw each other. Spring fever set in, and the two made plans to hang out. Friday after school, Cat came straight home. She emptied her backpack of all the school stuff to make room for clothes. She left a note on the fridge for Dad, 'Spending the night at Carrie's', and headed over to Carrie's house with a backpack full for the weekend. They'd planned to spend the entire weekend together. Then, when she arrived, she learned that Carrie had made plans with her new friends as well.

Carrie insisted that they get dressed up to go out. Deflated, Cat agreed to tag along as Carrie's "best friend." Cat pretended to be bothered by her fussiness when Carrie fawned on her, fixing her hair and make-up. She felt silly getting dolled up, but secretly liked Carrie's attention. As soon as they were done getting ready, Carrie rushed them out the door.

"I want to get out of here before my mom's boyfriend gets home." She whispered, as she coaxed Cat out the back door, pulling on her arm. She guided them around the back of the house to the north side, and along the property line to the street. Following the shadow of the trees, they made their way down the block. When they had gotten about a block away, she stopped to pull a cigarette and lighter out of her pocket. Cat stared silently. "Do you want one?" Cat shook her head 'No'. "That's cool. I wanted to get outta there before my mom's boyfriend showed up because I grabbed a couple of his beers!"

Carrie reached into her purse and pulled out two cans of beer. This time, Cat accepted when Carrie offered to share. They sat down in the gutter, under the cover of tree and shadow, and sipped on the room temperature beer. "We're going to hang out with Carol Ann tonight! I've got a surprise for you! You are gonna love this!" Carrie exclaimed as she put out her cigarette on the pavement in front of them. She got up and offered her hand down to help Cat up.

A moment later the two began a journey through the neighborhood, cutting down alleys and through backyards. Carrie wouldn't tell her what they were going to do. Carrie said it was a secret because they would get in trouble if they got caught. Carrie was very excited about doing it. That was enough of a thrill to get Cat excited, until they met up with the other girls.

Cat didn't pay much attention to which one was Carol Ann, staying focused on Carrie. Carrie bragged to her new friends about how Cat was her 'very best friend.' Still Cat never really felt like she had a place in Carrie's new world. *I feel like the tag along boyfriend.* Walking through the neighborhoods, the other three girls assured Cat that they were going to go do something really cool, but they had to be quiet about it. The girls got quiet when they stopped in front of a house Cat had never seen before.

———— ∞ ————

We got to a girl's house whose name I can't remember. Once we were in her bedroom, she made sure the door was locked. Nobody else was home. That was important. We gathered by her side table and she put some white powder on tin foil. I smoked off the foil with the other girls.

We all took turns until it was gone and then quickly disposed of the evidence. It made me feel funny and excited. We wandered around Pleasant Hill and Walnut Creek for hours that evening. We walked and talked and looked for fun trouble to get into. Eventually the other two girls went home and I spent the night at Carrie's house. We stayed up late talking. She stole some more beer and cigarettes from her mom's boyfriend. Carrie smoked Marlboro Reds, and I tried taking a drag but it just made me choke.

―⚬⚬⚬―

Cat would do anything to spend all night talking with Carrie. Trying to deal with her feelings for Carrie while keeping it a secret, she spent more time writing in her notebooks. Every other weekend Cat went to visit Mom, and on the alternating weekends, she went to stay with Carrie. It was the only time they got to see each other and Cat couldn't get enough of it. Staying up late during sleepover visits at Carrie's house, the two girls talked about all kinds of things. 'What would you do if you had the opportunity to make out with someone? How are you supposed to know you're doing it right?' They discussed these questions and agreed that neither one of them wanted to be embarrassed by being with someone and being identified as inexperienced. That idea seemed mortifying to the both of them.

―⚬⚬⚬―

Last night, Carrie and I decided to practice making out. I don't remember whose idea it was to

do it. My egotistical mind would like to believe that
I somehow had the nerve to try and talk her into
it. The truth is that I don't really recall the details.
I was too high on the situation and totally nervous.
We practiced for a while. Putting our hands over our
mouths, we made out with our own hands. But we did
it up against each other to pretend how we would be
if we were with someone else. I really wanted us
to take our hands away from our mouths, but I was
afraid what I would say. She might not ever want to
hang out with me again.

The subconscious mind has a strange way of interfering.
This was the closest Cat had gotten to making out with a girl
before and her emotions were focused intently on Carrie.
She was terrified, literally shaking. She got a little worked
up, sweating when they finally stopped. They tried to convince each other they were doing it right.

By Christmas Break, Cat had scrapped the whole hair bow
thing. She tried to create her own unique style. She sewed
finger-less gloves out of old fabric, creating a couple different versions. She always wore them with several rings and
bracelets. She switched it around depending on her mood
and outfit. It was her drag hand, her bit of flamboyance
that marked her as different from everyone else. She got
made fun of for it. People teased her with Michael Jackson

references. Cat dressed feminine sometimes, masculine other times. Mostly she tried to wear the tightest black jeans she could fit into. Her outfits were completed with black boots adorned with silver buckles.

During the break Cat went to visit Mom in Berkeley for a few days before Christmas. Staying with her at the Berkeley Inn was cramped. The room was tiny, and she slept on the floor. She didn't mind though, because the rest of the visit was so fun. There was a craft fair in the streets. The four blocks of Telegraph Ave, closest to UC Berkeley Campus were completely closed off to automobile traffic during the day. Mom's boyfriend was helping to work security for the street fair. Vendors lined the center of the street and the sidewalks filled up with people coming to shop and enjoy the holiday spirit. Musicians hung out on the corners with their instrument cases open for change.

It was a marvelous and stimulating environment for an 11 year old kid. Cat wandered the streets early in the morning when the vendors were getting set up. Many of the vendors already knew her as 'Maudie's Daughter,' but she wanted them to know her as a person for herself. She went from booth to booth, telling them "Good Morning," introducing herself, and asking them if they needed help with anything. By 10:00 am she had earned the trust of several vendors, and they were letting her help.

One vendor gave Cat money to go to the cafe and pick up a coffee. When she brought back the drinks and the change, they tipped her! Stuffing her earnings in a pocket, she moved onto the next vendor. Making her way up and down the street, she ran errands for vendors and babysat booths, while they left to use the bathroom. By the third day, she was helping different vendors with their sales. By the end of street fair, she had made enough money to buy Christmas presents for everyone on her list.

As a new Pagan, Mom chose not to celebrate Christmas. Mom explained, "before people celebrated Christmas, they celebrated the Winter Solstice." She shared the mythology and made the stories come alive. One afternoon, they hiked up to the Berkeley Hills. Instead of buying a tree (which would be too big for the little room at the Inn) they gathered small limbs from different trees. Each time, Mom would approach a tree, stroking its trunk gently, she would ask its permission to cut a limb. Taking out her ceremonial knife, Mom would cut a small branch, and thank the tree for its gift. Once they had gathered 12 or 13 small limbs, they made their way back down out of the hills.

When they got back to the Inn, Mom announced, "Now we will make our tree." They filled a 5-gallon bucket about a quarter full with small rocks, constructing a base for the tree. Limb-by-limb, they layered the branches like flowers in a bouquet. Anchoring the taller limbs in the rocks, they bound the shorter limbs to the larger ones with string and duct tape.

Filling the bucket with more rocks, Mom poured water into the rocks to keep their 'tree' green. When the tree was complete, Mom placed the full bucket on her table, wrapping it in purple velvet to hide the plastic. Cat got to decorate the limbs, and later gifts appeared on the table 'under the tree.'

When Cat returned home for Christmas, she was proud that she had worked for the money to buy gifts. She had taken initiative and it had paid off. On the drive home, she told Dad all about her experience working the street fair. "I made enough money to buy presents for everyone! I even got a handcrafted piece of jewelry for Margaret! But don't tell her. And of course I can't tell you what I got for you. But it's really cool!"

Dad made listening noises, but did not seem as excited about it as Cat was. After a little while she quieted down. *I could be talking about anything and he wouldn't listen. I don't even like his girlfriend and I took the time to pick something out for her. He could say something other than "that's nice". Forget it.*

Winter Break ended and Cat returned to Sixth Grade hoping she would be able to continue being brave, the way she had been in Berkeley. Still, there was something intimidating about her peer group. There were girls she wanted to talk to. She wanted them to like her. She wanted them to invite her to hang out after school. She got jealous when they had boyfriends.

How do I get to hang out with these girls? They won't even talk to me! I can't flirt with them. They will call me gay and then I'll want to die!

The word 'gay' was always used in a derogatory way. 'Why are you staring at me? What's wrong with you? Are you gay?' The concept of gay sex was discussed behind giggling uncomfortableness, embellished with 'eww gross!' and 'they do it like *that?*' It was never discussed in a positive or accepting manner. It was never presented as socially acceptable, and never in realistic detail. Being sheltered in middle class suburbia, Cat's upbringing failed to provide a category for the feelings she was experiencing. Providing no tangible point of reference, she was left feeling convinced that she must be doing something wrong.

Cat started talking to a boy who played saxophone. She thought the saxophone was really cool. He was the only person in band that was consistently nice to her. She had started playing the clarinet in the fourth grade and it seemed a logical choice to use her one elective class to take band. She thought that she would really enjoy the class because she liked to play clarinet so much. Instead, she ended up hating band class because she didn't feel included when nobody else would talk to her.

One day in January, the saxophone boy surprised Cat by asking, "Can I have your phone number so I can call you?"

Of course she said "Yes!" and gave him her number. She was so excited to get attention from someone in the band! He called her that afternoon at 4 o'clock. They talked on the telephone for a few minutes before she heard a child screaming in the background, followed by the sound of a frustrated mother. Saxophone boy apologized that he had to get off the phone, but assured her that he would see her the next day at school.

Cat started talking on the phone with Saxophone Boy a lot. She told him all about wanting to play as well as Benny Goodman when she grew up. She wanted to wear the snazzy suit and make her money making music like they did in the old black and white movies. *I want to be so good that the pretty singing ladies would swoon over me. But of course I can't tell him that! I feel so uncool.*

During a phone conversation, Saxophone Boy told her he chose the saxophone because he liked the theme song from the Pink Panther TV show. "I love that show too," she said into the phone, playing with the long phone cord. They talked on the phone several times a week and soon he was asking her to be his girlfriend. She couldn't honestly open up to him, but it felt good that someone liked her. She said yes, but it didn't really change much. They still just mostly talked on the phone.

Cat thought it would be really cool if they could jam together. The adults at Mom's house would often bust out their instruments and play music together, without sheet music. When visiting Mom, the social gatherings were always a lot of fun. People who liked to play with food would coordinate with each other in the kitchen to make a meal for everyone. People who liked to play music would jam with each other in the living room. Everyone laughed and had a good time. Cat was usually dancing in the middle of it all, or laying on the floor coloring, or playing the washboard or a hand drum while people jammed.

Cat tried to talk to Saxophone Boy about playing music. He seemed uncomfortable with the idea of playing without sheet music. The idea of just jamming together fizzled out and went nowhere. Determined to spark his musical interest, she went to the music store and bought him sheet music as a gift for Valentine's Day. She always tried to think about what other people would appreciate when she picked out gifts. Somewhere in her mind she could hear Mom saying, 'Remember, you are not getting a present for yourself.'

Cat liked talking to Saxophone Boy. She decided she should do something nice for him. *I do like him. He seems nice enough and he is nice to me. I think I'd like him better if he treated me like another boy. Or maybe if he was a girl. But that doesn't make any sense so I don't think I should tell him.*

Chapter 3

THE FIRE

Mom pursued her spiritual curiosity through self study. Spending hours at the library, and in bookstores, she consumed stories, essays, and textbooks about goddesses, mythology, European folklore, and Eastern mysticism. Her artwork was filled with goddesses and magic. Much of the time Cat was visiting her mother was spent hanging out in the studio, while Mom painted. Cat was engrossed in whatever Mom was doing. She saw her mother so rarely, she felt like there was always something new when she did get to visit.

Her mother shared stories about the goddess while she painted. Cat learned something new every visit. She got excited about what her mother was doing because Mom seemed happier. Her mother seemed to be doing better as a direct result of her renewed spirituality, which was cause enough to be supportive.

As she watched her mother's paintbrush glide across the canvas, she listened to her mother talk about meditation and finding your inner focus point. Sometimes she spoke about the Indians. Sometimes she spoke about Celtic faeries. Sometimes she spoke about channeling the grace of the goddess.

Eventually, Mom would always steer the conversation toward her daughter. Cat would complain with great animation, of the torture of living with Dad, and how the kids in the suburbs were so mean. She felt safe talking to her mother. She didn't like talking about school and the other kids with Dad, because all he was interested in was her grades. He just didn't get it. She appreciated being able to talk to her mom about that stuff. *At least she tries to understand.*

━━━━━)(◉)(━━━━━

Mama shifted the conversation. Cat sat legs outstretched in front of her, stretching and rubbing her legs while they talked. "So your father told me he took you shopping for your first bra." She paused, placing her paintbrush in a glass of water on the table to her left. She turned to look at her daughter, sitting on the floor. "He told me it didn't go so well."

"I don't like my body. It feels wrong. It feels uncomfortable." Cat responded without looking up. "I didn't like it. He's my Dad. You should have been the one to take me."

Cat's mother placed her hands on her knees and took a deep breath. "I am sorry that I couldn't be there for you when you needed me." Tiny tears threatened to overtake the mother, but she was fierce and strong. Instead, she got up out of her chair, lifted up the little girl, and hugged her mid air. Then she sat down on her bed with her daughter in her lap.

Mother and child held each other until Cat snuffled. "I love you Mama." She pulled away, climbing off her mother's lap to sit beside her on the bed. She wiped her face with her sleeve, before looking up at her mother. When her mother was standing, nearly six feet tall, the woman was almost always intimidating. Fierce and beautiful, she appeared royal and commanding to most who did not know her. Still, Cat knew that her mother was often depressed, poor, and sometimes too sick even for her to visit. Sitting next to her, Cat saw her mother as broken and immediately forgave her.

"And you know-" Mama seemed to pick up where they had left off three minutes prior. "Your father tries his very best." She reached out, moving a large clump of hair from Cat's eyes, and tucking it behind Cat's ear. "It isn't easy for him either.

"I know Mama." Cat responded, rubbing her hands on her knees. "It's just not fair. I don't like living with my dad. I'd rather live with you."

Mama reached out and hugged her daughter one more time. "Oh honey. I love you. Everything will be okay. Don't worry." She pulled away to look directly at her daughter. "Now, you need to get your stuff gathered up. Your father will be here soon to pick you up."

No matter what my Mama will always love me. I love to go visit her because she treats me like a real person. I can tell her anything and she wants me to feel better. And I want her to feel better too. I was worried about her. But the goddess is helping her get better. I love the Goddess.

———((O))———

Sleeping solid, Cat lay motionless in the darkness. Then, suddenly, she was sitting straight up, in a cold sweat. *Where's my mother?* She knew something terrible was happening. She was flooded with the overwhelming sensation that her mother was in danger. *What's wrong?!* Cat looked around the room. The clock said 2:30 am.; everything else was as it should be. Except she was awake, and positive that her mother was in danger.

Cat had always lived with Dad. *Why is this happening right now?* Her mother only lived a half hour away. She felt connected to her mother in ways she could not explain, but this was more than she could comprehend. She sat in bed, thinking about how everything had been the last time she visited.

Cat loved going to visit because Mama would send her downstairs and across the street to the busy cafe. Mama liked to drink hot tea. She always gave Cat enough money for 'something for herself' too. Cat usually ordered a hot chocolate or a mocha. It felt so grown-up to be in the city and go into the cafe. She loved to do things on her own.

In Berkeley, Cat went to the park and talked to people who were hanging out. Walking down the street, she learned all about the world from street corner poets. It felt glamorous. Living with her father consisted of going to school, coming home and doing her chores, going to her room, and going to bed early. She was always depressed or bored or lonely.

Cat looked around the room again. Taking a deep breath, she told herself out loud, "It was only a dream. You were only dreaming. It's okay. And you need to go back to sleep now, because you have school in the morning." She straightened out the blankets, pounded her pillow around a little, and laid back down.

Set on auto, the alarm clock woke Cat up every morning with the news on KNEW. A voice reported, "This morning at about 2:30 am, the Berkeley Inn Resident Hotel, home to several people, burned down." Cat sat bolt upright again in her bed. This time, she knew she wasn't imagining it. She was so worried that she turned off the radio. *I can't listen to this right now! All I want to do is call Mama! But I can't because of course her phone won't work if the building isn't there any more!*

Getting out of bed, she rushed through getting dressed and brushing her teeth. Going into the kitchen for breakfast, she resisted the urge to knock on Dad's door. *There is nothing he can do about it. He's probably still asleep. No need to make him angry first thing in the morning.* Tears sat dormant on the edge of her eye lids, waiting for just the right trigger. She poured her cereal and sat down at the dining room table. Forcing herself to eat felt pointless and she soon abandoned the half full bowl in the sink.

She couldn't stand it. She had to tell Dad. He had to know. *Dammit. Please don't be angry. I hope he is already awake.* Cat held her breath as she knocked on the door to Dad's room. When he opened the door, the story tumbled out of her mouth all mixed up. Dad perceived her fear and tried to assure her that there was nothing she could do about it right now.

It didn't make her feel any better. *What did you expect? It's not like he could magically pull your mom out of thin air. You're so stupid.* Shutting herself off from the worry, Cat pushed back her feelings until the only thing left was the normal hollow sadness of any other school day. Leaving the house early, she headed down the street to the bus stop.

Later that morning, Dad sent a message to the school office letting her know that Mama had contacted him. She was okay. Yes, the there was a fire at the Inn. The fire hadn't touched her room though. Cat had started the day worried, but the worry had been pushed back so far that by the time she got the news, it was too deeply lodged to move at all. She continued through the day focusing on the magical experience of waking up in the middle of the night knowing. She shared the story with her friends in the lunch yard. "It was like ESP or Magic!" Convinced something divine had saved her mother, Cat became even more interested in Mama's spiritual path.

⸺⸺◉⸺⸺

In an attempt to seem more cool with her peer group, Cat spent her time in the spotlight, talking about her weekend visits with Mama. After leaving Fairfield, Mama had moved to Berkeley. The adventures on Telegraph Avenue provided stepping stones that showed a path to the future. She was more excited about visiting Mama than she had been before. *Berkeley is such an interesting place!* There was colorful life all around and Cat wanted to soak it all in. *So much more exciting that my boring life in suburbia.*

The onset of hormonal madness had awakened some sort of extra sensory perception in Cat. She had spent time in the Elementary School library reading books on ESP. She had seen ghosts as a young child and believed in the supernatural. Friends started asking her questions, for advice in life situations and she seemed to have answers. They started asking her to interpret their dreams. Again, she seemed to know what to say without thinking. If she spent too much time thinking about it, then the answers became less clear.

I feel supernatural. I always seem to have answers, and I don't know where they are coming from. It feels like electricity running through me when it happens. Why can't I get answers to my own questions? Visiting Mama on the weekends gave Cat a safe space where she could talk more openly about her questions, and the thoughts running through her head. Mama seemed to be interested in her dreams and peculiar thoughts, and even encouraged her to explore them further.

As a practicing witch, Mama was more engaging when Cat started conversations with questions regarding spiritual and magical ideas. Mama's friends were also interested in the magical world. During the visits, Cat began to get accustomed to a feeling of community that she had not experienced anywhere else before. The combination of spirituality, community acceptance, and colorful diversity was attractive to her.

Mama's life had grown to be a lot richer than before. *Trying to escape the unhappiness that follows me like a storm cloud, I looked forward to visiting the alternate reality that is Mama's world.* The once new and exciting world of Berkeley now seemed shattered by the fire at the Inn. The knowledge that her mother was now homeless lingered in the back of her throat, pulling on invisible threads. Cat returned to worrying about her mother, and decided that it was time to work some magic.

Chapter 4

SAXOPHONE BOY

Cat knew she spent too much time hiding in the house watching TV. Being around other people seemed to be getting more difficult for her to handle. She couldn't explain how thing were different. It seemed important to her to know what was expected of her. Over and over, she felt rejected by her peers, ignored by her family, and worst of all, when she looked in the mirror, she couldn't see herself. I want to know how I'm supposed to act, how I'm supposed to feel. Everyone says something different and none of it matches what I'm feeling. But I don't understand. I don't know whats wrong with me."

Cat sat in the middle of her bedroom floor. Piles of clothes and blankets created a disaster scene. Head in her hands, tears poured down her face. Blotches of cheap make-up smeared green, gray, and black on her face and hands. She wiped her face with the bottom of her shirt. "It's not fair. Nobody understands. Nobody can help. Nobody cares." The empty house failed to respond.

Cat got up and went into the bathroom. She turned the faucet on, letting it run long enough for the warm water to arrive. As the water got warmer, she moved a washcloth under the stream, saturating it. She turned off the faucet and wrung out the washcloth loosely. Wiping her face with the warm cloth, she stared at her reflection. "What is wrong with me? That doesn't even look like me?" She turned the water back on to rinse the washcloth once more. She repeated the rinsing, wringing, and wiping ritual until her face was free of evidence.

"I don't know whats wrong with me. But I want it to go away. What the hell? I'm sick of this!" Cat straightened up and took a deep breath. *I just need to get some rest. I already washed my face. Now I need to brush my teeth, brush my hair and braid it, and then, I need to go to bed.* She fumbled under the sink to find her hair brush and mousse.

Cat closed the toilet seat, carefully placed a folded towel on top, and sat down on the seat. As she brushed her hair, she tried cheering herself up. "I can be pretty. I know I can." Matted sandy hair was slow to untangle. Cat gritted her teeth as she worked to break apart the little knots in her hair. Once smoothed, she filled her palms with flowery scented mousse. She worked the mouse through her hair thoroughly before separating it into sections and began braiding it.

Cat prepared herself for bed with two braids, one on either side of her head, curling down below her ears, like thick horse tails. *I have so much hair! I think my hair is beautiful. But the rest of me sucks.* She got up and looked in the mirror. She liked to separate her hair into several smaller braids, so she looked liked Medusa with snakes all over her head. But she never did that when she was going to leave the house.

Sometimes Cat would braid her in hair in several little braids, sleep with them, and unwrap them in the morning to make her hair wavy. Mostly she just braided her hair before bed to keep it from tangling. None of these tricks seemed to make her any prettier. "Shut up. Stop it. You are pretty! Other people are just stupid!" She put the towel back on the rack, but left her toothpaste, toothbrush, and hairbrush laying lazily on the bathroom counter. "Now you need to stop stewing and just go to bed. This day doesn't have anything good left in it."

Cat turned away from the mirror, turning off the bathroom light as she entered the hallway. With one great leap, she crossed the space between the bathroom and her bedroom,planting her toes firmly into the edge of the brown shag carpet in her open doorway. She stretched her legs out once more, spinning around gracefully, closing her bedroom door behind her as she turned. She smiled briefly at her momentary lapse of clumsiness.

Cat wanted to learn how to me cool. She wanted to be accepted. Most of all she wanted to stop feeling miserable all the time. People on the TV seemed happy. When they did have problems, there were always friends around to help solve whatever dilemma had arisen. It seemed like if she could just memorize the whit and charisma of the television characters, maybe she could learn how to be human?

Television presented the standard gender binary. Cat loved watching The Facts of Life. It was all girls. She wasn't into shows with girly topics necessarily, but she liked to watch the girls. Especially girls with boobs, and girls who would play dress-up and parade around the room. She didn't know why she liked to watch that, and would never admit it to anyone. She loved watching Wonder Woman as a kid too. Wow! Linda Carter was a knockout! Wonder Woman kicked butt and she was a smart, sexy woman. That was awesome! Even as a kick-ass superhero, she was still very feminine. She didn't look boyish. She dated men. She liked to be treated like a lady. The gender binary was still supported.

MTV was the coolest thing on television, in the eighties. Cat learned how to dance watching MTV Dance Party. Standing in the living room, in front of the television with the curtains drawn closed, she practiced dancing like the girls on the screen. She learned about fashion from the costumes in the music videos. She watched so much that reinforced the gender binary, that when she saw Boy George in his crazy drag on MTv, without a point of reference, she didn't understand what she was seeing. She just thought it was a creative, colorful costume. Clueless.

⸺◦《◦》◦⸺

Cat had noticed a small crowd of alternative kids at school. The front of the crowd was marked by a cute boy with a mohawk. Cat wanted to talk to them. She didn't know how to get their attention. *Why would they talk to me? I'm not cool.* She talked about them, and the cool clothes their wore, when visiting her mother. The next time she went to visit Mama, she was presented with a paper sack full of dresses.

"The punk rocker girls in the city wear dresses like this all the time." She informed her daughter, as the girl pulled fabric from the sack. "I see them up on the Ave, and when I'm riding the buses." Mama smiled a wide toothy grin. "Apparently they are all the rage right now!" She said, encouraging Cat to pull all the clothes out. "Of course, you'll try them on, right?"

Mama's enthusiasm was contagious and soon Cat was playing dress up with the new attire. Her favorite dress was a plain purple gunny sack style with a loose baby doll cut.

She proceeded to wear it so frequently that she got teased for not having enough clothes. Her face was stone as she walked passed the girls giggling and pointing. *I am getting sick and tired of hearing them call me ugly. Mama says if I just ignore them, they will stop. But they never stop. They're never going to stop because I look hideous. I must be a real joke.*

⸺⸺◈⸺⸺

Saxophone boy didn't seem to be phased by Cat's attempt to change her look. He still talked with her on the phone a couple times a week. She tried flirting with him a little but he never really responded the way boys did on television. They never made out.

When she gave him a peck on the cheek, on Valentine's Day, he blushed and asked her why she did it. She stammered something embarrassed and didn't try anything like that again. By the end of the sixth grade, they still hadn't broken up. In June, she convinced him to commit to spending the afternoon with her after school let out on the last day.

Their childish attempt at dating had fallen short of what she thought it should be. Cat knew she would like kissing. *I'm not sure how to start with him. I figure I should probably be doing that with him, since he is technically my boyfriend.*

Determined to figure out a way to be romantic, she planned a picnic. She packed a lunch and got fresh batteries for her cassette player. She packed a cassette of 'The Go Gos' because she remembered he'd mentioned liking their music. She tried to plan the day the way she wished someone would plan a date with her. *I have everything ready! I think the only thing that would make the day better was if he was a girl.* She shook her head violently, trying to shake the thought from her mind. *That's not right.*

Waiting for his arrival, Cat sat on the front porch watching the ants march by on the sidewalk. The warm sun filtered through the branches of the big oak tree in the front yard. She began to worry that he would flake out and not show up. She forced the thought out of her mind and replaced it with memories.

———

When we moved into this house, I was overwhelmed by how many kids in the neighborhood rode bicycles. I was embarrassed that I did not yet know how to ride a bike. I had a bright green banana seat bike that my parents gave me in Kindergarten. I had been terribly afraid of falling, and intimidated by Dad's frustration trying to teach me to ride.

He got mad at me for crying and not trying harder. He decided that since I gave up, he was going to give up trying to help me. The bike sat in the shed collecting dust for years. It moved with us to Oakland, and then again to Walnut Creek. Finally, with teary eyes of embarrassment and determination, I dragged the old bike out of the shed. I fell down a couple of times, but I kept trying. I didn't give up. I felt free!

I started roaming around the neighborhood on my bike. Soon Dad let me ride to Larkey Park by myself. Then I found the bike trail. At that point it didn't really matter where I was and was not allowed to go. As long as I was home by the time he got home from work, it didn't matter where I had gone. He never asked me. He barely talked to me. I started riding up the bike path to the open space. I'm so glad I found the creek. I've spent hours hiking up there. It's so beautiful and romantic. It seems like the perfect place to bring a date. I really hope Saxophone Boy likes it.

When Saxophone Boy arrived, Cat was bubbling over with excitement. She tried to remain reserved, to keep her cool. She told him that she had a surprise for him and he was really going to like it. Since he didn't have a bike, they would have to walk. She carried all the picnic stuff and tried to hold hands with him as they walked up bike path. His hands were sweaty and he complained about the heat and the long walk.

"It will be great. It's totally worth the walk! You'll see!" She encouraged him as they walked. "I've been going to the creek for a couple years. It's my favorite secret hiding place." He grumbled in response and wiped sweat off his forehead. She started to wonder whether she had brought too much stuff, as the bag seemed to get heavier as they walked.

I brought all the stuff I thought we'd need for a picnic. Geez. It would have been so much quicker if we were riding bikes! I wish he'd stop complaining and be as excited as I am.

When they got to the creek, Saxophone Boy sighed with relief. "Yes! There's shade here!" Cat responded dreamily,

"Yes! Isn't it beautiful?" She quickly began pulling things out of her bag. "Wait! Don't sit down yet! First let me lay out the picnic blanket." He looked a little irritated but waited a little longer to sit down. She spread out the blanket and he quickly took a seat.

As they sat in the shade she spread out the picnic stuff, naming each item as she placed it on the blanket. They listened to Belinda Carlisle's voice while eating sandwiches and twiddling their toes. Neither one of them knew what to say or do. *He is obviously not as excited about the creek as I thought he'd be. He's a Boy Scout! Boy Scouts are supposed to love nature!* Cat was disappointed when she realized he was obviously not going to turn into a mushy romantic anytime soon.

After they finished lunch, Cat packed everything up and they headed right back down the bike path. Saxophone Boy called his mother for a ride home as soon as they got back to Cat's house. He couldn't wait to leave. *Well that sucked.*

—————»((●))«—————

The following week, they attempted once more to have a date. This time, Saxophone Boy invited Cat to the movies. When the day arrived, the 'date' turned into a group activity. The awkward couple were accompanied by his little brother, and their mother. They parked at the Montgomery Wards shopping center. The mother announced that they would be stopping at the Ice Cream Parlor before heading to the theater, located at the center of the shopping center.

They entered the shopping center, and the family of three guided Cat to the left toward the creamery. The little brother terrorized the young couple while they sat at the checkered table, waiting for their order. His mother hit Cat with a barrage of questions she didn't know how to answer while they ate their ice cream sundaes. After the afternoon treat, the fumbling four made their way through the little mall to the theater. Saxophone Boy talked frequently throughout the movie, which she was not fond of. This time, she couldn't wait to go home.

When they brought Cat home, after some hushed urging, Saxophone Boy got out of the car and walked her to the door. She politely thanked him for a nice time, glancing back at the driveway before giving him a peck on the cheek. "I will be visiting my Mom a lot this summer, but I will call you." He shuffled his feet and nodded before turning and walking back to the driveway.

Cat put her key in the lock and opened the door to be greeted by an empty house. She let the door swing open, and sat down in the doorway. She waved at the station wagon as it pulled out of the driveway and disappeared over the eastern hill. "They probably can't see me anyway." She looked back down to find the ants were still working on the same line they'd been following for over a week. She sighed heavily. "Does anything ever get better? It's got to. It just has to." She looked back up at the street, but Saxophone Boy and his family were long gone.

I'm so glad its summer. I don't think I could handle seeing him every day at school. This totally sucked. She promised herself that she would remember to make nice and call him once or twice a week. She didn't want to hurt his feelings, but had lost any interest in trying to actually maintain a relationship with the boy.

The weekend after Father's Day, Cat went to visit her mom. She planned on spending the majority of her summer "free time" in Berkeley. Mama had moved into 'The Oasis', a group household in West Berkeley. Receiving money as a result of a class action lawsuit in response to the Berkeley Inn Fire, she cooperated with a few people to rent a pretty nice sized house with a huge back yard. It was just a few blocks from the railroad tracks and a pleasant walk to Aquatic Park.

At first, Mama had shared the front bedroom with a boyfriend. When the two of them began having problems, Mama moved downstairs into the immense basement. Then a very peaceful friend of Mama's moved into the front bedroom. He was quiet and kept to himself for the most part. He had long hair and a beard. He always had a calm and peaceful voice. Cat thought it was a little different that he was always wearing a flowing hippie skirt and Birkenstock sandals, but nobody acted different around him, so she just accepted it. She never really knew what to say around him because he said so very little.

Cleopatra lived in the back bedroom. She was a little gal, that had also been a tenant in the Berkeley Inn, when it burned down. Cat found her attractive and liked hanging out with her. She was an interesting person. Sometimes Cleo said things that sounded pretty fantastic, but Cat didn't care. She was only a little taller than Cat, and had great boobs. Cleo could talk about anything and it didn't really matter how ridiculous it sounded. Cat would stay entranced for hours.

For the first couple of months Mike lived in the middle

bedroom. When visiting her mother, Cat spent long hours hanging out with him. She talked with him about anything and everything. Watching him draw dragons, he let her play with his calligraphy pens and tips. She looked forward to spending time with him, and began to develop a crush on him. He seemed like a beautiful, gentle person to her. He never turned her away and never acted in a way that made her feel unsafe. She missed him greatly when he moved out to serve a prison sentence for a case of drunken violence.

———∞∞∞———

When I was eight years old, Mama took me with her to a Winter Solstice Ritual in John Hinkley Park. It was a joyous celebration. The spiritual family that Mama had developed was composed of many beautiful and accepting people. They were kind and creative. They seemed to recognize Mama as a great artist, and welcomed her with open arms. The ritual was comprised of many details that I did not fully understand, however I could feel the power of their collective belief. I recognized and respected the ceremony more than I had ever done in Grandmother's church.

Within the circle cast, I felt safe. We were untouchable. Protected by the gods and goddesses of Mama's new faith, we celebrated the joy of life in the darkest part of the season. As we came to part of the ritual that they referred to as "sacred bullshit", the wine began to flow. Passing the chalice around the great circle seemed to last for a long time. Nobody seemed to pay attention as I drank deeply from the chalice. By the end of the ritual, I was very sleepy and having a difficult time focusing.

As the crowd dispersed and moved into the neighborhood of parked cars, I was struck by how large our group had actually been. Perhaps it was more like 50 people? I was amazed at how strong the faith was in this group. This crowd was easily as large as the crowd that attended Grandmother's Episcopal church. I remembered Grandmother's accusations of the impending doom of hell that she claimed Mama would surely face if I didn't get her to pray to Jesus. I laughed inside at Grandmother's ignorance. These people were not bad. They were protectors.

Moving down toward the street where our ride was parked, Mama began to hold me back. There was a great commotion happening nearby. Bad men were yelling and Mike was there yelling back. Mama ushered me away to a friend's nearby car, where I promptly fell asleep. The story that I was told later was that a small group of the men had apparently accosted Mike's girlfriend. Yelling obscenities, accusing us of all being Devil-Worshipers, they had blocked him and his girlfriend from their car, and tried to force his girlfriend to go with them. When Mike had tried to protect her, a fight had broken out. In his drunken state, he had become very violent and reportedly put one of them the men in the hospital.

The accurate precision when using his knife had apparently dispelled any story of self defense. The judge did not believe that he could have caused so much damage simply by self defense. Despite the fact that there were several witnesses, he was found at fault. He had stabbed the man only once, and just slightly missed the man's heart. Mike, who had been blackout drunk on wine, could not remember enough details to support his own case. With reluctance and a sense of personal responsibility, he accepted the outcome of the court case. He was afraid of going to prison, and sorry for hurting someone so badly. Still, he had been protecting us all, as the people harassing him and his girlfriend could have targeted any of us. I'm angry he has to go away. I wonder if I will ever see him again.

The next guy that moved into the middle bedroom was apparently another friend of Mama's that had come to Berkeley to escape the unhealthy life he had been experiencing in Fairfield. He was in his 20's and his girlfriend Isabella was a really beautiful nineteen year old. Cat immediately fell in love with her.

Isabella talked to Cat like she was a person. She looked forward to visiting The Oasis, so that she could hang out with the new girl. They would spend hours talking. Isabella and her boyfriend took Cat to Chinatown and she got to hang out like a "teenager". Of course the couple got in trouble with Mama for bringing Cat home too late at night. Mama reminded them that she was 'only a kid.'

Chapter 5

TWELVE YEARS OLD

The Summer that Cat turned twelve, she spent mostly weekends at The Oasis, returning to the suburbs for the weekdays. Dad enrolled her in Summer School for the last time. The modified classes took place on Tuesday, Wednesday, and Thursdays on the school grounds of her Middle School. She found out that many other students had enrolled in Summer School for remedial classes. She was treated like she was stupid for *having* to take Summer School. As Summer programs had always been for fun in the past, it hadn't occurred to her that she would be judged for being there. She swore never to do it again.

Cat liked visiting The Oasis. She wanted to spend more time with Isabella. She and her boyfriend introduced Cat to alternative music and taught her how to dance. They treated her with acceptance and encouragement. Cat felt loved. She had friends. Going back to Walnut Creek and trying to hang out with kids her own age felt like she was stepping backwards. She wanted to move forward.

Returning to her Dad's house, Cat dove headfirst back into depression. She hid in her room and slept a lot. Most afternoons inside were spent alone in a manic state, crying and degrading herself. She believed that there was something wrong with her. *There must be something terribly wrong with me or people would want to be around me.* She pushed people away with erratic behavior. This reinforced her belief and therefore gave her security. Terrified of learning the truth about anything, she acted like she knew everything. There was still so much to hide from!

Cat spent a lot of time role-playing as herself talking with the kids who made fun of her. She practiced standing up for herself. She pretended telling the girls exactly how she felt. She pretended telling the boys exactly how she felt. She practiced telling Dad exactly how she felt. Hiding in her room, she was able to keep it all to herself.

When Cat got to visit Mama, she was as social as she could possibly get away with. She wanted to be with people who wanted to be with her. She wanted to be accepted. She wanted to have fun. She wanted someone to help her understand what the hell was going on.

Cat shifted back and forth between hating her depression, and taking comfort in its consistency. Visiting Mama at The Oasis provided an environment where she was free to be herself. She didn't really know what that was exactly. Still the openness was comforting and she looked forward to every opportunity to be part of it. She was so tired of being trapped with her loneliness.

Cat reached a point where she had almost given up on Carrie, when she was pleasantly surprised by the telephone. Carrie insisted that they needed to hang out. Cat agreed and before long, she was heading through the neighborhood to Carrie's place. The weekend flew by. After another episode of being dragged along as Carrie's token 'best friend', Cat was glad to retreat back to safety of her bedroom.

———— ∞ ————

I got finally got to visit Carrie and now I am even more convinced that I've lost her! She's been hanging out with trouble makers from her school. I already feel left behind. I'm empty and depressed. Everything is changing. What am I supposed to be changing into?

———— ∞ ————

Summer Solstice was an exciting event at The Oasis. There was a school bus in the driveway and droves of hippies and freaks camping out in the backyard and living room. The Grateful Dead were scheduled to play a concert at the Greek Theater and there were a lot of people who had arrived from various places to go to the show. As if the circus had come to town, the streets were peppered with school buses and VW Mini Vans covered with bumper stickers and elaborate murals.

Every street corner seemed to be overflowing with dead heads. Cat couldn't contain her excitement. A couple of Mama's house mates had managed to get signed on as Ushers for Bill Graham Presents. They had brought Cat along for a couple of shows at the Fillmore and the Oakland Coliseum. It was a fun way to pretend to be a grown-up. She dressed in a suit, was treated with respect, and got to show people their seats.

Ushering with Bill Graham Presents had provided her with the rare opportunity to attend a Pink Floyd concert earlier in the Spring. She worked through the entire show in the front section. She got to hear the band do sound check, and stay until after all the ticket holders had been emptied out of the stadium. They found all kinds of marvelous items after people left. Certainly an exciting experience, and one that she had shared in great detail with Carrie.

This time, Cat was going to usher a Grateful Dead Show. Unlike the Pink Floyd Concert, the seating at the Greek Theater was general admission. As ushers, they didn't have to police people as much. In fact, she was delighted to find out that they only really had to "work" from about two hours before the show started, until the third song. The rest of the show, she would be free to roam about and enjoy the show. She felt important being dressed up in a suit, being in a position of authority. Getting into the show free made it even better. Though, it felt awkward dancing in a suit, taking off her shoes certainly helped.

Over the course of the show, Cat wandered a path that covered every walkway she could find. Similar to the way she wound through the school grounds during lunch break at school, she followed the flowing path of people at the Greek. During the peak of the show, she found herself in the center of a swirling dervish of dancing bodies in the front pit area.

The movement of energy, air, and prayers washed over me. A warm wind of faith and praise and belief covered all of us like sunlight in a virgin field of wildflowers. Our hearts and souls bloomed under the radiance of Jerry's guitar. The notes carried themselves through the crowd and we soaked it all in.

For the first time Cat was able to fully perceive the intensity and interconnection that so many of the concert-goers were experiencing. The vibration of unconditional love was so vibrant and fulfilling, the evening felt like it could last forever.

Pouring out of the Greek, Cat recalled bits of the Summer before. Pouring out of the venue at Boreal Ridge had been overwhelming mayhem. Here at the Greek, she was not as overwhelmed. She knew the area. All the people carried the excitement of the evening with them back onto the streets.

Waking up the next day to all the out-of-town guests in and around The Oasis extended her excitement from the previous evening. It made her wish she could hop on a big hippie bus. She yearned to disappear into the world of the Grateful Dead traveling circus, and never return to her real world.

Everyone who was not able to get tickets into the concert could still enjoy the show. The local public radio station, KPFA, broadcast the concert live on-air. Saturday night inside the Greek had been an amazing experience. Even though they didn't have tickets to the concert for the Sunday night show, they got ready for the adventure anyway. This time, they didn't have far to go. Packed up with blankets and picnic supplies, Cat headed to the Greek with Mama. She was looking forward to the colorful people and all the excitement.

The tennis courts adjacent to the Greek Theater filled up with a crowd of people who would not be making it inside the show. When Cat arrived with her mother, she noticed right away that someone had set up great big speakers to play the live concert, via the radio. They didn't have tickets, so they joined the crowd and set up their blanket in the middle of the rainbow circus madness.

This time, Cat was able to come and go as she pleased. She wandered around, weaving through the crowd. The streets leading up to the venue were lined with hippies selling T-Shirts, kind grilled cheese sandwiches, and extra tickets. She saw people wandering around with a finger in the air. Groups of three and four people, arms connected, danced in the gutter singing 'All we need is One.' Some carried signs that said 'I need a Miracle.'

Every now and then, Cat would see someone jumping up and down, hugging another person in exuberant thanks. They had been gifted a "Miracle". It didn't take her long to learn that this "Miracle" was a free ticket into the concert. It was rumored that friends of the band were incognito, wandering around giving Miracles away to devoted followers.

By the time the music started, people had drifted away from the streets and piled into the Tennis Courts. It felt just as exciting to be there as it would have been inside. Folks played drums, and danced and enjoyed each other like a glorious family reunion. Cat wandered around taking it all in.

This is the family that I want to spend the rest of my life with. These people don't care about the rules of the rest of the world. They make their own rules. They feel kind and generous, vibrant and loving. She wandered through the crowds dancing and absorbing the euphoria of all of her surroundings. She found herself floating above the crowd, watching herself dancing below. Everyone was so full of feeling and she was overwhelmed with the stimulation.

Once July arrived, the Fourth of July, and Cat's birthday flew by. Before long Dad was talking about shopping for the new school year. Cat had been doing much of her self maintenance, shopping, cooking, laundry, on her own. She worked hard to convince Dad to let her do her own clothes shopping. Excited about creatively developing her personal style, she spent hours perusing the racks at the Buffalo Exchange. She looked for romantic and fanciful shirts like the ones worn by Howard Jones, The Thompson Twins, and members of The Cure.

In preparation for the big return, Cat played dress-up in her new clothes. She practiced applying eyeliner, and painting her fingernails like the guys in her favorite bands on MTV. Arriving back at school, Cat sought out Jennifer and Marie, seeking comfort in the familiarity of her sixth grade friends.

Cat was having a tough time. Every day was like walking into a war zone for her. She felt like she was fighting against the world. Secretly fighting against a person trapped inside her, she saw herself wandering lost in the dark with no landmarks for guidance. *It's like I'm in a strange place and all the street signs are in some foreign language. I might as well be on some other planet.* Sometimes Cat would tell people that she was really an alien. Stubborn and miserable, getting dressed every morning felt more like layering with emotional armor.

The school year provided a busy schedule. Cat tried to stay busy after school. She had given up band to join the school newspaper staff. Cat expressed a desire to continue playing the clarinet, so Dad agreed to pay for her to take private lessons. One afternoon every week, she rode two buses, transferring and running, to barely make it on time to her clarinet lesson after school. After her lesson, she still had a long transit journey back home. All winter, it was dark long before she got home. Arriving home from lessons by dinner time seemed irrelevant. Half the time she was eating TV Dinners by herself anyway.

On the days that Cat had to take the city bus across town

for orthodontist appointments, she often rode the bus all the way around the route just to kill more time. She didn't want to go home and be alone with herself and her depression, so on days without appointments, she tried to make plans with friends.

Marie and Cat hung out after school a couple days a week. It was a great adventure taking the bus to the Concord Library, where Marie waited for her mother to get off of work. When they spent the afternoon together, they actually got some homework done! Helping her friend with homework meant that Cat was staying focused on academics. It made her feel good to be helpful. It was certainly more fun than being stuck alone with her thoughts. Every day spent in Contra Costa County was a surreal state of limbo, the time in-between visits when she got to be happy in her mother's world.

Cat prepared herself for each day reminding herself that if she could just be strong enough to withstand the torture, eventually she would grow up and the world would be okay. *If only I could grow up and be a man. I already know how to cook my own food, and do dishes, and fill out welfare papers. I already go to the store to buy cigarettes for my mom. The world can't be any harder than that!* When Cat visited her mother, she felt like she was in a different world, where she was beautiful and loved and accepted.

The concept of moving into her mother's house was a dangling carrot, some kind of potential reward. She believed that if she could just be patient, her strength will would pay off. *When the time comes, I'll be living in a world where I can finally be myself without being degraded or teased.* Cat wanted desperately to be accepted, to feel loved.

⟫⟪◉⟫⟪

Cat's mother was a nudist. When Mama was in her own space she was often naked or not wearing very much. She tried to teach her daughter that there was nothing wrong with the human body, and one should not be ashamed of their body. When Cat went to visit her mother, she didn't have to wear clothing either. The Oasis was a safe space, and it did not occur to Cat that she ought to be cautious.

Sometime shortly after Mama moved into the basement, she helped arrange a "room" for Cat downstairs as well. A curtained section on the other side of the wall from Mama's bedroom became Cat's own basement room. When Spring Break arrived, she was excited to spend a whole week staying in her unique basement bedroom. She had privacy and freedom and was still able to be very close to Mama.

Saturday evening Cat took a shower after dinner. She returned to Mama's room for social time. She felt comfortable in her favorite purple dress. Wide and loose, the soft fabric was not constricting. With nothing else on, she felt air freely move between her legs. *Mama always says not to rush putting on underpants after a shower.* 'It's important to spend some time without underwear. You have to let your yoni breathe.'

Sitting still was not something Cat was good at. Her legs bothered her. It didn't take long for tingling and cramping to start in her legs, so she tried to rearrange the way she was sitting. Alternating from cross legged positions, to positions with one or more of her legs up was almost a constant. After a while of hanging out, one of her mother's lovers came over. He was not someone Cat was used to. She quickly lost interest in the conversation, wandering off to bed. Climbing into her loft bed, she fell asleep with her back and legs hurting.

The next morning Cat woke up early and went to take another shower. *If I let the hot water run on my back for a while maybe I will feel better.* Standing in the shower until the water began to get cold didn't seem to make much of a difference. The morning sun felt good on her face and shoulders as she walked down the back stairs wrapped in a towel. As she climbed down the short stairs into the basement, she was greeted by her mother's lover. "Good morning! You are already awake? Your mom is still asleep."

The man stood naked in the doorway that separated the entry side of the basement from her mother's bedroom. After staying up late on speed, Cat's mother had fallen asleep in the early morning hours. The visiting man had not, and seemed to be wide awake. With her right hand on her towel, Cat paused briefly to acknowledge him and respond. She rubbed her eyes with her left hand. "My back woke me up. I thought a shower might help, but it didn't." She continued toward her makeshift room in the corner.

"I know something that might help." The man ducked behind the curtain to Mama's room and quickly returned carrying a mirror in his left hand. White powder formed into small short lines lay on the dusty mirror. Cat looked at the mirror and the razor blade lying next to the lines. It looked vaguely familiar, but she couldn't place it. *That must be the drug that makes my mom so sick. This isn't happening. What do I do? What do I say?* He held out his right hand, motioning to hand her a straw. "It will take the pain away."

Cat shook her head. "No. Thank you anyway." Walking past his outstretched hand, she entered the corner room. He did not follow her and she heard him return to the cave. *I can't believe that just happened. I should be proud of myself. I said no to drugs. I could have said yes. I'm sure that's what that was. I wonder if I should tell my mom.* Closing the curtain to her room, she laid her towel on the floor. Positioning herself on the towel, she proceeded to stretch out her legs.

Cat's back and legs still hurt. With her legs spread wide, Cat leaned over and stretched out her back. She spent hours doing this on her bedroom floor at her father's house. It usually helped her feel better. Sometimes she even sat on the living room floor and stretched while watching television with her father. *It feels nice to be able to stretch naked. I can never get this comfortable with clothes on.* Methodically moving through each of her stretching positions, Cat tried to let go of her thoughts and focus only on the quiet. *Mama says I need to learn how to be quiet on the inside. How am I supposed to keep from thinking?*

The silence was broken when the naked man poked his head inside her curtain door. Bored, waiting for Mama to wake up, he asked what Cat was doing. "Stretching helps me feel better." She explained, legs together, reaching out to touch her wriggling toes. "When I stretch out my legs, it usually makes my back feel better." She frowned as she looked up at him. "But nothing seems to be working right this morning. My back still hurts."

"Do you want a back rub?" He offered, opening the curtain more. *I trade back rubs with Mama's friends all the time. It always feels good. That would be awesome!* Back rubs had never been intrusive. She had spent time working on other people's backs at summer camp too. Her camp counselors said she gave the best back rubs and suggested that she become a Masseuse when she grew up.

"Yes! Thank you!" Cat responded, smiling. She stood up from the towel on the cement floor. The naked man entered her room, letting the curtain door swing closed behind him. She climbed her ladder halfway, reaching for a pillow from her bed, to lay down on the floor.

"The cement floor can't be that comfortable." The man pointed to her bed. "Don't you think it would be more comfortable in your bed?" *It will totally be more comfortable on the futon! I love back rubs!* She nodded her head in agreement and finished climbing the ladder into the loft. Taking a moment to straighten out her blanket,she fluffed her pillow and placed it at the head of the bed. Positioning herself face down on, she laid on her belly with her head on the soft pillow. The naked man climbed up on her bed and straddled her back.

The nakedness did not frighten Cat. She had grown accustomed to nudity as being part of the normal freedom within her mother's world. Everything felt natural and peaceful. She felt his body pinning her down at the hips and tried to relax into the mattress. He started rubbing her back and she relaxed more. It felt good to have her muscles worked on. He asked where specifically it was hurting her. Cat answered that her lower back and legs bothered her the most.

Moving down her back his hands continued to move down her body. His weight shifted as he reached her lower back, pinning down her legs as he worked on her hips. He began to talk to her while he rubbed her body. She started to get nervous. "You are a real tease aren't you?" She didn't respond. All of a sudden Cat was scared and she didn't know why. "You are dirty tease. You were teasing me last night. Flashing your tight little pink pussy at me before you went to bed."

Cat's muscles tightened up. *What's happening? He has me pinned and I don't feel good anymore.* She started to feel sick to her stomach and sharp pains shot through her legs. She heard her mother's voice in her head, "If you fight someone, they will hurt you more fighting back." Cat stayed quiet and still. The man shifted his weight again. This time, he forced her legs open, and kept her weight pinned with his hands.

"You are a dirty little bitch just like your mother." Cat clenched her muscles. *I want this to be over. I won't make a sound, just pretend like I'm dead.* She was terrified of what would happen next. "I fucked her all night, but her pussy isn't pink like yours." She let out a whimper and tried to move her legs. He was starting to hurt her.

"Don't you dare move, you dirty like bitch. You tortured me last night, you are going to get yours now." Her legs cramped up as he tightened his grip on her thighs. Moving his body down, his hands made sure she could not move. "Don't worry about making noise. Your mother is out cold." She swallowed hard and squeezed her eyes shut tight, holding back tears. "I bet you are going to like this. Dirty little tease."

His hands moved to grasp the skin where her thighs met her ass, and pushed her labia open. Cat could feel his breath on her legs, as he buried his mouth in her vagina. His mouth moved and his fingers twitched as he licked and bit her. She felt the same feeling in her body as she did when she played with herself, only she usually stopped when her legs started to get twitchy.

The man wasn't stopping. Cat was scared. She didn't like the way he was talking to her. She felt violated and didn't completely understand what was happening. Her body was responding differently than her mind. Her heart pounded as she prayed for it to be over.

Cat felt wet like she needed to go to the bathroom. This

seemed to make it worse. He became more emphatic and rubbed his penis against the inside of her thigh. She was terrified. *Is he going to rape me right here? Please Mama wake up. Wake up and walk in right now. Please.* He rubbed himself up against her until she felt a hot sticky wetness on her back. He pressed his hands hard against her ass to push himself up off her. Climbing down the ladder, he left her corner room without saying another word to her.

Cat laid there completely still, hiding from the whole experience. She listened carefully as he went into Mama's room. She heard a rustling noise. *Is he getting dressed? Is he leaving? I hope he's leaving.* She held her breath in anticipation. Soon she heard him leave the basement and she clambered down from her bed shaking. Picking up her towel she shook it out and wrapped herself up, trying to wipe off her back.

Now Cat was afraid to be naked. Holding the towel firmly at her armpit, she gathered clean clothes with one hand. After getting completely dressed, she cautiously dared to leave the basement. Peeking around the house, down the driveway, she looked to see if anyone was around. Climbing the back stairs, she held her breath, and ventured into the house upstairs. *People are still sleeping. At least he isn't here.* A sadness filled her and tears swelled in her eyes. *This house is not safe anymore.* She walked out the front door and down the street.

After a long walk, all the way around Aquatic Park, Cat decided she was getting tired and she had better head back to The Oasis. When she got back, her mother was sitting in the chair at her painting desk drinking her morning tea. Cat stood pensively next to the desk. "I didn't like that man, Mama." Mama looked at her sleepily and asked why. "He offered me some white powder on a mirror. I said 'No Thank

You'.'" Mama became irritated and Cat left the room.

Cat returned to her basement corner room. She cleaned up her room and prepared her weekend bag for the return trip to her father's house. She stayed quiet in her room until her father arrived. Shocked and quiet, she rode back to Walnut Creek, staring out the window of his truck. *I wonder if there is a safe place anywhere?*

It took several weeks before Cat finally told Mama what happened. She was scared that Mama would be mad at her. The man had told her so many times how bad she was, Cat thought it was her fault. When she finally shared the experience, Mama got very angry. Crying, Mama hugged Cat. "You are always more important than any guest. I will never let him come over again." Still, Cat had learned that she had to be cautious about wearing clothing, even at her mother's house.

———≈«◉»≈———

Cat's depression hit a new low. She had been depressed before, even suicidal. But hormones were hitting her harder now, and her brain was all mixed up and confused. She was angry and bitter and determined to make sure that everyone knew she was completely crazy. She moved vacantly through the school year. Every minute spent alone fed her depression.

Cat hated Margaret, mostly because she believed Margaret hated her. She was determined not to get to know her father's girlfriend. Dad had been dating Margaret for four years already. They were buying a home together. She appeared to be a permanent part of Dad's life. From what Cat could see, he seemed to be a lot happier with his girlfriend than with his daughter.

Most evenings, Margaret got home from work before Dad. Cat would emerge from the safety of her bedroom just to check and see who else was in the house. The two would butt heads over something little. It always ended with Margaret yelling "go to your room". The angry tween would storm back to the room, slamming the door behind her. When Dad got home, he'd come in to talk to his daughter. Worn out, he begged Cat to try and get along with Margaret better. Then he would leave her alone with only depression for company.

The school year dragged by slowly. Cat spent very little time paying attention to what she was supposed to be doing. Miserable in her body and mind, she strove to escape as often as possible. She got up early every morning, leaving the house by 7:00 am Playing chicken with the cars as they passed the bus stop in the early morning light, she prayed that one of them would hit her. Other kids at the bus stop laughed at her. "You're crazy Cat!" She made a joke out of it, but inside, she really wanted to die. One neighbor girl was nice to her. But they never talked except at the bus stop.

Cat had known Hannah since they first moved in. They had played together for a little while in fourth grade but the friendship never seemed to go anywhere. *Hannah is a nice girl. She is smarter than me. She always has perfect clothes and perfect hair. She is too good for me. Why is she being nice to me now?* The girl seemed a little concerned about Cat jumping in the street. She never laughed or got loud like the boys did. Once off the bus, Hannah disappeared into the crowd and Cat didn't see her again until the next school morning at the bus stop.

Nobody was happy with Cat. Teachers complained about her daydreaming. Margaret complained about how little she paid attention to her actions and words. Putting herself to bed early on weeknights, she would fall asleep, praying that she'd never wake up. Lying in bed at night, she discovered how to leave her body intentionally.

Closing her eyes, Cat breathed in deeply. With each breath, she felt herself expand and contract. With each contraction, she felt her spirit separate from her body, diving deep into herself beyond the shell of her body. Upon expansion, she pushed her spirit up, past the limits of her skin. Repeating this process, until she could see herself lying below, Cat left her body an empty shell.

Chapter 6

INITIATION RITUAL

Cat spent almost the entire Summer of 1987 visiting her mother. Turning 13 was a really big deal. Mama kept going on and on about how her daughter was 'becoming a woman.' Cat didn't feel anything like what she imagined being a woman must have felt like. She was busy trying to figure out what it was supposed to feel like being thirteen.

The Grateful Dead returned to the Greek Theater for Summer Solstice. This time Cat was not ushering. She spent both Friday and Saturday evenings hanging out in the Soccer Fields, listening to the show with all the others who did not have tickets. Mama supervised her less than the previous Summer. Spending the evening wandering around through the crowd of Deadheads, Cat found the marvelous circus of hippies and travelers to be both distracting and stimulating. She could walk up to anyone and talk to them. She never felt judged.

Dancing away the hours, her legs felt like they never wanted to stop moving. She felt like she was searching for something, but she didn't know exactly what she was looking for. Cat knew she wanted to be accepted. These people were accepting, and yet, they sought no attachments. She would talk with someone for a while and then they'd get distracted and wander off to talk with someone else. *I want someone to decide that I am important enough to stick around for.* Despite the exciting experience of being immersed in the crowd, Cat felt isolated and alone. Eventually depression overcame her excitement, and she wandered down the streets away from the crowds. Getting lost in narrow streets of double parked cars, she continued to follow the labyrinth until she again recognized her surroundings.

Sometime late in the evening, Cat arrived back at The Oasis. Mama was very angry with her. *She had been worried about me?* Apparently, getting lost in the crowd, and then wandering down through town had taken several hours. After wandering for at least ten miles, her legs were no longer restless. She acknowledged her mother's concern, apologized for her poor judgment, and retired to bed. The next day was spent with another houseful of hippies playing music in the living room and cooking delicious food in the kitchen. Cat's poor judgment of the previous evening already forgotten, Sunday was spent celebrating friendship and freedom.

<hr>

Mama's spirituality was very important to Cat. Mom believed that turning thirteen was a coming of age that deserved special attention. She planned an entire ritual for the purpose of baptizing her daughter as a young woman and accepting her into the world as an adult. The initiation ceremony carried a heavy burden of expectation. Cat was now expected to act like an adult in all ways. She didn't even understand what a teenager was supposed to feel or act like, let alone an adult. The whole event was well-intended. Still, it did not inspire in her daughter what Mama had been hoping for.

The coming of age ceremony took place at an isolated beach just north of Goat Rock. Loaded up with all the necessary camping equipment, the caravan of vehicles made the journey out to the coast. Cat rode in the back of the truck, like she had done on the trip to Boreal Ridge two Summers prior. At one point, they stopped at a pullout to stretch their legs. One of Mama's friends decided that it would be helpful to clean a bit of garbage out of the floorboard of the truck.

With an armload of paper trash, the dark-haired man approached the dumpster. Upon reaching the dumpster, he found it padlocked. Next to the locked dumpster, there was a "No Littering" sign posted. He was outraged. Long hair flying in the wind, he began beating the dumpster in an effort to break it open. While the irony of the situation was apparent, it became more important to calm him down and remove him from the situation. Eventually, Mama was able to calm down the dark-haired man. Coaxing him back into the truck took some effort, but soon they were loaded back up and continuing on their journey.

Reaching their destination point, the caravan of cars parked along the side of the road. Cat could see no beach. She was disappointed to learn they still had a good mile to hike down the path with all of their gear before reaching the beach. At first the path was easy. Nearing the cliffs, the path grew steep and narrow. She was relieved when they all managed to get down to the beach without falling off the cliff.

As far as cat could tell, nobody else was there on the beach. Their own private cove was covered with great pieces of driftwood. Previous visitors had constructed a small room made of driftwood, complete with windows and a doorway. They set up camp right next the driftwood room. All of the kitchen gear and food was placed inside the room. The men set up the camp area, constructing a great fire circle out of driftwood. The women proceeded to set up a ceremonial area a short distance south of the camping circle. Mama set up a bower of driftwood, creating a special room just above the fire circle.

The ritual began at sunset. While the the men made fire and played music in the fire circle, Cat's mother led all the women to the southern ritual area. The women had their own ceremonial chanting and prayers to perform. Leading her daughter down to the sea, she stripped the child of all clothing. "You are being stripped of your childhood." Mother explained, and began a prayer to the Ocean Goddess. She bathed Cat in the cold ocean, as if to baptize her with the blessing of the Goddess. It was bitterly cold. As the moon rose, and the fog slowly moved in toward them, Cat felt the painful bite of salt and sand on her naked body.

After the baptism, Cat was brought back to the women's circle. They formed a tunnel with their arms, pushing her through, as if she was being birthed. Emerging from the tunnel of arms, she was clothed in a prayer robe and welcomed into the women's circle as one of their peers. After dancing around her, chanting prayers, and embracing her, the group moved together and rejoined the men's circle. Together, they were a clan and Cat was to be treated as a peer, rather than a child.

A ceramic teapot sat on the edge of the fire. Sharing of bread and wine commenced. One of the men played guitar, and people began approaching Cat with gifts. One by one, gifts were presented and words of acceptance were shared. One of the last gifts presented was a very large bag of dried mushrooms.

Everyone fell silent and looked at Mama, waiting for a reaction. Cat didn't know much about hallucinogens, but she did understand that was what she was being handed. Cat was so surprised, she didn't know what to think. *Mama is in shock. She does not approve. What can she say? After coordinating such a big ceremony to recognize me as adult, she can't very well take them away from me. What is she going to do?*

Mother discreetly shared some words with the gift-giver. Listening intently, Firecat overheard, "I really wish you would have consulted me first." *Mama didn't take them away. What happens next?* The mother looked at her daughter and asked "Well, what are you going to do with them?"

Cat motioned toward the teapot. A man came out of the shadows and fetched the teapot with hot pads, bringing it to her. She opened the gallon size zippered bag, grabbed a large handful of mushrooms, and placed them in the teapot. The man returned the teapot to the base of the fire and returned to his seat, in the shadows of the fire circle. Cat went to the bower and carefully put all of her gifts away in her camping bag. She fell asleep under the bower, listening to the music and chatter around the fire.

The next morning, Cat awoke early. She ate a few of the mushrooms. They tasted awful. Still in her prayer robe, she went out exploring the peaceful early morning beach. The cool moist sand filled in the spaces between her toes. Salty air filled her lungs and time stood still. Wandering along the coastline she played with seaweed and shells, making abstract pictures in the sand. She continued to wander south down the beach until reaching a point where the rocky coast stretched far into the sea, and the beach disappeared completely.

Turning around, Cat started to head back toward their

encampment. Smoke rose from the campfire in the distance. She could see other people were starting to wake up and move around. Iridescent colors reflected in the salty air. Nothing seemed out of the ordinary. Everything was exactly the way it should be. She felt free and accepted by the ocean breeze.

Today is the day I turn 13. My family is here with me. She expected the feeling to last forever. When Cat reached the circle, folks were starting to make breakfast on the fire. Thomas was playing the guitar. As she sat down on a log near him, he proceeded to play 'The Birthday Song,' by The Beatles. She smiled and moved with the music. *There is so much love here. I want everyone to know how much I appreciate this acceptance.* Watching the fire grow, smoke and flames dancing with each other, she felt content in the space between the worlds.

The contents of the ceramic teapot had been emptied the night before. Cat watched Mama fill the teapot with fresh water for the new day and replace it on the edge of the fire. The young woman went to her bower and pulled out the bag of mushrooms. Grabbing another handful, she approached the edge of the fire and reached for the teapot. Pausing for a moment, she glanced around, taking notice of Mama's eyes intently watching. Lifting the lid, she pushed the handful down into the cool water. She watched them float to the top, then replaced the lid. Turning to look directly at her mother, she spoke with intention. "We can all share my birthday together."

As the morning progressed the mist receded and the sun broke through. Uncharacteristic of the Pacific ocean, the day offered the gentlest of breezes. Most of their party refrained from wearing clothing, or wore very little. Wandering up and down the beach, they played in the sand with each other. Not children, not adults, not men or women, they were simply human. They were family. They were love. All together, they made music and sand art, stacked rocks and driftwood, and frolicked through the day as if it would last forever.

Unfortunately, it did not last forever. As the afternoon progressed, folks began to clean up and pack gear away. The breeze picked up and folks began layering in skirts and sweaters. By sunset, they group was hiking back up the path with all the gear, uneaten food, and their garbage. Cat fell asleep on the ride home and woke up at The Oasis. A hazy Sunday morning left scattered bits and pieces of the weekend playing hide-and-seek in the nooks and crannies of her brain.

Chapter 7

TOO YOUNG ADULT

I was about 10 years old, riding a public bus with Mama the first time I saw someone with a brightly colored mohawk. I had seen them in the movies, but this was real life. I noticed the guy and was startled and interested in his hair. This was certainly different than what everyone else was doing. It occurred to me that he must be very brave to do that. I was afraid to stand out as different. Mama was delighted to see the color. She saw artistic deviance from the norm to be a thing to appreciate. She spoke to me about the wonderful diversity of nature and people. She talked about how they were all connected. I got lost in her words, but I enjoyed spending time with her.

Cat's thirteenth birthday celebration had felt like a dream. She wasn't sure how she was supposed to be different now. *I don't feel different. I still feel clumsy all the time.* She went to talk to her mother about the experience. Mama thought it had all gone quite well. *If I am supposed to be an adult now, I'm embarrassed about how fearful a child I have been.*

"I should tell you something, Mama." Mother nodded her head and waited for her daughter to continue speaking. "I never told you before. I guess I was embarrassed." She proceeded to share the story of the tree house.

The little girl wanted so badly to be accepted. She wanted to be like the other boys. Following the boys down the road, along the creek, she grasped at bugs and tadpoles in the trickling water. The neighborhood boys teased and taunted the little girl. "You're just a sissy! You're just a cry baby!" The words stung, and she held back tears that fiercely protested behind her eyelids.

They threw rocks and dirt at the little girl and ran ahead of her. "I'm just as brave as you are!" She shouted, wiping dirt from her face. She stumbled in the gravel and scraped her knees. She briskly returned to her feet and ran after them. This particular afternoon, the group followed the creek all the way to a meadow shadowed by a great oak tree.

Running to lose the little girl, the boys scrambled up a makeshift ladder nailed to the side of the tree. High above she saw a tree house. She wasn't afraid of climbing. She loved to climb trees! Struggling to keep up with them, she was the last to reach the great oak. The ladder was tall, and she got a little nervous, but she did not want them to see her fear. Swallowing hard, and holding her breath, she proceeded to climb the ladder to the clubhouse in the tree.

When she reached the platform of the tree house, the boys were panting and catching their breath. As she climbed through the hole in the floor and took a place in the circle of boys, they all laughed and congratulated her for catching up to them. For a while, they laughed and played. She began to forget their differences.

Then one of the boys jumped up. "You think this is cool? Wait'll you see the second floor!" Pointing to another hole in the roof, he began climbing up a rope to the mysterious second floor.

The rest of the group followed up the rope, including the little girl. Standing on the second platform, they peered down from high in the tree branches. "This is too high! It makes me dizzy." One boy commented, and returned down the rope to the first platform.

Another boy teased him, calling him a sissy-girl, and then turned to the girl. "What about you? Are you a boy or a sissy-girl?"

The girl stood with her back straight, brushing dirt off her dress and wiping her face. "I'm brave, alright. I can even stand by the edge!" The boy coaxed her closer to the edge of the second floor platform. Looking down her stomach turned. She was terrified. It was so high up and she was afraid of falling, but she didn't want the other kids to know. Tight lipped, she peered around the great meadow. From behind her, the loudmouthed boy taunted her. "You ARE scared! You're just a sissy-girl!"

With her hands on her hips, the little girl stomped her foot. "I am not a sissy-girl! I am more brave than you are. I can prove it! I will jump out of this tree! I bet you are too much of sissy to do THAT!" From the first floor platform, she heard one of the boys gasping "That's not brave. That's Crazy!" She turned to face her tormentors, and slipped.

Falling backwards through the air, she watched the boys scrambling down the ladder of the tree house. There was no time to panic, because she hit the ground too quickly. Eagle spread on hard packed dirt, her head and back made a blinding impact. Dizzy, she was flooded with pain through her entire body. The pain was quickly overshadowed with shame and embarrassment. She was just a sissy-girl and the boys had just proven it. Standing astonished in a circle around her, the boys asked if she was okay.

Completely winded, swimming through a spinning world of dust and nausea, she shakily got up. She wiped dust off her dress and addressed the blurry circle of children in front her. "I am Just Fine! And you are all very mean! I am going home now!" She could hear their voices begging her to keep it a secret as she wobbled home. When their voices had disappeared completely, she stopped holding back the tears. She hurt really badly. Her head was spinning and her back felt broken. Worst of all she had proven to everyone, that she really was just a sissy-girl. And now her heart was broken too. When she got home, she went straight to her room. She didn't want to tell her parents. She didn't want to tell anyone. She put on her pajamas, crawled into bed, and prayed that she would fall asleep and never wake up.

As the girl shared the story with her mother, tears streamed down her face. Cat felt so bad for keeping the secret. She didn't know why, but it felt really important. She had never gone to the doctor. She had never been willing to admit that boys teasing her could have impacted her so much. She knew it was really stupid to jump from so high up. None of that really seemed to matter as much as the relief of sharing the story with her mother.

Mama, watched her daughter crying over the memory from being five years old. She chuckled a little, and gently wiped her daughter's eyes dry. "Oh honey. I love you."

—◦«‹◉›»◦—

Cat straightened up, sniffling a little. She stopped crying and corrected her posture. "Also, I want to know about my grandfather." Mama looked at her funny. "I never met Dad's father. I have heard a vague story about Grandma and Grandpa getting a divorce. There is nothing else. He never calls or sends birthday cards. Dad doesn't talk about him. What happened to him? I want to know." Mama stiffened up a little and took a deep breath. "I suppose I should tell *you* a story now. "

Sitting and talking with Mama in the cave, Cat learned the truth about her Grandfather. It was a great relief to learn that he had not abandoned his family. "When your father was about 15 years old, your grandparents got divorced. Your grandmother had caught Maurice trying on her clothes. It was disturbing to your grandmother. She was very religious." Cat had personally experienced the hatefulness of her grandmother's "religion". She felt bad for her grandfather. *But why would that keep him from visiting me?* Silent and attentive, she waited for Mama to continue. "After your grandparents divorced, your grandpa got a sex change." Mama concluded. She didn't elaborate further.

Cat waited for more to the story. *There has to be more to tell.* "But I don't understand. Why doesn't he visit? Doesn't he want to see me? Why doesn't anyone talk about him?" Mama hesitated before answering.

"*She* did visit once. You were too young to remember. As a woman, she changed her name to Maureen and dyed her hair red. When she came to visit us, you were just a toddler. I think that's why your father didn't like it when I dyed my hair red. It probably reminded him of the awkward situation with his father." Cat repeated her questions. It didn't make sense to her. Mama made it sound like something you could just go out and buy! "Your Uncle made your Dad promise not to tell you. He was afraid you'd tell your cousins and he didn't want his children to know." *The skeleton in the closet. My grandfather is a transsexual.*

Mama didn't explain why Grandpa had done this. She didn't know what had since happened to *her.* The conversation didn't last that long, and was not very informative. Cat sensed that her mother was uncomfortable talking about this. "But you are going to be a beautiful woman! If you want to dye your hair every color of the rainbow, I don't think you should worry about what your father thinks." Cat couldn't tell if her Grandpa had run away or been exiled. Either way, the conversation was clearly over.

Mama shifted the conversation by changing the subject. It was clear that she was more interested in focusing on the points of personal responsibility that came with being a woman. It was difficult for Cat to take this part seriously, although she couldn't clearly express herself. She had liked the attention she gotten for her birthday. It was a great party. She liked hanging out with people older than her.

Kids her age were judgmental and mean. Mama's friends were acting as guardians, mentors, and peers. Mama reminded her daughter that despite her coming of age ritual, the rest of society would still recognize her as a child. "Being a teenager is a time of transition and learning. It is essential that you keep yourself open to the experience of learning and growing."

Mother explained "I was disturbed by the large gift of mushrooms you have been given. However," she paused, momentarily questioning her own words, then thoughtfully continued, "I believe that it can be a great learning experience for you. I will not take them away, and will allow you to keep them." Rules of conduct were then laid out.

Cat would not be allowed to bring them back to her father's suburban home. She was forbidden to discuss them with anyone outside the safe circle of people who had attended the initiation ceremony. "They are illegal. You would be endangering yourself and others to share the information." Mother concluded the talk by reminding her daughter that "what is between the worlds does not concern the world."

At the end of the weekend, Dad picked up his daughter and brought her back home to Walnut Creek. She was quick to make plans to hang out with Carrie. Spending the night at her friend's house, they stayed up late talking. Cat shared stories of the experience of the initiation ritual. As far as she was concerned, if there was anyone she should be able to be honest with, it was Carrie.

As Cat told the story of the evening, and the following day on the beach, Carrie listened in awe. The experiences with Mother seemed so magical and surreal. Carrie asked many questions. It was exciting for Cat to answer the questions. She loved the attention. *I love when she is so interested in me. Right now, I feel like I am the center of her universe. I wish I could feel like this forever. With Carrie right here next to me.*

＝＝●＝＝

When Cat returned to visit her mother later in the month, more excitement circled The Oasis. It was another concert weekend! Bob Dylan was going to be playing with The

Grateful Dead at the Oakland Coliseum. The household was again alive with a school bus in the driveway, and many traveling deadheads occupying the living room and backyard. She was excited. Cat wanted to actually get inside the show. Mama didn't have the money for tickets. Many of the others were going to be able make it inside the concert. Cat was determined to figure out a way to not be left behind.

Brainstorming for ways to get tickets, one of the people offered Cat money for some of her mushrooms. Mother was not pleased with the idea of her daughter selling mushrooms. However, she gave in and allowed it, since ultimately, it was done specifically to buy tickets for them to get into the concert. In the process, Cat learned the value of the enormous birthday gift she had been given, and her surprise and excitement about the Summer was renewed.

Going to the show was amazing. The Oakland Coliseum was much bigger than The Greek Theater. For all the interesting activity that Cat experienced hanging out in the Soccer Fields the previous month, being inside the coliseum show was exponentially more thrilling. The loving and accepting family feeling was multiplied by the huge crowd. Everyone danced in the halls, in the rows, and on the grass in front of the stage. This was clearly a place between the worlds. The music echoed in their bones, moving their muscles as if by magic. The movement was fluid, the people were a river, and every drop of water was holy water. She was touched by the vivid spirituality of the music and color and bodies merging into one great being of love and light.

We danced together. Electricity lights up the space between the dancers. Everyone moved as one great being. Arms and legs moving wildly, beautifully moving in between each other like a great mechanism. Fluid as a natural organism, wild grasses moving in the wind. No one runs into each other. Eyes closed, their perception of each other's cooperative parts of the great whole.

She smiles wide, showing her broken teeth. Thin lips stretch across her face, lighting up her eyes to reveal the fire within. Glowing like a great magic firefly, she bounds across the stream and merges into another current of dancing nymphs.

Going back to the suburbs was like a form of punishment. Cat wanted to spend all her time between the worlds. She no longer had any interest in concerning herself with the real world of the suburbs. Instead, she began focusing on the sky. There seemed to be no limit to the sky. The clouds moved freely, undisturbed by the laws of man, they exhibited limitless grace. The colors of the sun reflected in the clouds at sunset renewed her yearning to carry with her the colorful magic that she had experienced dancing at the Dead Show.

In an effort to capture that feeling, she began painting watercolor pictures of sky. Using cotton balls instead of paintbrushes, she meditated on the feeling of freedom. She channeled her yearning for freedom into the pictures. This newfound interest in art pleased Mama and she gladly shared art supplies with her daughter.

Sometime in late summer, after the big birthday, Cat decided that she wanted to try the mushrooms again. She had eaten them on the beach and hadn't been aware of any changes in her the mental state. So she decided that she must not have eaten enough. Not sure exactly how much was the right amount, she grabbed a handful.

They were getting ready to take a trip to the laundromat. She didn't say anything to her mother about it. It didn't occur to her that she needed to say anything. The experience on the beach had been so relaxed and comfortable, she had no idea that she was taking too much for being in the real world.

At the laundromat with her mother and her roommates, Cat found herself extraordinarily interested in watching the dryers spin the clothes. At this point, Mama realized what must have happened. One of her roommates discreetly ushered Cat out of the laundromat, and hung out with the tripping teen in their van, while the rest of the group finished their laundry. When they got back home, Mama tried to ask her daughter how much she had eaten. Cat couldn't speak properly. All the muscles in her body felt as if they were made of soft rubber.

The adults decided the best thing to do would be to join the girl on her trip. A few of them ate some mushrooms as well, and began choosing music that they thought she would enjoy. She watched the record spin around and around as the sounds of Piper at the Gates of Dawn echoed through the living room. The music was liquid in the air, and she felt as if she was swimming. *Too many clothes for swimming.* Cat began to remove her clothes.

Lying naked on the living room floor, Cat kept saying that she was melting, like butter. A pool of warm liquid on the floor, she began to feel different parts of her body. She tried to explain to her mother "This is not my body." Cat floated above the girl's body below. Mother laughed at her daughter, and assured her that it was she definitely in the right body. She told her daughter not to worry. "we are all here with you dear."

They spent the afternoon and evening tripping together. Listening to music, dancing, and being lucid in between the worlds. This was nothing like what she had experienced on her birthday at the beach. This was so much more vivid. Cat was thankful that she was not alone.

In the days following, Mama took the time to explain to Cat that tripping was not something that should be done in a laundromat. Nor is it something that should be done in secret. She had been upset with Cat for doing what she had done. She explained that not everyone in the city would understand, and that it was dangerous to be in public in that state. For future reference, Cat was expected to talk with Mama about tripping before actually doing so. In this way, Mother could ensure that her daughter was in a safe environment before she became incapacitated.

"I don't understand. Why didn't it happen that way at the beach?" Cat inquired. Mama explained that they had all been high at the beach as well. In a natural environment the goddess could watch over her and cradle her, therefore the effects were likely much more subtle. In the city, there was a lot more contrast. Also, she had probably eaten twice as many as she should have. Lesson learned, tripping at a laundromat is not a good idea.

Chapter 8

THE DEVIL IN SCHOOL

With each school year, depression seemed to hit an all-new low. Cat's depression seemed to push past suicidal thoughts and had developed into an apathetic waking coma. Like a zombie, she moved through her classes in a daze. As hormones hit her harder, the brain jumble began to form a maze. Doodling instead of taking notes in class, she seemed to be unconsciously searching for a pathway to clarity. Like the mazes she created for the school newspaper, there were more dead-ends than anything else. Angry and bitter, she was determined to convince everyone that she was completely crazy.

Cat stopped caring altogether about her academic success. Time that should have been spent working on homework was instead spent lost in thought or writing in her notebook. Unlike the previous year, she spent many afternoons alone. Regardless of how long she hung out in front of the school talking with people, eventually she would be the last one left. Inevitably she'd get bored and head home. Sometimes she went to the Library. Sometimes she wandered around at the mall. Sometimes she would ride the bus all the way around the route. Eventually, she would always go home.

Dad worked long hours, combined with the time it took for him to fight with commute traffic, he was away from home even longer. Cat frequently ate TV dinners by herself. She cooked them in the microwave. *Eating alone wouldn't be so boring if I could use the stove. They don't trust me. They think I am going to burn down the house.* Her cooking was limited to the microwave and the toaster. Dad told her to pick out several frozen dinners when they went grocery shopping, in preparation for the nights he was working late.

Cat discovered that intoxicants helped her hide from the pain. She took up the habit of stealing a very small amount of alcohol from each bottle in her dad's liquor cabinet. That way, the levels did not appear to go down, and she would still get enough volume to have an effect. Mixing the liquors in a bottle half full with Koala brand mixed juice, she carried the concoction to school.

Though she had begun to make friends on the newspaper staff, she felt incredibly lonely. Everyone knew who she was and many of her peers made fun of her. They called her 'Waterdog.' She did not like that. *My name is Firecat.* She really didn't like anything about herself. She tried her very best to get a good buzz on by the time the first bell rang. She did not want to feel present in her life and this was the best escape she had found so far.

One Friday in Spring, Cat was so disgusted with her world, she packed up for the weekend and headed to the BART station. Adventuring on the subway and bus with her backpack and boombox, took a few hours. Sitting at the Rockridge station, music kept her company as she waited for the bus. When she finally arrived at The Oasis, Mama had received notification from Dad to be on the lookout for Cat. Both parents were unhappy with the decision, and relieved that nothing bad had happened to their child. She got in trouble, of course. But since she was there anyway, Dad let her stay for the weekend.

Sunday morning, Cat left her mother's house before anyone woke up. Making her way uptown, she headed for Telegraph Ave, where she was sure to find people who would talk to her. Hanging out with random people, bumming change and making conversation felt like freedom. By the afternoon, she had made friends with enough people to make plans that redirected them to a more remote location.

Sitting in an alley behind the bakery, Cat talked to another girl. The girl was beautiful, with dark hair and big eyes. She wanted to be close to the girl. The girl was interested in a guy. Cat wanted the guys to disappear, but put up with them for the sake of the pretty girl. "He has a friend," the dark haired girl explained. "If you can just keep him busy for a little while, I'd really appreciate it. I'm sure everything will be fine." She heard herself agreeing to keep some random guy company, when what she really wanted to do was disappear into the afternoon sun with the girl sitting next to her. "They should be here soon with something to drink!"

Cat didn't care about anything anymore. She had already drank a couple of beers sitting on the sidewalk by the pizza place earlier. Now, she was ready for anything. Anything was good, as long as she was with this beautiful girl. "For you, I will do it." She smiled, putting her hand on the soft thigh next to hers. Soon the dark haired girl was lighting another cigarette and greeting the boys as they returned to the alley with wine in brown paper wrappers.

The old battered mattress was just fine for sitting down. Quietly questioning how it had arrived there, she nursed the bottle of Night Train in brown paper. Cat's dark haired friend had quickly become distracted by the young man she had been expecting. The two of them were partnered nearby lip-locked and groping, oblivious to the rest of the world. Stuck with the random stranger she had agreed to "keep occupied", Cat proceeded to follow the example of her dark haired friend.

After making out and necking for a while, the fellow seemed to think that the obvious next move would be sex. Cat was not interested in having sex with the stranger. She had been drinking enough to begin getting dizzy and was not entirely sure that she might not begin throwing up soon. Mortified by the prospect of potentially vomiting while kissing someone, she began to get up. He was not happy with her for trying to get up and protested. "I have to get home. I was supposed to be home hours ago!" She pointed to the darkening skies. "I have to go back to West Berkeley. I'm going to be in so much trouble!"

The fellow insisted on walking with her. The dark haired girl had long since disappeared with her kissing partner. Somewhere back in another alley, they may have been having sex. Cat wasn't sure exactly what was going on, as everything seemed blurry and her stomach was doing somersaults. "I have to walk. You have to stop kissing me because I have to go." She pushed his hands off her breasts, and tried to straighten out her clothes. Soon she was stumbling south on Dwight with the fellow close behind. *God I hope I can sober up before I get back to my Mom's house. When is this guy going to get bored walking with me and just go away? He can't show up with me! I am going to be in so much trouble!*

He walked with Cat south from the downtown area toward her mother's place in West Berkeley. Every few blocks they stopped to neck somewhere. He would attempt to talk her into more. She would insist that she couldn't. It was late.

She had to get back to her mom's house. They repeated this ritual three times until finally they made it to San Pablo Ave.

"We are really close. You can not come with me to my Mom's house. I have to show up alone." He protested one last time. "No! I promise to call you next time I am in town, but you have to go back now. You can't come with me!" She insisted that he stop walking with her.

It was really late. In fact, it was long after dark by the time she made it back to The Oasis. Dad was waiting, and apparently had been for quite some time. Cat was reeking of cheap wine and malt liquor. Covered in hickeys, she stumbled in blurry eyed. She was in a lot of trouble with both her parents this time. Dad, sternly instructed her to gather her belongings and steered her toward his truck. The ride home was quiet. *Please don't throw up in the truck. Please, I don't want to throw up in the truck. Oh god, I just want to get home and crawl into bed.*

The next time Cat got to visit her mom, she got the alcoholic talk. Her mother was convinced she had become an alcoholic, or was going to become one. Of course, she rolled her eyes, which only made Mama angry. *She is being ridiculous! She does a lot worse than drink. I barely drink. So I got drunk once. Who cares!* Cat made listening noises and then made empty promises to her mother about alcohol. *Clearly she is just paranoid.*

<hr />

For her eighth grade elective, Cat had signed up to be on the school newspaper staff again. She enjoyed the class. It was a loosely supervised social group with a somewhat focused goal. They put out a newspaper called The Jaguar, named after the school mascot. She wasn't really focused on writing much. Too nervous to be very vocal, she ended up working primarily on proofreading, editing, layout, and publishing. The production and supervision aspects of the newspaper were right up her alley.

Cat was thankful that the teacher let her do these things. He tried to foster inspiration by encouraging students to do what came to them naturally. Even though she was using the black and orange dumb terminal screen of the IBM, she fell in love with the act of working together as part of a team. She also drew illustrations for some of the articles, created a word search, and a maze, near the comics section.

Making friends with a really cute girl that was a first year staff member had been a great way to start the school year. The teacher partnered Jill up with Cat because she was a second year member. They were given an assignment to go interview a teacher together. Cat had fun hanging out with Jill. After that assignment, they sort of became friends. They started hanging out a little more often and even exchanged phone numbers.

That was a big deal to Cat. She could talk on the phone for hours if she liked who she was talking to. It was the next best thing to actually hanging out. Sometimes it was better than hanging out, because they couldn't see how awkward she felt when it was a phone conversation. They would just look for things to talk about.

Once Jill had decided Cat was cool, she introduced her to the cool crowd. They had cool clothes and listened to cool music. They had heard of some of the bands that she'd learned about in Berkeley. She got to be more like herself around these kids. Cat wasn't convinced that she could tell them everything, but it became clear that it was okay to "not fit in". Some of them would get high before school.

Some of them drank alcohol. Some of them smoked ciga-rettes. All of them were alternative or punk rock in some way. All them had their own style.

Cat began get more creative in the way she combined her clothes. She talked Dad into letting her buy clothes at the Buffalo Exchange instead of the mall. When she bought used clothes they were cheaper. She could get more for the money, and she could get creative. She wanted to sew her own cool outfits like Molly Ringwald's character did in Pretty in Pink. She thought that if her clothes were cool that, peo-ple would be more likely to talk to her. It was fun to feel included. Still, she was afraid to be completely herself. Still not sure what that was, she was convinced that nobody would want to be her friend if they really got to know her.

Cat began talking with Jill about her mother's spiritual-ity. Jill seemed interested, and Cat was eager for the atten-tion. Cat had been writing a note to Jill, during Math class. They were not in the same class, and it had been her inten-tion to pass the note in the hall between classes. However, she dropped the note on the floor. Being easily distracted Cat forgot about the note, when she did not see Jill in the halls. Coincidentally, Jill had math in the same classroom, the following period. She walked in, saw the note with her name on it, and picked it up.

As students were not supposed to be writing, passing, or reading notes in class, the teacher confiscated the note when he caught Jill reading it. Instead of punishing either one of the girls for the crime which they had committed, he attacked the content of the note. What was worse, he sent the note to the school counselors office. Apparently, to him, witchcraft, meditation, and candle-gazing was the equiva-lent to Devil-Worshiping. He seemed to forget all about what they had actually done wrong, and instead focused entirely on the content.

Cat was called into the office, as she had penned and signed the note. The counselor explained to her that educators had a legal responsibility to make sure the students were safe. Devil Worshiping was not safe and surely her parents needed to be called, to be informed. According to the counselor, our teacher had been very distraught upon reading the note. He was concerned that not only was she putting herself in danger, but she was also endangering another student.

Cat was furious and became very defensive. Paganism was Not the same Thing as Devil-Worshiping! She was insulted. The counselor tried to explain to her how she was incorrect, and revisited the teachers' concern for their well being. Cat began yelling at the counselor, in anger, "What about freedom of religion? Whose business is it what I believe spiritually?" She told the teacher that she understood that they had broken school rules with the note, and she would be fine accepting whatever punishment was appropriate for writing and passing notes. However, she was outraged that she was being misjudged for the content.

The counselor didn't seem at all interested in punishing her for the error in conduct. She kept refocusing on Devil-Worshiping. Then she said that she would have to contact Jill's parents as well. Jill had been sitting quietly next to Cat for the beginning of the meeting, but was clearly frightened by the prospect of getting her parents involved. She remembered Jill describing her parents as conservative Christians who would have expressed just as close-minded a response.

Cat wanted to protect Jill from getting in trouble. She looked at the pretty girl turning white in the chair next to her, tightly clutching the sides of her chair. She redirected the conversation by again asking "What about my freedom of religion?" The counselor responded that as a minor, the student didn't have any rights. Therefore the 'freedom of religion' that she kept referring to did not apply.

Absolute bullshit. Finally, Cat burst out, "Fine, call my mother! In fact, I will call her myself and tell her right now." The counselor agreed that it would be responsible and appropriate for her to call her mother. Cat did not the mention that she did not currently live with her mom. The counselor handed her the phone and she dialed her mom's number. Once on the phone, she briefly explained what had happened with the note.

The counselor watched the girl on the phone, face contorting as Cat explained that she didn't want Jill's parents to be contacted, because she was concerned that they would be as close-minded as her math teacher was. Hearing this, the counselor began to protest, but the student cut her off. "My mother wants to talk to you." Cat handed the telephone receiver to the school counselor.

Mama's voice was so loud that both students could hear her from where they sat. Mama repeated the same 'freedom of religion rights' that Cat had already claimed to the counselor previously. She explained that 'Paganism was not devil-worshiping' and that as educators, 'they should know better.' In addition, she explained that if the school contacted Jill's parents, or further harassed either of the students regarding their choice of spirituality, the school would be receiving a call from her attorney.

Mama made it clear that she was insulted by the situation. She had an attorney on her phone list from the recent Berkeley Inn lawsuit. While she was bluffing a little, reading them the riot act was enough to put the fear of publicity in anyone. The school counselor responded very stiffly.

"Yes ma'am, I understand. Thank you for taking the time

to speak with us today."

Both students were sent back to class after the phone call. The school never notified Cat's father or Jill's parents. They never messed with either student about anything again. Mama had put the fear of lawsuit in their minds. The last thing they wanted was a crazy parent filing a suit against them for harassing children. The two never got in trouble for passing notes. They never got in trouble for anything again that year. Cat became untouchable and she bragged about it to her friends.

———————•«(◊)»•———————

Cat didn't see Carrie as often during eighth grade. Every time Cat saw her, she was thinner and her boobs were bigger. She was ashamed of how ugly she felt standing next to Carrie. *She's so pretty.* Cat was totally smitten. It hurt in an indescribable way to be around Carrie, so Cat didn't try as hard to make plans with her. This left her alone on alternating weekends. The lonelier she got, the more depressed she got.

Chapter 9

PARTY CRASHERS

Dad was getting frustrated. Cat had actually come to him months before asking about getting back into counseling. Busy with working, commuting, and trying to keep up with everything life threw at him, he kept forgetting to look for a counselor. His daughter kept getting in trouble and was doing poorly in school. His peers suggested she would benefit from tutoring. He knew that she was smart, but something had to be done.

Dad finally gave into the nagging memory of unfinished business and did some hunting. Once he found a local counselor that worked with teenagers, he immediately got Cat scheduled with weekly counseling appointments. When he mentioned the upcoming schedule change at the dinner table one Saturday morning, her response was less than enthusiastic.

Cat had given up on Clarinet lessons. She got tired of having to run to catch a bus, just to spend almost an hour waiting at the transfer station. Repeating the process after lessons meant she got home long after dark. Walking home in the cold alone after lessons had been exhausting and depressing in seventh grade. She was glad to give that up, and now she would have to ride the city bus to a new appointment once a week after school. Dad pointed out that it would be an easier ride because she didn't have to transfer buses.

Cat decided early on that she didn't trust the counselor. She was convinced that the counselor didn't care, and was only putting up with Cat because she wanted Dad's money. She spent most of the sessions staring at the woman's leg hair poking out through tiny holes in her pantyhose. Cat thought it looked rather odd. It kind of creeped her out. *It would be better not to wear the hose. Or just shave your legs.*

In counseling sessions, Cat ranted and raved about various things, trying to be extra melodramatic. She figured her dad better get his money's worth. She was determined to make the woman work hard for Dad's money. No matter how many appointments she had, she never seemed to get comfortable with the counselor. However, she did like that it gave her a reason to go to downtown Walnut Creek. Lots of teenagers hung out downtown. She wanted to see what it was all about. Dad didn't want her hanging out downtown. So of course, that's where she went. Still, she didn't linger for very long, as she was terrified of being caught breaking the rules.

Cat had a great deal of leeway space. There were several hours of each day that Dad had no contact with her. He did not return from work until at least 6 pm, most often later, and he had no way of knowing whether she was going home or not. It was only the fear of what Dad might do if he caught her doing something wrong that kept her from pushing the boundaries too far. She wanted to do her own thing, but was terrified that if she went too far, he would give up on her. While she took her time going home, she always made sure to be there long before he was expected back.

When Cat had counseling appointments, she had an excuse to go downtown, even though she was grounded. She would get downtown early, and stop by McDonald's for an ice cream cone. Hanging out and eating her ice cream, she watched the kids that she didn't know. They were all having fun with each other. They all knew each other. She wanted to be part of a group of friends like that. She was starting to develop that with Jill and her friends, but still, she always felt removed. She always felt isolated, even in their small crowd. *What do these kids have that I am missing?*

After her appointment, she'd walk through the downtown area. If she had enough money, she'd stop at the cafe' and get a coffee. Sitting quietly on the patio, she'd watch the teens hanging out. Situated with her notebook, she doodled and wrote rambling words illustrating whatever she was feeling at the time. *I wish they'd talk to me. Just come up and introduce yourself. "Hey, I see you here every Thursday. What's your name?"*

Nobody ever talked to her. Eventually, she'd pack up her things and quietly leave the cafe'. Arriving at the empty house, she'd make a TV dinner, do her chores, and retire to her room.

⸻ ((◦)) ⸻

Over the course of eighth grade, Cat managed to end up being grounded for the rest of her life. Or so it seemed at the time. She would get in trouble for something, ride out her punishment, and then get in trouble for something else. It seemed to happen over and over again. Mostly she lied a lot, and then got caught a lot. At one point, when she was in between restrictions, she got Dad to agree to let her throw an 'End-of-Eighth-Grade Party.'

Thanks to being a two-year staff member with the school newspaper, Cat had managed to gain face and name recognition with what felt like a lot of people. She didn't feel especially close to many of them, but still, it was a pretty large social crowd! Throwing a party could be really fun! *People might actually show up!* So when she got grounded again, Cat was very disappointed. Her smart mind went to work on Dad. "If I'm grounded that means I can't go anywhere. But I am not leaving to have a party." Somehow she managed to get her dad to agree. Amazing!

The last Saturday evening before the end of school, Cat would get to host a big party. She decided she would invite *everybody* she could think of. She wanted her party to be the "It" Party, the party that everyone would talk about in school. She thought maybe it would anchor her position in the cool crowd. Of course none of it would matter if she moved to Berkeley.

Despite my growing social life, in school, I am becoming more and more depressed and isolated from myself. I have feelings going on inside me that are confusing and I have nobody that I trust enough to talk to about them. I can't even find the words to adequately share the feelings I am experiencing. I try to explore myself as often as I have chances to sneak off. It feels like a trial and error process, something like a grand adventure. Each step I take is a question. In the direction of the rough and colorful Telegraph Avenue, I stumble along a path of self exploration in little bits and pieces on the weekends that I get to leave the suburbs.

I breathe in the counterculture like sweet apricot nectar from the grocery store, with whipped cream on top because mom's food stamps will pay for it. Like a dog on an invisible leash, unaware of which direction my anchor lay behind me. I can't see it, and don't know for sure where it's hiding. I am afraid of failing, afraid of being seen and being judged insufficient, unacceptable. I spend as much time hanging out on the Ave as I can get away with, during my weekends at Mama's place. I sit, invisible to the world and just take it all in. Drawing pictures, and asking for change, not because I need it really, but just to give me a purpose for being there. I hold down the edges of my pictures with the change I collect from passers by. Sometimes I sell a picture for five or ten dollars.

I talk to people who live on the street, and to college students. Occasionally I have to talk to police. I avoid these opportunities as much as possible. Sometimes, I bring my clarinet with me and play with the box open for money. I don't really expect anyone to give much, because I know I'm not good. Still, it gives me an excuse to be there, to spend hours in front of Rexall Drugs, without anyone else questioning my existence. I'm busy trying to find clues on my personal search for existence. I don't want to have to shift my reality quickly and this place seems safe to me.

The street vendors begin to get to know me as a regular face on the street. I am glad to talk to anyone that seems to acknowledge me as a human being. This strange kind of unquestioning acceptance feels very different than the judgmental looks that greet me in the suburbs. I am ashamed of my past. I am ashamed of my present. Afraid that I will some how miss some great clue and die in the midst of a police state disruption, I have little hope for the future. The moment is always the most important thing for me. I want to feel everything, perceive everything, understand everything, or at least something.

Everything and nothing and little bits of something that I can not explain, swirl in a great mass of emotion. I always feel like a rabbit on its haunches, ready at any moment to sprint away to some unseen cave of safety. I feel compelled to be alert to any possible detail that might be the key to the unidentified mystery I am trying to discover. Every day I have to return to Dad's home, a great blue burden of misery waits in the shadows of my bedroom. Returning to my room, my weekend bag landing upside down on my floor, I collapse exhausted and crying into my blankets in the corner under the shuttered windows. I feel isolated, like Contra Costa County is a prison, and my room is Solitary Confinement. Every bus driver, teacher, and convenience store clerk looks down on me. I can read disgust in their faces. They all despise me, seeing me as untrustworthy, a trouble making freak. I will never be anything, to anyone. I will never be a well respected man like Dad.

When the night finally came for her big party, Cat was really excited. Some of the girls made mix tapes of music just for the party. They listened to Love & Rockets and The Cure over and over again. Lots of people showed up. One person smuggled in a couple of wine coolers. Another person appeared with some pot. It was really low grade shaky stuff. They took turns hiding in Cat's bedroom closet for the sneaky stuff, because they didn't want to get caught.

Dad was home and hiding in his room. He was pretty good about not embarrassing Cat in front of her friends. Relaxing in his room, he didn't show any interest in being in a room full of teenagers. Cat was thankful that it was all going well. At one point, some guys showed up that had not been invited. *We have party crashers?!* A couple of the guys from the cool group went outside down the walkway toward where the other boys were.

Cat could see that things might get ugly so she went inside and knocked on Dad's door. She quickly explained what was going on. Dad went outside to the boys on the walkway and informed them they were going to have to leave because they were not invited. Then he went back in his room.

They all cheered! "That was awesome!" The evening went on for several hours. The party was a big success. Kids would be talking about her big party at school on Monday. Despite all the miserable hell that puberty and middle school had been for her up to that point, for that one night, Cat felt accepted. The living room had been completely full, and she had felt loved by her peers. In the moment, she felt like she had friends.

Later in the evening several of the Cat's friends went for a late night walk to the local park. They wanted her to go with them, but she insisted that she couldn't leave the house. That was the rule that Dad had stuck to, so she had to as well. Ignoring the posted hours on the park sign, the group enjoyed a game of dodge the sprinklers and returned victorious and sopping wet. Eventually all the parents came and she passed out, in her room happy and exhausted.

My mother moved out the day after I finished first grade. I was surprised and confused. I'd been hearing their arguments through the walls. For a long time, but I didn't know how long. I can't remember that far back. My memories floated in bits and pieces. Sometimes I can pull them out of the pool and recall details. It takes a lot of conjuring to make that happen and I usually prefer to forget. Sometimes they surprise me.

I remember being in Kindergarten. Some kids at

school had been talking about divorce. I didn't know what that was. I didn't want to feel stupid in front of the other kids at school. I didn't want to give them another reason to tease me. Still, I wanted to know what they knew.

I wanted to understand everything, and be smart and cool, and blend in. I really wanted other kids to stop teasing me. It was a sad and lonely existence, to be the one that everyone teased. I always looked forward to coming home to Mama. She was my whole world. If there was anything or anyone that I put on a pedestal when I was little, it was Mama. I could do no wrong in her eyes. She was always there for me. She always had words of acceptance and love and big hugs for me.

Everyday when I got home from school, we had a snack. Then we had cuddle and nap time. I recall sitting on my parents' big water-bed and talking with Mama. Then we'd snuggle and take a nap in the big bed. I didn't mind that I had to take a nap, because I was with Mama. It felt safe.

So I went home to find the answer. I waited until we were sitting in the big comfy bed to ask the scary question. I remember that the color left my mother's face when I asked "What is divorce?"

―∞―

Cat put down the pen and closed her notebook. She couldn't write anymore. Tears streamed down her face. Had so much time passed already? Looking back, she imagined what Mama must have been thinking. Her parents had been fighting for a while. *They were clearly not happy. Despite how shaken Mom was by the question, she had answered it with grace and poise.*

Mother had explained to the little girl, that sometimes mom's and dad's just can't get along. "They try a lot and it isn't enough. So they agree to not live with each other anymore." She said that sometimes it's the best thing but it can be hard on kids. She said that it was important to understand that it didn't have anything to do with the kids, and it was probably pretty confusing for everyone involved. Cat understood, and it sounded terrible to her. "Will you and Dad ever do that?" Mother assured her daughter that she would always be there for her. "I'm not going anywhere," she responded. Then they hugged and snuggled and took a nap.

———————⸺«(•)»⸺———————

The 1986 fire at the Berkeley Inn was a blessing in disguise for Cat's mother. Agoraphobia had really done a number on her. If the fire had never happened, Mama would never have moved into The Oasis. She would still be hiding in that tiny apartment room. She hid in the comfort of regular habits. She didn't leave her apartment room very often. When she left it was only to go to familiar places. She followed the same walking paths through the same parks. She always went to the same grocery stores, and the same Cafe' where she always ordered the same thing.

Mama would go for walks, moving gracefully, and almost silently on the memorized routes. Only the rhythmic tapping of her walking stick echoed as she disappeared from the populated areas. She liked quiet tree lined residential streets. She liked going up to the hills and spending time with the trees. She still liked it, but after moving to the south side of town, she didn't go up there as often. The view from the Berkeley Hills shows how large the San Francisco Bay Area is, while presenting it as small and separate. Often the fog covers it up entirely and one could pretend like the city didn't even exist.

The Berkeley Inn had been purchased by some people who were not Americans. They were from somewhere from the Middle East. They wore turbans on their heads, and had funny mustaches. Cat never got to know the details as they were not pertinent to her visits with her mom.

The hotel was in great disrepair. Cat remembered there being mattresses lying in the halls. The apartments in the resident hotel were just a room. Some had toilets, some did not. Her mother's had a little half bath with a sink and a toilet. She cooked her food on a hot plate and did her dishes in the the bathroom sink. When it was time to take a shower, there was one bathroom per floor that was a full bath with shower. The bathroom on her floor didn't always work though. Sometimes when she went to visit Mama, she had to go all the way down to the first floor to use the bathtub.

It was creepy wandering around in a hotel with her bath stuff. Having to come back up through the main lobby in her bathrobe, all wet from the bath was especially unnerving. The men behind the counter made her uncomfortable. Some of the other tenants made her uncomfortable.

Cat recalled a time when she went down to the lobby bathroom to take a bath. There was a dead mouse lying next to the tub. She very carefully avoided it while she bathed. She bathed quickly and scurried back up stairs to tell her mom. She was frightened but didn't want to let that stop her. She always wanted to prove her strength somehow. She wanted to be a tough guy. She didn't want to be afraid of anything. What Cat was most afraid of, was losing her mother's approval.

When the Berkeley Inn burned down, it was rumored that it was an arson job, to enable the owners to cash in on their insurance. The owners, of course, filed an insurance claim on their business loss and tried to flee the country with the money. Unfortunately, the local law enforcement had other ideas.

With a possible arson charge hanging over their heads, they were encouraged to stick around. They stuck around long enough for a class-action lawsuit, presented by a band of disgruntled tenants, led by none-other-than Cat's own mother. Once the legal battle had been lost and paid, they ran, tails between their legs, back to their home country. At least, that was the story Cat was told. The property continued to develop its own story after the owners left.

Being suddenly homeless forced Cat's mother to face her fears of being outside around other people. She could not avoid her neighbors or the outside world, because she was alone in the world. Yet she was not alone. All her neighbors were in the same situation. Rather than avoiding them, she talked with them. She actually got to know some of them. She made friends and gained personal strength from the experience that carried her a lot farther than she had expected. The momentum she gained propelled her forward for long enough that finally, Dad agreed to let Cat move in with Mama.

Mother was a natural artist. She incorporated her passion for creativity into everything she did. In Cat's eyes, she was amazing. She made big calendars for every month. *I remember, when I was little, getting to color the pictures that illustrated each month on her home made calendars.* She wrote everything important for school on the calendar, along with her own appointments. This had made the younger child feel important, like a big kid. Now, remembering them made the present Cat nostalgic.

Mama made everything fun. She hand painted eggs for Easter, and she blew eggs out hollow and painted them for Christmas ornaments. She made detailed ornaments for the tree. We got to do it together. When Halloween time came, she made the best costumes. She would take me to the thrift store at the town square by the park. We'd search to find clothes that she would then snip, and sew, and modify into the perfect costume.

Downtown Sonoma has a lot of character. Although it isn't as charming as it used to be, as it has become a hotbed of B&B's and restaurants. I liked the Sonoma of my childhood, when the theater really showed the latest movie. There wasn't a line to get into the museum, and the clothes at the thrift store were still cheap. In my memory, that park was the biggest and prettiest park ever. Sonoma is still worth visiting, but it will never again be as beautiful as my childhood memories of going to the town square for lunch, a trip to the thrift store, and a trip to the park.

When my mother left, I lost all those afternoon trips to the park. I lost the Christmas cookies with icing and the decorated calendars. I lost the afternoon snuggles and talks that we had every day after school. I lost my best friend. I remember feeling my heart breaking as she left our house with her bags.

Chapter 10

THE OASIS

Moving in with her mother was something Cat had been dreaming about for years. Now that it was happening, she was sure that her whole world would change forever. Being in Berkeley provided a completely alternate reality. Mama's friends got Cat high.

Mama shared with her daughter. "I expect you are going to experiment with drugs. It's only natural. But I would rather you come to me. If you go getting something from strangers on a street corner, they could be selling you Drano or rat poison. I don't want you accidentally killing yourself." This was Mama's way of trying to be a practical and effective parent to a teen in a big city. She assumed her daughter would want to try everything.

Cat just needed to rebel. She needed to push the boundaries set before her, and to figure out what *her boundaries* were. She had to practice standing her ground. Mama gave her so much room that Cat practically had to try and kill herself to rebel. By the time, Cat got to move in, her mother had already spent over a year practicing so much patience with her daughter that she very little patience left. When Mama hit her limit, she'd explode like a volcano.

Cat didn't want to be around Mama when she yelled and screamed. It was a pretty frightening experience to be present for. She would shriek and wave her arms around and the ranting and high volume with all the tears and anger and frustration was enough to scare anyone into the smallest hole they could find. Explosions are often messy. Not only did she terrify the girl, but Mama also terrified her house mates and problems began to arise in her household. The timing directly corresponded with Cat's hormonal tension. The housemates that began to act poisonously vindictive toward her mother, were the same people that Cat had begun partying with. Her tension and confusion spilled out, affecting the situation as she searched for boundaries to cross.

It was Father's Day when Cat moved in with her mom. With a lack of tact that only a 13 year old can truly master, she happily packed all her stuff. She was looking forward to having her own little cave in her mother's basement. She was going to have a loft in her room and it was so cool! Anything that was different from the norm, that was alternative from the standard suburban lifestyle was cool to her. *I want to be free from the expectations of being normal. I want to be free to find myself!*

Fantasy is not always the same as reality, and in most cases differs greatly. Her adolescence was no exception to this rule. Dad helped his daughter pack her stuff into his truck and delivered her to The Oasis. There were three bedrooms upstairs, all occupied by other housemates. Some of them were leftovers from the Berkeley Inn.

They had used some of their class action lawsuit money to get the house and had been renting it for a couple years by that time. The landlord seemed cool enough. He never gave them a hard time, even when they were late on the rent. Dad had been sufficiently satisfied with Mama's ability to stay in the same house for a while.

The downstairs was as big as the upstairs, only the ceilings were taller. The basement had one of those angled cellar doors that was accessed from the back yard. When Cat went out the basement door, she had to climb the back stairs to go into the house. There was no bathroom in the basement, so that meant going to the bathroom in the middle of the night required going outside, up the stairs, in the back door and down the hall, and then repeating, in reverse, the whole process to get back to bed. Cat didn't mind having to do it during the day. She did not enjoy this process in the middle of the night. She thought it would be especially unpleasant in the winter.

There was a wall that divided the basement into two great rooms, with a large doorway cut out in the middle. Mama hung thick drapery style curtains in the doorway for privacy and warmth. This gave her a room equivalent to the size of half the house. She hung tapestries and blankets on the walls for insulation and decor. Paintings were affixed to nails that had been hammered through the tapestries. She hung tree roots from the ceiling to emphasize the allusion of being underground. Her art was everywhere. It felt like a surreal cave. And in fact, it was nicknamed "The Cave" by all those who entered, including her mom.

The south side of the basement was the side with the door. There were shelves up to the ceiling for storage. The south wall was lined with windows. This made it bright enough to do lots of projects during the day. The need for lamps was nearly eliminated. A long work table lined the wall under the windows. In the far corner, at the end opposite the entrance to the basement, was Cat's area. Over a year ago, one of her mother's lovers helped to build the loft bed. She had spent hours arranging and rearranging the "room" during previous visits.

A curtain hung from the ceiling, offering privacy in her bed. Underneath she set up a little living room area for herself. She used a dresser and curtains to create the illusion of a wall and doorway. This gave it a room within a room feel. She was happy! She loved her room there and was overjoyed to move her stuff into it that Father's Day.

Dad stayed and talked to her mom. Margaret did not like him spending time with other women, especially Cat's Mama. She was not pleased at the amount of help he had given Mama over the years already. Margaret and Cat did not get along, and the girl assumed that Dad's girlfriend was happy to see her go. Still, it was tough for her dad, a slap in the face to move his daughter on Father's Day. He had tried his very best to be a good father to her, and she had not been very responsive.

———— ((◦)) ————

Mama had already gotten used to letting Cat ride the bus. She had been taking the city bus to school since she was ten years old. Cat had taken the bus and subway to come to visit her mother several times. The high school she would be attending was a few miles away from the house, near the downtown area, and conveniently, across the street from the UC Berkeley campus. She would have to take the public bus to school every day! She felt free. She immediately started taking off during the day that Summer. She couldn't get away with it every day. Not at first.

That first summer Mama would make her daughter stay home every couple of days. "You've been gone a lot lately, honey, it won't hurt you to spend some time at home." She would tell her all this while making tea & toast. Then she would take the tea & toast on her tray, and head out the back door and down the stairs to The Cave. She would disappear in there for hours at a time. If anyone wanted to spend time with Mama, they would have to come to see her, because she almost never came out of her cave. It was no different with Cat.

At first, Cat was excited about getting to live with her mom, thinking it was going to be just like a long visit. She brought Mama tea and toast in the morning. They would drink their tea and eat their toast, talking about what the day might have in store while they enjoyed breakfast together. It didn't take long to begin feeling like a chore. She had to go upstairs and make the tea and toast. She had to bring the tray downstairs. She had to serve her mother. Often because Mama was too depressed to leave and Cat was afraid Mama would not eat if Cat did not feed her.

The girl began to feel burdened by the necessity to take care of her mother. She was almost 14 years old and she knew everything. Cat was all grown up, or so she thought. *I can ride the bus. I can go anywhere.* Mama couldn't stop her, and now Dad couldn't either. *I am free. It's unfair that I have to take care of my mom.* She would be grumpy at Cat about taking too long, or not making breakfast correctly. *It is ridiculous for her to get mad at me for doing something, that I started doing, just to be nice.* She didn't want it to become a chore. There had never been any discussion. There was no agreement. So Cat didn't bring her breakfast one day. Just to see what would happen.

Some days when Cat had left before Mama woke up, Cat had prepared tea and toast, leaving the tray by her mother's bed with a good morning note. But for one day, she decided not to do anything. She left the house without saying good morning. She was fed up with feeling taken for granted and wanted to see what Mama would say. She went on with her day, not returning home until after dinner time.

Mama was furious when Cat returned home. She ranted about being gone from home so often and so long. And then... It was the breakfast. Mama was actually mad at her for not making her tea and toast before Cat left for the day. "And what was so important that you had to leave without having breakfast with me first?" Mama scolded. *I knew it! She expects me to wait on her!* Cat was feeling justified. Her experiment had produced exactly the results she had expected. Cat was feeling even more like she knew everything.

"It's not my job to bring you breakfast every day!" Her response cut into Mama like a knife. "It's a nice thing for me to do, but you shouldn't expect it!" *It's totally unfair for her to be mad at me for not making her breakfast!* Mama held her face in her hands. Tears poured out of puffy red eyes. Her feelings were hurt. She felt rejected and unwanted by her daughter. Cat was too proud and defensive to understand.

They each went to their separate rooms. This was the beginning of the real turmoil. True, they had hit some rough spots since Cat had turned twelve. Limits had been pushed in the past, but the young girl had never before shown such bold rebellion. Mama was at a loss. In the past, this attitude had been saved for Dad. When Cat moved to Berkeley, the balance of good parent/ bad parent shifted. Cat was able to begin talking to her dad a little more. The fairy tale image of her mother quickly faded to black.

Despite the fact that Mama's feelings were hurt, she admitted defeat. She had been beat. It was not her daughters job to bring her breakfast. Once they both had time to calm down and think, the young woman and her mother had another talk. Cat apologized for being mean and hurting Mama's feelings. "I acknowledge that it was not fair for me to expect you to wait on me." Mama explained that it was just her missing her daughter being little and wanting to spend so much time with her mother. "I understand that you are becoming a young woman," Mama said, "but you still need to learn some manners."

A young woman. That made Cat shudder. She didn't know what about becoming a young woman that she didn't like, but hearing that made her want to do everything opposite that Mama said a young woman was supposed to do. *But I don't like Mama being angry because she gets scary when she's angry.* When Mama was angry, she would shriek loudly, waving her hands around violently, screaming at the top of her lungs, until she was sobbing and hyperventilating. *Then of course it becomes my fault for making her get like that.* By the time that arguments escalated to this point, Cat would be so worried about her mother, and so exhausted from the whole experience that she usually succumbed to taking the blame and was apologizing. *I will try to be the responsible young woman she wants me to be.* It never stuck.

━━━━━❈━━━━━

Cat spent a lot of time hanging out on Telegraph Ave. Walking five miles across town to be there did not seem like a chore to her. Once she started walking her legs began to move rhythmically, as if they had their own power. She went first to the bus stop, but could not stay still to sit and wait for a bus. Instead she moved quickly up through the neighborhoods in pursuit of a feeling of freedom.

The Summer between Middle School and High School,

there seemed to be more deadheads and hippies hanging around than she had noticed before. The Grateful Dead would be returning to the Greek Theater the weekend after her 14th birthday. She had spent the weeks leading up to her birthday immersing herself in their subculture whenever possible. She decided that her birthday would be fantastic.

Cat spent the better part of her birthday hanging out in front of Fat Slice Pizza with a couple of deadheads. Occasionally she would announce to passersby that it was her birthday. By the end of the day, she had convinced her "new friends" that they should come home with her. She spent the evening tripping with a head called Cosmo and making out with him.

Cat wanted attention. She wanted acceptance. She wanted to feel good. Her new friend didn't seem to mind the opportunity and obliged freely. Without any arguments from Mama, he was allowed to spend the night in Cat's bed. As a birthday present to herself, she had intercourse for the first time. It didn't feel dirty or forced. She enjoyed the closeness and didn't feel bad about it.

By the weekend, Cosmo had moved on and Cat was meeting new people. Her feelings weren't hurt. They were all free of attachments and simply enjoying the world in the moment. She went to The Grateful Dead Show at the Greek Theater. She didn't get in, and consequently spent a large portion of time hanging out in the adjacent Soccer Fields. She met a boy named Bryan, and ended up bringing him home with her like a stray puppy.

Cat really liked him. They talked and drew pictures together. They seemed to connect in a way that felt natural and not forced. He hung out with her and stayed at The Oasis for about a week. Then he took off with a guy. It turned out that Bryan was attracted to guys. Her feelings were hurt and she was confused. If he liked guys, then why did he spend so much time with her? *Was I a terrible girl? Is there something wrong with me?*

Cat wore revealing clothes when she went out. She tried to make them creative. She put together her outfits to mimic the pretty girls on Telegraph Ave. She thought they were cool. She wanted to be accepted by them. *In Middle School, girls wouldn't really talk to me until I looked like them. Maybe if I can look enough like the pretty girls on the Ave, they will talk to me.* She didn't feel like a young woman. *I don't know what I feel like, except confused. But I know I like girls and I like boys too.*

Cat decided that she needed to be more sexy to make the guys like her. It didn't seem to work out the way she wanted though. The guys who were attracted to her didn't seem to want to hang out for very long. She was more physically attracted to the girls. Too terrified of being found out, she refrained from talking with them much. It was much easier to hang out with the guys because they didn't intimidate her. She could relate to them.

The guys seem to like hanging out with me, because I act like them. Added bonus, I've got tits! Once the guys realize that I might be willing to get sexual, they get kind of boring. She was thoroughly confused.

Cat liked the attention. She liked feeling wanted. *If this is what feeling pretty is supposed to feel like, then I like it sometimes. So why do I spend so much time feeling all fake and empty. Why can't I escape being depressed all the time?* She would try to find guys who would get her drunk or high, so she could hide from the sadness. When she went up to the Ave, she'd pace up and down the street until she found a couple of guys spare changing. Sitting down next to them, conversation was quick to follow. Soon she'd join them in the effort to beg for money.

Eventually, the collected money would go to buy them all food and some kind of intoxicant. It was usually cheap beer or wine, depending on who she was keeping company with. She hung out and talked to everyone that would talk to her. She was as loud and boisterous and visible as she could be. It was terrifying. She wanted so badly to be accepted that she threw herself directly into the fire. In the process she got burned pretty badly.

The experience of hanging out on the streets fed Cat's cocky attitude. *I know a lot more about the world than my parents give me credit for. They don't believe in me at all. I wonder if they even care what happens to me?* Naive and pompous, her snarling teenager attitude was like a slap in the face to Mama. She started really having a difficult time understanding how to deal with her daughter.

———— ◆ ————

The next big concert that the clan from The Oasis packed up for was Laguna Seca. This time, Mama and her friends traveled in a great caravan. Similar to the previous trips up to Goat Rock, and Boreal Ridge, they piled into multiple vehicles with camping gear and people. This time they headed south. The trip seemed to last forever. By the time they pulled onto Dead Lot Friday night, it had already started getting dark.

This time, they were camping in the parking lot. It was the first time Cat really got to immerse herself in the subculture of the Deadheads as a traveling city. She fell asleep in a sleeping bag on the ground as folks set up camp all around her. When she awoke everything was quiet and she was damp from the early morning mist. Walking up and down the rows of cars and encampments was like wandering the streets of the city. Only in this city, she could walk barefoot and feel dirt and grass beneath her feet.

Different camps each offered something unique. Many of the camps were still quiet with sleeping people. Cat wandered the aisles until she found a camp that was stirring with hot coffee. Reaching into her hip bag, she found a crystal to trade for coffee. Sitting and drinking coffee she talked with folks that wandered by. She remained for a while after her cup was empty. Finally, thanking the folks for their company and coffee she handed them back the empty coffee cup.

Legs feeling twitchy, Cat went back to roaming again. This time she found a camp offering pancakes. As more people woke up, she could see more and more "shops" open up. Everyone had something different to offer. As the sun rose higher in the sky, the air began to warm up and so did the crowd. Returning back to her base camp, Mama didn't seem at all disturbed by her daughter's coming and going. She knew Cat would be staying on the lot. As long as the girl was here on Deadlot, she was safe.

Mama had been given a ticket to get into the Saturday evening show and Cat would be hanging outside while the show was going on. There were plenty of other people who would be outside during the show. She would not be bored. She changed clothes out of her pajamas, putting on a sun dress more appropriate for the Summer day. Digging through her weekend bag, she assessed what else she might have to offer for trade.

Locating a box of watercolor crayons and a water bottle, she added them to her hip bag. Then she wandered off, back down Shakedown Street, to make more friends. Stopping to talk to different people, Cat began offering body painting to different people. Dipping the crayons into her water bottle, she drew rainbows and swirly designs on folks in exchange for various different items. She gained new crystals and trinkets, adding them to her bag of stuff that she could use for barter later on. She bartered for food and drinks. She talked with people. She moved on throughout the crowd.

As the sun grew hotter, Cat felt her skin burning. The sting of sunburn on her chest encouraged her to move the elastic top farther and farther down her chest. By late afternoon, she had put on a soft cloak and moved her sun dress down as if it were only a skirt. Bare chested underneath her cloak, the sting of the sunburn was comforted with the gentle brush of soft fake fur.

As the sun set, Cat could hear the sound of the concert playing in the distance. She had settled down to talk to a boy who seemed to be pleased with her openness and half nudity. Again, she thrived on the attention and let him get closer to her. The boy introduced her to 'Rush', a bottle of something that they took turns huffing, and then laid down together in the midst of their heads spinning. After a while it made her head hurt, and they began making out instead. Eventually she got tired of it all and wandered off to find her base camp.

In the morning Cat awoke to the painful itching of a gloriously bright red chest. Her breasts were burnt so badly that it hurt to wear anything at all. She wandered the aisles of camps bare chested, wrapped in her cloak. Talking with people that she had met the day before, she hunted down coffee and a grilled cheese sandwich. Returning back to base camp, Mama informed her that they would be packing up and heading home early in the day. She teased her daughter about the sunburn and suggested that perhaps she had learned a lesson about running around half naked in the hot Summer sun.

Cat was not appreciative. Mama's comments did not make the sunburn feel better. Short tempered from exhaustion, she was not as helpful as she could have been with the packing of the camping gear. She wandered off several times. The boy from the previous night found her and gave her his bottle of Rush. She tucked it in her bag, and kissed him in thanks. Eventually, she made her way back to their vehicles.

Loading gear and people, the caravan attempted to leave Deadlot before that afternoon's concert began. They anticipated a great deal of traffic and were eager to get back home. The weekend had been fun and seemed to float by like a dream. Cat was asleep in the car long before they actually made it home. Within a week of the show, she decided that the Rush was a bad idea. It was fun for a minute, but then it made her head hurt and she got nauseous. She threw the bottle away with no regrets.

Despite the fact that Cat had been practicing being a teenager for a year now, she still didn't know what she was supposed to be doing, or if she was doing it right. She presented herself as an awkward person who was used to be abused by their peers. She continued to receive abuse from her peers. Her fantasy about being able to do whatever she wanted was not properly nourished by her mother's bedside parenting. Once she actually got to go live with her mother, it didn't take long for fantasy to turn into reality. That's about the time Cat stopped coming home on a regular basis.

Chapter 11

FRESHMAN YEAR

Cat lay in the quiet silence of her loft room. *I've moved so many times!* She hadn't minded too much, because getting made fun of by her peers got old quickly. Every time they moved to a new place, she tried to convince herself that "this new place will be different." *Middle School was the first time that I stayed at the same school for more than two years. I wonder if any of the kids will notice I'm gone when they get to high school. Probably not.* Social anxieties compounded with her awkward self-presentation added to the challenge of making friends. She felt like other kids didn't like her. She was sure they knew she cried a lot, and judged her for it.

Cat's life had started in Alaska, but they hadn't stayed there long either. Dad had been drafted and was in Boot Camp stationed at Anchorage. Mama lived with him in housing for the families of folks stationed nearby. Mama used to tell her daughter stories about the winter she had spent in Alaska. Cat liked looking at the beautiful photographs. *I bet the sunset and sunrise that far north is amazing. Someday I want to go there to see where I was born and paint the sky.*

When Cat was a baby, they moved to Oregon. Hazy

memories of picking blackberries along the edge of a near-by canyon hung like old spiderwebs in her mind. *I remember wandering around the neighborhood with a couple of other kids. Of course the world seemed huge to me then, so it may have simply been the neighbors yard. But I remember the neighbor had a toilet in his backyard with plants growing out of it and I remember watching guys riding their motorcycles through the canyon. It was loud, but it was so cool!* She recalled telling her Mama, "When I get big, I'm gonna ride a motorcycle too!" After a couple of years living in Milwaukee, her family headed south to California.

Cat's family stayed with her Aunt for a while in Fairfield. Combing through her timeline, she tried to recall memories from living with her Aunt. All she could remember was that she had argued with her cousin a lot. When they moved again, it was into a little place in Hayward. She wasn't allowed to play outside because the street was very busy. Mama said the cars drove very fast and she didn't want Cat to get hurt. *There was a Subaru dealership across the street from our house.* She pictured in her mind numbers on brightly colored banners across car windows. *I remember falling asleep listening to my parents watch television. My bedroom had no door, so it was never quiet or absolutely dark.*

Cat was almost five years old when her family finally moved into the house on Hyde Road. It was beautiful there, with a big yard to play in. There were other kids down the lane. It was actually safe to go wandering! She found a creek, and woods, and had daydreamed about all kinds of possible adventures. That's when she started having trouble relating to the other kids. *Why were they so mean to me? I just wanted to play with them.* Bits and pieces of memories hung around and poked her sometimes when she was feeling lonely.

Cat was rejected by her peers in Kindergarten and First Grade. Kids teased her about her name and her homemade clothes. When Mama moved out, Dad enrolled her in a different school. After two years in a school walking distance from her Aunt's Daycare center, Dad moved them yet again. This time they moved to the city for a six month lease. She was teased there too. "Firecats not a "real name", the kids would say. "You're a liar!" Nobody wanted to be friends with "a liar".

Finally Dad succeeded in his search for a place to stay put. He was very excited about being able to buy a home instead of just renting. They moved into the house just in time for Christmas of her fourth grade year. Once they landed in Walnut Creek, Dad finally stopped moving.

Of course, Cat didn't stay that long. *Walnut Creek was no better than any other place I've been.* She left as soon as she was done with Middle School. *Starting High School will be a great adventure! I hope the kids like me this time.* Excited and terrified, she counted the days until she started her newest school.

———— ((•)) ————

Mama had made it clear she didn't like alcohol. When Cat drank alcohol, she forgot to be scared to talk to people. Everyone seemed to like her more when alcohol was involved. *Mom is just being ridiculous. Just because her Dad drank whiskey, doesn't mean that I'm automatically going to become an alcoholic. She just doesn't want me to have fun. She doesn't want me to be happy because she is never happy. It's not my fault.* She did not take her Mom's "No Alcohol" rule seriously and would joke about it with people while she was drinking.

Cheap, sweet, syrupy wine always felt like cough syrup coming back up. When Cat drank, it was too much too fast. She frequently embarrassed herself by throwing up. She'd get the spins and stumble across town to get home. Sometimes she'd be so drunk that she would take a nap on the way home. She'd look for a bush that was big enough that she could crawl underneath. She'd nestle underneath in a ball and go to sleep, trying to escape the spins and sober up a bit before she got home. Sometimes it worked and sometimes it didn't.

Arriving back at The Oasis, Cat would try to sneak into her room without having to interact with Mama. Climbing up the ladder into her hideaway bed, she'd pass out under cover of the mountain of blankets and pillows. The curtain hanging from the ceiling would block out the light, and the whole world, as far as she was concerned. Mama didn't usually come in her room. She'd just holler through the wall. "Come in and talk to me!" Cat would pretend to be asleep and it usually worked. Eventually Mama would give up and stop.

Once the school year started, Cat didn't drink as much. During the week, she'd only have a couple of beers after school in the park. Hanging out with other kids from school, she'd sit in the grass & talk about school with them, homework sprawled across the grass in front of her. When it started to get too dark to do homework, Cat excused herself and headed back across town. She arrived home late enough that it was easy to disappear into her room. If she was still tipsy, she'd lie and tell Mama that she'd been smoking pot. Mama would dismissively ask her about homework. Cat would mumble something and crawl into her loft bed, disappearing behind the curtain.

For the first time in her life, Cat made friends quickly. She became quite a social person. Every day she left home early. She took the bus up to Telegraph Ave and headed straight for the Cafe' Bottega. Everyone who was anyone hung out at the Cafe'! It was a social scene similar to downtown Walnut Creek, only way cooler. *The punk rockers here are way more punk rock that the suburban kids. These guys are hardcore!*

The biggest difference was, in Berkeley, people actually talked to her. She was able to become part of the scene. She developed a routine that included being social with other people on a daily basis. Here it was cool to be different to an extreme that she had never experienced before. For just a little while, she started to feel a little less isolated. Weird hit a new plateau.

Cat worked hard to become a regular fixture in the scene at the Cafe'. *People look forward to seeing me.* She even met a guy who she ended up dating. She spent the night at his house. He spent the night at her house. Her mom talked to his mom. They made an agreement. And before she knew it, the parents had decided to take turns hosting the couple. The afternoon routine of hanging out in the park changed and she began spending afternoons with her new boyfriend. Most days she would eventually end up at his house, or bringing him home to her place.

Cat's boyfriend lived in a community household in North Berkeley. It was another social hub where people went to hang out and meet up with other people. She really liked going there. *It's so cool that people are allowed to paint their bedroom walls. People can be themselves here and be accepted despite their differences.* She began to develop a friendship with one of the girls who lived there. Maureen was a year older than her. *She is so independent and so tough! I can't believe she actually likes me!*

One night when Cat's boyfriend was sleeping over at The Oasis, they were awakened in the middle of the night by the sounds of her mother having sex loudly. It was awkward for her. Sexuality was awkward for her anyway. *It's bad enough knowing that it's my mother on the other side of the wall, but laying next my boyfriend while I have to listen?! I wonder what he is thinking.* She pretended to be asleep, and not to notice. *Oh my god! I hope this never happens again.*

The next night Cat was sleeping alone. Sometime in the early morning hours she was again awakened from her sleep by the sound of her mother's moaning and screaming. This time she was irritated. It felt like an invasion of privacy, as if they were having sex right in front of her. She had school the next day and knew it would be hard to fall back to sleep. She waited until her mother was climaxing, and then Cat began to applaud. She kept clapping until she only heard silence from the room next door.

A few days later, a conversation occurred between Cat, her mother, and her new lover. Mama was attempting to address some recent irresponsible behavior patterns. Cat was not responding in a mature manner. Becoming irritated, Mama seemed to think that was a good time to bring up the applause. "And by the way, what was *that* the other night?" Her lover, Will, had been waiting in the shadows for the parental altercation to conclude. His interest in the conversation increased and he moved slightly forward to pay more attention.

"What was that all about?" Cat retorted. "I am trying to sleep, have to get up early for school, and you wake me up in the middle of the night with your sex? I don't want to have to listen to that! Why don't you learn to put a pillow in it?! That's what I do!" Mama turned bright red. The response caught her completely off guard.

Clearly she was the one being irresponsible in this particular situation. Although her daughter had not shown much tact, she had not done much better. Cat took the silence as an opportunity to excuse herself from the conversation. Will was a little shocked by the direct answer. He seemed to be amused by the situation, almost proud.

———◦((�))◦———

By Winter Break of ninth grade, Mama's lover had moved in. Mama and Will were off on adventures together almost as much as Cat was off on her own adventures. The new couple left town on a road trip the week before Christmas. Mama made arrangements with "the other mother", and soon it was agreed that Cat would spend a week at the North Berkeley house. With very little supervision, Cat was free to conduct herself with as much independence as she so desired.

Much of the week was spent on hallucinogens. Cat and many others came and went over the course of the week, helping to cover the better part of Maureen's room with a collage of detailed psychedelic murals. By the time they were done, the pictures were so dizzying that nobody really wanted to hang out in her room much anymore. It was a whole lot of fun making it that way though!

The experience helped to deepen the bond between the two girls. Cat spent the majority of the time with Maureen, returning to her boyfriend's room mostly for bed. Soon her boyfriend was feeling neglected and made a point of showing it. They argued, saying hurtful things to one another. Other friends hanging out provided enough of a distraction that soon they were making up. Their world seemed to revolve around loud music, intoxication, and sexual innuendos. Occasional interaction with adults occurred only when they ventured downstairs into the kitchen near mealtimes.

When the noise and commotion of the eternal party in her boyfriend's room became too overwhelming, Cat wandered the house in search of quiet spaces. She found interesting conversation with some of the older adults living there. *They seem so wise. I hope that one day I will be that worldly and have such a great understanding of life. Not all adults are this wise. These people seem to be something extraordinary. They aren't like the boring sheeple that live in suburbia. These folks actually think about things and discuss things with one another.*

Cat was especially impressed that they had a living room without a television. The television was locked away in a small room off of the kitchen, where the door was often closed. Folks in the rest of the house were not subjected to the sounds coming from the TV room. Instead of focusing on a television, their living room walls were lined with books. The lighting was soft. The chairs were comfortable, and people could actually hear each other when they conversed.

When Mama and Will returned from their adventure, there was very little conversation exchanged. Cat had no interest in where they had been or what they had done. Mama showed little interest in Cat's activities in her absence. When she went to visit Dad for Christmas, she refrained from informing her father of Mama's absence. Winter break passed without a hitch and soon school was back in session.

Cat made several friends over the course of the school year. Many of them did not actually go to her school. She was promiscuous and irresponsible, constantly chasing her next high. While she had started the year doing most of her homework and going to all her classes, she got into the habit of getting high at lunchtime, going to Algebra, and then cutting her last two classes of the day.

Cat wanted people to like her and certainly developed a reputation. She liked hanging out with the guys. She was attracted to the girls. Still, she flirted with the guys more. *The guys are less intimidating I can relate to them. I just can't understand the girls at all!* Wanting to be accepted by the guys, she let them fondle her and use her body. Still, she wasn't terribly attracted to most of them. It felt more like a power trip than anything else.

Most of the friends that Cat made were superficial. They weren't real friends. People to party with helped her to feel less alone. She never really let them get to know her very well. As soon as they were gone, and not paying attention to her, the loneliness crept back up into her chest. She moved from one social group to the next. The only constant was the big house. No matter who she hung out with over the course of the week, she usually ended up in North Berkeley at least a couple days a week.

Only a couple of the friendships that Cat made when she was fourteen outlasted her freshman year. One in particular was Katie. She was also promiscuous and often chasing intoxication. The day Cat met her, Katie had been taking phenobarbital and drinking heavily. The beautiful redhead was totally wasted. Unable to walk, and depressed about a recent breakup with a guy she had been seeing, she was clearly in no state to be left alone. Cat ended up babysitting the hot mess for hours.

Later, Cat found out that Katie was well-known throughout her new circle of friends. The redhead had a reputation for being a bad girl, a troublemaker, and a rowdy drunk.

Cat's new friend seemed to appreciate that she had taken such good care of Katie when she clearly could not take care of herself. Their friendship developed slowly, and would outlast many of the other friendships she developed in her freshman year.

Cat also spent a lot of time hanging out with Maureen. One day at school, Maureen had brought a pair of clippers with her to school. Cat wanted something to change, so she asked Maureen to shave her hair into a mohawk. When Cat showed up at home with a mohawk, Mama was pleased. *So much for rebellion.* "I can't wait to see it put up!" Mama exclaimed. Cat dyed it bright red. Still Mama was not phased. "It looks beautiful." Mama proclaimed, fawning over her daughter.

Cat was disgusted when Mama went so far as to put brilliant shades of color in her own hair as well. *She is trying too hard to be cool. Why can't she just be my mother? Why can't she stop trying to act like a teenager? This "acceptance" feels fake. Why can't she just be a normal mom?* She wanted acceptance from her peers. She expected acceptance from her parents. *They are supposed to accept me, to love me, no matter what.* When Mama tried so hard to show acceptance, it made Cat uncomfortable, as if it wasn't real. The big show made it hard for her to trust Mama.

When Dad was disappointed with her, he didn't fake it. Still, she always knew that she could count on him to be there for her if it was really important. He might not seem to have very much feeling, but he was steadfast. She could trust him to always be there. She was beginning to feel like she could not trust her mother the same way.

Maureen took Cat to her first punk show. They went to the Gilman Street Project on the edge of West Berkeley and Albany. They walked all the way across town to the club.

Drinking outside with all the rowdy punk rockers was a lot of fun and depressing at the same time. They never made it inside, but the party seemed to be happening outside anyway. Later on, she came to regret not going inside, as it turned out to be the last time that Operation Ivy played a show there before they disbanded.

One afternoon Cat was hanging out at the Cafe', working on homework and wishing for a distraction. Katie showed up and hung out for several hours. Cat didn't get much homework done, but she really enjoyed spending time with Katie. She found herself hanging out in the afternoon, hoping that Katie would show up again. The time they spent together increased every week.

Running around with Katie was fun. Together they were "the two red-headed mohican girls". The more time Cat spent with Katie, the more she grew fond of her. When she learned that Katie had been the person who "had broken her boyfriend's virginity", she was not intimidated. *I am surprised this doesn't bother me. Strange. It makes me feel closer to Katie.*

One night when they were drinking together, Katie asked for permission to sleep with her boyfriend. "That won't bother me" she answered, "because you are special to me. He is special to me." Katie smiled as Cat continued. "Sharing two people who I care about seems natural. As long as you are both honest about it..." She paused and then hugged Katie and kissed her on the cheek. "Thank you for asking me. I love you." The two girls hugged and kissed each other briefly, giggling about it.

One Saturday morning Cat arrived at the North Berkeley house to find another girl had spent the night with her boyfriend. Without communicating a break-up, he had replaced replaced her. Her feelings were hurt. She had made several friends at the house, and decided to continue hanging around. *Just because he's a jerk, doesn't mean that I have to lose all my friends.* Pretending to be unaffected by this sudden change, she made a point to get to know the new girl. At first, it was out of revenge, but then Cat started to develop a crush on her.

Christina was very attractive, physically, and socially. She was creative and beautiful, and Cat really enjoyed being around her. The two girls started showing each other physical affection, snuggling and sleeping next to each other in his bed while he was busy hanging out with the guys. When the "new couple" had a falling out, the ex-boyfriend called Cat.

Christina called too. It was a huge ego stroke. She began spending more time with Christina. *I can make out with her, and snuggle and touch her. Without any guys being involved! I can be greedy and totally focus on her. She doesn't have a problem with it. She actually enjoys my company!*

They didn't date. It wasn't necessary. The two girls acted freely themselves without pretenses. There was no expectation. They talked like friends, and slept like lovers. It wasn't frightening. Cat spent a couple weeks following her like a puppy. Spending time with her, she got to meet people from an entirely different social circle. She didn't really get to know them all terribly well, and felt a little intimidated by them. She was welcomed back into her boyfriend's bed when Christina became distracted by her other crowd of friends.

This new crowd of folks were all a few years older than

Cat. Many of them were actively involved in The Rocky Horror Picture Show that played on Saturday nights. New Years Eve arrived and several of them were hanging out at the North Berkeley house. Christina convinced Cat to go with them to Rocky. They had gotten a hold of some gel tabs and decided that it was a great night to spend tripping.

Hanging out backstage before the show, Cat saw so many things that she didn't understand. Her trip became really intense and she ended up staying backstage for most of the show, too high to move. Cat was not familiar with the cult scene surrounding Rocky, even though she had half the songs memorized from listening to her mother's records. She could recite the words, and still didn't understand what they referred to.

The players got dressed up and acted out the movie in front of the screen while the movie was playing. These folks were different than the street punks that Cat was used to partying with. These folks were intelligent, educated, drama geeks. They seemed to be a pretty tight knit social group and she felt like a stranger. As the new year progressed, she tried to get to know some of them a little better. She was impressed by the fact that the guys weren't afraid to dress in drag, and the girls were not deterred by sexual variance.

The Rocky crowd seemed pretty self assured. Cat was not. She ended up partying with some of the Rocky crowd a few more times over the course of the year. Sometimes they would talk to her when they saw her at the Cafe'. Still, she was clearly not part of their crowd. She didn't feel intelligent enough to keep up with their conversations and often had no idea what they were talking about.

For a short time, Cat got officially 'got back together' with her boyfriend, but he got bored with her. They made plans for Valentine's Day, and he never showed up. She found out later that he flaked out on her to go out with some other girl who had a nice car. She heard second hand stories about him having sex with her, on top of her car. Cat was really depressed about it. That didn't stop her from going over to the North Berkeley house and hanging out with Maureen.

————))•((————

Cat started having sex with older guys who also lived in the big house. Moving from room to room she made her way through most of the community searching for acceptance. She had no respect for herself. Unable to accept herself, the temporary feelings she experienced with others served as a distraction from her own personal misery.

Sex helped Cat leave her body. The guys that she actually enjoyed being intimate with were the ones that were bisexual, or embodied some feminine qualities. She started getting into group sex scenarios with Maureen and other guys. She found that she could actually be physical with girls if there were other guys involved. Too afraid to try and flirt with a girl by herself, she continued to encourage group sex encounters, as a safe way to be with girls. It was not as threatening when there were three or four of them, guys and girls together. She ended up having sex with several guys, just so she could get physical with girls.

Cat's fondness for Maureen grew. One day, she made the mistake of telling Maureen that she was attracted to her. "I'd like to be with you, without the guys, just once." This seemed to make Maureen uncomfortable. Almost immediately, she began spending substantially less time with Cat. Both were terribly embarrassed by the whole scenario.

The community house in North Berkeley was big enough that she could be on one side of the house hanging out and never run into people on the other side of the house. Different people moved in and out of the house. There were a few older folks that were a root part of the community. They were a circle of friends that had originally come together to form the big house two decades prior. Older than her mother, she looked up to them as elders.

Every now and then she would be around during a quiet time when she would sit and talk with one of the elders. Or more accurately, she would listen to them talk. They were educated and rich with many life experiences. Awestruck, Cat sat with full attention, studying every silver hair and every wrinkle as she listened to their insight. *I hope that when I'm older, I'll be just as rich with knowledge and wisdom. If I actually live long enough to be an adult, I'm going to make sure that my life never becomes a stagnant pattern.* Cat decided she wanted to die a wise bohemian scholar like these shiny people.

Chapter 12

LOST AND FOUND

When Chinese New Year arrived, The Grateful Dead came back to town for a show at the Henry J Kaiser Memorial Stadium in Oakland. Cat took BART out to the show, following the stream of people all the way to the stadium. Everywhere the Dead went, a roaming subculture followed. It was easy to find her way. She looked for familiar faces. She moved throughout the crowd, up and down the aisles of cars and encampments. Surrounded by people that had brought her joy in the past, she felt isolated.

Feeling like a stranger, Cat followed a path that circled through the greater circumference of the the city of deadheads. She continued to follow the same path, repeating her steps similar to the way she had patrolled the campus of her middle school, as if searching for some familiarity. Eventually, her sadness overcame her. *I can't walk through these crowds. I don't want anyone to see me crying.*

Cat didn't want anyone else to approach her saying "Hey little sister, Gimme a smile!" *I can't force any more smiles. I feel trapped.* She was confused. This place was supposed to feel like family, still all she could feel was a thick, heavy sadness. *Something is seriously wrong with me.*

Talking to herself as she wandered away from the crowd outside the Kaiser, Cat tried to work through the confusion, like a math problem. She could not begin to explain what was causing her dysphoria. The more she failed to understand, the more anxious she became. *I don't understand. Anything.* She followed sidewalks through neighborhoods that no longer looked familiar.

Glancing up from her hysteria, Cat realized she had wandered into a part of town that was not safe. Scanning the horizon before her, she took inventory of her surroundings. Crack dealers standing on shadowy corners eyed her as she walked by crying and ranting. Cars pulled over with scary people, trying to coax her toward their cars. Turning a corner, she quickly changed her direction. Disoriented by the new surroundings, her heart pounded fiercely in her chest. *I have no idea where I am.* She turned another corner, searching for some kind of landmark.

She saw a glimmer of lights on water. *That must be Lake Merritt!* Crossing the street, she moved past a large building to get a better view. Far down the hills from the her current location the lake glistened in the darkness. *How far away is that? How long have I been walking?* Straining her eyes, she focused on the concert lights on the far side of the lake. *If I can get to the lake, I can follow it all the way around back to the Kaiser.*

Cat carefully navigated the littered streets back down the hills, avoiding conflict with drunks and drug dealers. Women in short skirts and too much make-up stood in the light of a corner liquor store. Cat felt their eyes on her as she walked by. As she passed she heard them talking with someone parked at the curb. *Don't look at me. I don't exist. I am invisible.* Eventually she found her way back to Lake Merritt near the Zoo.

Back on the path around the lake, she felt a little safer. Exhaustion began to course through Cat's body. *I remember being a little kid. My dad brought me here to the kids amusement park. I remember asking if we could walk all the way around the lake and Dad said 'No, that would take hours". Now I get to find out for myself. I sure hope it doesn't take hours. All I want to do is go to sleep. And never wake up.* Her legs began to cramp up.

Cat stopped at a bench to sit down and rub the cramps out of her legs. I have to keep going. It doesn't matter if it hurts, I have to get back before *the concert is over or I will be stuck here.* Returning to the path, she continued to walk. Soon she was crying and again swimming through her dysphoria as her legs moved on autopilot.

When Cat once again found herself wandering through the crowd at the Dead Lot, she knew she had made it back. *It must be very late. The show is letting out.* Long past sunset, the cold wind added to her discomfort. The mayhem of all the people reconnecting with other people after the show was disorienting. She followed the river of people as they left Dead Lot. *I don't even know how I am going to get home. Maybe I will see someone I know and I can get a ride from them? Or maybe I can bum enough change to ride the train?* Traffic picked up slowly as cars tried to leave the area.

Lines of police cars waited outside the area. Every driver prayed that they would make it past the police line safely. As Cat followed the dancing river toward the BART station, she saw cars being pulled over. Coming out of a Dead show seemed to be automatic cause for search. Hippies lined up against their vans, while policemen frisked them and tore apart their homes. She pushed her hands deep in her pockets and walked briskly, keeping her head down and her path straight.

Cat hoped for the comfort of a familiar face, but none appeared so she began asking for change for the subway from folks passing by. When she reached the train station, she counted her change. *Yes! Enough for the train and maybe a coffee in the morning!* In the subway, the BART trains were full of colorful hippies heading back to wherever they would be spending their night.

As the train approached Cat queued up. Double doors slid open and she looked for a spot to sit down on the floor. People played drums and chatted with each other as if they were still on the lot. *These gypsies carry home with them everywhere they go. Seems like it would be a great way to live, if only the police would leave them alone.* Still, she felt detached from them. Something was out of place and she was pretty sure it was her.

———— «◉» ————

As springtime progressed, Cat's mother found out she was pregnant. Her new lover, Will, had become a permanent fixture and the girl was not terribly fond of him. She strove to become more socially active and therefore less present at home. Determined to numb herself from all the uncomfortable feelings, she moved farther and farther away from her own personal dignity. In doing so, she began failing classes at school.

Dad received a notice in the mail informing him of Cat's academic status. The school warned him that if she didn't clean up her act, she would not be allowed to return the following school year. He was livid. He had paid a great deal of money for her to attend a private school and she was wasting it. After getting the riot act read to her from both parents, she knuckled down on her homework some.

This did not encourage Cat to go home any more frequently. Instead, she spent time at the North Berkeley house hiding in quiet rooms to focus on homework. Maureen was also trying to catch up. By the end of the semester there were several other teens hanging out doing their homework. With less partying and more studying, she felt supported by her environment and it encouraged her to try harder. But she kept falling asleep in the middle of her books and papers.

Waking up frustrated with herself, Cat would shuffle off to school without returning home for several days at a time. *I keep falling asleep. I am trying to focus on my work. But I get so tired.* She drank coffee several times each day. With finals coming soon, the drunken parties had turned into study parties with coffee for everyone. Determined to pull it together at the last minute, she stayed relatively sober.

Still Cat kept falling asleep. The weekend before finals week, one of the guys hanging out at the North Berkeley house offered her some Speed. This time around, she recognized the white powder. She meekly declined. *My mother has been addicted to this off and on for years. I am not going to make the same mistake. This is a terrible drug. I am strong. I will make it through all this homework without falling prey to the powders.* They didn't push it on her, and accepted her answer. She returned to her efforts to do her catch-up work and soon fell back asleep.

Waking up in Maureen's room sometime in the wee hours, she looked down at the mountains of work she still had left to do. She was overwhelmed. *I am never going to accomplish all this if I keep falling asleep.* She got up and went into the kitchen to see if anyone else was awake. She could hear noise coming from the TV room, and pushed the door open. Walking into the TV room, she was greeted by bright eyed teens, engulfed in mountains of school work. Clearly they had not fallen asleep. *I have to get this work done.* Swallowing hard, she took in a deep breath and asked, "Is that offer still good? I don't think I am going to make it."

The guy who had offered earlier responded "Absolutely. I was just waiting for you to ask. I didn't want to push you." He chuckled, picked up his fanny pack, and ushered her back into Maureen's empty bedroom.

Lining out some powder for her, he explained what to do. He warned her that it would burn and then laughed at her as she grabbed her face "Holy shit!"

"I told you it would burn." He added.

Cat thanked him and went back to her pile of catch-up work. He said "No problem. Anytime." and headed back into the room where his homework was waiting. She analyzed the work in front of her. She had 5 essays to rewrite. Her final for English Composition was 11am and she had to have them all done by then. *I am barely done with the first one. If I am going to get this done, I am going to need a plan.* She outlined her time line for the morning, and stacked her papers in an organized fashion.

When the sun rose, she had made a lot of progress. Cat packed up all her stuff, and headed toward campus. She had been sitting for hours. *My legs are all cramped up. I need to walk it off.* She walked faster than usual and before she knew it, she was a block away from school. *Bottega will be a distraction. But I'm not done yet. I need a place to sit and work where I won't run into anyone I know.* She stepped into a Cafe' near the school, where her classmates did not frequent. She ordered a Latte and sat down at a table by the window.

Surrounded by college students working on their own

final projects, Cat set down her Latte and pulled out her binder. Hours passed quickly, as she poured herself into her writing. As soon as she completed the last assignment, she packed up her supplies, and left the Cafe'. She hurried down the block, ran up the stairs into her school building and walked into her Comp class just in time to take the final test. She flew through the test with ample time left. Spending the rest of the class period doodling in her notebook, she thought about how wonderful this success had been for her. *Now if I can just get through the rest of the week, the school year will be over.*

Later in the week Cat found out that not only had she aced her test, but she had gotten a good grade on all of her final draft essays. The experience was so positive that she shed all of her fears about Speed. The next time she was offered, she gladly accepted and allowed herself to get distracted by whatever creative direction her brain decided to go.

⸺⸺»《◉》«⸺⸺

The end of the school year meant another party at the North Berkeley house. This time, folks arrived from all the different social circles of friends that Cat had met over the course of the year. Like a great reunion, the house and courtyard overflowed with intoxication and teenage hormones. They all had a great time. The adults seemed to hide in their bedrooms, only emerging to attend to issues when absolutely necessary. The rest of the time, they appeared to be completely absent.

Cat ended up spending the evening hanging out with a guy from the other edge of the Rocky crowd. Chris was short like her, a young adult and a really good kisser. She ended up going home with him. The next couple of weeks, she began spending the night at his house often. Drinking and partying with the crowd of friends that frequented his house, she quickly began playing the role of his girlfriend.

Katie had landed a job working for Kirkle Enterprises, an assembly line warehouse in Emeryville, it was basically a sweat shop. She helped Cat get hired, and soon she began working her first regular job. She never filled out any paperwork, or obtained a work permit. It never occurred to her that she would need to. Working in an assembly line for five dollars an hour, she folded clothes, stuffed envelopes, and made MTV key-chains with a terribly smelly glue. The warehouse was hot and sweaty and she was always glad when the workday was over. When payday came Cat was excited to have so much money at once.

After cashing her check at the check-cashing center, Cat gave some of her money to Mama to help with groceries and bills. She spent the rest of it partying with Chris and his friends. She developed a habit of carrying a bottle of vodka in her purse. She thought it made her cool and more grown-up to always have alcohol on hand. Carrying with her a quiet misery, she tried to drown herself in a false glory.

——————————«(●)»——————————

The landlord of The Oasis had sold the property and informed Mama that they would all have to move. Since the new owners were going to be remodeling, Mama was entitled to a settlement. He agreed to pay her a few thousand dollars to move out. Many of the other tenants had already moved out. In fact several of Mama's old friends had stopped coming around entirely. They did not approve of her mother's decision to be with Will. He was judged to be untrustworthy and "bad" for her.

Instead of listening to her friends' concerns, Mama dismissed them all as selfish and close-minded. The new crowd of people that he brought with him, were ultimately his crew. Lackeys that jumped at his command, Will put them all to work packing up the household. Cat wanted no part in it. She packed up the items of personal importance, and left the rest for other people.

Cat's 15th birthday was a rowdy celebration of alcohol and sex. When Chris delivered her back home with a new kitten, they were greeted by Will's demanding instructions. Immediately put to work packing things up in the trucks, she found it very difficult to escape this time. The family seemed to have more vehicles than drivers, and Chris was talked into helping drive them up North.

When the time came to leave The Oasis, Cat was glad to have Chris coming along. He didn't seem to be as happy about it. Arriving in the the Mendocino area without a house to move into meant that much of their stuff had to be packed into a storage locker. After all the work had been done, Mama and Cat were left in the woods with their pets and each other. Will returned to the Bay Area with a van full of lackeys, and Chris returned with them, concerned about getting back to his job.

Chapter 13

NEW TOWN

The dislocated family landed in their new world by way of a bumpy gravel road up on Albion Ridge. The ridge was one of many little ridges that wind up into the hills of the Pacific Coastal range. Like a fan of rib bones attached to the spine that is Highway 1, the Pacific Coastal range lays the land down at the edge of the sea. With sharp rocky edges, the two worlds collide, leaving very little sand by the sea.

Will raved about how wonderful a place Albion would be for raising his son. He insisted that Mama and Cat would be happier there. They went to stay with friends of Mama's who had four acres in woods. Pulling into their driveway, the tall redwoods formed a majestic view of the new fairy tale reality. The van was parked in the meadow, next to an outdoor kitchen completed with fire-pit. Cat set up her own "room" across the meadow on the outdoor stage covered with moss and old carpets.

Sleeping under the stars was pleasant, and a little chilly. Early mornings she awoke with her blankets wet from the nightly fog. Walking to the outhouse in the middle of the night was less comfortable than having to go out the back door and up the stairs, the way she had done in Berkeley.

The basement bathroom situation seemed a little more favorable now. Also, the outhouse stunk. And there was no sink to wash her hands afterwards, just a little pitcher of water for splashing on her hands. Being so cold, the last thing she wanted to do was get her hands wet.

Walking around in the woods with her kitten, the morning was quiet and moist. Cat liked exploring and there were a few trails for walking around. It was peaceful and the everything was shadowed in early morning fog. She saw so many trees taller than the sky with beautiful little clover patches covering the ground. Large ferns made her feel like she might walk around a corner and discover a dinosaur walking through the mist.

I remember being a kid visiting Mama. We had somehow made our way to San Francisco for a big concert happening in Golden Gate Park. I don't remember what the name of the concert was. There were several bands and Dinosaur Jr was one of the bands playing. I must have been somewhere around ten years old.

Its funny how I remember that particular band name. We had been roaming around the park. We happened down a path that led to a turtle pond. There were great hostas and ferns everywhere. I remember expecting to see dinosaurs there because the whole scene felt prehistoric. I imagined that must have been what the world looked like everywhere when the dinosaurs were alive.

I was hot and tired at the concert. I was hungry. Some of Mama's friends were there. I was hanging out on a blanket and someone gave me some brownie crumbs to eat. Everything got better later in the afternoon. I don't remember which part of the day included going to the turtle pond. Everything is sort of squished together, like the brownie crumbs. Sweet and crumbly and squished into a ball.

———— ∞ ————

Mornings in Albion were slow and still. People woke up slowly and quietly. So did the woods. It was a huge contrast to the life Cat had been accustomed to in Berkeley. The Oasis had been busy. There was always a van or bus in the driveway. People would sleep in the living room and often two, if not all three of the bedrooms, would have more than one person sleeping in them. The mornings were a noisy bustle of warm drinks and food smells and 'good morning's. Here, the quiet was crisp and creaky in her bones. The hustle and bustle was far away, back in the city. She found it pleasant and lonely in the morning mist.

It warmed up nicely, and by noon all the fog would be gone. It never got terribly warm though, with the cover of the trees, everything stayed shady and damp. The ocean was beautiful and she could see for miles when they drove down the ridge to the grocery store. Clear skies for miles and beautiful waves were very misleading. As soon as they got out of the van, she was hit by the cool ocean breeze, and reminded of the fact that they did not get the inland heat here.

———— ∞ ————

When Mama moved out of our home on Hyde Road, she was experiencing a lot of pain. She stayed with her older sister in Fairfield for a while. Trying to piece together a new path, a new plan for her life, must have been very challenging. I visited her at my Aunt's house several times inconsistently. I don't remember much from those visits except fighting with my younger cousin.

Eventually, she moved out into her own apartment, and I celebrated my 8th birthday in a park down the street from Mama's new apartment. The neighborhood was rough, and her life got rougher. Sometime in the next couple years she moved out of the apartment, into the home of some of her old high school friends, and their six children.

When Mama moved into the house on Sycamore Street, she took over a large studio bedroom above the garage of the big family house. The big family was comprised of a couple of people she had known separately from high school. At some point she ended up introducing them, which eventually resulted in a long tumultuous marriage and several children. It was during the peak of their marriage, they opened up their home to Mama. That was also an interesting place to visit her, as I had a lot opportunities to play with other kids. There were six little boys, ages ranging from two to ten. Often there were cousins there as well. I got plenty of boy time.

The house on Sycamore was a madhouse. The two story house was covered with stacks of everything everywhere. I remember walking into the kitchen and seeing all the counters creatively stacked with what seemed to be hundreds of dishes. It looked at first like someone getting ready to have a giant yard sale. Upon closer observation, I would discover that all the dishes were dirty. There was a comical sign in the kitchen that said something like "Complain about the food, and You get to do the dishes." The rest of the house was stacked with books, and laundry, and anything else you could think of. Roaming the house in the early morning hours, was like tiptoeing through a treasure hunt.

The mess was a constant. Between the two parents, six little boys, the revolving gang of neighborhood children, and local cousins, it was like visiting a zoo. The difference there at Sycamore Street, was that the children were the animals, and they ran wild. The adults locked themselves in the cages of their rooms, to hide from the madness. When they did emerge, it usually meant that cleaning was happening. Any children caught hanging around were immediately put to work.

Consequently, they never had much of a problem going outside to play. Hide & Seek and Tag were soon replaced with Cops & Robbers, Cowboys & Indians, or Girls Against Boys. While the games were energetic, I always ended up getting stuck with a role that did not thrill me. I was often the "token girl" and the boys argued with me. Apparently the roles that I wanted to play were for boys only. Eventually I would get bored of it, and go upstairs to visit with Mama..

It didn't take Cat long to get tired of the isolation of Albion. She was bored and didn't like being trapped with her own thoughts so much. Also, her pregnant mother was becoming more and more emotional. Cat couldn't handle being around Mama in her condition. Cat was also very emotional. She started to get worried because her period was late. She ate Black Cohosh capsules for a few days, trying to bring on her period. Nothing happened.

Frustrated and feeling trapped, Cat decided that she would trek down to the Bay Area. Catching a bus from Albion to Philo gave her a head start. In Philo, she stuck out her thumb and caught a ride to Santa Rosa. From there she was able to catch public transit to San Francisco. Once in the city she took the subway. After a very long day, she managed to get back to Berkeley. Exiting the subway at Ashby station, she immediately took off to go find Chris.

Cat wanted to surprise him. She walked to his house and saw him talking on the pay phone across the street from his place. It had been a couple weeks since she had seen him and she missed his attention. Throwing down her bag and bedroll next to the phone booth excitedly, she tried to grab his attention. Without taking the time to acknowledge who she was, he covered the receiver of the phone and responded quickly. "I can't talk right now. I'm on the phone with my girlfriend." Stunned from the blow, she staggered backwards. She picked up her bag and walked away quickly.

Cat kept walking until she was back on Telegraph Ave. She headed to Cafe' Bottega to see who she might find. Running into Katie, she was glad to find someone who she could talk to. She gushed out all of her unpleasant emotions while Katie listened sympathetically. Katie told her friend that Chris was an asshole that didn't deserve her. As the two girls hugged, Katie added "He might not care, but I am glad that you are here to visit! Why don't you come home with me? I haven't been home in a while anyway."

Feeling the love of her friend, she agreed to go with Katie. The two girls set off back across town again. Walking past Chris' place, she felt a surge of emotion in her belly. *What an asshole. He doesn't deserve me anyway.* Katie noticed her glancing at the big building on the corner. "Don't worry about him. You get to come to my house today! It's only a few more blocks." She grabbed Cat's hand and squeezed it as they picked up their pace.

Arriving in the early evening with Katie at her mother's house, Cat felt the exhaustion of a long day of travel starting to catch up with her. It was nice to be inside a real house and be able to just sit down for a while. Katie showed Cat her bedroom and eagerly played records for her. Despite how often they had hung out before the move north, she had never been to Katie's house.

Katie's mother was very nice to Cat. She seemed pleased that Katie had brought her home. Apparently Katie did not come home often, and brought friends there even less often. Her mom was a lesbian and did not approve of most of Katie's friends but she seemed to like Cat a lot. Sitting in the dining room, she listened to her mother talk while Katie brought her snacks and pop. Her mother stood by the table talking to both of the girls.

Katie's mother asked pointedly "Have you actually looked at a penis?"

Katie rolled her eyes. Apparently, she was not comfortable with the topics that her mother liked to bring up. "I happen to like penises mother." Katie commented.

Her mother responded "But have you ever *really looked* at a penis? Its ugly! Do you really want to put something that ugly inside you? I certainly don't! Now a vagina is beautiful, like a flower." She smiled. Cat chuckled. At this point Katie decided she had heard enough and ushered her friend out of the dining room.

Leaving Cat's bag and bedroll at the house, the two girls headed back out to see what kind of fun they could get into. There was some kind of demonstration going on when they arrived back on Telegraph. On their way up to the Ave, they had devised a plan. They intended to see how many random strangers they could make out with. It would be fun to blow people's minds. They'd just walk up to someone and tell them they wanted to make out. Dragging them to the nearest wall, Cat and Katie could push them up against the wall together and blow their mind. Then, when they started to realize what was going on, the girls would just walk away.

It wasn't really about teasing people. They were going for shock value. They had been discussing how it seemed to be okay for guys to be pushy. However, when girls tried to do that, it was not acceptable. Together they wanted to challenge the norm. They wanted to be shocking. They wanted to feel good, and be completely in control of the situation.

They managed to get liquor and in their drunken stupor,

the two girls blew minds right out of the crowd. Eventually, too drunk to have the energy for it all, they stumbled back across town to Katie's house.

Cat really liked being with Katie. She felt like she would go through any shenanigan if it was with her. She was so glad that Katie accepted her. She was so glad that Katie was there for her when Chris had hurt her feelings so badly. *I had only been gone for a couple of weeks and he had already replaced me! What an asshole. I am better off without him.* She fell asleep spinning from intoxication. Drowning in the emotions of the day, she smiled as she fell asleep in Katie's arms.

In the early morning hours, Cat woke up in excruciating pain. She tried to be quiet as she made her way to the bathroom. She was bleeding heavily. *At least I'm not pregnant! No matter how much it hurts, just remember, this is a good thing.* But the pain was dizzying. Combined with her hangover, Cat felt like she was dying. She was afraid. She did what she always did when she was scared. She ran away. She didn't want to wake anyone up, so she quietly packed up her stuff and slipped out the back door.

Stumbling from bus stop to bus stop, Cat rested on each bench she passed. She was in so much pain that she was frightened. She thought about how connected she was to her mother. *If I am experiencing so much pain, it must mean that Mama is in labor.* She felt like her insides were being ripped out of her. Bleeding all over herself, she was embarrassed. *I'm so glad I'm wearing a skirt, so nobody can see the blood all over my legs.*

After the sun had risen, Cat began watching for a

phone. The next pay phone she reached, she attempted to call Mama at the Albion house. There was no answer. She moved on. She kept moving until she reached the BART station. This time she called Katie. She apologized for leaving the way she did. "I was worried about you." Katie responded on the line. Cat told her not to worry, thanked her for the wonderful visit and told her that she had to go back home.

Lost in a haze of pain, Cat left her body, navigating on autopilot. When she came back to reality, she was calling the Albion house from the grocery store at the bottom of the ridge. Mama asked how she had gotten home. *I don't remember exactly how I got back. I must have bummed change and taken public transit. Or maybe I hitchhiked part of the way. I really don't know for sure. I don't even know what day it is.*

She told Mama that she had taken public transit from subway to bus, and bus to bus until she made it as far as Santa Rosa. "I hitchhiked the rest of the way, and it only took one ride. They were going all the way to Fort Bragg." *The last thing I need is to have her stressing out about me right now. What I really want to know is what has been happening with her?* "'I was worried about you. I tried to call. Are you okay?"

Mama had been worried about her daughter as well. Apparently, while Cat was experiencing her first miscarriage, Mama ended up going into the hospital as well. She had not gone into labor, but got very sick experiencing somewhat of an early false-labor start. Mama had been worried about her daughter as much as Cat was worried about her mother. The hospital sent Mama home, as she was not in labor. Convinced that it was their connection telling her something was wrong with her daughter, she had tried to find a way to contact her, to no avail.

The town of Albion was just her size, but Cat didn't know it yet. She was bored out of her mind with nobody to talk to, and no place to go. Taking the bus or walking could only get her so far. She was used to being in the suburbs and the city where the bus gave her freedom. In the city, she could walk in whatever direction she needed to go and feel confident that she would eventually get there. This place had few roads, many dead ends, and if she went too far it was just cliffs and the ocean. She felt trapped and yet, as she stayed longer, she would fall in love with the area and keep coming back for years.

"Want to go to town?" Will asked. Without thinking twice Cat jumped up. *I don't like going anywhere with you, but I am so bored! Anything has got to be better than being stuck here all day.* She found out quickly that "going to town" consisted of driving down the ridge road to the main store. They pulled into the parking lot and she was not impressed.

After going into the store and returning with two cups of coffee, Will opened up the side doors of the van. He began hanging out tye-dye t-shirts in the open van doors. "Now hang out and look cute. That will help with sales." He said, organizing the remaining shirts on a blanket in the van. She grimaced. *That's great. If you are relying on my looks you're not going to sell anything.*

Hanging out in the parking lot, trying to sell shirts lasted hours. Watching people come and go began to feel like watching a television show. The first time was boring. After a few days of this routine, she began to recognize some regular faces. Cat realized that other people "came to town" by hanging out in the parking lot too. She started looking forward to the routine of "going to town". She used the shirt sales as a purpose for socialization, much the way hanging out with vendors on the Telegraph had been social.

Cat spoke fearlessly with whomever would take the time. Hoping to make a few dollars in the process, it was a great way to get to know new people in this new place. Will would take her with him to "town" to "help him". *I think he is just trying to keep Mama and me from tearing into each other.* Will was counting on a young busty female as being a great sales pitch. "Sex sells merchandising all the way baby." He winked as he tossed her a candy bar. *Kind of gross when I think about my mother's boyfriend cashing in on this with me.*

Cat wasn't paying as much attention to the shirt sales as Will would have liked. Then again, he was easily distracted and often wandered off to talk with people. Cat started wandering around and searching for people that looked her age. She saw a kid that was shorter than her. He had dark hair, like brown hair dyed black, and dark eyes. He was smoking a cigarette. He looked very young, and she decided to give him a hard time about it. *Maybe I can get him to give me a smoke? And possibly some conversation?*

"You're too young to be smoking." Cat spoke to him as she approached. "You should just give your cigarettes to me." He immediately responded about how he was older than she thought he was. In turn he harassed her for looking so young. They smiled at each other and he reached in his pocket for his cigarettes. She dug in her pocket to pull out a lighter.

Sitting together smoking, they exchanged names and compared birthdays. It was friendship right away. Cat found out that Cole was a just little older that her. Their birthdays were very close. She started looking for him whenever Will took her to town. After a few days of running into each other, they started making plans to meet up and hang out.

Cole introduced Cat to Touchstone, which had a lasting impact on her. Touchstone was a community center located off the road just past the north end of the grocery store parking lot. She had seen people hanging out there as they drove by, but didn't venture there alone until after Cole took her there. Run by an older Christian man, it appeared to be a small house on the side of a hill.

Upon entering, Cat found herself in a great room with couches and a pool table. There was a refrigerator and a simple kitchen space. Another room was set up with video games and a Foosball table. There was also a quiet room for studying, with a chalk board, chairs, and tables, leading to the back office where the owner hung out most of the time.

Touchstone also offered a walk-in closet where people could donate clothes, shoes, and other reusable items. Anyone could go through the stuff and take what they needed. There was no sign-up, or qualifications. If you were in need, you took what you needed. If you had something to share, you could do that too. Cat had never seen anything like it before. She was impressed.

The community center was a wonderful resource for many people in the area. Not only was it a safe space for young people to be, it was also a place for homeless, or transient folks to come and prepare food. It was a place to get warm when it was cold outside. It was a place to meet up with other folks in the community.

Tuesday night was movie night at Touchstone. The man running it rented two movies from the hardware store every Tuesday afternoon. At 6pm he turned on the first movie, and the second at 8pm. Anyone in the community could come watch the movies for free. Many families would come. It was a regular routine for folks to gather at the movie nights.

Also, there was a potluck jam for adults only on Saturday nights. Cat didn't know how many people attended, as she was not in that age group. Still, she marveled at how wonderful it was to have such a fixture within the community. Sometimes, there were free vegetables and loaves of bread lining the kitchen counter for folks to come and take home as they needed. *If I ever have the money, I want to open a community center one day. When I am older, I want to live out in the country and provide a community center that brings people together like this.*

Cat spent the rest of the Summer catching rides to Albion with Will. Sometimes he would drop her off on his way to work. As his work days became more frequent, the t-shirt selling days became less frequent. Occasionally, he would drive ten miles farther to Mendocino. She welcomed the ride and the excuse to leave the quiet meadow.

The same routine in a bigger town, Cat still felt nervous. Getting to know the locals was slow. She was shy around people she didn't know. She spent time watching other people and not talking to them. Making friends with Cole gave her something to look forward to. Slowly she began to meet new people when she was with him.

Mama's pregnancy dragged on. She was due any day and they were still camping in the meadow. They had not found their own place to live yet. Mama's stress started to get out of hand. Will couldn't take it, and started working really hard to try and find them a place to live. Mid-August, one of his bosses agreed to rent the family a piece of property four miles up Navarro Ridge Road. It had a little two-bedroom double wide trailer with a one-room cabin in the back that Cat immediately claimed as her bedroom.

There was an outhouse in the back by a little cabin room. *So I don't have to go into the house to use the bathroom if I don't want to. Funny that I have gotten so used to using an outhouse. But still, it's my own bathroom.* She immediately claimed the little cabin room for her bedroom and got to work making the space feel like home.

With no insulation, the cabin got chilly at night. It would get colder as the season progressed into winter. When she talked to Dad about it, he agreed to buy her a wood stove for heating her room. That was exciting. It made her love the room all the more. It took a couple weeks emptying out the storage locker, but soon they were settled into their new home.

Chapter 14

LITTLE BROTHER

When Mama finally went into labor, there was a circus of hippies camped out in the living room and on the property. Everyone, including the midwife, had come up to visit for several days, in anticipation of a birthing that should happen any day. The midwife ended up giving her mother herbs to stimulate contractions. When the day came that her mother was in labor, everyone was there to help her, to take turns coaching her, to take care of the house, and anything else that might come up. It was a celebration of magic and new life.

Apparently, that meant it was a good time to trip. Everyone was tripping, except the midwife. Mama always tripped for ritual, and this seemed to be a monumental experience, and therefore appropriate to her. The altar was set up in the bedroom, for a ritual birthing ceremony. Unfortunately, midway through the experience, Will decided to run to town and came back with a young girl named Melody.

Melody was probably eighteen or nineteen years old. While he should have been paying attention to Mama and the ritual birthing of his child, Will was busy getting distracted by Melody. When she got too high and freaked out, he focused much of his attention on her, and this upset Mama greatly. It was incredibly disrespectful. Many of the house guests were disgusted with Will's behavior.

Cat was pretty oblivious. As she was also tripping and overwhelmed by all the people and stimulus, she removed herself from the house for much of the day. Four acres in the redwoods is easy to hide in. There were great big trees that she could sit inside, completely hidden. Pathways through the woods made for pleasant quiet time.

There was a great field in the front of the property, big enough for a spiral dance. There was a little goat shed, and adjacent to the wide driveway, there was another grassy clearing. With a fire pit in the center, this clearing was much more lush, surrounded by tall grasses and flowering bushes. Walking up the path through the redwoods, she ended up back at the fire pit.

People were sitting around the fire. People were wandering in and out of the house. *Too many people.* Cat went in the house to check in ,and see how things were going. *Too many people.* She retreated back to her room again. It was overwhelming hearing her mother in so much pain. She didn't really know what to think of the whole experience. Later in the evening, her mother began to get really sick. Mama had been in labor for hours and did not seem to be dilating properly. The midwife was concerned about her mother and the baby. It was long after dark when they ended up rushing to the hospital, about 25 miles away.

Cat piled in the van with her mother and a couple others, including the loud and confused Melody. Her presence seemed to increase the tension in the van. While Will drove two and three times the speed limit on the winding coastal highway, Mama threw up in the back of the van. A caravan of vehicles raced to keep up with him.

Will drove recklessly. Cat squeezed her eyes shut and held her breath as the van passed between vehicles in a space too narrow for a lane. Clipping one of the side windows in the process, Will cursed breathlessly without slowing his pace. *Oh my god. We are going to die before we make it to the hospital!*

A crazy crew of hippies and pagans in ritual garb, emerged from the dark foggy parking lot. Mama signed papers at the intake desk, while Will and midwife explained hastily the context of their visit. Multi-colored disciples noisily hovered behind them. Cat stayed close, but not too close. *The bright lights in this hospital are intimidating. I feel like someone is staring at me from above. Like I am being examined under a microscope. I would leave but I know that this is supposed to be important to me. I'd really rather just be at home in my bedroom alone.*

Trailing far behind, a lost Melody wandered aimlessly, without Will or direction. A nurse appeared from behind the intake desk with a wheelchair for Mama. The midwife helped her sit down. Mama's disciples followed as the nurse guided them down a long bright hall. As they entered the delivery room, more nurses were quick to help her onto the bed. Cat stood next to the doorway watching the nurses become frustrated. There were so many people trying to cram into the delivery room that the nurses had no room to move around.

The whole crowd tried piling in the room, but the room was too small. A doctor appeared, asking people to clear the doorway as he tried to enter the room. As Mama screamed out in agony the doctor tried to address the mass occupancy. "You cannot all be here! Only family members allowed!"

A choral round of murmured responses "We are all

family" further confused the doctor and nurses. "Who is the father? Where is the father?" Staff inquired while forcing the motley crew out of the hospital room. Cat stood next to the doorway. *Where is Will? This is hilarious. Everyone wants to be part of this miraculous birth of the anti-Christ, and the father is nowhere to be found!* After a great deal of commotion, hospital staff were able to reduce the number of extra people to a meager four. The midwife, Mama's sister and close friends remained.

Those who remained in the Emergency Room with Mama, chanted prayers while the midwife tried to help her remember to breathe through the pain of contractions. The hospital staff struggled to stay focused on their jobs, clearly distracted by the uncommon ritual taking place in the midst of their evening shift. In the distance, the extra people had only slightly dispersed. Some remained in the hallway close to the birthing room. Some had gone outside to smoke cigarettes. Some wandered the hospital halls in search of a cafeteria.

In the midst of all the madness, a totally confused Melody was catching the attention of the hospital security. A staff member had identified Melody as being high on *something*. After being detained by security for a short period of time, police appeared. Accompanied by hospital staff, a small group of people questioned her at great length. Will, who had been following her previously, quietly slunk off to the birthing room. Slipping into the back of the room just in time to respond when Mama called out for him. He pretended to have been present all along, trying hard to distance himself from the potential legal hazard of the soaring Melody. Fortunately Melody couldn't remember anyone's name, or how she had come to be in the hospital. Nobody stepped forward to offer explanations.

The hospital staff were able to gather the necessary information from the midwife. "She had planned a home birthing. Having gone a month past full term, we have been trying to induce labor. She has been in hard labor for over fifteen hours. She had been losing too much blood and was in bad shape. So I urged the party to move to the hospital. The baby's skull has begun to harden and seems to be stuck in the birth canal. I was concerned that the baby was in danger of suffering brain damage from the experience." The staff half listened in between the screaming, chanting, and loud breathing.

Cat sat in the hallway watching Melody's interrogation out of the corner of her eye. Across the hall, she knew Mama was on the edge of dying. The scene in the hospital room moved like a patchwork slideshow peeking through the half open doorway. *You asshole. Why did you have to show up in our life? Why did you have to get Mama pregnant? What are you going to do if she dies? If you think you are going to be my father, you've got another thing coming.*

After a few hours, Will came to sit next to Cat. "It's done. You're mother is asleep and I am going to go pass out in the van for a while." He got back up and wandered out toward the hospital exit.

Next the midwife came to sit next to Cat. "You're mother is fine. She is resting. You have a baby brother. He is resting too. I suspect you also need rest. I'm glad we came in. If we had tried to stay at the house, they both could have died." She got up and wandered down the hall toward the exit.

So much for the magical ritual home-birth. I bet none of the staff were expecting this mayhem when they came to work. Lucky to live huh? I need a cigarette. Cat got up and wandered out of the hospital in search of someone who might be able to give her a smoke and a ride home.

—————⦿(❋)⦿—————

The beginning of September was cool and misty in the woods. Cat fell in love with the new property. Despite the mayhem that surrounded their family, she felt drawn to their homestead on the ridge. Wandering in the melancholy woods, she searched for a glimmer of hope and motivation. *This is a beautiful place to call home. There is magic in these trees. They have been here long before me and will live longer that I can imagine. My secrets are safe here. I just have to believe that everything is going to be okay. School starts tomorrow. A whole new beginning! I will be okay. Everything is going to be okay.*

It was overwhelming starting the year at Mendocino High School. The halls were loud, bright, and crowded. The stimulus was too much to handle. Cat felt hate and judgment everywhere. *This is like middle school only worse! And these people clearly don't tolerate outsiders. They know I am an outsider. Look at the way they stare at me. I just want to tell them all to "Fuck Off."*

Hanging out with Cole, Cat began making new friends more quickly than she would have on her own. Her new friends tried to help. "Come to the Community School! The High School sucks. You will like the Community School a lot better!" She came home distraught, crying to Mama about the terrible place. Mama tried to help. She made a few phone calls, and soon Cat was transferring down to the Community High School Annex.

Cat was immediately welcomed by the students and staff at the Community School. Classrooms were less formal and more social. Every morning, during second period, the whole school crammed into the largest portable classroom, full of couches and big pillows. With about fifty students enrolled, it was a cozy rowdy family. This was a daily check-in, between students and staff. In an attempt to run their school democratically, morning meeting offered an opportunity to communicate openly that was embraced by most present.

The head teacher was a Buddhist and a reformed alcoholic. His patience was outstanding. *These teachers all seem pretty open-minded and accepting. They are clearly here because they care. Not like any school I have attended before!* Despite the fact that Maybeck had also been run democratically, it had been two to three times as large. Additionally, she had witnessed somewhat of a cliquish bias between some of the teachers and students. In Berkeley, inclusivity had been an ideal, a dangling carrot in the distance – never reached. Here at the Community School, the feeling of inclusivity was an immediate reality.

Cat still had a couple of classes up the hill, at the big High School. Running across town between classes meant that she was often late. Fortunately her teachers took this into consideration and were a bit lax on reporting tardies. However, walking through town provided an opportunity for distraction. She skipped a couple of her classes on the hill, opting to hang out at the cafe. But she made sure to return to school for her classes at the Community School.

Cat had enrolled in Driver's Education for the fall of her sophomore year. She went to class only a couple of times and decided that she didn't like the teacher. He seemed gruff and discriminatory. She learned from other students that "only the girls with the shortest skirts passed his class". Disgusted with the rumors, and his attitude, she stopped going altogether. She was dropped from the class, and received an F. There was no argument when she explained to Mama why she had stopped going.

Mama suffered severe postpartum depression. She had found out shortly after getting pregnant that Will did not find pregnant women sexually attractive. Mama's already low self esteem had suffered several blows since getting together with him. Feeling lonely and unwanted throughout much of the pregnancy, she was looking forward to feeling wanted again. He informed her that he wouldn't have sex with her until after the doctor gave the go ahead. So she waited several weeks more to feel love from him.

In the meantime, baby brother just wanted to be loved and taken care of. The novelty of the new baby was short lived, as Will escaped the home front to go to work. He brought one of his friends up from the Bay Area to help him on a job. Cat had started school just two days after the birthing, so she wasn't around much either. The school bus picked her at 7am, at the end of the driveway. She learned very quickly that the school bus waits for no one. It didn't take her long to get used to hitchhiking into town.

As the weather got colder and wetter, Cat's attendance improved. The alternative wasn't all that fun. *I'm in town to go to school, so I might as well.* She took to cutting only her PE class to go downtown to the bakery. She made more friends hanging out at the bakery than she did in school. After school, she rarely made the school bus back home, and would consequently end up hitching a ride back to Albion. She quickly learned that it was common practice for locals to hitchhike as a regular means of transportation.

Definitely different than what I'm used to.

Mama was very excited about her follow-up appointment with the doctor in Fort Bragg. She had been looking forward to "getting the okay from the doctor" to have sex again. She felt rejected and unwanted. Her mood swings and physical exhaustion added to her low self esteem. Feeling useless, she really wanted some recognition from Will regarding her value. She made a point to declare this in detail to Cat the evening before the doctor's visit. "... And so, it would be a good idea if you make yourself scarce tomorrow afternoon. Come home as late as you like, or stay with a friend if you want. I would rather not have any interruptions."

That morning, after Cat left for school, Mama and Will loaded the baby up in the van with all the laundry. Heading into town for the day's errands, their first stop in Fort Bragg was the doctor's office. After the doctor's visit, they went grocery shopping and headed to the laundromat. It was there at the laundromat, that the police decided to approach Will.

Apparently Will had a warrant out for his arrest. The local police had been aware of him being in the area, since the family had moved there over the summer. They had interacted with him at the hospital when her brother was born. Still, they seemed to be turning the other cheek and ignoring his warrant. It was almost as if they were waiting for the baby to be born, waiting for Mama to be healed enough to cope without him. The time had come, and so he was arrested.

Cat stayed in town for a while after school. Hitching as far as downtown Albion, she lingered for a few hours at Touchstone. When she finally caught a ride up the ridge, it was well after dark. She entered the house cautiously and was greeted by a furious mother. "Where have you been?

I needed your help and you came home so late! Take your brother please. I need a cigarette." Cat put down her bag and received the fussy baby.

Mama was in shambles. *What the hell? She told me to stay away. What the hell is going on?* Mama cried and fussed with her tobacco can, struggling to roll a cigarette. Lighting her smoke, she proceeded to tell the story of the day. She had not driven in a very long time and was not comfortable driving the van back home. "Somehow I made it home. I don't know. It's all a blur right now." She said, shaking her head and puffing on her cigarette. Her friends from the neighboring ridge had come and helped her. After spending hours crying she had barely been able to care for the baby boy.

The girl was immediately put to work. The entire school year proceeded as a battle of emotions for Mama, for Cat, and for the miserable and confused baby boy. Isolated four miles off the coast in a little trailer, Mama felt completely alone. "I am really going to need your help. I can't do this by myself! What was he thinking bringing us here? If we were in Berkeley, I would have friends, I would have family, I would have a bus system. Now I have nothing... but *you* to help me." Mama rattled off her frustration, while she fumbled to roll another cigarette. Overwhelmed by Mama's sadness, Cat huddled on floor pillows snuggling her now sleeping baby brother and nodded in agreement. "Of course I will take care of you Mama."

Cat began running many household errands with her backpack and her thumb out. Mama would send her to school with the food stamps and a list. She used food stamps to buy breakfast and lunch at the grocery store, saving the change. After school, she would go to the grocery store and pick up what they needed at home. Then, if she had enough change altogether, she'd go to the movie store and rent a movie for the night. Heavily loaded down with all the things, she'd hitchhike home, often arriving after dark.

When Cat arrived, Mama didn't ask her about school much. Instead she unloaded all her stress about the day. "The baby wouldn't stop crying. All I wanted to do was have a little break." Mama whined. Cat put all the grocery bags on the kitchen table and headed to the living room. *You think you've got it rough! It's exhausting carrying all that stuff for miles!* Hitchhiking included a lot of walking. It was cold and windy on the coast and she felt like a pack-horse. Getting home meant that she could unload all the weight and finally relax someplace warm.

Mama would get up and go in the kitchen. While putting away the groceries, she hollered into the living room, "Play with your brother! He's been missing you all day!" *You know what I think? All he was really wanting was for someone to play with him. He's a baby! He just wants someone to pay attention to him, to love him.*

What Mama really wanted was for someone else to play with him, feed him, and change his diapers. She looked forward to the arrival of her daughter and a break from the constant responsibility. Cat began to resent being the alternative parent. *Nobody ever asked my permission. Nobody ever asked me what I wanted. If they had, I would have said that Mama isn't in good enough physical or mental condition to take care of a baby, and I certainly wouldn't have signed up to pick up the slack!*

Mama's friends helped her with transportation, taking her into town occasionally for laundry, or appointments. She began relying on Cat for more and more of her daily needs. Cat bought Mama her tobacco, her groceries, her medicine.

"It's too hard to roll my cigarettes with your brother on my lap." Mama announced to Cat. "Come over here and roll me a couple of cigarettes." Clumsily, she fumbled with Mama's rolling machine. "You did that much quicker than I can! Thank you!" Mama picked up one of the rollies and lit a smoke with baby brother on her lap. Handing the gurgling baby over, she instructed her daughter. "Now go feed your brother. The formula is on top of the fridge."

Cat laid her brother down on the floor pillows and went to the kitchen to prepare his bottle. When she returned, he had pulled a stuffed animal onto his face and was waving his arms wildly in frustration. She removed the toy and held the bottle in his mouth. He quickly began to suckle on the nipple, emptying the bottle of formula. Propped up on pillows, Cat lay down beside the baby and listened to her mother.

"You roll cigarettes a lot better than I do! Where did you learn that? Well it doesn't matter." Mama got up from the chair to refill her teacup in the kitchen, continuing her one sided conversation from the other room. "I have such a hard time doing that while I am taking care of the baby. He gives me enough time to roll one or smoke one, but never both." Returning to the comfort of her chair, she set down her teacup and lit another rollie. "Before you go to school in the morning, please make sure to roll me enough smokes for the day. I just can't do this by myself."

And so it became a regular chore for Cat to roll a day's worth of cigarettes for Mama. There wasn't enough time before she left for school in the mornings. Cat ended up making it to the bus stop late more frequently. She began to get more comfortable with hitchhiking and would hang around town later, avoiding going home. She knew that as soon as she walked in the door, she would be put to work.

Cat discovered quite by accident that Mama didn't get

as upset when she brought friends home to spend the night. Cat and her mother both liked it because then they had more people to talk to than just each other. Cat's friends like Mama's artwork, and thought she was really cool. Baby brother liked it also, as this increased the number of smiling faces giving him attention. They all loved taking care of the cute baby. He was always in the same place when they arrived. Propped on pillows, surrounded by stuffed animals, baby brother lay desperately trying to get Mama's attention.

Chapter 15

COMPANY

A small, cast iron, pot belly stove was used to heat the little trailer in the woods. Cat didn't mind splitting firewood. She enjoyed going out and swinging the ax. She looked forward to the release. *I can take out my anger and frustration when I am splitting wood.* She began using it as therapy when she couldn't handle the crying from Mama and the baby. She looked forward Mama's reminder "You have to keep enough wood split and stacked in the house, and by the front door. I can't go out and split wood myself. It's just too difficult to do with a baby."

The hot water heater and stove ran on propane. They had a little five-gallon propane tank. When it ran empty, they had no hot water and no way to cook. Mama's friends had helped with this chore on errand days. The tank sat outside between the back porch and Cat's bedroom shed. It had to be unhooked from the propane line and taken down to the grocery store to be refilled.

It was cold and rainy the first day that Cat had to help with the propane tank. The tank was heavy empty, and even heavier full. Hitchhiking the five miles to the store in the rain was a miserable experience. She was gone several hours round trip and soaked to the bone when she finally arrived home with the filled tank.

With the rainy season in full gear, Cat was aware that she would likely be expected to repeat this chore again. Determined to improve the speed and efficiency of the chore, she convinced her mother to let her practice driving the van on the ridge. Cat was not a good driver. It didn't help that she hadn't really had many driving lessons ever. So she taught herself how to drive on the ridge.

Mama was concerned about her getting pulled over and made her daughter promise not to take the van off the ridge. "I promise Mama. I will keep it to the ridge." She began by driving up the ridge a little ways, turning around and driving back down to the house. Each trip she explored a little farther up the ridge. In doing so, she discovered a wonderful place about four miles up the ridge from their house.

Cat began going up there when she needed to be someplace peaceful and quiet. The property looked like it may have been a homestead a hundred or more years prior. There were old buildings that had long since collapsed on themselves. She began taking her friends up there as a place to drink and smoke and hang out without prying eyes.

By the time Cat had to refill the propane tank again, she had plenty of time to get more comfortable driving. Despite her promise and fear of the open road, Cat got brave and drove the van all the way to the store. While there, she backed into the side of a shiny white Cadillac in the parking lot. The driver was furious. The girl was mortified.

She got into a lot of trouble for driving it all the way to the store. "The rule was that you were not to leave the ridge with the van! You don't have a license! Nor is the vehicle properly tagged or insured!" Mama tore into her daughter.

"Now I have to figure out a way to pay for this person's damages!"

After that, Cat resigned herself to driving the van to the end of the ridge. There she would park, and hitchhike the remaining mile to the grocery store. Having access to the van made trips for propane a little easier. Even if she had to hitch the last mile, it was still easier to get a ride on the main highway than it was up on the less traveled road. *The tank is really heavy when its full! Way too difficult to carry very far!*

The more Mama relied on her, the more Cat grew to hate going home. She felt used. She was exhausted by all the chores. She was exhausted trying to provide emotional support for her mother who almost never stopped being depressed. She hated that her brother was always crying. There was little that Cat could do to make him happy. *I shouldn't have to ask my mother to take care my baby brother so that I can do my homework. She just assumes I am here to serve her.* Cat resented the whole scenario.

------((◉))------

A young blond man who had previously come up from the Bay Area to help Will with work, began returning regularly to visit and help mother. He was in his early twenties and very pretty. The blond man and a guy who Cat only knew as "Mushroom" came up a few different times. When the two men visited they would promise to stay for a few days. They brought more firewood and took Mama to town for shopping and errands. Cat took a fancy to the blond man, and began figuratively throwing herself at him. He was hesitant only briefly, and soon allowed her to be affectionate with him.

The two the men decided it would be amusing to get the girl drunk. "Let's see how much she'll do once she's had a few." Cat explained to them that her mother must not know. *Mama thinks alcohol is the devil.* She took the two guys up the ridge to the old homestead site. The three spent hours hanging out drinking, smoking and joking around. At bedtime, she opted for sleeping in the living room because it was "too cold in the cabin." Laying on the living room floor next to the blond man, she fondled and teased him while everyone else slept. Eventually, he gave in and had sex with the girl.

After a couple of visits, Mushroom became jealous. He seemed to think that if Cat was more drunk, perhaps he could get into her pants as well. Instead of driving up to the homestead and returning home only slightly tipsy, they boldly locked themselves away in her cabin room to drink. Listening to music and stoking the fire in her little wood stove was fun for a while.

In response to their coaxing, she drank until she was throwing up. Still she showed no interest in being intimate with Mushroom. He began to grow impatient. Skipping past subtle flirting, he tried outright to negotiate with her, suggesting that she owed him sex after "all he had done". She responded curtly, "I am not comfortable with that. I didn't ask you to do anything. You chose to, of your own accord."

He became pushy, and tried to force her. "Are you going to let him do this?" She asked, cozying up to the young blond man. Relying on him to "protect her" did not work out to her benefit. Instead, Mushroom convinced him to assist in the effort. Eventually the two of them cornered her in the cabin room. She left her body lying in the bed while they used her. Unable to handle the situation she left the only way she knew how.

The next morning she left early for town without saying anything to her mother or the house guests. *I've had enough. From now on, when they come to town, I am just going to visit friends.* When she did see them again, they suggested getting a bottle of tequila. "Nope. I'm not interested in drinking with either of you." Mushroom was angry. He acted as if somehow he had been cheated. Cat felt violated by his pushiness. *It's my body. I should be able to say no without repercussion.* The blond young man avoided her gaze. She was disappointed by his lack of backbone. *If you are stupid enough to just follow his orders, then you can go to hell with him.*

⸺«◍»⸺

As the days grew longer Cat began coming home later and later, and sometimes not at all. She preferred spending time with her girlfriend. They had met early in the year downtown at the bakery. *She is so beautiful and funny. I really like hanging out with her.* Marigold was boyish, and still very feminine. They had begun developing a friendship soon after meeting. She started coming home with Cat sometimes. Marigold was her "first girlfriend". They never really talked about their relationship in serious terms. The two girls were just together naturally.

Although Cat made several casual friends during the school year, she had just a few really close friends. Marigold started calling her "Kitty" and the rest of the folks in their closest circle followed suit. At first she winced when the nickname started, but she got used to it. It felt like more of a term of endearment, than an actual name.

Cat wasn't comfortable with casual friends or new

friends calling her "Kitty." When someone that wasn't in their close circle to her tried to call her that, Marigold was quick to draw the line. "You are not allowed to call her that! Her name is Firecat. Only her closest friends can call her "Kitty". She'd wrap her arms around Cat, protectively and kiss her on the cheek as if marking her territory.

Mama loved it when Cat brought friends home to spend the night. She grew fond of all of the people in their close circle and they all seemed to really like Mama. It was a rare occurrence that Cat arrived home without Marigold or another close friend. They would stay up late in the living room unless baby brother was being especially fussy. Then the teens would be banished out to the cabin room because they were "keeping up the baby".

Cat shared a different part of herself with each one of her closest friends when it was just one on one. They also all hung out as a group frequently. The boys treated her like "one of the guys" so naturally that she forgot their differences. That is until their girlfriends came around! *Why do these girls give me dirty looks? It's not like I am going to steal one of their boyfriends! The guys don't even notice that I am a girl!*

There were only a couple other female friends in the group. Neither of them ever seemed interested in dating. Nor did they ever seem very interested in spending alone time hanging out one-on-one with Cat.

In the months that passed throughout the second half of Cat's sophomore year she spent more time absent from school. She went to her classes when the weather was too unpleasant to be outside, or if it was a teacher she didn't want to disappoint. In the mornings she went downtown to the bakery and hung out. If she had any money, she'd buy a steamed milk with almond.

Hanging out and bumming cigarettes, she'd wait for Cole and the other guys to show up. When enough of the gang had arrived, they'd all walk down to the headlands to smoke and play D&D or just hang out and talk. Sometimes they'd climb trees, or sword fight with sticks.

Cat started the semester with good intentions. "This semester, I am going to go to school for at least a couple of classes every day." Her motivation was not consistent and she'd often forget the importance of this goal, gradually skipping out at least one or two full days every week. *It's a really good school. If I can just stay focused, I can keep from failing.*

Unfortunately, Cat was too busy hiding from depression, hiding from herself, and most often from responsibility. Terrified to be alone with herself, she tried to make sure there was always at least one person around. More often than she liked, Cat spent hours sitting around town by herself, "waiting to see who might show up". She used food stamps at the grocery store, to buy snacks. Sitting in front of the store, nibbling on her food gave her an excuse to hang around for a while.

Sometimes when she could scrape up a dollar, she'd buy a burrito from the liquor store. They were great on a cold day because she could use the microwave in the liquor store to heat it up. *Nothing beats a hot burrito on a cold day.*

In the afternoon, if Cat hadn't found someone to come home with her, she would take the school bus to Albion, or simply catch a ride with someone. She'd hang out at Touchstone for a while, again, waiting to see who might show up. Playing pool with random folks kept her active. There were usually enough people around that she would end up taking turns. When it wasn't her turn, she'd sit on the couch and work on homework. After a while the routine would get boring and she'd try to talk someone into giving her a ride home.

The lonely days were better for schoolwork but worse for the mood swings. Social days put Cat in a better mood, but were not good for school attendance and even worse for getting homework done. Spending a couple hours in the morning with the guys, then going to a couple of classes proved to be a strained attempt at academic focus. When she hooked up with the female friends during lunch, she began trying early to talk them into coming home with her after school. Once she had solid plans for the evening, she stayed happy for hours.

Some afternoons in the spring, Cole and Cat spent time hanging out on the front lawn of the school. If she hadn't found someone to take home with her, she headed back toward the school by the graveyard. It was a quiet sunny patch of grass, perfect for some good old fashioned rough housing. There, she enjoyed playing in the grass. She didn't put too much thought into it, just let her feelings level out with the competition. For just a little while, she could play like a kid, entirely in the moment.

The two were close to the same size. Everyone else was too big, not an equal match. Cat liked wrestling with Cole. She felt like an equal. The interaction was competitive and energetic. She would usually start it by picking on him. It would evolve into them rolling around in the grass play-fighting and sort of trying to kick each other's ass, but not really. They didn't hit each other, just wrestled. Then one day he told her to stop.

Cat was surprised and hurt. *This doesn't make any sense. Why does this bother me so much? Why does it bother him so much?* Cole backed up, telling her "No Kitty, I don't want to hurt you." Up to that point Cat had felt like he had accepted her "just like one of the guys". Cole referenced her gender as though that somehow emphasized the need for him to not play rough with her.

"This has never been a problem before. Why does it matter? So what if I am girl!" She argued. Cole was insistent, refusing to participate in the game that they had played so many times before. After it became clear that he was serious, she admitted defeat. She tried to respect his boundaries. Still, she felt rejected and couldn't understand why.

After that day in the grass, Cole seemed to be around less frequently. Cat became aware of them actually spending less time together. When they were both hanging out within a larger group of people, he seemed to have little interest in talking with her. Not only had he stopped playing with her, but he seemed to have stopped *wanting to* play with her. Thinking about their friendship, Cat's sadness deepened. *Why did he reject my friendship? What is wrong with me? I miss my good friend. What is it about me that always drives people away?*

Downtown with Marigold, Cat sat perched on the steps by the toy store. Drinking coffee and chatting, their hips so close, they could have been attached, the couple pondered the potential options for the coming evening. Some random guy from the high school walked by, stopping to say hello. They vaguely recognized his face, but did not recall his name. *No reason not to be social, though he doesn't look like someone we'd normally party with.*

"What's your name?" Marigold asked him, following it up with, "you got a cigarette?"

The guy dug in his pockets and emptied them out to show there was nothing to share. Instead of moving on, he hovered at arms length, near the foot of the stairs. "I'm sure I could find something better to put in your mouths."

Adding, "Why do you want my name? You don't need to know my name to have a good time."

Cat quickly responded. "I need to know who you are, so I know who I'm avoiding." *You feel like an asshole. Move along asshole.*

Random guy deflected Cat's comment and shifted his stance to focus more on Marigold. "Oh come on girls. I bet you both know how to party! You got a boyfriend? A date for the party at the Quarry tonight?" His gaze was fixed on Marigold, as he shifted his weight, swaying a little. She was quick to respond.

"Neither of us are interested! Because we are both taken." Marigold wrapped her arms around Cat, kissed her cheek, and added "by each other". Random guy made a comment about her not having a penis, and Marigold corrected him. "She *does* have a penis. *You* just can't see it. But she knows how to use it, so it's none of your business." Glowing, Cat puffed out her chest. *Put that in your mouth asshole! She loves me and you will never understand! So just fuck off and move along!*

———••(())••———

Cat was having trouble with reading. She would read her books for school, but nothing was sinking in. Mama thought perhaps it was a reading comprehension problem, so Cat began reading homework aloud to Mama. In doing this, they discovered that it was not her reading comprehension, but rather her eyesight. Mama decided that Cat would have to make an appointment to visit an eye doctor.

Cat took herself to the appointment after school. It turned out that she needed glasses for reading. Being on welfare, she was given 3 or 4 frames to choose from. All of them were ugly to her. She didn't like her glasses, and was not consistent about wearing them. When she had once had no problem letting hours slip by with her nose deeply planted in a book, now she was hesitant to even try. The glasses made her feel ugly and awkward. She often stuffed them in her pocket, or let them get lost in the bottom of her bag.

Spring in school meant time for exams. Mama reminded Cat that she ought to go into the regular doctor for check-up. Again Cat had to make her own appointment. She took herself to the doctor alone, after school. This time, it was not as simple as getting glasses. She didn't realize that going in for a check-up would be a "well-woman examination."

The doctor was not gentle with the girl. Cat lay on the cold table. The doctor asked her questions while she examined the girl. "Are you sexually active?" The girl responded "yes", while staring at the ceiling. She pinched her eyes shut tight and prayed for the exam to be over. The metal speculum was cold and pinched inside her. Tears welled up in her eyes and she whimpered.

The doctor scraped something along the inside of the girl while brashly commenting, "If you are sexually active then you should be used to this." The girl winced again, half-whispering, "It hurts." The doctor continued. "It doesn't really hurt that much. You'll be fine." Cat held her breath, tense from head to toe. The doctor removed the speculum and Cat let the breath out, trying to relax. Then the doctor jammed her fingers inside the girl to feel around and Cat held her breath again.

The girl was was angry. Cat had been drunk or high pretty much every time she had sex with a guy. She never really enjoyed it that much but she had little feeling of discomfort.

This poking, prodding, and jamming was so intrusive and the doctors conversation did little to comfort her. *I like sex with my girlfriend. It never hurts like this.* She felt violated. She tried not to speak and prayed for the exam to be over quickly. *I am never ever going back to a doctor like that again.*

⪻⪼

Cat made an acquaintance with a pretty hippie girl who had a boyfriend and a station wagon. She suspected that they did powders but she never asked them about it. She had not done any powders or pills since she left the city. *I am not in a hurry to do that now.* Her boyfriend was old enough to buy beer and also happened to be a self-proclaimed tattoo artist.

Cat was interested when the girl bragged about how her boyfriend had made a homemade tattoo gun with a guitar string. Cat talked him into giving her a tattoo. She drew what she wanted on a napkin while they hung out on the picnic tables outside the burger dive. "It's too complicated, but I'll do my best." He indicated that there were too many distractions downtown.

The group went down to the headlands to find a secluded place. Drinking beer and smoking, the small group gathered with Cat's tattoo in the center of the circle. Getting a tattoo was a real social event! Cat certainly thought it was special. *My first tattoo. Hurts like hell, but I'm tough. I can do this. I can do anything.*

The fellow didn't do a very good job. Bloody and dirty, her arm hurt really bad. She decided that she was going to wait a long time before getting another tattoo. Next time she wanted the person to listen to her more about what she wanted. Still she was proud to have withstood the pain for the picture of a snake wrapped around a rose, proof that she was tough enough to withstand any challenge.

Chapter 16

HOMECOMING

May arrived. Will was released from the penitentiary and sent home on a greyhound bus. When he arrived Mama was temporarily happy. She was exuberant about seeing him. Dutifully, she had sent him packages of food as often as she could. She had written him letters. She still hadn't had sex since he had rejected her during pregnancy and she had been waiting the whole time he was gone. When Will got home from the pen, Cat became invisible. So she stopped caring about what time she went home and started spending more nights away from home.

May was a beautiful month in Mendocino. It seemed that this was the one month that it warmed up without getting too cold and foggy on the beach. Many of the kids would go down to the beach at lunchtime and often would remain through the afternoon class time.

The head teacher was Cat's instructor for Psychology and also for Government. At one point, he asked her why she always showed up for Psychology class, but almost never to Government. To which Cat responded, "Psych is a cool class, and its before lunch. By the time Government class happens, I am too busy getting drunk on the beach to come back up to the school." He shook his head. At least she was honest.

By the end of May, they had retreated from the coastline to spend days up the river at a swimming hole several miles up Big River. It was too foggy at the coast for swimming and the days inland were much warmer. This required transportation. While it was easy to walk down the headland paths to the beach, the swimming hole was about 20 minutes drive inland from town. You had to know exactly which road to turn on, as nothing was marked. It had been a local hangout spot for years and when she first arrived, Cat realized why town had seemed so quiet. Everyone must have been at the swimming hole!

Cat liked swimming, drinking, snacking, and hanging out, and most of all, being included in the group. *This was carefree, the way the Sunday afternoon on the Yuba River had been when I went with Mama. Only here, I'm not hanging out with my mother's friends. These are my people.* At least, she wanted them to be. Cat really only spent quality time with a few individuals, and this social crowd was much larger.

Between all of the transients she was usually able to find a ride up to the river. It was the nicest there late morning. By two in the afternoon, the water was completely in shadow, and too chilly. Gradually all the people would head back down to town. Some would continue on down to the Navarro River where the late afternoon sun shone on the water.

Cat had made it through her sophomore year. She'd spent at least half her waking hours of the school year walking along the headlands or through the woods, crying and talking to herself. And still, she had managed to make a relatively large group of friends. She had no idea what they thought of her. Often depressed and lost in thought, she questioned whether people were hanging out with her because they liked her or because they had nothing else to do.

At first when school let out for summer, Cat just continued with her regular routine of going to town and looking for people to hang out with. Instead of going home in the evenings, she looked for the party to go to. Most days there was some kind of party happening somewhere, even if it was just a bunch of people hanging out at the river or the beach. She spent more time at Touchstone. She spent days at a time with friends instead of hours a time. She did make a point to go home for her birthday.

Cat's sixteenth birthday was a pretty huge deal. It was was even more psychedelic than her thirteenth had been. Most of her friends from the school year showed up. Several of Mama's close friends that had been at her initiation ritual arrived to camp out for a few days. She was excited to see learn that Mike would be showing up. Mike had already done his prison time, spent a year on the east coast, and returned to the West Coast, to live in Oakland.

Some friends from her freshman year in Berkeley piled into a car and drove up from the Bay Area for a few days. The party gradually developed, pulsing with a symbiotic ebb and flow as though the group of people and their movements were simply moving parts of a whole living being. What started as a BBQ in the fire pit, turned into a campfire as the evening progressed.

Despite the absence of a formal ritual, Mama took time to set up an altar. Guests visited the altar, carefully placing special gifts there, as though it were a great game of Elvin Chess. Occasionally, Cat would take notice of something that had appeared or shifted when passing by the altar. She'd pick something up, add something to it, or simply rearrange the pieces. Once the arrangement felt done, she'd dance off to the next distraction and completely forget about the altar of gifts.

Cat was delighted to be surrounded by so many familiar people. *So many people care about me!* The birthday girl moved fluidly through the evening, taking care to spend time thanking each and every guest for their presence. *Moving through the air is like swimming.* Words echoed and bounced back between smiles and laughter. People and objects so completely transformed that Cat discovered herself exploring a new planet for several hours. "The moon is blue, the air is silver and four acres to play in!" Not entirely different from her home, and yet somehow ethereal and hidden.

As Cat continued thanking each new guest, she was reminded of the guests she had thanked hours before, and yet these folks were somehow different. Their costumes were more elaborate, as if they had wandered through the looking glass and stumbled upon a midnight Tea Party in the high court of Wonderland. "It's a beautiful place that keeps changing." She smiled back at the Cheshire as she explained her surroundings to the guests by the fire.

The location was so secluded, that Cat felt safe the whole night. She was very relaxed when she finally fell asleep, her dreams continued as if she were still awake. By the sun's early mist, everyone was sleeping in various places all over the property. Some lay by the fire, some in the grass, some in the house, and some in her cabin. Nobody was in a hurry to get moving.

When she did awake, she reminisced the evening's events and found it difficult to determine when she had actually fallen asleep. *What part had been the party and which bits were actually a dream?* She concluded that it had all been between the worlds and therefore all were valid and without concern to the real world.

Soon after the birthday visit from her Berkeley friends, Cat convinced Marigold to venture down to Berkeley with her. They spent about a week in the Bay Area. Much of the week disappeared into partying really hard, drinking and doing powders. Marigold got tired of the scene and they headed back up to Mendocino. Within a couple days of returning, Cat was itching to go back down to the city.

"You can go back if you want to, but I am not interested." Marigold made it clear that the city was bad news. "Anything that is going to make me happy can be found right here in Mendo." The two girls did not share the same opinion, or desires, and soon Cat was heading South on her own.

Cat took public transit as far as possible and then hitched the rest of the way. She made a couple trips between Mendocino and Berkeley the same way. She didn't have any problems hitching once she got away from the city. The closer to the city she got, the more difficult it was to get rides. When she had enough money to catch buses, she opted for the safer option. The bus didn't go all the way to the Mendocino very often though. Eventually, it stopped running altogether.

⸺◈⸺

When Cat spent time in the Bay Area, she tried to make a point to visit her dad. It gave her a landing target, and a justified purpose for the visit. Still, it was more of a loose structure of housing and she didn't give her father much notice. He was often busy, and didn't seem to mind the random visits. Cat was gone in Berkeley and San Francisco wandering around visiting friends and partying most of the time.

Sometimes, she would meet Dad at his office when he got off work and ride back home with him to spend the night.

During one of the random visits, Cat decided to try to talk about sexuality with Dad. It was awkward, like the first time she had told him that she was sexually active. It had only been a couple of years since the last discussion. His respect and approval was immensely important to her. She wanted him to see that she was being herself and that she was okay.

Cat had approached him a couple of years prior. When it had become clear to Mama that she was sexually active, Mama had insisted on taking her daughter to the clinic for an exam. She did not feel comfortable discussing the exact details of her sex life with Mama. She tried to protest, because she knew that she was not actually having intercourse, and therefore could not be getting pregnant. Mama insisted that when you are sexually active, you need to be prepared for anything. Things that you don't plan may occur despite your best intentions and being prepared is always the best option. Since Mama used a diaphragm for birth control, she insisted that Cat should try the same.

Using a diaphragm was exceptionally challenging for the girl. More complicated than using tampons, she had to become fully comfortable with her own body inside and out. She had to manipulate this odd contraption to enter her body and be able to remove it again. Mama insisted that if she was sexually active, then she should have no problems with this. She insisted that there was no shame in practicing. Cat felt strange "practicing" with a diaphragm, and was thankful it was something she could do behind the locked door of the bathroom.

When she decided she needed to tell Dad what was going on in her life, Cat brought her diaphragm to the discussion. When she tried to speak, and her words ran dry, she had thrust the diaphragm case into his hands. Blinking wide eyed, she said "I thought you should know."

Expecting the plastic case to say all the things that Cat didn't know how to say, she waited for a response from him. She hadn't known what to expect from the conversation. Ultimately, Dad was more concerned about boys using his daughter for her body, than the choices that she made herself. Cat had been surprised and strangely comforted by his response.

Now, Cat needed to talk to Dad again about her sexuality. This time, she had no props to hand him. She didn't know exactly how to describe what she was feeling. "I'm confused." She started to explain, "because I like girls too." His response was not as comforting this time. Cat felt like he was too quick to dismiss the conversation. "It's just a phase. It's normal to experiment when you are young but you will grow out of it." She awkwardly backed out of the conversation with little protest. *Obviously, he doesn't want to listen. He isn't going to be any help this time.*

━━━━◈◉◈━━━━

Cat spent a week partying in Berkeley at the big house. Visiting her ex-boyfriend always led to meeting new people. This time, she met his most recent love affliction. Abby was a student at UC Berkeley. She was beautiful and very affectionate. Cat spent time with Abby and a couple of other college girls that had moved into the big house.

Abby and her friends seemed to be very comfortable with casual nudity. Cat was entranced with their inviting and affectionate behavior. Spending time playing dress-up, flirting, and making out with the college girls was an intoxicating experience. She spent several days following them like a lost puppy. They seemed to giggle about the whole experience. Cat enjoyed the attention and they seemed to enjoy the company.

Cat spent a week with some guys in a band. She talked them into letting her sing with them. Every day she was over there, waiting for them to be ready to practice. *They always seem more interested in getting drunk or high, than actually playing music.* She liked partying, but really wanted to sing! "Come on guys! Don't drink too much or you won't be able to play music! I want to jam! What's the point of being in a band if you're never going to play music?"

Cat had songs she'd been working on and had briefly entertained the daydream that she'd actually get to be the singer in a band. All it took was one week of hanging out with the band guys, to decide they were too lazy to be successful musicians. Cat left the band house, dismissing the temporary dream of singing in a band. After visiting Dad one last time, she took the subway to San Francisco.

Leaving the subway station, Cat was greeted by the edgy poetry of a street musician. She smiled as she walked by. Walking up the steps onto the sidewalk, one foot in front of the other kept moving. An hour and a half later, Cat found herself sitting down in front of the Ben and Jerry's at the corner of Haight and Ashbury. Powders and booze had bridged the gaps between nights and days for a couple of weeks. Coming down hard, she found herself in the company of many others who were strung out and jonesing.

Cat spent a couple of days hanging out. It didn't take long spending time with the drunks and junkies in Golden Gate Park for her to be done with the city. Cat missed Marigold. She missed the peaceful redwoods behind her little cabin room. *Sleeping on the ground is getting old. I need a shower, a bed, and a healthy meal. Time for another transit adventure.* Taking buses North, she transferred first in San Rafael, then Santa Rosa.

It was dark when the last bus dropped her in Philo. Spending the night in the edge of the redwood forest, Cat awoke early in the mist. She wandered past the Navarro River swimming hole as she hitched back up to Albion. *I wonder whether anyone I know will be heading this way to the river today. Maybe I should just hang out here and see who shows up? I wonder whether anyone here has missed me, or even noticed I have been gone.*

Dropping her bag and bedroll, Cat used them as a cushion to sit and rest. She briefly entertained the idea of heading down to the swimming hole. *I wonder if Marigold is there? It's probably too early in the day.* She paused on the shoulder of the highway, staring across the road at the little path that she knew would lead to the Navarro River. *Who am I kidding? She won't care about seeing me. I've been gone a month. She's already forgotten about me.* A great sadness filled her chest and her empty belly growled.

Cat got up and continued walking along the shoulder of the highway, carrying her bag and bedroll. The last month had worn her down. She hadn't had a good night sleep since her last visit with Dad. "I just want to go home. I wish someone I know would drive by and recognize me." The trees did not respond. The cars did not come. "They'll be driving by and recognize me, and pull over, and give me a ride. I really just need a friend to be happy to see me right now."

Cat's face was flushed. Choking on salty tears did not keep her legs from moving. *I really need to feel loved. I should be happy that there are no cars. I would be embarrassed if someone actually saw me this way.* Occasionally a car would pass by, but no one slowed down for Cat. Her legs hurt, her stomach hurt, and her heart hurt. *What the fuck is wrong with me?*

Several hours passed before Cat made it to Highway 1. She dared not try to walk up the windy shoulder of the coastal highway. *That would get me killed. There is not enough room to walk. Besides, I don't think I have enough strength to walk up that hill!* She resigned herself to waiting on her bedroll.

Cat had spent the better part of the summer in the Bay Area. Partying with different people that she had met during previous visits or during Freshman year. By the time she came running back to Mendocino, she was burnt out, strung out, and had no idea what she was running from.

Shuddering vibrations of painful stimulus. Lights every nerve on fire. Cold, numb, aching convulsions hide in a dark shadow of calm. Fire washes over my temples. Boring deep through, cauterizing. Essence of human thought and emotion. Deceive. Guiding the unaware into a trap of crevices oozing. Illumination of life, shattered. Blood pours out into bottomless holes in the floor. Hands, strangling ankles as they reach up. Grasping for air. But it isn't there. In this black cave, darkness is bitter and unfulfilling. Emptiness so dense it becomes a void. A black hole, enveloping and consuming.

Coming back to Mendocino after being gone for so long, was not easy to do. Cat's friends didn't seem to care that she had been gone. She wasn't unwelcome, but they certainly weren't concerned with the details of her absence. Things had changed. Cole didn't talk to her as much. Marigold was mad at her.

Cat was clearly hung down and burnt around the edges. People who had been comforting in the past, now didn't seem interested in being around her all that much. The talk of her party was old news, having been replaced with the everyday gossip of the past five weeks. She felt like everyone had something better to do that to hang out with her.

Chapter 17

LEAVING SCHOOL

Cat began her Junior year muddled with depression. She was feeling the recoil of sobering up from a summer of intoxication. Spending every day searching for some kind of high to escape her misery had worn her ragged. Marigold had replaced Cat with a new boyfriend. Many of the friends with whom she had felt emotionally safe, had become detached or unavailable. Drinking got heavier. She started hanging out with a rougher crowd, floating from one group to the next, searching for attention, for acceptance, for some kind of positive stimulation.

In an anxious search for the false confidence Cat had experienced with powders over the summer, she continued to expand the crowd of people that she spent little bits of time with. Having Will home added to her anxiety. Mama had convinced Will that powders were the most effective medicine for her chronic fatigue. So the air was abuzz with static at home. Nothing was sacred. Nothing was safe.

Cat stayed with different people, and had sex with people that she knew might not remember or recognize her. She sought out guys who just wanted to have sex with her. The instant high of physical attention gave her temporary relief from a strong feeling of self hate. She struggled with an overwhelming feeling of dread each day.

I wish I would just die in my sleep. Wouldn't that be interesting? I wonder what they would do if they came back to the bedroom to find me dead on their pillow? Though she did not consciously attempt suicide, Cat fed herself an arsenic of slow emotional suicide. Powders affected her ability to retain the details of her experiences. *Blurry road sign ahead, just add alcohol.*

Cat was miserable at home since Will had returned from prison. At first it had been okay, because Mama relived the honeymoon phase of their relationship. Cat's freedom to be herself with Mama was quickly lost as a result of the change in the household dynamic. She went home less and less frequently.

One afternoon, she decided to go home on the school bus right after school instead of arriving late at night. *I am not feeling terrible today. Maybe I ought to go be around my family.* Cat needed a shower, a warm meal, and a good night sleep. *Won't my mother be surprised if I show up and actually try and do some homework!*

Cat opened the front door and was surprised to see the living room full of naked people. This wasn't the river on a hot August afternoon. This was her living room on a cool September afternoon. Mama was so startled by her presence that she blurted out, "What are you doing here?"

Cat responded, "I live here." The heavy weight of being quickly forgotten hit her hard in the gut. "It's 4:30 in the afternoon and it's a school day. I come home from school and you ask me what am I doing here?" She walked right back out and slammed the door. *I can't handle living at home anymore. It does not feel safe walking into an orgy at 4:30 in the afternoon.*

Cat was overwhelmed by the startling fact that she knew all the people in the living room. She had been physically intimate with at least one or two of them previously. She knew that walking in on her mother in the middle of an orgy was something that would be burned in her brain forever.

Cat walked around the yard to her cabin in the back. She started going through her stuff and repacking her bag. She spent the next few hours hiding in her room and planning her escape. *What will I do? Where will I go?* At some point Mama knocked at her bedroom door, trying to talk to her. "I don't want to talk. I'm going to sleep." She didn't force herself in, and Cat was thankful when Mama abandoned the effort.

Cat tossed and turned in her brain, while she paced around the small room. It was so small, pacing was more like fidgeting. She rearranged little knick-knacks and treasures on her shelves, picking random things to bring with her. *I can't stay here. I don't want to be a failure. I don't want to be miserable.* She didn't want to be alone. She wanted to feel safe.

Cat sifted through her stuff and eventually packed two bags and a bed roll. She knew that she could no longer come home regularly. Still, she wanted to continue at school. She wasn't trying very hard to get good grades. Still, she knew that she needed *something* positive to focus on. She knew that she felt safe at the school. Eventually, she fell into a broken and tormented sleep.

Cat's bladder ensured her early rising. Before the first light of dawn, she was up and getting ready to go. She considered sneaking into the house to try and grab some food and decided against taking the risk. With two bags and a bedroll, Cat headed out to the road. She hitched into town and walked up the main drag to the coffee shop. *It's still too early.* Foggy, cold, and depressed, she headed all the way into school.

Cat set her bags up against the classroom that housed the morning meetings. She got out her notebooks and a pen dropping them on the ground beside her bags. She got out her cigarettes and a lighter and sat down on the ground. Her mind was a swirling vortex of emotional toxins. She lit a smoke, took a puff, and vigorously began to write:

Sanity is lost, like the morning frost, come from the evening dew. I know I'm crazy. So are you. I'm writing this for the fuck of it. Same as sucking on a liquor tit. Get real drunk, don't try to flunk the test of life by doing junk. But some yummy crank. I know I'm rank, when I've been smokin base. But sometimes that's the case. Cough and hack. Black in back or in front. Not a pig. Not a cunt. Who knows why? Who knows what? You show me, and I'll show you what I've got.

Cat started crying onto her paper. Her writing was sloppy, hands shaking, legs numb. She wiped her face, rearranged her bedroll, giving her a fresh position and lit another cigarette. She knew she was not okay. She felt terrible in her skin. *Nothing feels good.* She prayed that nobody would come by and tell her everything was okay. *It is NOT okay. I don't want to be pacified. I want to be accepted. I want someone to actually care about me.*

Cat knew what she wanted to feel, but she wasn't able

to communicate that to anyone. She tried to put her feelings into words and they came out in shards of glass. Again, the girl left her body. Half slumped on her bags in a sleepy daze, she rested limp in the gravel.

Cat could feel the clean green life of the trees. *People don't matter.* Cars passing below her were like bugs crawling along the edge of the headlands. Floating above her body she was free to smell the ocean. She recalled an afternoon when she had gone skinny dipping in the ocean with Marigold. *She was so beautiful. I was freezing, and the salt bit little holes into my skin.* The sun had been glorious.

Her heart had felt warm with love for Marigold. *She was always happy to see me. She brought me home and smuggled me into her bed.* That day on the beach had been a wonderful experience with the romance of the sea. Shrieks of chilly laughter echoed in her head as she watched the waves from cold foggy atmosphere.

An hour or so passed, and the arrival of cars yanked Cat back into her body. Cold and numb she fumbled with her surroundings for something familiar. Taking the last cigarette out of the pack, she lit it with shaking hands.

Cat knew that, in theory, if she couldn't find anything else to do, she could always do school work. It was in the back of her mind, and difficult to focus on. Only going home two or three nights a week, she would spend the rest of the nights away. She called from friends houses at first. By the end of September, she was running out of places to crash and failing to call at least half the nights she stayed out. She started sleeping out in the utility shack behind the school. She'd hang out on the beach or in town until it was dark.

By shadow of night, Cat would sneak into the shack, curl up, and go to sleep. She started leaving her bedroll in the shack, hidden away. Early in the morning, the sun would wake her up. Her cold achy body would remind her that she needed to move quickly, before other people started waking up. Tucking her bed away, throwing on her jacket, and tying her shoes was accomplished in practiced fluidity.

Creeping quietly around the back of the property, Cat headed through the field to the graveyard. There, she could take a little more time to make sure her clothes were straight and her bag was neatly tied up. Walking into the downtown area from lower streets made it less obvious where she had slept.

Heading to the bakery, she'd hang out and wait to see who she might be able to bum a cup of coffee from. *At least I can start asking for quarters. It only takes a few to get some coffee.* Then she had a purpose. And a warm cup to hold onto and sip.

Waiting for folks to come into town, seemed to take longer this year. Sophomore year Cat had felt like she had more friends. Now she felt lonely again. She didn't really make plans that nurtured friendships, as much as she searched for the next party. She spent a few more mid morning breakfasts of hash browns with cheese and refillable coffee at the Sea Gull Inn with random people, and then they all just started to run out of money.

———⋙⟨⟨◍⟩⟩⋘———

It only took a couple of weeks of staying in the utility shed, before a janitor found her stuff, or saw her, or both. The head teacher discreetly approached Cat about it. He was a kind hearted man. He recognized that if a student was doing something like sleeping in the utility shed in the back of their school, they probably needed some kind of help. He did not call Mama. Instead he calmly listened to his student.

Cat poured out her misery. She told him that she was depressed and she didn't feel good at home. Mama was always depressed, and yelled at her a lot. Will was bossy and made things worse. Baby brother gets neglected and she gets him dumped on her. "I can't handle going home. I just want to feel okay, and school is the only place I feel safe."

Instead of calling Mama, he told Cat that she could stay in one of the classrooms at night. "You have to keep it secret. Do not tell any of the other students, and under no circumstances are you ever to bring anyone else in." She did not tell him about her addictive struggle with powders. She was afraid to be judged and thankful for his compassion.

True to his word, he left the door unlocked for her every night. Cat stayed in there most nights for almost a month. She actually did do some homework. She tried to stay a little more sober. She spent nights detoxing, crying, writing, and praying for some great change. She was miserable. She was sure nobody cared. *Yet, I'm in here in the safe place so obviously someone cares.*

Cat dreaded the obligatory trip back to the ridge every few days. Mama had stopped grilling for details of her absence. Instead she went directly into the guilt trip. Cat couldn't handle it. It was too much emotion to defend herself against. When she showed up, she'd try to quietly go straight to her room. Avoiding a trip into the trailer was a little easier, since the outhouse was right next to her cabin.

Cat would try to slip in late, undetected. She'd empty out her bag, refresh it with cleaner clothes and whatever seemed to grab her attention, and then burrow herself under as many blankets as possible. Hiding in the sweaty darkness of her bed-nest, sleep would eventually find her. Sometimes she would get up very early to sneak into the trailer, shower, and perhaps grab a little food for her bag. *As long as Mama hears me leaving for school in the morning, she'll know that I've been home, that I spent the night.*

Halloween was a miserable night spent chasing a high that never happened. There were supposedly parties happening several different places. Nothing ever really panned out. Everyone seemed to have plans with someone else and Cat ended up depressed and passing out at someone's house.

Cat had been traipsing around town in an old hand-me-down beaver coat. The costume beneath the coat was minimal, and was meant to resemble some perverse adult version of a cat. Freezing and melancholy, she managed a ride home with friends who were intoxicated and ready to call it a night.

Waking up with a hangover from lack of good sleep and nourishment. Shivering, sleeping curled in a ball with only the coat as a blanket, had not been sufficient. *I thought fur coats were supposed to be warm!* She found herself apologizing as bumming normal clothes to wear became important. She received a severe lecture on the travesty of the fur industry and subsequently forget to bring the beaver coat when she left. She felt guilty for losing it and she felt guilty for having it. *I can't win.* She made her way back to town.

By the weekend, Cat was ready for some good solid friend time. Cat missed the times that she had hung out with Cole and Richard and the other guys, the previous year. She had felt like just one of the guys. Everything had felt normal while Will was gone, comparatively. She missed that feeling of normal friendship, without such a heavy emphasis on partying.

When Cat ran into Richard, she tried to talk to him about it. They used to talk on the phone about everything and nothing. They had gotten really close. Now, he seemed to be willing to talk again. She relished the opportunity and they she spent the better part of the afternoon hitchhiking up to Comptche.

When the two friends reached Richards house, Cat used the phone to call Mama and check in. Feeling better from her talk with Richard, she was brave enough to actually try and talk to her mother. *I guess it's important to at least check in sometimes.*

Cat's phone call was not well received. Her mother was not appreciative.

Mama got very angry with her on the phone, insisting that Cat come home right away. "I'm stressed out. You need to come home and watch your brother so Will and I can go to the hot tubs!"

Impossible. Even if I was driving it would take at least an hour! Cat tried to explain that she didn't have a ride. "It's getting dark and hitchhiking out of here after dark is practically impossible!" Mama got angrier. "If you're not going to be coming home tonight, don't bother coming home at all."

Cat took it as an ultimatum. Distraught and glad to be in a place that she felt safe, she allowed herself to enjoy the evening hanging out with Richard and his mom. She briefly shared her misery regarding her current relationship with her mother. Richard's mom was very nice. "You are always welcome here, even if Richard isn't around."

Cat spent the rest of the weekend visiting with Richard and his mom. They rode the school bus back into town on Monday morning. That day she went to school and searched for a solution. Cat spent time with the friends that had time for her. She walked around the streets of Mendocino for hours. Wracking her brain for the right answer, she decided that it was just getting too cold to be on the streets. *I can't keep up with school without the stability of a regular place to go back to. It's just not working.*

Cat felt trapped. She walked out of town to the highway mid-afternoon. Mesmerized, she stared at the waves of ocean crashing against the sand, constantly recreating the shape of the beach. *I wonder what it must feel like to know your purpose. What does it feel like when you know exactly what you are supposed to do, and can find peace in that repetition?* There was something mystical and free about the coastline. She felt strong emotions pulling her south down the coastline.

Walking with her thumb out, she was quick to get a ride. It was the head teacher of her school. Cat was afraid to ask him for a ride all the way home, even though she suspected he would say yes if she asked. She didn't want him to come in and talk to Mama. She didn't want him to judge her for her decisions. She just wanted him to support her. "I'm leaving. I have tried to keep going to school, but it's all too much." She told him that she was going home to pack her bag for the road, and then she would be heading south. Instead of telling her all the reasons why that was a bad idea, he responded gently.

"I'm heading to Santa Rosa for evening classes at the College." He said as he dropped her off at the bottom of her ridge. "You just be careful." He urged Cat to seek her own truth. They were reassuring words, coming from him. *He has always been a kind man. Truly a blessing.* She got out of his car, and tears well up in her eyes as his car pulled away. *I wonder whether I will ever see him again.* She started up the ridge, thumb out, and picked up a local ride that dropped her at the driveway.

Walking up the driveway, Cat was quiet and cautious. She wanted to make sure that she wasn't seen. She had no patience for confrontation. Slipping into her room, she repeated the ritual of dumping her bag out. This time, she repacked for a long haul. She chose basics that were easy to layer, some crystals, notebooks, pens, colored pencils, a couple of sharpies and a shaggy hard bound copy of *The Complete Works of Shakespeare*.

Some people carry a Bible, and I've got Shakespeare. Laughing at herself, Cat dubbed it "her bible". She put her grandfather's long overcoat on, and tucked her little sheathed dagger into the inside breast pocket. *Hopefully I won't need to use it, but just in case I run into trouble, I could do some damage with this little double edge blade. And perhaps reading Shakespeare will help me find some great hidden meaning that will enlighten me.*

With a patchwork backpack, bedroll, and her little Army green knapsack, Cat half-ran down the driveway and out of sight. Back to the road, she walked west for a couple of miles before she was able to get another lift. A couple of drivers later, she found herself getting dropped off in Booneville after dark. *I will be waiting here for a very long time. Especially after dark. If it's not a straight shot all the way to Cloverdale, I'm pretty much screwed until morning.* Cold and hungry she sat down on her bags.

Chapter 18

MIKE AND ABBY

Every now and then, cars full of local, drunk, redneck boys would drive past jeering at her. After about two hours of waiting, a logging truck pulled over. Cat was nervous. It was too dark to really see the driver well.

He didn't feel safe but she really wanted to get out of there, so she took the ride. His truck was old and small. The cab was tiny and not designed for overnight hauls.

The truck rattled and wobbled around every corner. His driving made Cat nervous as he flew around tight corners on the winding highway. He began talking to her. She kept her answers short, trying not to encourage further conversation. The driver started asking her if she did favors for guys who gave her rides.

Cat responded that she had a strict moral structure that did not accommodate such activities. He verbally attacked her, while hurtling the logging truck through the darkness. "You're not one of them Less-Beins are you? I hate those bitches. They just tease you and then say that shit at the end like it's some kind of bullshit excuse to not put out. I hate those less-bein tease bitches. You're not one of them are you??"

His driving made her nauseous, and the conversation made it worse. Being cramped and cold in the cab of the truck, Cat was curled up in a ball in the seat, protected only by the seat belt. Her left hand tucked into her right armpit for warmth, her right hand shook inside her breast pocket, sweaty fingers clung to the handle of her little dagger. Her toes twitched. Her legs cramped.

"I don't know about all that. I just know that I gotta really know somebody well to be close like that. I mean, I want to love someone and marry them before I get physical with them."

It was a half-lie. It was too dark to see her face. It was too dark to see him clearly. He rambled and spewed hateful and demeaning talk at her about all the terrible "less-bein" bitches in the world as he flew his old logging rig on auto-pilot all the way to Cloverdale. Cat just kept repeating that she had her morals and she had to stick to them, rocking and twitching in her seat.

She had to go to the bathroom. She was scared of what this old guy might do to her. She was even more terrified of being dumped off so incredibly in the middle of nowhere and at night. Fortunately, neither happened.

When they pulled into Cloverdale, he drove to the south end of town. Pulling into the parking lot adjacent to the Owl Cafe, the trucker handed Cat a five dollar bill. As he handed it to her, he told her "You're a good kid. Stick to your morals and you might get somewhere. Here's five bucks. Go get yourself something to eat." He pointed to a corner about a half block up the street. "Then go stand on that corner and you will get a ride within a half hour." He dropped her off and left her standing in a cloud of dust as his truck pulled away.

Shocked, hungry and shaking, Cat had nearly pissed

herself. Her heart was racing as she went into the cafe She used the bathroom and glanced at the menu. Five dollars wouldn't go very far and it was already pretty late. She politely excused herself and walked out to the corner. Just like predicted, thirty minutes and someone pulled over for her. She was amazed.

This time, the driver was a younger man, perhaps in his late twenties. He was overweight and smelled of meatloaf. In fact, the whole car stunk of meatloaf. The driver was nice enough. He didn't really talk much. The strong smell of food when she was over hungry made her nauseous. The car was clean and comfortable.

Cat stared out the window and fell in and out of sleep. She woke up when the car was approaching San Rafael. She politely asked the driver if he could drop her off somewhere with a pay phone. He dropped her off downtown. It was a couple of blocks from the freeway, at an all night donut shop.

Here Cat could afford to get a cup of coffee and a snack! She thanked him politely for the ride and he left with a muffled "You're welcome." She went in and unloaded all her bags into a heap, under a table by the window. It was nice to not be in a car. She took her jacket off and set it on the window seat. A wave of relief washed over her. *I'm free. I'm hours away from my mothers house and going back is no longer necessary. Everything I do from here on out is all for me! What should I do now?*

Cat bought a cup of coffee and two donuts. She asked for all of her change back in coins, for the pay phone. Sitting down with her coffee, she started to go through her knapsack, taking inventory. She found her phone book. *Who should I call?* She was exhausted. *I have hitchhiked enough for one day. I can't stay here all night. I want a warm bed.*

I want to feel safe. She went outside to use the pay phone. She bummed a cigarette off a local drunk.

Calling Mike, Cat explained breathlessly that she was in San Rafael, and could he please come pick her up. He was worried. He asked her where she was, and how she had gotten there. "I couldn't stay in Mendocino anymore." She explained how Mama had kicked her out, and how it had taken her six hours to hitchhike this far. He told her to stay put and headed out to get her. She got off the phone, smoked the cigarette, sipping slowly on her coffee. After the smoke burned out to nothing, she headed back inside.

Picking at her second donut slowly, Cat killed time in the warmth of the donut shop. She thought about how she had crushed on Mike when she was younger. She remembered how affectionately he had responded to her when he visited over the Summer. When he arrived, he greeted her with a warm hug and a she responded with a wet kiss. He took her home to his studio in Oakland.

Cat passed out quickly in his car. This was someone familiar. She could trust him. She awoke when they arrived at his place. He smuggled her in past potentially prying eyes of roommates, and poured her into his bed. Without asking anymore questions, he wrapped his blankets around her and fell asleep to the smell of her road dust.

—————«(❂)»—————

When Cat awoke, everything was bright and shiny. Mike's room was a large studio room with big bay windows. He had a big bed with soft blankets and sheets. She snuggled up to him and thanked him graciously with physical affection that may have been more appropriate if he had not been twice her age. That didn't seem to matter. They spent the better part of the next couple of days in and out of his bed. She needed someone to show her love and he seemed overjoyed and honored by her presence. He kept petting her hair, kissing her forehead, and asking her why she chose him to run to.

By the second day she had her fill of the lotus of physical affection. She wanted to go out for coffee. Cat got cleaned up and dressed up as sexy as she could muster with her small repertoire of costumery. Emblazoned with hickies, they went to Telegraph Ave for some cafe time. Mike walked in presenting her as he would a girlfriend. Some of his older friends recognized her. They had met her as 'Maudie's Daughter', when she used to accompany Mama during weekend visits at the Berkeley Inn. Their discouraging looks directed at Mike, challenged her to grasp his arm more tightly.

Cat publicly fawned over him. Feeding his ego made her feel powerful. They stayed for a while. When they left, they drove around, running a few errands. She teased him in the car as he drove. The rush of the power was like a high. As long as she emasculated him, he would protect her and take care of her.

Cat quickly fell into a relationship pattern with him. They talked for hours in each other's arms about their hopes and aspirations in life. Their conversations were random and dreamy, not directly associated with each other, instead sparking off each others ideas. They talked about gardens and big kitchens, about freedom and dreams and happiness. By the end of the week, they were heading back up to Mendocino to pick up the rest of her stuff.

Pulling in the driveway on Navarro Ridge Road, Mike's car was greeted by the barking dog, and her mother blinking in the sunlight of the front porch. She was glad to see her daughter, and glad to see Mike, and confused. So many emotions flooded her face as she realized what was happening. Cat got out of the car with the intention of going directly to her room to pack. Instead she had to defend herself against tearful pleadings.

"Why haven't you called? Where have you been?" Mama demanded answers. "Why are you doing this to me?"

Cat responded to the questions with short answers. *Why was I doing this to her?* "You kicked me out! You made an unreasonable request and told me that I was not welcome back home if I did not comply." Mama insisted that was not true. *I don't want to argue with you. I just want to be able to pick up more of my stuff.* "I'm going to live with Mike now. You don't have to worry about me anymore."

Mama was hurt and confused. She insisted that they at least spend the night before driving back to the Bay Area. Cat and Mike agreed to do so. Under different circumstances, Mike would have enjoyed a visit with her mother. They had been friends for years. However, the tensity of this situation made conversation a little more challenging. He explained to Mama that it was better this way. "I will take good care of her. I will make sure she is okay." He assured her that Cat would be in a loving home. "You know me. You know that I will take good care of her."

The next morning, Mama drafted a letter that gave Mike legal authority, as a guardian, to sign on her behalf for emergency legal and medical reasons. They all drove down to the post office where Mama had it notarized. She handed it over to Mike and told him that she was entrusting her daughter into his care. The three drove back up the ridge in silence.

As Cat was packing her stuff up into Mike's station

wagon, Mama started crying again. Mike tried to calm her with his soothing voice, her sobs came and went in intervals. She kept repeating, "But I just don't understand." Finally, he gave up, told her that he loved her, and got into the driver's seat.

"I'm ready. Let's go." Cat said, as she closed the passenger door.

They pulled away, listening to Mama screaming, "Why are you doing this to me??"

Cat was excited to be free. She was excited to be with someone who appreciated her. She was eager for whatever the future might hold for her. Ready for adventure, she put her bare feet up on the dashboard and lit a cigarette. The salty ocean breeze blew through her hair as they wound down the curvy highway approaching the head of the Navarro River.

⸻ «◉» ⸻

Both Cat and Mike were excited driving back down to the Bay Area. It didn't even occur to Cat to wonder what Mike was thinking. She felt like anything was possible. *Everything will be better now.* She had no idea what that "better" would look like. She only knew that for the first time in a while, she felt truly loved.

When they arrived back at Mike's studio in Oakland, both were exhausted from the long trip. They didn't bother to unload much from the station wagon. Instead, they retired for the evening, agreeing that the unloading of stuff could wait another day. Collapsing into his bed, the two made love and fell asleep in each other's arms.

The following morning, Cat awoke before him and

quietly proceeded to the kitchen. She tried to make hash browns the way he had shown her, but they didn't turn out as well as they had when Mike was cooking. She woke him up with her attempt at breakfast. He was warm and affectionate. After eating breakfast, they cleaned up the dishes together and made plans to go out for coffee.

Mike was unemployed, and had been actively looking for work prior to her arrival. Her presence was a distraction from job hunting. After a couple weeks it became apparent that he needed to hurry up and find a job. The honeymoon period that they had been experiencing was fading quickly as he stressed about money. Once he knuckled down and started really looking for a job, he was quick to land a night job at a local bakery. He began bringing home leftovers and seconds from his baking job, which ensured that they always had delicious bread to eat.

As soon as Mike got the job, Cat realized that she too would need to find something to do with her extra alone time. She contacted Katie to let her know that she was back in the Bay Area. Katie was excited to hear from Cat and informed her that she was still working for Kirkle. "Do you think that I could get back on there?"

Katie thought it wouldn't be a problem. Cat went to visit Katie at work the next day, and talked with the boss. He had no problem taking her back. Soon she was working everyday.

Thanksgiving arrived and Mike brought Cat to his parents house for the holiday meal. Very little was discussed regarding the nature of their interactions. He introduced her as Maudie's Daughter. It made her squirm. She felt judged. She stayed relatively quiet. She didn't know what to say.

They regarded her oddly, as if they didn't know exactly what to think about the situation. Still, they were kind enough, and everyone ate plenty. After the meal, the two helped clean up a little. They didn't hang around very long though. Clearly, he was just as uncomfortable as she was, if not more.

The month of November had passed quickly and the studio that Mike had been renting was no longer an option for them. Despite the fact that she never seemed to see anyone else in the house, Mike did in fact have roommates. He was supposed to be renting the large studio room by himself. It was not going to be okay for him to stay there with her. She didn't have anywhere else to go, and he didn't want her to leave. So they began looking for an apartment that they could share.

They found a place just two blocks away from his current studio. It was a one bedroom apartment. They both agreed that sharing the same bed all the time was a bit of a distraction. They both needed their own space. Cat stated firmly that she required privacy and space that was entirely her own. So they agreed that she would have the bedroom. Mike was satisfied to set his futon up in the living room.

Mike's station wagon was not cooperative. They managed to get a lot of stuff packed up in the car. After limping the car two blocks to the new apartment, it remained in the parking garage awaiting repair. The rest of the move couldn't wait for the car to function properly. With a looming deadline they had to get creative.

Absconding a shopping cart from the local grocery store, Cat began loading up boxes. The two of them made several small trips down the bumpy sidewalk. It took some time and they got plenty of funny looks. Every time they passed someone along the way, they had to explain what they were doing. The scene was especially entertaining when they were trying to move furniture. Once the move was finally completed, they were tired and excited about settling into the new apartment.

When Mike was sleeping during the day, Cat was at work. When Mike got ready for work at night, he folded the futon into a couch and magically, they had a living room. Between their work schedules and separate sleeping arrangements, the time that they spent together dwindled quickly. Mike was gone to work before Cat got home in the evening. He usually arrived back shortly after she left for her bus adventure commute. Communicating with notes on the fridge evolved into the most common form of exchange.

When their days off matched up well enough to actually spend waking hours together, Mike whined about how much he missed his roomie. He began talking dreamily about how he wanted Cat to be around forever. Occasionally he mentioned the thought of her growing older and having children. The thought made her sick to her stomach.

Cat's enchantment with her older lover had faded. He felt needy. She missed spending time with him, and enjoyed the time they did spend together. Still, she felt weighed down. *I want to be appreciated, but this is too much to handle. I am not trying to plan a family with this man. I am not ready.*

⸻ ⵙⵙ ⸻

Working at the warehouse, showing up on time was expected and arriving a couple of minutes late was tolerated. There was no apparent award for showing up early to work. Still, Katie and Cat seemed to earn some respect from the boss. Reading him was like interpreting a convoluted definition of opposites. It was the absence of disrespect that led to exchanged looks between the two girls.

They hated the job, but enjoyed some of their cowork-ers. Cat especially liked that she got to spend five days a week with her good friend. Katie was commuting on public transit from Concord, where she was living with her boy-friend. She wanted to spend social time with Cat outside of work, but he was jealous and controlling. Katie assured Cat that everything was fine, and besides they got to spend five days a week together.

Katie was totally enamored with the controlling boy-friend and refrained from speaking ill about him. She inter-preted his abusive nature as a sign of his true love for her. Cat was jealous of their weekends together. *I wish we could spend an evening hanging out. He treats her like garbage and still she goes home to him. Why? I would treat her like gold! But that's okay. I get to spend all week with Katie, and he only gets the weekends.* Cat wasn't terribly fond of the job, but she adored spending so much time with Katie. Cat felt like she would do anything to keep her beautiful friend smiling.

Christmastime arrived, and Cat was proud to be able to invite Dad to the apartment. He came over for dinner on Christmas Eve. The two roommates cooked together and the three of them shared a meal. Dad was careful not to criticize or question the situation. He could see that his daughter had her own room. Her and Mike each took turns illustrating the busy schedule and living agreement that they were balancing. They showed no signs of being physi-cally intimate. *I'm sure that Dad would not approve if he knew what was really going on.*

After dinner, Cat rode with Dad to his house in Walnut Creek. Spending the night in the guest room of the house she grew up in was strange. Waking up Christmas morning before had been normal when she was a kid. Now she didn't know what to do with herself. She ate a little food. She watched a little television. Eventually, she went into the computer room and played on the Mac until Dad woke up.

Their Christmas was nice enough. She felt awkward the whole time. Eventually, she called Abby who agreed to come pick Cat up. After leaving the last boyfriend, Abby was not spending as much time at the big house in Berkeley. Their ex-in-common insisted Abby was crazy. Cat thought she was wonderful. Just as she had done in the past, Cat developed a friendship that outlasted the short period of dating.

Now Abby is coming to pick me up in Walnut Creek! Cat told her that it didn't matter where she went, she just couldn't handle staying there. Abby was delighted to see Cat. Dad wasn't surprised to see her go. They had spent the better part of the day mulling around the house and her departure was inevitable anyway. When she picked her up, Abby told Cat, "I'm taking you to meet my parents." Cat got nervous. What would they think of her? Abby assured her that it was "no big deal."

Abby's parents lived in Marin County. When they pulled up to the driveway, Cat was astonished. There was a security gate. The young woman entered a password prompting the large iron gate to creak open slowly. Pulling past the gate toward the house, Cat's jaw dropped. Abby laughed at her and she closed her mouth.

"This is where your parents live?" Cat gasped. *This is the biggest house that I have ever seen!*

Abby laughed again as she answered "yes". Getting out of the car, Cat looked up at the estate house and asked her if it was a mansion. "Are your parents rich? I'm not dressed nice enough to go in here. You should have warned me!"

Abby laughed as she pulled her toward the door. She

insisted, "Everything is going to be fine. Nobody will judge you." Cat held tightly to her warm hand and followed with interest.

Walking in the door, Abby hollered out to her invisible parents that she was home. The house was even bigger on the inside. The carpets were pristine, the ceilings extraordinarily high, and all the rooms were spacious. Abby walked into the kitchen and opened up the fridge. There was no big celebration happening here. It could have been any day, except for the huge decorated tree in the family room. The fridge was packed full of food. While Abby pulled food out of the fridge, Cat stared at her new surroundings.

Abby's mother walked into the kitchen and casual introductions were immediately exchanged. She didn't seem to notice that the guest looked out of place. She didn't bother to ask Cat her age or any personal information. She simply accepted her daughter's guest without question. It was exactly the opposite of what Cat had been afraid of.

Abby talked briefly with her mother about various family members and what they had all been doing for the holiday. Apparently everyone had gone somewhere different and no celebration had occurred in this big house. *If I lived in a house this big, I would have a party bigger than the movies! They are so casual about this whole exchange. I wonder whether they know that today is still Christmas.*

After Abby's mother left the room, Abby proceeded to fix them a big plate of food. Next she went to the liquor cabinet and made them each a drink. She handed one of the drinks to Cat, and instructed her to follow. Winding through the labyrinth of the huge building, they found their way upstairs in another large room. This was Abby's bedroom. *This is bigger than my dad's living room.* There was a large television, a large bed, and everything matched. Cat felt totally out of her own element. *I feel like I'm on the set of some old black & white movie.* Abby was so casual and upbeat, and laughing at her astonished guest.

Abby kicked off her shoes, turned on some music, and climbed on to the middle of her bed. "Come on" she said, "I can't eat all this myself" and coaxed Cat to do the same. She kicked off her shoes, and took off her jacket. *It's so nice and warm here. Her bed is soft. She is so beautiful. I feel like I am in a dream.*

They sat on the bed eating and drinking and listening to music. After the girls were done with the plate of food, they ventured back downstairs in sock feet. Placing the empty plate in the kitchen sink, Abby opened the fridge to look for dessert. They stood in the kitchen eating pie and talking about nothing important at all. Then, refilling their drink glasses, Abby grabbed Cat's hand again and led her back upstairs.

Sitting on the soft bed, they finished their second round of drinks and began to play around. Tickling and wrestling turned into kissing and wrestling. The two spent hours kissing. It was wonderful. Cat was sure that she was in heaven and wanted the night to last forever. Eventually they fell asleep in each other's arms.

Waking up in the bed next to the empty space that had been Abby's warm body, Cat got nervous. Was she alone here? She didn't know what to do. She didn't know where she was. Her short-lived panic subsided when Abby emerged from her bathroom with a toothbrush in her hand. "Good morning sleepy head" she said, smiling at her house guest. She was already getting ready to leave. Despite the luxurious setting, Abby didn't seemed very enthusiastic about staying long. Cat needed to go back home as well. When Abby brought her back to the apartment, Cat introduced her to Mike.

Mike and Abby seemed to get along well. Cat was pleased. In fact, she felt like she was glowing. She was sure Mike could see it too. After her Christmas lover left, Mike commented on how fantastically beautiful Abby was. Cat agreed. He didn't seem threatened by the apparent adoration for her. Instead, he was intrigued. She began to brag about all the wonderful reasons why he would enjoy being friends with Abby.

Chapter 19

LOVE YOU FOREVER

Returning to work after the holiday, Cat was thankful for a regular routine. She looked forward to a routine that included laughing and joking with Katie. *She is so beautiful to me.* They were always happy together. Even when one of them was depressed, the company of the other was uplifting. With Katie's birthday coming up, they had plenty to talk about.

Katie would be turning 17 on New Year's Eve and Cat wanted to give Katie the world for her birthday. Her boyfriend was not as nice to her. She got to hear all about the fights and the makeup sex. Cat assured her friend, "You are a magnificent person and deserve to be treated like a queen for your birthday."

Katie had recently gone into the clinic for her annual panel of tests. While neither one of them was as responsible as would have been prudent in terms of their sexual activity and drug use, Katie was very careful to get tested regularly. She talked about it at work with her friend, while they folded cotton shirts, and stuffed them into plastic bags for shipment. Placing the "examined by" stickers on the mail order bags, she admitted that she was scared. "What are you scared of?" Cat asked her.

Katie explained that she was scheduled to go pick up her test results later that week. "I'm sure everything will be fine." Cat tried to reassure her. The fear was evident as the muscles in her face and hands tensed.

She continued, "I don't know what I am nervous about. I've gotten this test done a hundred times before and I was never scared about it. But this time, I am really anxious." Cat didn't know what to say to make her friend feel better. After a little while, she managed to change the subject.

A couple of days later, Katie was waiting at the BART station in the morning. She rode the subway from Concord, where she lived with her boyfriend. Cat rode the bus from her apartment near Lake Merritt. They always met up at MacArthur BART and rode the shuttle bus together to the Emeryville warehouse. As Cat approached her friend, coming out of the subway station, she saw tears streaming down Katie's face. *Something is terribly wrong.*

When Cat reached her, she wrapped her arms around Katie and let all of her love for her friend cover her like a blanket. *What had happened? Did she get in a fight with her boyfriend again?* She didn't ask any questions, and instead waited for her friend to speak. "I got my test results yesterday," she sobbed. Cat petted her hair. "I knew there was something wrong. I knew it was going to be bad, but I didn't expect this," Katie continued.

Cat pulled back a bit, to wipe the tears from Katie's face. Mascara dripped down her cheeks. Using the edge of her jacket, Cat tried to clean her face. Katie looked directly in her eyes and said, "I came up HIV positive. My life is ruined." The stream of tears flowed freely down her face. "And now my boyfriend hates me." Cat pulled her close again.

"Oh babe. I love you so much." Cat told her, as she pulled

Katie close against her and squeezed her tight. Commuters standing around the subway station awkwardly tried not to look at them. Cat shot protective looks of warning at prying eyes. They pulled away from each other. Katie pulled out her cigarettes and handed one to her friend. Lighting her cigarette, and Cat's, she pulled her toward a nearby bench. Sitting down, smoking their cigarettes, they waited together for the shuttle bus to arrive.

When the two girls were at work, Katie spent the better part of their work day rambling about her dreams of a life with children. Though she didn't mention her test results directly, Cat knew that her mind would not falter from the topic for long. All Katie had ever really wanted to do was be a housewife and a mother. She wanted the white picket fence with children running in the yard. She wanted a garden and a dog. She wanted the happy suburban life that she had not experienced in her own childhood. Now, she was sure that would never happen. She could not have children. If she did, they would be born diseased.

Love for Katie filled Cat's chest. It was so strong that she felt she would burst from it. Cat told her friend, "I'm sure you would make a wonderful mother."

Katie responded, "But I can't now." Tears flowed again, and their coworkers kept their eyes down, focused on their own work. Nobody dared intrude on their conversation. Even the boss, who regularly complained about a lack of productivity, tiptoed around Katie that day.

"When you get to a place in your life that you are ready to be a mother, I will be your surrogate." Cat was amazed as she heard the words spill out of her own mouth. *I have no desire to be a parent. I am sure I would be a terrible parent. Still, I would give anything to make Katie happy, even carry a child for her.*

Katie's face lit up temporarily. She looked at her friend, digesting the words in disbelief. For a brief moment, Cat thought perhaps Katie truly understood how much she cared for her.

⸺⸺«◉»⸺

As the new year progressed, Cat began using powders again. Going home to an empty apartment was lonely and depressing. With money in her pocket, she began going to the Ave after work, looking for other people to hang out with. Falling back into the habit of using powders and drinking was easier with a source of income. In the past, it had been a challenge to come up with intoxicants. Now, she was able to pay for them and people were hanging out with her for the party. She felt wanted. She felt sexy.

Cat often tried to get someone to come home with her. She didn't want to make the trek across town alone. She didn't want to sleep alone. She didn't want to be alone. This often ended up with her up late, wasted and having sex until the wee hours of the morning. Then, when it was time for her to go to work, she kicked out whomever had kept her company the night before. The rate with which she was consuming intoxicants increased too fast. She was quickly back to the same place of insobriety that she had been the previous summer.

Late in January, after a week straight binge on powders, Cat finally came down. She came down so hard that she slept for a whole day. When she awoke, she was very sick. She got up just long enough to go to the bathroom and promptly, she returned her hot achy body back to bed. Tossing and turning, her body choked in tangled sweaty blankets. Mike began to get concerned about her. His blurry face appeared, forcing tea and water into her. Her throat swollen almost entirely shut, she could not speak. She gasped for air. Delirious, she sobbed, choking on her tears.

Tossing and turning, hallucinations swarmed around her. Placing damp towels on her forehead, Mike tried to cool her down. Still, her fever persisted. Peeling off her sweaty clothes, he covered her with wet towels. Taking her temperature, his fear shone through the haze like a piercing light in the darkness of her fever. Her scalding tears frightened him. He poured her into the shower, trying desperately to bring down the 104 degree fever. Cursing him as the cool water cut into her, a million knives escalated the pain that shot through her body.

Holding her in his arms like a baby, Mike carried Cat from the bathroom to her bedroom. Laying her quaking, wet body back in her bed, he covered her with more damp towels. It had been almost forty-eight hours without relief from the high fever. Cat could hear his voice in the distance, telling someone that her fever had not dropped below 103 for two days. She felt like she was drowning in lava.

In and out of consciousness, Cat's eyes closed and she prayed they would never open again. Her life had been a series of miserable events and feelings. She had prayed that her life would end and she was sure her prayers would finally be answered. *I only wish that death comes mercifully. Please without so much pain.* She could feel terrifying figures swarming the room. She knew they were not real. Too weak to fight them, her will to live was completely gone.

Mike returned to the room. This time his voice was strong and focused. He was taking her to the hospital. She silently protested, her empty voice failing to escape constricted throat muscles. He removed the wet towels, steamed from the heat of her skin. Her naked body shivered. Cat tried to pull the blankets over her, and Mike pulled them back. Again she protested and his voice became firm, almost frightening. Crying in a slump on her wet bed, she didn't want to be saved. Determined, he forced clothes onto her wet body. She was too weak to fight and went limp in his arms.

Bundled in blankets, Mike carried the feverish girl to his car. Pouring her into the back of his station wagon, Mike didn't even attempt to seat belt her. Instead, he laid her down and covered her with more blankets. Being in motion made Cat nauseous. *Why won't he just let me die?* She felt like there was nothing worth living for. *I don't belong here. I don't belong anywhere. I feel completely lost.* The brightness of the street lights shot past the windows. As they catapulted through the city streets, she returned to the hot darkness of her inner mind.

Bright lights forced Cat's eyes open as the car pulled up to the Emergency Room doors. Cold air pushed itself into the back of the car, as Mike opened the door to the back seat. Whimpering, the girl clung to the blankets. His arms reached in and pulled out her limp body. Leaving the car sitting in the unloading zone, he carried her bundled body into Oakland Children's Hospital. This time, the swarming bodies around her were real. She couldn't fight them and had no will to protest. Sitting in a wheelchair next to the intake desk, he stood tall above her, signing paperwork.

Briefly touching her forehead, the nurse glanced at Mike. "How long has she had this fever?" She tried to speak. Rasping, her voice cut against the inside of her throat. Tears rolled down her flushed face. His response faded as another nurse wheeled her quickly through the double doors into a blinding hall. The rolling stopped in a small exam room.

The nurse seemed to disappear as quickly as she had

appeared. Cat was left sitting in the wheelchair alone in this bright miserable room. Shaking, she tried to climb onto the hospital bed. Losing her balance, she felt herself falling. Out of nowhere, Mike appeared, catching her, and helping her onto the bed. She curled up in a ball, and he covered her with the blankets as he had done in the back of his station wagon. Time seemed to move too slowly. This cold bright hell was not where she wanted to be.

The feverish girl begged for darkness. Hoarse indecipherable noises forced themselves out of her swollen throat. She felt Mike's hand brush her hair back, as he urged her to stop trying to speak. Hot tears rolled down her face in stark contrast from the freezing air that pushed through the ventilation system. Closing her eyes, she allowed herself to fall back into the comfort of weary sleep.

Someone else entered the room, and Cat felt Mike's focus shift from her to the new person. She heard the word *shot* and terror swept through her entire being. The blankets were being removed. She was too cold. She tried to say "NO NEEDLES!" Neither of them could understand her words. Still, Mike understood her fear. He told her to look directly at him. Another person appeared in the room, to hold her body steady.

With both hands, Cat held onto Mike. Rasping, her quiet voice pleaded with him. "Sshhh. Stop trying to speak. Just hold my hands tight." She weakly grasped his hands. As the needle entered her skin, she screamed. This time Mike heard her voice clearly echo through the halls of the hospital.

Time stopped. Cat felt truly betrayed. *Why had he let them do this to her?* Slumped back down on the hospital bed, she felt violated. She was already in so much pain. Confused and exhausted, she left her body and floated down the hall searching for a way to escape altogether. In the exam room, Mike sat by her empty body, tucking the blankets back around her and petting her hair.

Merging with the lights pouring out of the ceiling, the floating girl knew that none of the staff could see her. She saw a nurse wheeling her crumpled body in a chair. She saw Mike talking with the staff. She had Beta Strep. Strep Throat was highly contagious. Alpha Strep was the most common form of Strep Throat. Beta Strep was much more dangerous. Additionally, it could cause brain damage to have such a high fever for so long. They scolded him for not bringing her in sooner.

Handing him a prescription and a list of instructions, they asked Mike if he understood. Nodding, he signed paperwork and hurried out of the sliding doors into the cold darkness of night. Bundled, Cat's body remained in the wheelchair while he left to retrieve the station wagon. The nurse wheeled her out to the curb. The station wagon pulled up to the yellow curb. With the car still running, Mike left the driver door open. Moving around the back of the car, he quickly opened the door to the back seat. Lifting her tenderly out of the chair, he kissed her forehead and spoke quietly. "Everything is going to be okay. I am taking you home now."

Moving through rushing wind, Cat followed the station wagon that carried her infected body. When they returned to the apartment, she heard Mike speaking to her limp body. She could feel his exhaustion. This had been a thoroughly frightening experience for him. She felt bad that he had tried so hard to save her when she did not want to be saved. Moving through the doors that separated the outside world from the hall of apartment doors, she watched him carry her body to the door that opened into their apartment.

In her bedroom, the girl sat, an empty shell crumpled on the ground. The body waited for Mike's warm arms to pick it up again. She watched him with curiosity. *What motivates him to care for me so dearly?* Making her bed up with fresh sheets and soft blankets, Mike prepared the bed for her return. Placing her body back in the bed, he pulled the blankets over Cat and again kissed her forehead.

Cat felt gravity forcing herself back into the body, feelings of hot pain moved through her. Her eyes opened and looked up to see small tears hiding in the corners of Mike's eyes. Forcing words through her swollen throat, Cat told him that she had to call her boss. Leaving the room briefly, he returned with the cordless phone. Dialing the number for Kirkle, she waited for the sound of the answering machine. She had to shout into the phone to make sounds into raspy words for the recording mechanism. "Cat. Sick. Strep throat. Call tomorrow." *Click*. She heard the phone hit the floor as she passed out.

━━●━━

Sometime later in the evening, Cat awoke with an urgency. Getting up to use the bathroom, she realized that she was no longer hallucinating. Looking in the bathroom mirror, her face was pale. Washing her hands, she touched her wet hands to her forehead. She shivered. Her hands were cold. Her forehead was no longer as hot. Her throat was still swollen too much to eat but she was famished.

Cat wandered into the kitchen to find a note on the fridge. She was alone in the apartment again. She made some ramen and sipped the broth. She tried to eat the noodles and failed. She could barely swallow the broth. Dumping the noodles into the garbage, she placed her empty bowl in the sink. Returning to her room, she crawled back into bed and allowed sleep to take her.

Several hours passed. When Cat woke again, Mike was asleep on his futon in the living room. This time, her throat was not as swollen and she was able to swallow without sharp pain. She felt like she hadn't eaten for days. She got up to use the bathroom and then moved quietly through the living room into the kitchen. Searching for something to eat, she found bread from the bakery. She spread a thick layer of butter on the soft bread and peeled the hard crust off the edges. Stuffing the soft buttered bread into her mouth, she started to heat water for coffee. Mike heard her moving in the kitchen and got up to greet her.

Coming up behind her, he wrapped his arms around the girl and hugged her long and hard. "I was afraid I was going to lose you!" She let him wrap her with love. Feeling his bare chest push up against her back, she shuddered. Glad that she was no longer in extreme pain, she thanked him for taking care of her. Still, she was apprehensive of his expectations. She dared not linger too long in his arms. His grip loosened as he became aware of the tenseness of her muscles. Abandoning the prospect of coffee, she returned to her bedroom leaving him confused and alone in the kitchen.

Cat's boss called her back later that day. When she explained what her ailment had been, he encouraged her to stay home for several days to recuperate. Apparently he had contracted Beta Strep in his youth and was concerned about catching it from her. The dangers of this rare strain had imprinted him with a genuine fear of the illness. The following week he allowed her return to work with no harsh words regarding her absence from the warehouse.

Mike had become extraordinarily protective of Cat as a result of her recent sickness. Distinctly aware of his strong feelings toward her, she continued to create more distance between them. His moods became more sullen as his loneliness grew stronger. When the opportunity arose, she made a coffee date with Abby and Mike together. Since they had gotten along so well, she thought that perhaps she could nurture a new friendship between the two of them, thereby helping to fill in the empty space she had created with her intentional distance.

The result was exactly what she had hoped for. Abby and Mike began spending more time together. Though Cat was somewhat envious of the time he got to spend with Abby, she dismissed her internal feelings. Cat had gotten what she wanted. Mike was distracted and less lonely. His focused had shifted from her. It was liberating and she quickly returned to her habit of going out after work. This time, she was more cautious about using powders and she no longer tried so hard to bring someone home with her in the evenings.

Chapter 20

LONG BLACK HAIR

Valentine's Day arrived, and loneliness set in like a deep cold in her bones. Cat missed the affection that Mike had directed toward her. Yet, she did not wish to return to the frightening confines of his expectations, of a future with her. While he spent Valentine's Day with Abby, she spent the evening alone in her room crying.

What am I missing? What am I trying to find? Happiness? What exactly is that supposed to look like? How will I know when I have found it? Or will it be disguised? With my luck, I will pass it right by and never know that I ever had the chance to be happy. I don't believe I am meant to be happy.

Cat wanted someone to love her. She knew that Katie was spending the holiday with her boyfriend. He had not abandoned her, despite the recent changes in their life. The people with whom Cat had been partying were not really friends. They didn't care for her. Their interactions would never be endearing or supportive. *Am I even worth loving?* Cat did not love herself. She hated herself. Looking at her reflection, she saw ugliness. She stared at a reflection of someone who didn't feel at all like her.

The next day, Cat woke up in a better mood. *Today, I am going to cheer myself up. Today, I am going to take myself out. I can be my own date.* She got up in the morning and took a shower. Taking time to scrub down every part of her body, and shaving her legs smooth. She would make herself a beautiful woman. If it took hours, she would force it into her reflection. Someone would see her and recognize that she was worth getting to know. *If I take the time to truly nurture myself, then perhaps someone else will be able to see my value.* After the long shower, she got dressed up in the prettiest outfit she could put together.

Making her way across town on the bus, Cat headed back to Telegraph Avenue. Notebooks in her satchel, she decided she'd go back to Bottega. *Maybe I will see some-one there that knows me?* Getting off the Bus 40, she crossed the street heading toward the UC Berkeley campus. Headphones in her ears, the Violent Femmes provided a tempo for her footsteps. Watching out for people she might wish to avoid, she kept her pace steady.

A few blocks later, Cat walked up the ramp into the cafe The patio was empty. *Its early.* She ordered a latte in a tall pint glass. Grabbing a spoon and several packets of sugar, she headed out to the patio. Sitting at a round stone table by the black iron railing, she proceeded to empty a large pile of sugar into her latte. She knew the drink would get cold quickly, but she didn't care. *As long as I have a drink, I can hang out. I could spend hours here with a cold half empty glass and they won't tell me to leave.*

Grabbing an ashtray from a nearby table, Cat pulled out her cigarettes and a lighter. After lighting a smoke, she pulled out her notebook and a pen. She laid them on the table in front of her. *I don't know what to write. I'm sure something will come eventually.* She took a sip of her latte. Still hot. Crossing her legs, her skirt edged itself up her leg and she tugged at it to go down. Taking a drag off her cigarette and another sip of the hot coffee, she directed her gaze toward the passing people.

What am I doing here? Cat could pretend that she belonged here all day long, but it didn't change how she felt. She was an alien and positive everyone that glanced in her direction could see it. Doodling abstract lines on the lined paper made her look busy. *There's no answer hiding in this notebook. Who am I kidding?* She laid the pen on the open notebook. Taking another sip of her coffee, she placed the cigarette in an empty ashtray notch. The pint glass made a hard knock against the marble patio table. She picked up the pen and began to write.

As the afternoon moved slowly, people she knew moved in and out of the patio. Some of her past lovers came by and talked with her. Nothing really inspired Cat by the interactions. *It is nice to be distracted with idle conversation. But really. This is all fake.* Aware of the emptiness in her interactions, she made no attempt to engage deeply with anyone. Then Jasper walked into the Cafe'.

Cat had seen him before. She didn't really know him, but she thought he was absolutely beautiful. She had been too intimidated by his beauty and self composure to approach him when she had seen him at the North Berkeley House. *I have only seen him a couple of times, but I could never forget him!* This time, she swallowed her fear and decided she would strike up a conversation with him.

Emerging from the Cafe' with his coffee, Jasper took a seat at the table next to her. Cat drank in the image of perfection that she witnessed sitting nearby and reached out with as much courage as she could muster. "Haven't I seen you before?" A long black trench coat covered his t-shirt. Beat up black combat boots wrapped tightly around the bottom of his black jeans. Long black hair poured down his back. The visage was complete with a black top hat. She reached out for her coffee, took a sip, and put it back down. "Cold already."

Cat lit another cigarette and focused her attention on him directly. Jasper turned his chair to return her conversation. They exchanged names and began their conversation with relatively empty and meaningless chatter. Time passed slowly as they continued to talk about everything and nothing in particular. She dared to flirt a little and allowed her words to take her further. She felt her cheeks flush as she realized that this beautiful young man was in no hurry to leave their conversation.

Eventually, they got bored with the Cafe'. Jasper invited her to spend more time with him. Cat's heart raced. This beautiful man actually *wanted* her company. *Is this really happening?* She was giddy. She had observed Jasper before and wondered what it would be like to run her hands through his long beautiful hair. Now she was walking down the street with him, heading across town to his apartment.

Jasper told her that he shared an apartment with his best friend Sage. Sage's boyfriend was old enough to buy alcohol and there was probably whiskey left over at his place already. As they walked, their conversation continued to become more intimate. By the time they reached his apartment by the subway station, their flirting had set the stage for the prospect of a very passionate evening.

Arriving at his apartment just after dark, Sage had already gotten a head start drinking. Cat felt awkward sitting on the couch underneath the front window. She wasn't confident that his roommate was platonic. Sage seemed to pick up on her nervousness, and fed it by teasing her. Jasper came to her rescue with a drink. She swallowed hard, attempting to drown her anxiety with whiskey. Sage laughed at her. "You're such a kid."

Jasper was a year older than Cat, and Sage was another year older still. *Two years difference isn't enough for her to call me a kid.* Their conflict became abundantly clear when Cat responded defensively to the jabs. Settling into the couch next to her, Jasper protected her from her seemingly harsh judgment with warm hands of approval.

The night proceeded with intoxication and hours of making out. The next day, they woke up late with hangovers and warm words. Intimately greeting the morning together, Jasper's interest had not waned. As the day progressed, sobering up was inevitable. Eventually, they made their way back across town to the theater where he worked. Cat kissed him goodbye and wished him a good night at work.

Returning to the apartment in Oakland, Cat's glow seemed to disturb her roommate. Mike questioned her, as to where she had been. Cat answered with vague empty words. Despite his recent distraction with Abby, Mike was still clearly attached to her. He began to prattle on about the problems that were beginning to come up between himself and Abby.

"She's flaky." Mike complained that Abby's frequent cancellations were distressing to him. He reached out to try and put his hands around Cat's waist. She stepped backwards, just out of reach. "And now I'm losing you too." Cat shook off the knee-jerk response that she felt bubbling up inside her chest.

Over the course of the next few weeks, Cat began spending most nights with Jasper. Working at the movie theater meant that he was able to get free passes pretty often. She went to the movies several times with him. Almost overnight, they had become a couple and his friends seemed to accept her as part of his life. Included in his group of friends, Cat began hanging out frequently and looked forward to the company. Going to work during the day, she took the bus downtown to the theater to greet him in the evenings.

Cat began letting some of her clothes pile up in his bedroom, so she would always have something to wear to work in the mornings. Going to work from his place in the morning was a little easier than taking the bus from her apartment. Several days would pass without returning to the apartment in Oakland. When she did return, she brought Jasper with her.

Mike was there, drowning in the sadness of abandonment. "What happened to you?" In response, Cat introduced Mike to her new boyfriend. Mike shuffled his words around with his feet as they retired to her bedroom and closed the door.

Although Jasper's roommate gave Cat a hard time a lot, she came to realize that Sage didn't have a problem with her. Her personality was simply a little sharper edged than Cat was used to. *No matter, I'm glad to be here.* Sage was beautiful, intelligent, well composed, and her discriminatory words were not to be taken as a judgment, as much as a critical analysis. She did point out that Cat was there so often that perhaps she should be paying part of the rent. Cat couldn't afford to pay rent in two different places. The point was valid. Jasper had no interest in limiting the time that they spent together, so the couple began discussing getting a place together.

Their love affair was rampant with drinking, fighting, and making up. Cat gushed about him at work to Katie. In return, Katie gushed about her boyfriend to Cat. "He proposed to me! And of course I said yes!" Cat's internal response was not positive, but she hid it with a supportive 'Congratulations'. Katie continued, "We are going to get married as soon as I turn 18."

I'm not sure this is a good thing. After witnessing the terrible mood swings that their arguments have already triggered so many times... He treats her like shit! Still, Cat was quickly distracted with her own rowdy new love. *Who am I to judge? Maybe it will be okay. Everyone just wants to be happy, right?*

Katie already knew Jasper from previous social encounters and showed no signs of disapproval. Coming to work with a hangover became a fairly regular occurrence. Though Cat was not using powders frequently, they occasionally made their way into her system. A variety of intoxicants kept her from attaching herself to any one particular habit except insobriety. Laughing at the roller coaster of sex and drugs, the two girls reveled in the wonders of their youth.

There was always lot to talk about. Katie rarely brought up her illness, except occasionally, when she had good news to share, like meeting with a Nutritionist. The girls shifted their focus from the monotony of the mindless job. They complained about their partners, their weight, and spent cigarette breaks complimenting each other, flirting, and telling each other how highly they cared for one another. Then, at the end of the day, they went their separate ways to re-enter the habits of their respective love relationships.

This routine lasted only a couple of months before Jasper succeeded in finding a place for them to move. His roommate would be moving as well. Collectively, the three of them agreed that moving out meant that one last party together was necessary. The night of the party arrived as did a large crowd of friends. The partying was loud and rowdy. Inevitably, sometime late in the evening the police were called. Fortunately, most of the guests had left or passed out by then. Cat had been dizzy with drunkenness and was half-dressed in Jasper's room when they heard the knock on the door.

The remaining guests got quiet. The loud knocking persisted. Wearing only a long shirt and panties, Cat made her way down the stairs to the front door. Answering the door half naked and bleary eyed, she asked the officer what she could do for him. He pointed to a chair in the street, surrounded by broken glass from the living room window. He asked her if she knew anything about it. She nodded her head no.

"I'm sorry sir, I don't. I was sleeping. Is there anything I can do for you?" He indicated that he had received a complaint about noise. Cat repeated that she had been sleeping and had not been aware of any noise. He peered up the dark stairs with his flashlight and saw no sign of a party. No sounds were coming out of the apartment, except the sound of their two voices. After a couple of minutes of questions, and no change in her story, the officer apologized for bothering her, and left her alone in the doorway. She closed the door, walked back up the stairs, and crawled back into bed.

For a brief moment, she felt like a superstar. She had made the police go away!

Soon after that evening, Cat and Jasper had successfully moved his stuff into their new place. She returned to the apartment in Oakland to gather up what stuff she had to bring with her. Mike was disappointed, but not alone. He had moved another old friend in. They were mutually helping each other out. *So this is closure.* With a sadness in his eyes, he wished her well. She gushed about how much she was in love with Jasper and thanked him one more time for helping her so much.

Cat and Jasper had rented a room in a six-bedroom flat on Emerald Street in Oakland. The flat was one of four in a fourplex that shared a common front yard. There were already several people living there and the couple did not socialize with them very much. They kept to their own bedroom most of the time. The room opened up onto a patio, where the two were able to go outside and smoke in the moonlight together.

The unit below their flat was vacant. Soon some of the Berkeley Gutter Punks found out about the place. They started coming over and partying in vacant flat below their room. At first, Jasper and Cat thought it was pretty cool. Then, the punks decided they would start squatting in the empty unit. It became a problem directly reflecting on the couple, especially since they were hanging out downstairs with the BGP frequently.

The pair only lived on Emerald Street for a couple of months. The housemates did not appreciate the loud parties. Nor did they enjoy listening to the arguing that inevitably occurred after the couple became belligerently drunk. The roommates collectively agreed that the new couple were not a good fit for the household. Additionally, the housemates did not like it when the police were called multiple times by perturbed neighbors.

The final party that decided their fate on Emerald Street ended up bringing the police into the upstairs flat. One of the roommates had a beautiful marijuana plant in the front room. Cat was terrified that they were all going to jail because of it. The police just walked right by it without a second glance. The plant stood three to four feet tall in a large pot sitting in a front bay window. All the tenants agreed the male plant with large fan leaves was aesthetically "the perfect house plant." It did not produce flowers, but the living room smelled lovely. The police didn't even notice the plant.

Cat's love affair with Jasper had been tumultuous between all the arguments and make-up sex. Lots of partying, lots of drinking, lots of passion, and lots of arguing. They really couldn't get enough of spending time together. They also didn't give each other enough space. Pretty soon, Cat decided she had been there long enough. *I have to get back on the road. This place is strangling me. I need to get away from the parties. I can't go on pretending that everything is okay.*

With the couple moving out of the Emerald Street house, Jasper would be going to stay with his mother again. Burned out and ready for change, Cat no longer had the temperament to continue pushing her way through workdays at the warehouse. She got the bright idea that leaving town would solve her problems. Strung out and worn down, she had thus far maintained her job through all kinds of partying.

Cat had survived moving and gutter punks invasions and still made it to work most of the time. She hated her job. It was hot as Hades in that warehouse. Insufficient air flow assured an unpleasant environment for all. The boss was psychotic and bipolar. She had seen coffee cups and screwdrivers thrown across the room and had no patience for it. She once again felt trapped, and demanded to be set free.

Part Two

Chapter 21

RANDOM DIRECTIONS

Last Summer is already a mashup of memories that has proved somewhat challenging to sift through. However, the life that started when I moved in with Mike seems to be a blazing collection of drug induced memory splashes that are having a great impact on my artwork. Joining the world of transients increases my feeling of being utterly alone. Still, I believe that the freedom to roam will help me find myself.

I called into work leaving a message that I was quitting my job and not coming back. I've returned to a cycle of using powders too frequently for my own good. Drinking until I'm sick or passing out has become a regular habit. Having money from a job has made it all too easy to obtain. Every payday I splurge a little more liberally than the previous payday. The scene is getting too thick and salty and I'm starting to grasp for air. This isn't running away, because I am free. I am free to stay, and free to leave. My life is my choice and I am choosing to make a change!

——— ✿ ———

Everything really was too much for Cat to process and she was running away from it. She had hitchhiked to and from Mendocino several times. She felt confident that she could travel anywhere with her feet and her thumb. She went down to the Gilman Street on-ramp in the warehouse section of the Berkeley/Albany border. It was a spot that got traffic going out of town, without too much police visibility. Nervous and anxious, she really wanted to fly as far as possible.

Cat decided that she would go to Colorado. She had talked with many really kind Deadheads that spoke highly of Boulder, Colorado, so she chose that as her target. She found that much of her travel was taken up with time spent by herself, lost in thought on the side of the road. Sometimes she walked, sometimes she just sat on her bag. If she could find shade, she would stay there longer. She didn't feel anxious during the day unless she was stuck in need of food or a bathroom for too long. At night, she felt more vulnerable being on the road.

Cat developed the habit of trying to find a place to make camp by sunset. Trying to find a place to sleep, and set up a discreet bed was more challenging in absolute darkness. Sometimes sleeping under a highway overpass, sometimes in a storefront, sometimes she simply camped by the road she had been traveling on. Days and nights seemed to shift between one another with no regard to the movement of time. It was a wonderful relief to only have herself to talk with.

The traveling girl moved in and out of manic and depressive waves. Talking and singing and crying with herself, as she spent her days on the road. Some rides she would talk to the driver a lot. With other folks she was very quiet. Some rides were short and some were longer. Sometimes people would give her a couple dollars or buy her some food.

Every city she stopped in had a street scene subculture. Going to the local Cafe' and park, she looked for the place where people were just hanging out. She looked for the punks and the hippies. When she saw someone playing guitar for change, she would stop and talk to them. Street musicians always seemed to be a good focal point in any city's street scene subculture. She spent time sitting by herself, observing and begging for change.

Cat talked to people. She was outgoing and adventurous and almost reckless. She was free. She was hungry. She was cold. She had no idea what she was doing. She got high. She got drunk. She stayed with people she barely knew. Sometimes she just slept outside in a park, or behind a building. She met interesting people with different ideas about the world. She learned about trust, and intuition. She learned how much the universe takes care of you if you provide kindness toward others.

Cat liked Boulder. It was a beautiful town with a pleasant atmosphere. She started to make friends. She even looked around for a possible job, entertaining the idea that she might find happiness if she stayed there. After a couple of days, she began to feel stagnant. The voices in her head told her that if she stayed too long, she would end up getting into trouble just like she had in Berkeley. No great romance tied her to this place. She had not found the answer to the incessant questioning voices underneath the ivy in which she slept. Without a word of goodbye to her new friends, she headed back to the road.

⟫⟨⟨◍⟩⟩⟪

Cat headed South from Boulder. Somehow she managed to find herself walking down a long road with nothing in every direction. She looked up at the crossing. *So this is Four Corners? I have heard about this place... Where Colorado, Utah, New Mexico, and Arizona all meet. There is nothing here. So desolate.* Traveling through the reservations, she found it difficult to get rides.

It was hot on the plain, and she walked in shorts and a loose blouse. Bare legs poked out from beneath her frame pack as she walked. Few cars passed. When they did, Cat was sure that the drivers were staring at her. Some hollered at her, like a prostitute. *Mama always said that Native Americans were kind and spiritual people. All I can feel from these guys is hate.* Between the sparse passing cars, the wind on the plain was almost silent.

Walking in the sun, Cat's thoughts struggled to populate the emptiness. *If I walked far enough along that side road, I bet there are houses out there. I can't see anything. I wonder if I just started walking down one of these driveways if I would just disappear forever. Would anyone notice that I am gone?*

She had no reason to venture down any of the dusty detours. The main road was enough of a detour for her. With no idea where she was, or where she was going, she continued to put one foot in front of the other. After several hours of walking, a truck filled with Native Americans pulled over, creating a small dust cloud. They stared at her like she was an alien. She felt threatened and did not understand why. A man hung his arm out of the window peering through dark sunglasses at the girl on the side of the road.

"Where are you headed girl?" the passenger asked. He tipped back a beer can to capture any last drops before crunching it in his hand. He tossed the crumpled can in the dry grass behind Cat. "Well? Do you want a ride or not?"

Cat heard the other passenger laugh and the driver grunt. She put her hand above her eyes to block the glare of the late afternoon sun. "West. I'm heading West." *Anywhere that gets me out of here is good. God, I hope these guys don't rape me.* The first passenger turned and spoke something indecipherable to the driver before turning back to Cat.

"Well come on girl. If you want a ride, you better hurry up. We don't got all day!" The middle passenger laughed again as she hurried to throw her bag into the back of the pickup truck. As she was climbing into the truck, the truck began to move and she fell onto her bag.

Another man sat in the back of the truck next to an ice chest. He looked at her bare thighs, eyes moving across her body, like a map. He opened up the ice chest, pulled out a beer, and handed it to Cat. She thanked him as she received the lukewarm can. *Anything to drink is better than nothing.* He turned to tap the sliding window to the cab of the truck. The middle passenger slid the window open. The man in the back of the truck silently handed two more cans of beer through the window. Leaning against her backpack, she guzzled down the beer and laid the empty can in the bed of the truck.

Cat closed her eyes and let time pass. When she opened them, the truck was pulling into a town. They pulled over to a curb and the men in the front of the truck hollered something. Cat figured this meant her ride was over. With her back pack on one shoulder, she climbed out of the truck onto the curb. She waved to the truck and hollered "Thank you." The truck pulled away birthing another dust cloud. She squinted and waited for the dust to clear.

A moment later, Cat began to assess her surroundings. Standing in front of what appeared to be a hardware store confirmed that she had reached civilization. Colors were muted and dingy. The sunset had almost disappeared beyond the horizon and the store was clearly closed. As she began walking down the street, she realized that most of the businesses appeared to be closed. *Where am I? Is this The Twilight Zone?* A little more investigation determined that she had arrived in Farmington.

⸺⸺●⸺⸺

Finally landing in Santa Monica, Cat spent about a week hanging out on the boardwalk. Partying on the beach was fun. She met new people. Nothing really compelled her to stay, and she missed being around people with whom she felt a real connection. Also, the hippies there were talking about upcoming Dead shows. She missed people that knew her. She missed family. Most of all, she missed her mother.

Over the course of the year, Will had returned to the Bay Area in search of work. Mendocino had not provided enough work for him to support her mother and little brother. After a few months of being back in the Bay, her mother and brother followed closely behind. When Cat returned to the Bay Area, she went to visit her mother and found her accomplishing a great deal of housework and painting, with the help of the powders that Cat had been running so fiercely away from. In an effort to bond with her daughter, Mama offered to share. The girl hesitated only briefly, and then accepted the offer.

After spending several hours visiting with her mother, Cat decided she had better leave. With more energy than should be contained in a small stucco box, she proceeded to walk 6 miles across town to the UC Berkeley campus. Slowing down when she got near the Ave, she made her rounds, checking every nook and cranny where she might find people that felt like family. She checked the People's Park, the Cafe' Med, Fat Slice, and Bottega. Eventually, she settled into a pile of people in front of the Outpost. Spending the evening talking with the usual suspects, it didn't take long for her to feel as if she had never left.

It took a couple of days for Cat to find Jasper. He was staying with his best friend and old roommate, Sage. They were staying in a squat in the Rockridge area with a handful of people Cat did not know. Jasper invited her to come and stay there with him. Rekindling their romance was almost automatic. The roller coaster of partying, fighting, and fucking seemed to pick up right where they had left it. It didn't take long for this to get old. Cat was getting nowhere fast. After a week or so of spending evenings with him, she left the squat and went back to spending more time with the hippies on the Ave.

Every few days Cat went to visit Mama. They would have dinner together. Cat would get a shower, and spend a night sleeping on the floor next to her brother's bed. He would wake up in the middle of the night screaming from nightmares. Crying for Mama, he'd try to climb out of bed. Still, he was just a toddler. Cat felt sorry for him. Half-asleep, she would reach up into his bed and rub his back and hair until he fell back into dreaming.

Soon, Cat felt the need to leave again. Feeling stagnant, she was hoping that somehow her travels would ease her discomfort. She hitchhiked north to the Mendocino, searching for old friends. Wandering down the main street, she saw nobody that seemed to care about her presence there. Saddened by her failed attempt to reconnect, she headed back out to the road. Catching Highway 20 in Fort Bragg, she headed inland to Willits.

In Willits, Cat was picked up and was offered dinner, a shower, and a place to sleep for the night from some kind hippies in the woods. The following day she was again on the road. This kindness was repeated in Fortuna. It was beautiful country with not a lot of traffic. She kept traveling north and zigzagging up California until she found herself in Arcada.

Cat got better at finding kind locals in each town where she stopped. In Trinidad, just north of Arcada, she found herself in with a group of people who were drinking and doing powders. This triggered more sadness and feelings of being trapped, so she headed back on the road.

After going farther north in California than she ever had before, Cat decided to turn around and head south again. She hitched straight down the coast without stopping until she landed in Santa Cruz. That was an interesting scene. Walking through downtown toward the boardwalk, she was in search for the neighborhood where the hustle was happening. Also, Cat was curious to see what the town was like after the effect of the Loma Prieta earthquake of 1989.

Santa Cruz was a strange and interesting place after the earthquake. There were many houses that had been so badly damaged that they were technically uninhabitable. Many of these houses had turned into squats. Cat was partying and looking around for a group of people to crash with and found some guys that seemed pretty nice. She didn't feel threatened by them, and they didn't seem to be jerks. They seemed more intelligent and less drunk, than a lot of the folks hanging on the streets.

Hours after the sun set, the skinheads started lingering. There appeared to be a territory issue going on between social groups with the street scene. The police seemed aware and unhappy about this. They also began increasing in number. Cat decided it was a good time to get lost and her new friends felt the same way. The guys invited Cat to go with them and she was happy to oblige. The group walked across town to a quieter neighborhood. Her new friends warned her that "not all the people in this squat were of their group."

"We've got the attic area, which, thanks to Loma Prieta, has a huge skylight of a hole in the roof," they explained. "This is helpful as it provides light. The rest of the house is dark." When they arrived, it was just as the guys had described. The lower levels of the house were in total darkness, save the candlelight. All the windows on the house had been boarded up so it was a challenge to navigate through, especially at night.

Moving through the squat, Cat was astonished at the group of people that she met. The folks squatting in the lower, darker levels of the house, claimed to be Satanists. *I've met hard rockers who joked about their music being referred to as the devil's music. I've met gothic rockers who wore symbols that were commonly misinterpreted as Satanic. I have never met people that actually go through the motions of giving religious or spiritual credence to the Devil on a tangible level.* Symbols and words were written in blood on the dining room wall. An altar was set up, that looked like it was being used regularly.

This is a crazy contradiction! If someone is recognizing and acknowledging the fallen angel as a deity, they must therefore be acknowledging the Christian dogma which supports the concepts of God and Satan. If, in fact, that is the case, then it seems to me that these are really just pissed off Christians. Cat shared her opinion with her new friends as they set up camp in the attic that night.

"I don't think they would appreciate that interpretation," they responded. Regardless, she decided that there was something pretty creepy about the whole situation. She didn't feel comfortable or safe being there. *Just one night. I am not spending two nights here!*

⚯

The next day, Cat got a strong feeling that she ought to leave Santa Cruz as soon as possible. She had been on the road for several weeks and was getting pretty tired. She needed a shower. She needed to sleep somewhere that she knew was safe. She was starting to miss Jasper, and people who felt familiar to her. Early in the morning, she headed out to the Denny's by the Highway 17 on-ramp. After getting some breakfast, she went out to the road to try her luck at getting a ride.

Cat hadn't been out there long when a biker pulled over. He was having some trouble with his motorcycle, and she was curious. She liked motorcycles. She had enjoyed getting rides from bikers in the past. She walked over to him and started making conversation. She offered an extra hand, to help him tinker on his bike and get it going again. She convinced him into giving her a ride. He said that his Harley was a hard-tail and she wouldn't be able to handle riding for very long at a time. He didn't like taking it on the freeway, and since it was a nice day for a ride, he agreed to take her over the hill.

They went the back way through the hills from Santa Cruz to Daly City via Boulder, CA. The two would ride for about 30 minutes, stop to buy a couple beers, and smoke a cigarette. Then they drove for another 30 minutes, stopped and drank the beers and smoked a couple more cigarettes. They repeated this process to stop at another store, and then again to drink the second set of beers.

Up in the middle of nowhere, drinking beer, having a smoke and talking about traveling with this biker felt like a wonderful way to spend the afternoon. He asked Cat if she was ever nervous about traveling by herself. She responded that she hadn't had any trouble yet. "I have pretty good intuition, and stand my ground when necessary." He complimented her by telling her that she 'had more balls than most guys he knew.' *Coming from an old grizzled biker, that's a big compliment!* After a couple lazy hours, he dropped her at a subway station and wished her luck on her travels.

Cat bummed change until she had enough to ride the train back to Berkeley. When she got back to Berkeley, she was exhausted. *It feels good to be back home.* Then again, she didn't really have a home now. She wasn't sure what to do with herself. She wandered Telegraph Ave until she found people she knew.

Perched atop her bags and bedroll, she took in her surroundings and started to catch up on the "who's in town" and "what's happening now" gossip of the street scene. She killed time for a while until she was able to catch up with Jasper. Eventually she ended up back at his mom's place in Albany, sleeping on the couch with him.

Cat spent a couple of weeks hanging out in the street scene during the day while Jasper was at work. Spending evenings and his days off with him was comforting to her for a little while. Though it didn't take long for the couple to fall back into the habits of intoxication, arguments and makeup sex. *I am tired of feeling like I'm in limbo.* Nothing really seemed to have meaning for her, so she abandoned him to revisit the road.

Hanging out with heads and freaks on the Ave, Cat met a very feminine guy from Salt Lake City. He convinced her that there was money to be made in Utah. She was getting anxious about becoming stagnant. Deciding that she needed leave again, she agreed to hitch with her new friend to Salt Lake City. After arriving in Utah she spent a week there partying with people she barely knew.

Salt Lake City was nothing like he had described. She was not making money. It was too hot to move during the day, and nighttime was all about the party. The fourth of July reminded her that her birthday was coming soon. Cat knew she did not want to celebrate her birthday in this foreign and uncomfortable locale. Everyone in the scene there was pretty much nocturnal. They went to a club one night, when School of Fish was playing a concert. She spent most of the evening hanging out by the door, flirting with the doorman, with the sole purpose of trying to con her way into the show.

Cat's tits were a blessing and a curse. She could use them to manipulate people. It made her feel dirty. It felt totally fake. When she got dressed up to go out, she felt like she was dressing up in drag. Most of the time she wished her breasts were gone. She walked a lot, which made her back hurt. She found a record store that had things she liked and started talking to people. She got a tape of the Revolting Cocks. That made her happy. A week in this place was enough to make her want to move on though.

Chapter 22

NOWHERE LAND

Hitchhiking out of Salt Lake City was a nightmare that Cat didn't know how to conquer. Hitchhiking was clearly posted as being illegal by all the freeway on ramps. The ramps all led to a confusing mix of interchanges. Frustrated, she talked to a local bum, trying to determine which off ramp would be safe and effective to get her heading West.

The shabby gentleman explained that there was "no hitching out of SLC" and suggested she accompany him on a bus north to Ogden. There, he showed her how to get to the train yard, so she could hop a train going west. He showed her how to find places to hide on the train where the bulls would not spot you, when they are patrolling the cars. "It's important to put yourself in a place where you won't cast a shadow when they shine their light your way." She crammed herself in a small opening at the end of a grain car. There was very little room to move around once she was in there. There was no going anywhere. No going to the bathroom. No stretching her legs.

At night in the high desert on a freight train, the cold wind reminded the girl why travelers carry flasks of whiskey. After a couple hours of riding, Cat lost most of the feeling in her body and passed out completely. She regained consciousness when the train started slowing down early in the morning. *I have to piss so badly!* Her body hurt in an indescribable way.

As soon as the train slowed down enough for her to consider trying to jump off, Cat started wiggling her way around trying to get out of the small cranny she had been hiding in. She panicked a little. The urgency in her bladder, combined with her sudden fear that she might not be able to get back out of the end of the grain car terrified her.

Cat was shaking and hyperventilating as she pried herself out. Without any thought as to whether she would be seen or get caught, she pulled her bag out, and jumped off the train. Her legs were wobbly and sharp pains shot through her body. She stumbled a little and took off in run. The fear that someone might see her, re-entered her mind. She didn't have to run very far, because the train sped up and continued on its way.

Where am I now? A vast scape of bleak dusty emptiness showed no threat to privacy. She squatted and went to the bathroom in the dust, right there in the middle of the desert. After relieving herself, she realized that she was hungry. Cat walked until she found something that looked like the direction of a highway. There was no little store, no travelers diner. It seemed like there was no town there at all. But there was a freeway on ramp. The sign by the road told her she was in Carlsbad, Nevada. *Never heard of it. Now that I'm standing in Carlsbad Nevada, where am I going? And where can I find some food?*

It took her a while, but she did eventually get one ride. They dropped her somewhere else in the middle of nowhere. *Who takes these exits anyway? There must be some kind of a side road heading off into the desert, or some mystery junction. I don't see a town, or any place to try and find food.* Cat wandered out to the highway, near the merging of the on ramp, to try and increase her visibility.

She was there for a while. Her sense of time was almost non existent. It could have been a half hour or three hours and whether it felt like a long time to her depended more on her environment and the way she was feeling than actual time passing. Here is was hot, dry, windy, and desolate. Cat sat on her backpack and played with the dry grasses poking out of the sand. She watched an ant colony conduct their business, uninterrupted by the passing cars. She talked to herself and discussed the possibilities of where her next ride might take her, and which direction should she say she is going.

⸻

Sometime in the late afternoon she got a ride with a gal who was going all the way to Vacaville, California. *Jackpot! I won't have to hitchhike again in Nevada! This is definitely not my favorite place to be.*

Cat got to talking with the driver. It turned out that her boyfriend was none other than an old family friend! She offered for Cat to stay with them for the night, as it would be very late by the time they got to Vacaville. *A shower, meal, and a warm place to sleep sound great! What a surprise it will be when I show up!*

The drive lasted several hours. They talked some. After the sun had set, the girl fell asleep with her head against the window. She awoke in the early morning hours when the driver pulled into the Vacaville driveway.

When the two travelers walked in the door of the

little house, the driver announced to the seemingly empty house, "Hi honey! I'm home! And I brought you a surprise!" As her boyfriend turned the corner, his jaw dropped seeing a 16 year old Cat standing in his living room. She had not seen him since her mother had lived above his garage on Sycamore Street. He pulled out a bottle of liquor, as his partner retired to bed for the remainder of the evening.

The two spent several hours drinking and catching up on stories of the last few years. After several drinks, the man began flirting with the Cat. Commenting on how much of a woman she grown into did not encourage her to respond to his advances. She shrugged them off casually, as if they were a great big joke. *He is almost as much of a pervert as I am! How can I be offended?* She brushed it off as a mildly creepy compliment. He didn't force himself, and the dynamic shifted into more of a mutual joke.

The next day, Cat woke up on the couch. The house stayed quiet while her hosts slept late. After going to the bathroom and eating a bowl of cereal, she went back to sleep on the couch. *It's a real luxury to be able to sleep half the day! I never get to do this when I am traveling!*

The hangover ensured a late start. By the afternoon, she was up and visiting more with her old family friend. They made peanut butter and dill pickle sandwiches for her to take along in her bag. They laughed about their similarly odd taste buds and the strange luck that had landed her there in the first place. Eventually, sometime in the afternoon, he drove her back to the Highway.

⸺⸺◦((◉))◦⸺⸺

Trying to get out of Vacaville, Cat had a difficult time getting a ride. *At least it isn't the Nevada desert.* She got a ride as far as Fairfield. Waiting with her thumb out for a couple of hours was frustrating. *I don't know what's worse, no traffic, or hundreds of cars passing me without anyone slowing down.* It was hot and windy. She was sick of being there already. *Get me out of this city of misery.* Mama had been miserable when she lived in Fairfield, and everyone she had met there seemed unhappy.

The first ride she was able to get said they were heading up to Marysville. The driver headed north up Hwy 99, the old Golden State Highway. Getting dropped off in the late afternoon, she found that once again, she had no idea where she was.

Landing on a quiet back road highway with dusty shoulders, her feet hit the ground happy. She was hungry and needed to go to the bathroom. *I am out of the city!* Long fences showed where the dusty grassy shoulder stopped and private property began. These were large farms. The houses were too far off in the distance to see, but she knew they were there. She could see barns in the distance peppering great golden fields. There were no bushes to take cover in so she had to hope that no cars drove by while she was pissing.

The limited traffic made it easier to be private in the wide open. This also drastically decreased the probability of getting a ride out of there anytime soon. The sun would be setting soon. Propping her bags up against a fence post, Cat sat down on the ground to think and rest. Pulling a peanut butter and pickle sandwich out of her bag, she settled down to enjoy a quiet dinner.

I am a walking contradiction. Cat needed rest, and to sort out her thoughts. Upon achieving the time and space she was frightened. *I am afraid to be alone, but I can't stand to be around people for very long.* Her loneliness always brought sadness. She felt like there was something wrong with her.

Facing unrecognizable demons brought tears to her eyes. Rehashing memories of persecution, rejection, and depression pushed her into a downward spiral. If there was some great lesson she was supposed to learn from all these experiences of pain, she couldn't see what it was. She succumbed to the confusion and streams ran from her eyes, with only the dusty breeze as witness.

Cat's emotional state was pure roller coaster She was happy to be free. On the road she had nobody to which she had to answer. She could not fail to meet anyone's expectations because there was nobody else involved. Finding her freedom left her with her own expectations. *What are my expectations for myself? What is it that I'm searching for?*

The traveler was searching for what it meant to be Firecat, searching for her true self. Everywhere she looked, she failed to find what she was looking for. When she looked inside herself, she felt miserable hollow pain. She wanted so badly to be more than pain, more than sadness. "I want to be joy and creative inspiration." She shouted, hands outstretched. *I want to feel love. I want to be loved.* She hated her emptiness.

After crying her eyes dry, Cat got up and danced wildly in the dry grass. Shaking her arms and legs, helped circulate her energy and get her blood flowing. "I can't just stay here and wallow in my misery. I've got to keep moving or I will never get anywhere." Loading her pack onto her back, she headed north along the side of the quiet highway.

Several hours passed as she watched the sunset over fields of waving golden grasses. Every now and then she would stop and rest. Occasionally a passing car would bring her quickly to attention, thumb out and hair flying. Drivers passed without slowing and she was again alone with her thoughts. *I'll be turning 17 in a couple of days.* She wondered if the day would pass with any recognition. *Will I be somewhere where I can celebrate or will it be just another day on a highway somewhere? Would anyone notice if I just disappeared completely?*

The wind began to get colder and Cat considered setting up her bedroll along the dusty grass shoulder. As the last drops of sunlight faded off into indigo, a truck slowed down to pick her up. She remembered the trucker on Highway 128. *I've gotten rides with other truckers since then that have been okay.* She climbed into the cab with her backpack.

The driver asked, "Where ya headed?"

Cat responded "North. As far as you can take me."

She rode with him for a while. Maybe an hour or so had passed, when he began to start asking questions she didn't like. "So I'm helping you. What are you going to do to help me?" He was a large man and smelled of hours of driving. She was sure she was not strong enough to fight him off, if she had to.

"You stopped for me. If its a problem, you can drop me off anywhere. I don't want to be a problem."

This was not the answer he was looking for and began to recite to her the "my way or the highway" rules. He said "Nothing comes for free. Everyone eventually has to pay up or put out." At that point, she apologized, explaining that if she had known that was the condition for riding with him, she would not have taken the ride. She asked him politely if he could drop her off as soon as possible. He became irritated.

The trucker pulled over on the shoulder. Cat could feel

his anger and wanted out of the truck. Terrified he would get out and chase her down, she moved as quickly as she could with her pack. He was yelling at her as she opened the door. She threw her bag out and jumped out of the cab in a fluid motion that landed her half on top of her pack.

The driver slammed the door closed and kicked up a cloud of dust as he pulled back on the road. Cat thanked the universe for her luck. He had not laid a hand on her. He had not chased her down. She was free again. She was alone again. This time it was the middle of the night. It was cold. And once again, she had no idea where she was.

Cat knew she was exhausted. She expected getting a ride in the dark would be impossible. *Blessings in disguise.* Dusting herself off, she moved farther away from the road and sat down to go through her pack. Getting another layer of clothes from out of her bag, she bundled up. She laid out her bedroll, and laid down her head using her backpack as a pillow. *This day has been long enough.*

<hr />

First light forced Cat to give up on staying warm and asleep. She tried to gather her thoughts as she repacked her bag, rolled up her blankets and headed back to the road. Rides were slow to come, but covered a good distance. Through winding connecting roads she made her way all the way up to Oregon. She didn't know what she wanted to do or where she was going, so she just kept going north.

It was the middle of the night when she got dropped in a grocery store parking lot in Medford, Oregon. She needed to use a bathroom. She needed to eat something. She needed sleep in a warm place. It was clear that was not going to happen here. Dust and rocks moved through the air as she assessed her surroundings.

Searching for a sidewalk in the darkness was almost as challenging as finding a bathroom. Eventually she found the back of a building that could at least provide a little relief. Walking back toward the highway, she found that the cloverleaf style of the on and off ramps provided great hills of grass as dividers. Setting up camp conspicuously in the middle of a dark place provided sufficient camouflage until the sun began to rise.

Packing her bag and bedroll quickly, the morning's first rays caressed her back. She walked down the grassy hill to the interstate, in an attempt to catch an early ride. Rides were short, and people were hesitant to stop for her. Perhaps they were too busy. She created a variety of narratives in the hours that followed, as she strolled slowly north through Oregon. Promising herself that she would write it all down someday, she talked through details as though devising a great recitation.

Late in the afternoon, Cat was dropped off in the quaint town of Rogue Valley. Walking through the small downtown area, she felt like she was visiting the ghost set of an old movie. She was searching for a public restroom and perhaps a place that she could sleep for the night. Someplace with cheap food would have been helpful too. There didn't seem to be anyone in this town. *All the stores are closed. Is it Sunday?* Still, it felt unreal to her.

Sitting in front of a closed store, perched on her bedroll, she held a sign asking for help. A man pulled up and began talking to her. Driving a clean, nondescript looking, white compact car, the middle aged man seemed bland and tame. He asked her if she 'knew the Lord'. He offered food and shelter for the night. She was so exhausted, she felt compelled to accept.

The man was not a cook, nor was he well off. He didn't share much personal information about himself. She tried not to share much about herself. An odd bachelor, his house was simple and strangely organized in an almost obsessive way. She sat in his dining room in awkward silence, while he prepared TV Dinners for the both of them. She showed very little response to his mild attempt at conversation over the short meal.

After dinner, the strange man brought her a clean towel, pillow, and a blanket. Suggesting that she would sleep better with a shower first, he laid the pillow and blanket on the couch for her. Going into the bathroom, she locked the door behind her. Nervous about being naked in this man's house, her intention was to bathe quickly. Once the warm water began to flow down her back, the feeling of urgency lost momentum.

Cat's thoughts sped up as time slowed down in the shower. Despite her awareness of danger, being clean helped her feel a little more capable of taking care of herself in what could potentially become an unstable situation. Slipping out of the bathroom into the dimly lit living room, she tucked herself under the blankets. The strange man came out of his bedroom, still fully clothed, including his shoes. He asked if she needed anything else, and then said goodnight and excused himself to the bedroom.

Laying in the darkness, Cat imagined the worst. Thoughts of her odd host approaching her half naked in the middle of the night kept her half alert as she moved in and out of sleep. When morning came, she was quick to pack up her things. Her host was also up early. He offered her a bowl of cereal and milk. Pensively watching her eat, he gathered his keys and jacket.

The strange man dropped Cat off in front of the store where he had picked her up the evening before. He handed her a twenty dollar bill and wished her luck as he drove away. *Thank you universe, for protecting me from what could have been a horror story. That guy was unreal!*

———◈———

Cat wandered back out toward the highway, setting up post on the edge of the on ramp. Walking along the interstate had not proven very successful, and she was nervous about the local police. This place seemed too sterile for compassionate law enforcement. Cautious about testing her luck, she remained on the edge of the on ramp for several hours before getting a lift.

Hopping from one truck to the next, Cat ended up riding with a fellow who she felt a little more comfortable talking with. This guy engaged her in conversation without making her feel threatened. He seemed to relate to her almost like a guy and this put her at ease. Only briefly did he make reference to her gender as it related to traveling. He asked her how she stayed safe, when there were so many people out there that could potentially cause her harm.

"People assume I'm either easy, crazy or stupid when they pick me up. I make it clear from the start that I'm not easy or stupid, and people generally leave it at that." He chuckled and commended her for her gumption.

It was late in the evening when they approached Eugene. The trucker explained that he had a few more hours to drive North. Then he would unload, and turn back around to head South.

"It's already late. Not a great time to get dropped off.

If you wanna ride along with me, I could use the company. It helps me stay awake, having someone to talk to." *I don't really know where I'm going anyway. The cab of this truck would be a little warmer than getting dropped off in the middle of the night.*

Cat agreed to ride the rest of the loop with him after he explained that he could still drop her in Eugene on his way back. To sweeten the deal, he offered to pay her for her time. He gave her a cents per mile offer, and she agreed. His points were valid, and she felt he had already proven to be safe. She felt pretty strongly that the driver would not physically assault her.

The ride was long. The trucker and traveler talked about all kinds of things. He did not refer to her gender again. Although after a while, Cat began to wonder, since he had been so respectful, if he did bring up some kind of physical exchange, whether she might actually consider it. When they approached his unloading destination, the driver instructed Cat to hide in the back of his cab. Cozy in the back, there was a television and a small comfortable bed. She fell asleep for a little while.

When Cat awoke, they were already on the road again. He asked her if she had a good nap. "Welcome to the land of the living," he chuckled as she climbed into the passenger seat. Soon after, they pulled into a truck stop at the edge of Eugene. Pulling in, the fellow thanked Cat for keeping him company. The morning sun sliced through her eyelids as she looked through his dusty windshield.

Cat was only partly thankful for the end of the ride, as they had sort of run out of things to talk about. *If he asks me to continue riding with him, I think I will.* She paused before grasping her bag, and reaching for the handle of the door.

"Maybe we will run into each other again." The driver

suggested and handed her forty dollars. "Good luck kid." She smiled at the driver, stuffed the money in her pocket and clambered out of the cab. He leaned over to pull the door shut all the way. Cat waved goodbye and turned away from the truck as he pulled out of the parking lot.

Chapter 23

THE NAMING

Walking into town, Cat felt empty and lost. *I've been traveling for a while. I should know where I am going by now!* She was searching for something that would have meaning to her. She remembered the way her mother described shopping in a thrift store. "You don't really know what you are looking for. You simply wander around, taking it all in, and wait until you hear that little voice trying to get your attention. Follow that little voice and you will find the treasure you are meant to find. If you go looking for it, you will pass it by."

What treasure am I passing by? What am I missing? A strong feeling of emptiness, where she knew her self worth was supposed to live, loomed just below the surface of her skin. Deep sadness weighed her down, making her backpack heavier with every step.

When Cat reached the University of Oregon campus area, she perched herself on a newspaper stand. Her backpack and bedroll leaned on the bottom of the newspaper box, half hiding below the metal framework. She looked at the newspaper through the plexiglass. *Today is my birthday!* Watching the people passing in the mid-morning sun, Cat wished for a positive and eventful day. Her travels had uncovered an undercurrent of gypsies that drew her curiosity. She wanted them to accept her into their culture.

Cat was a stranger here and everywhere she went. Each stop she made, she witnessed people immersed in an already active community of family and support. Reminded of the activity that used to move in and out of The Oasis, she longed to see an old friend's face pass by. She wanted someone who knew her, to accidentally find her, and take her under their wing.

She daydreamed about being to be part of a bus family. She watched buses pull up in front of campus. Hippies who seemed to know their ride was coming, were waiting and quick to load up. She watched this happen a couple of times and worked up the nerve to go over and talk with some of the hippies hanging out.

Cat learned that she had just missed the Oregon Country Fair the previous weekend. There had been a great concert and hippies had come from far and wide to camp out at the fair. Now many were heading out to Cougar Hot Springs for a regional rainbow gathering. *A rainbow gathering? That seems like a better place than hanging out on a street corner.* She talked with folks until she was able to score a ride east to the encampment.

The ride heading east provided her with a seat crammed in the back of a VW Bus, with several others that she did not know. Nobody seemed to mind the tight quarters. Everyone was already used to this kind of travel. The familiarity with which folks conducted themselves in this environment felt more like traveling with her mother and her friends when she was younger. Strangers didn't feel quite like strangers, and she began to loosen up a little. *I'm safe in this world.* She daydreamed about how long this might last and if she could somehow find a stronger family on this leg of her journey.

They stopped in a small roadside town to stretch their legs. The driver went into the little store to pay for some gas and grab a drink. Cat looked up at the city limit sign. Rainbow, Oregon. Population almost nothing. *A town name like that sounds like a town founded by hippies.* The looks that the travelers got from passing locals did not support her hypothesis. By the time they loaded back up and hit the road, she felt like they were being watched all the way out of town. *Had we stayed much longer, they might have planned a lynching.* Looks can be very deceiving sometimes.

The winding road along the waterway seemed to last forever in the dark. Pulling into the campground by starlight, Cat was thankful for the ride to be over. She didn't stay to camp with the folks she had ridden with. Instead, she headed for the smell of smoke, and the sound of people drumming and singing. Setting her bag in a small alcove of bushes somewhat near the campfire, she set out her bedroll. She wanted to go and talk with people. She wanted to be accepted right away. Road exhaustion overtook her, as she replayed the possible ways she could introduce herself to this new group of potential family.

The sound of drumming and acoustic guitar floated lightly on the mountain breeze. The sweet smell of campfire cradled Cat into heavy sleep. Cold aching bones and a full bladder woke her as early sunlight brushed her eyelids. She turned over to assess her surroundings. The faint smell of last night's fire still tickled her nose. Something about the place made her feel safe. She was finally able to breathe deeply without anxiety.

Leaving her belongings where she had slept, Cat got up and began to explore. Finding a place to go to the bathroom was not going to happen here in the campground.

She needed to find a place that was more secluded from people. She followed the sound of water down a rocky path just south of her. Coconut sized rocks with flat sides and sharp edges piled the ground along the edge of the river. Finding a place private enough to escape from prying eyes did not seem to be readily available, but everyone in the campground was asleep.

Ducking below the campground's line of sight, Cat removed her shoes and pants halfway down the natural rock wall that bordered the Mackenzie River. Continuing down the rocks toward the river, she relieved herself on the rocks a couple feet from the river's edge. Layered with two shirts, her ragged sweatshirt, and a thin tie-dyed skirt, she went down a little farther to clean herself with the river water.

Using all the muscles in her feet and toes, she carefully traversed the rocky shore. Squatting down low over the water's edge, she splashed fresh cool water on herself. Pulling down the edge of her sweatshirt, she dried the inside of her thighs and shivered. The water was so cold. The cold rocks against her bare feet felt like tiny needles penetrating the nerve pathways all the way up her legs and back. Reaching the top of the rock path, Cat was quick to put her pants back on underneath her thin skirt.

Replacing her shoes made walking on the rocks less challenging. Cat wandered the rocky border of the river, heading east for a while. When she could no longer see signs of the campground, she cut a path up the hillside from the river. Everything was crisp here. The quiet rushing water echoed louder on the early morning breeze. *How do the fish survive in such cold water? Perhaps they never sleep?* She decided that she would attempt to go back in the water later in the day.

Wandering the pathways back through the campground,

Cat discovered several small encampments scattered throughout the woods. Some folks had tents. Some had vans or trucks set up like little houses. Many people were simply sleeping under the trees in the open air. As Cat wound her way in and out of the encampments, she searched for folks she might recognize from her travels elsewhere. Arriving back at the front of the campground, she was pleased to see signs of life emerging from the peppered encampments.

The smell of campfire coffee renewed an indescribable joy within the cavity of her chest. She stopped to say hello to folks along the path back to her backpack. Greetings were jovial and a sense of family was present in every interaction. Wishing that this feeling of belonging could last forever, she immersed herself in each moment as it passed. Praying that time would stand still, she blinked. Wiping away the tears that nobody else could see, her heart ached.

⸻ «(0)» ⸻

Cat spent about a week at the gathering. The hot springs was actually a couple of miles down the road. During the day, some of the folks staying at the campground would make their pilgrimage to the hot springs. Then after a couple of hours, folks would begin to return to the campground. It was easy to find a ride in either direction, every day she was there.

Despite the beautiful environment of the Hot Springs, Cat opted for staying at the campground most of the time. The first day she made the trek to the springs, she read the posted sign clearly stating "Clothing Optional." At first, she thought the freedom would be refreshing and comfortable. Certainly other people there seemed to enjoy the experience. Still, being naked reminded Cat how uncomfortable she was in her own skin. Stripping her clothing off, to soak in the natural flow of hot spring water had raised her anxiety beyond a point of pleasure.

Spending several hours with the comfort of kind people close by, Cat allowed herself to spend alone time with herself. She felt secure focusing on herself, knowing that at any time, she could go and join the group. Loneliness did not overtake her here in this beautiful place. She thought about what it must have been like for natives living here, before white man came along. *They washed in this river. It is so cold! I wonder how they did it.* She became more courageous, and decided she too would bath and wash her clothes in the cold river.

Stripping down to nothing, she dismissed the feelings of anxiety associated with her nakedness. Instead, Cat chose to focus on the task at hand. Starting with her dirty clothes in a pile by the river, she soaked them all one by one. With soapstone that she had collected at the Hot Springs, she laid the wet clothing out on flat rocks and scrubbed them with the soft stones. Then, after rinsing them in the river, she laid them out on the rocks to dry. She repeated the process with her own body, lathering up everything including her hair, with the soft soap stone.

Cat allowed her naked body to dry within the warmth of her poncho blanket. Wearing it for the better part of the day, she waited for her clothes to dry. Later, she moved her damp clothes away from the river and hung them on tree branches above her camp. By the end of the day, enough of her clothes were dry, to redress for the evening chill.

Evening arrived and a large fire circle developed. Many of the travelers gathered around the evening fire circle. Folks had hand drums, various noise making instruments, and one remarkable young woman played guitar. Libations were shared. Some of the smoking kind, and some hallucinogens were shared. They played music and talked.

Cat watched the young woman with the guitar. She said she was from Alaska. *She is from Alaska? I was born in Alaska. I wish I was brave enough to approach her, to talk to her. I would love to hear more about Alaska.*

Cat was enamored with the young woman's voice. Everyone loved the music she played. Still, Cat was intimidated. She didn't want this woman to be afraid of her. She didn't want anyone in the circle to know that she was attracted to women. She stayed on her side of the circle and instead talked directly with the people sitting next to her.

It was the longest evening that Cat had stayed awake and participated in the community of the gathering. They spoke about many things.

"If you were an animal, what kind would you be?" One of the men asked the group.

She thought about cats as the round-table conversation continued. *I've always felt a kinship to cats. Maybe because of my name? Maybe there are other reasons.*

When the discussion moved around the circle toward her, rabbit came up. She was surprised. Still, the general consensus was agreed. One of the older men spoke through the smoky campfire. "You are most like a Rabbit. Always on the move, skittish, keeping to herself. You never let anyone get too close." Murmuring of agreement followed and the man beside her said, "From now on, you are Rabbit."

⸺◦《●》◦⸺

Within a couple of days, the girl decided that she had accomplished everything that she could at the gathering. People were starting to migrate back to town. She didn't want to be left behind alone. Most days during her stay, someone with a van or school bus would announce in the morning, that they were making a trip to "town". Anyone who wanted or needed to go to Eugene was invited to ride along. When the bus returned in the evenings, they always brought someone new to the gathering. Now the people were thinning out. Less people were arriving than leaving and she decided it was time to catch the next bus back into town. With it, the new nickname "Rabbit" traveled with her.

Chapter 24

GYPSIES AND ALIENS

Back in Eugene, Rabbit was hanging out on the streets again. This time, the girl didn't feel as alone. She had made friends at the gathering. Some of them were here on the streets of Eugene with her. She wasn't as afraid to talk to people. Through the network of people, she learned about a Barter Fair happening the following week in southern Oregon.

Rabbit spent the rest of the week hanging out in Eugene, until it was time to go to the Barter Fair. Catching a ride with folks heading to the fair, she followed along the stream of travelers. Setting up camp in the parking lot, with so many other folks, she investigated how she could get into the fair without money. Rabbit successfully negotiated with the right people. She arranged to pay her way by helping with set up in the mornings. Helping to pick up garbage, and be an extra hand when necessary, she worked her way through the weekend.

It was exhilarating to accomplish what she had set out to do. Rabbit had made a place for herself, found a purpose in being there. During the early morning on the last day, she met some gypsies camping in the middle of the parking lot. She was mystified. These folks were not just hippies in traditional garb. They were actually Romany Gypsies. There was an older man, a younger man, and one woman. When she left the Barter Fair at the end of the weekend, Rabbit traveled back to Eugene with her new gypsy friends.

Rabbit thought their traditional clothing was romantic. Their religion seemed very similar to the neo-pagan practices with which her mother had raised her. Returning to their apartment in Eugene, they taught her more about their beliefs and practices. Rabbit spent a couple of days in their apartment studying, resting, and being intimate with the younger man.

On the third day, the older man decided that she was fair game and intruded when she was in bed with the younger man. She tried to protest, but she was quickly corrected. Afterward, Rabbit laid on the living room floor, crying. The woman tried to calm her down, explaining that "all the women in the Romany tradition were the property of their the men," and she should consider it a blessing to be cherished by both the men at once. She told Rabbit quietly that "she too, had been blessed accordingly." Rabbit was not happy about it. She did not feel cherished. She felt violated.

When she talked with the young man about her feelings, he said he understood. She wanted to leave, but was not allowed to do so, unless she was dressed in the traditional garb. Also, they would all have to go out as a group. She was informed that this was the common practice. A woman was not allowed to go out by themselves. Rabbit was frightened. *What has happened? How did I end up in this awkward position?* She pleaded with the young man, "Help me get out, please." Finally, he agreed to help her.

When the older gypsy man was asleep, the younger one accompanied her out of the apartment. Underneath her gypsy dress, Rabbit wore boy's clothes. As soon as they had gotten far enough away from the apartment for her to feel secure, she stripped the fancy dress off, leaving pants and a loose shirt showing underneath. She handed him back the gypsy dress and thanked him for his help. Giving him one last kiss, she scampered away. He turned around and headed back to the apartment they had left behind.

Rabbit was so happy to be free, she climbed up on a newspaper stand and began to sing. She sang and joked with people walking by. Tipping her hat for any change she could get, she warbled for hours like a robin at the first sign of spring. A newspaper reporter came by and asked if he could take her picture.

"You can if you give me a dollar!" She responded smartly.

He asked her some questions, took her picture, and put a five dollar bill in her hat. As the sun began to move lower toward the horizon, she began to get chilly. Afraid of staying in Eugene for too long, for fear of being dragged back to the apartment, Rabbit headed toward the highway with her backpack and bedroll.

Spending the night in some ivy below the on-ramp, Rabbit was awake and on the road at first light. Hitching south now, it occurred to her that she had been away from California for a couple of months. She got rides as far south as Medford, arriving before the end of the day. She headed into town. Searching for a place that offered food and services for the homeless, she found a community center near the railroad tracks.

Rabbit was able to use the bathroom and sit inside for a while. They offered enough food for a couple of days of traveling. As she was leaving, she met a family of people who seemed very nice. Their oldest son, Snake, was an extraordinarily beautiful man with long black hair. She was sad to see them go, wishing she could talk with them more. They shared a few words and then went their separate ways. Heading back out to the road, she was glad for the food she had obtained at the community center.

Rabbit hitchhiked back down to California. She found Jasper. He didn't seem to be doing anything differently than when she had seen him last. She checked in with her mother. *My parents had actually been worried about me?* The couple of months she had been on the road had been the longest she had gone without contacting them. Mama was especially worried. She said that Dad had even contacted her trying to figure out 'where their daughter was.'

"I'm fine! I was just fine! I was at a Rainbow Gathering!" Making the rounds visiting people only took her a couple of weeks and soon Rabbit was back on the road. Something told her to go back and find Snake and his family. Without saying goodbye to Jasper or her parents, she headed back out to the highway on-ramp.

Hitchhiking to Medford was pretty direct this time around. She got just a couple of rides that took her long distances. Within two days Rabbit was back in Medford. She headed to the community center where she had met Snake and his family. She was able to reconnect with them relatively quickly. "I came back here to look for you." She told him, smiling. Snake promptly responded by taking Rabbit home with him.

They spent several days partying at night and hanging around the house during the day. Halloween arrived and they enjoyed a rowdy night of drunken intimacy. The next day, he informed her, "This has been enough time in the city. My family is going to be returning to the hills where we babysit a gold-mining claim outside of Jackson." *How exciting!* Rabbit gladly agreed to go with them.

Hidden away in the hills, a week or two passed by without leaving the privacy of the forested home. They didn't go wandering much because it had gotten cold and icy. He also warned her that the neighbors were not used to people traipsing around in the woods. "If we get too close to the neighbor's property, they will likely greet us with a shotgun." Rabbit was satisfied to stay in the warmth, romancing with the beautiful Blackfoot man. They talked about hopes and dreams, all the things that they wished for in the future.

Snake began making warm jokes about sexy, barefoot, pregnant hippie women. Suddenly she felt threatened. *I am not his woman. This is simply what's happening in the moment. Nobody owns me! I'm certainly not pregnant. Am I?* Rabbit felt trapped. Paranoid and anxious, she told him that she had stayed long enough.

"I have to get back to California. I have to check on my mother and my little brother."

He was unhappy with her decision. His parents seemed indifferent. Snake's father would be heading to Medford for supplies in the next couple of days. Rabbit insisted that she needed to ride back with him. Reluctant to let her go, Snake tried to convince her to stay. She refused and he let go of the argument.

"You're right. You don't owe me anything." He stroked her hip and smiled. "I've enjoyed your company though." She smiled at him, leaning down to kiss his forehead. "Look me up again next time you're passing through."

Rabbit assured him that she would. When they arrived at the community center in Medford, she courteously thanked him for the hospitality and ride. Snake's father wished her the best of luck and continued along with his errands in town.

At the community center, Rabbit told them that she needed to get back to California. "Do you have a telephone I can use? I need to get in touch with someone that can help me."

She felt a strange desperation to get back to the Bay Area. *Something is wrong.* She felt scared and didn't know why. They tried to be helpful. Eventually, she was able to get in touch with Jasper. "It's too cold to hitchhike back over the pass. I need to come home now!" Between the folks at the community center, and Jasper, she was able to get a bus ticket from Medford to Oakland.

Rabbit's bus was scheduled to leave in the very early hours of the morning. She made her way across town to the bus station to wait. *There are some very strange people that hang out in bus stations. This should be interesting.* With hours left to wait, not having anywhere else to go, she amused herself with interesting conversations.

One fellow talked with Rabbit for hours. He explained that he had a space ship. "I am actually an alien in disguise." He confided in her. "My ship is hidden for now because I don't want anything bad to happen to my ship while I'm gathering information about people on Earth." He tried to convince her that if she returned on a certain day, he would take her with him into space.

Clearly this man is crazy. Yet, as they talked for hours, it became apparent that he truly believed what he was saying. After a while, she started to actually believe him. She even began considering the idea of leaving the planet behind. *I feel like an alien in my body. I've never really felt like I belonged anywhere. Perhaps leaving the planet altogether would be a good idea?*

She knew that they were not alone in the universe. *People from other planets probably avoid us because we are so dysfunctional. Maybe this guy is the answer I've been looking for. Still, the idea of being trapped in a spaceship with this strange character might get old after a while. It's not as though I could just hitchhike back to Earth.*

When Rabbit's bus finally pulled in, the alien man handed her a piece of paper with a date and time for reuniting with him. She thanked him for the offer and told him she would try her best to make it back in time. Sitting back in the greyhound seat, Rabbit closed her eyes. *If I literally disappeared off the face of the planet, would anyone notice I was gone? Would I actually be missed?*

Her heart sank heavy in her chest. She wanted to feel loved and accepted. For now, she would go back and visit Jasper. *Perhaps he will have missed me.* Cold canned air filled her nose with the smell of air freshener and exhaust as she fell into dreaming about leaving forever.

Chapter 25

UNEXPECTED LOVE

Arriving at the Oakland Bus Station was hot and noisy. Crammed in a line down the aisle, everyone was glad to be getting off the bus. It had been a long ride and her legs were cramping. Feeling a little nauseous, Rabbit stumbled down the stairs into the light of the afternoon. She waited by the bus, watching for her traveling bags and bedroll. She lit a cigarette. Smoking it halfway, she changed her mind and stomped it out on the ground. This was not helping her feel better. Perhaps if she ate something she would feel better?

As her gear was removed from the bottom of the bus, Rabbit saw Jasper. She gave him a huge hug. It felt wonderful seeing someone she knew she could trust! She had not expected him to meet her at the bus station. She picked up her bags, layering them with the intent of carrying everything. He insisted on helping her, taking one of her larger bags. "I promised your mother that I would make sure you made it to her place safely." *Had they actually been worried about her?* She wanted to cry but kept it to herself.

As the couple walked up Grand Ave toward Mama's apartment, Jasper told her that he had been visiting her mother in her absence. "She was worried about you," he said, repositioning the bag on his shoulder as they walked. "And I missed you. I don't want you to keep leaving."

She didn't know what to say. She wanted to feel loved. She wanted to feel *wanted.* Here and now, he was telling her exactly what she wanted to hear. Maybe this time she would be able to stay?

Rabbit felt uneasy and incredibly hungry. She didn't tell him about Snake. She suddenly felt like she had somehow been cheating on him with the Blackfoot in Oregon. Voices protested inside her head. *But you broke up. You weren't actually dating. But he still loves you.* She felt ashamed and tried hush the voices in her head so she could listen to Jasper.

Arriving at her mom's place, Jasper greeted Mama with a big hug. In Rabbit's absence, Mama and Jasper had continued to develop a friendship. She thought it a bit odd, and yet, it was comforting to think that these two very important people had commiserated together about her absence. She announced that she was starving and Mama headed straight to the kitchen.

Rabbit dug through her bag for cleaner clothes. "I am going to take a shower!" she told Jasper. "Stick around, I won't be forever." He assured her that he wasn't planning on leaving anytime soon.

Crying in the shower, Rabbit let all her tears run down the drain with the dirty water. *What is wrong with me?* She felt so much confusion. All this traveling and she didn't feel any closer to an answer. Emerging from the shower barefoot in a loose hippie dress, her hair dripped down her back. She sat on the floor at Jasper's feet and teased him with the wet hair. Mama brought food into the living room and they all ate together. She thanked Jasper again for delivering her daughter back safely and then focused on Rabbit. "You had better call your father and let him know you are okay."

Several hours passed and Jasper had to leave. She decided to stay and visit longer. Despite her lack of interest in seeing Will, it was somehow comforting to stay with her family. *I am not ready for sleeping in the cold again. I need to just stay here with Mama for a little while.* Jasper promised to come back and visit again soon. With hugs and kisses, he left her in the company of her family.

Rabbit stayed for a couple of days. She found herself sleeping a lot. Too exhausted to make the journey across town, she felt no motivation to leave. She alternated between hunger and nausea. She didn't feel good and was starting to get nervous that she had not yet started her period. In fact, she was more than a couple of days late. She began to fear that she really was pregnant. The mornings were especially rough.

Mama suggested that she go get tested. "There is a clinic where you can get tested for free," she offered.

Jasper came to visit again. Rabbit was feeling weak and afraid. Morning sickness had started hitting her hard and she was terrified of what to do about it. Promising Mama that he would take good care of her, Jasper accompanied Rabbit across town to the clinic. As they walked, she shared her fears with him. "I'm pretty positive that I am pregnant." She was afraid that with all the partying that she had been doing, carrying a child would likely kill her. She was convinced that she was not in good enough health to make it through such an ordeal as pregnancy and childbirth.

Jasper listened to her, holding her hand as they walked. Professing his love to her, he told her that he would be there for her no matter what happened. "I know that it isn't my child and I don't care. If you wanted to keep the baby, I would be there for you. I would love you and help you raise the child as if it were my own."

Rabbit squeezed his hand, as tears poured out of her face. Was this the unconditional love she had been searching for? *It wouldn't work though. We always ended up fighting too much.*

She was honest with him. "Jasper, I love you too, but you know that it would never work. You drink too much. You drink every day. You are an alcoholic and I can't raise a child with an alcoholic." He didn't seem offended by her honesty. He admitted the truth in her words. He did have a problem with alcohol. Loving her couldn't change that. They walked in temporary silence, their hands clasped tightly together. She was blown away by his words and terrified of what the future might have in store for her.

Arriving at the clinic, Rabbit was nervous. She took a number and sat down in a chair next to Jasper. When it was her turn, she walked up to the counter and took the clipboard, pen, and intake form. With the paperwork in hand, she sat back down next to him, hands shaking. She could feel her breath hot and tight in her chest. Filling out the paperwork, she tried to remember the last time she had her period. It had been a couple of months.

Finishing the paperwork, she returned to the intake window. The woman behind the counter took the clipboard from her, and handed her a specimen cup and a handi-wipe. Pointing toward the bathroom, she instructed Rabbit, "Put the cup in the collection window after you're finished. It will be a little while but," the woman assured Rabbit, "I will call you back to the window as soon as we have the results."

Walking into the bathroom, Rabbit saw the little metal window the nurse had described. A small sliding door opened up into something like a cabinet. Rabbit sat awkwardly on the toilet. Following the directions posted on the wall beside the toilet, she tried to aim into the little cup. Twisting the lid onto the specimen cup, she used some toilet paper to wipe the outside of the cup dry. Sliding open the little wooden door, she placed the full cup in the tiny, silver collection cabinet. After washing her hands, she returned to the waiting room and sat down at Jasper's feet. A wave of nausea washed over her and she laid her head in his lap.

Rabbit felt weak. *This is a terrible experience. I want it to be over now.* She remembered Halloween night. *They had been careful. They had used protection. What had she done wrong?* She remembered Snake's comment about how beautiful pregnant women were. She shuddered. Jasper petted her hair as she cried silently into his lap. Then the woman at the window called her name. "Miss Burnell?"

This time Rabbit was wobbly. Jasper helped her get up. "I can do this." She said, mostly to convince herself. She walked quickly up to the counter.

"Well, Miss Burnell, congratulations, you are not pregnant." As the words came out of the woman's mouth, Rabbit used all of her strength to not vomit in her window.

She was angry. "What? I don't understand! If I am not pregnant, then why am I so sick?" The woman answered that she didn't know. Perplexed, the nurse offered, "Sometimes the first test is wrong. You can always come back next week and test again."

Why am I so upset? I should be happy about the test results? Rabbit wasn't happy though. She was scared. "If I'm not pregnant then something worse might be happening to me? Am I dying? Why do I feel so weak?"

Jasper got up and urged her away from the window. "Come on. We're done here. Let's go."

Heading back across town toward Mama's apartment, Rabbit expressed her confusion and fear. She was angry.

They had made a mistake. She was sure they had. Jasper didn't know what to say. Accompanying her for the trek across town helped a lot. She thanked him over and over, for being her friend and caring so much. By the time they got back to the apartment, she was exhausted. When Rabbit told Mama what had happened, she responded simply "go back next week and test again."

She tried to go out to the Ave a couple of times over the next week. Riding along with Will made it a little easier. She was able to get out of the apartment for a couple of hours, and could return easily to the safety of the apartment without having to walk for hours.

Talking with the hippies on Telegraph was strange for her. She wasn't sure how she felt about their interactions. They were all focused on partying and tour. She wasn't interested in partying right now. She had done so much to her body in the last couple of years, she began to wonder whether she needed to stop altogether.

Rabbit had never actually been on Dead Tour before. She felt like it would be a great adventure, but she was afraid to go alone. Every time she went out, someone inevitably asked her if she was pregnant. She hated the words. She felt weak and moody. Everything made her cry. Despite her intention to stay away longer, she ended up returning to the apartment with Will. He made her uncomfortable but she had learned how to be around people who made her uneasy.

Another week of morning sickness and crying passed, and Rabbit returned to the clinic for a second test. This time, the results showed she was pregnant. In fact, according to their results, she was likely over two months along.

She was angry! *Why did they tell me last week that I'm not pregnant and now they're saying I'm two months along!*

What in the holy hell? How come they couldn't get it right?

The woman behind the counter gave her a piece of paper with pertinent information about getting an abortion. She told Rabbit not to worry. "We can take care of everything here in the clinic." Taking the paper from her hand, she stared at the woman in disbelief and walked out of the clinic.

Rabbit returned to Mama's apartment in tears. What was she going to do? She couldn't have a baby. She was in terrible physical condition. *I am too small to carry a baby. It would break me in two!* She knew it was a terrible idea.

"I could carry the baby and then give it up for adoption, but that would be a terrible thing for the child. The baby would surely be born with defects from all the toxins I have been putting in my body." She allowed all her fear and anger to pour out of her, as Mama listened.

Rabbit paused for breath and Mama took the opportunity to interject. "I think you should call your father."

Rabbit was mortified. *Did she actually say that?* Mama insisted that if she really needed help, the child should call her father. "He will be able to help you. He's probably the only one who can help you. Call him."

The night passed slowly with restless sleep. Finally, daybreak came with more nausea and tears. Pulling the crumpled clinic paper from yesterday's pocket, Rabbit tried to flatten out the wrinkles. Her baby brother came into the living room. His hair was wild and he was eager for attention. She looked at him and was reminded how terrified she was of her situation. It was too much for her to handle. They laid on the living room floor playing underneath the Solstice tree for a while, until she heard her mother moving in the kitchen.

Mama entered the living room, setting a cup of tea on

the table next to her daughter. Gathering up the little boy, the two of them disappeared into the bedroom for the morning ritual of clean diapers and getting dressed. Rabbit picked up the cup of tea and took a sip, choking on dry tears in her chest. *Today I will call Dad.* She swallowed hard. She didn't want to disappoint her father. *How will I tell him? What should I say? What will he say?*

Hours passed slowly. Finally, Rabbit got dressed and ready leave. She told Mama she was going out. "Don't worry, I'm leaving my stuff. I'm coming back later."

Mama made acknowledging sounds from the other room, where she was feeding little brother. Walking down Grand Avenue, Rabbit recited what she would say to Dad. Every time she neared a pay phone, she slowed down. Getting too choked up to talk, she would pass the phone, telling herself that by the time she reached the next phone, she would be ready to call. She headed through town, toward the office where Dad worked.

Rabbit was almost to his office when she decided she had to suck it up. She stopped at a pay phone just a few blocks from Dad's office. Leaning up against the phone box, she picked up the receiver. Dropping coins into the metal slot, she waited for the dial tone. Punching in the numbers to his office phone, she held her breath. When he picked up the phone and answered, storm clouds raged in her face.

"Dad?" He could hear her crying. "I'm in trouble. I need help. I didn't know who else to call."

Rabbit could hear his calmness on the other line. "How much do you need?"

She read him the details provided on the clinic sheet. He said okay, that he would take care of it. She thanked him, still crying, and hung up the phone. She had expected him to question her further. She had expected him to tell her all about the mistakes she had been making. She had expected a terrible reaction. Yet, he was there for her, just like Mama had predicted.

Rabbit put another quarter in the pay phone and dialed the number to the clinic. She had to get an appointment quickly. She was almost three months along now, and if she didn't get it taken care for soon, it would be too late. She swallowed hard, providing the woman on the phone with all her pertinent information. She thanked the voice on the phone for helping and hung up the receiver.

Shaking, crying, and swimming through nausea, Rabbit made her way back to Mama's apartment. It was almost Christmas. She felt no cause for celebration. She felt trapped and too exhausted to enjoy a holiday. When she arrived, Mama saw that she had been crying for a long time.

"Well?" She looked at her daughter and waited for an explosion of emotions.

"I have an appointment on December 30th." With no more breath for speaking or crying, the girl curled up in a ball on the living room floor and rested under the bright green tree.

———— ⊸(◍)⊶ ————

Rabbit had been staying mostly inside for a couple of weeks now. The cabin fever was too much for her. Promising to return in a couple of days, she left on Christmas Eve and headed to Berkeley. When she got to Telegraph, she headed back to the Outpost. Sitting with a group of hippies, she spent the evening talking with folks about subjects that had nothing to do with what was in her head. She needed distraction.

Finally, in the early hours of the morning, she fell asleep

with a couple of other people in a doorway. She felt protected being a group. Nobody would mess with her because she was not alone.

Christmas morning was quiet on Telegraph Ave. Most businesses were closed. The street vendors were not coming out today. It was mostly silent except for the people who lived here in the alleys and parks. Rabbit was sitting with a group of people in front of the Bank of America, when a newer compact car pulled up to the curb in front of them. Two women got out of the car and approached their group. In their hands, the women carried an armful of wrapped gifts. The women handed each of them a gift and wished them all a Merry Christmas. Returning to their car, they drove away as quickly as they had arrived.

Everyone was excited. They all opened their gifts. Some got socks. Some got gloves. A few people traded with each other. Rabbit pulled her shoes off and put on a new pair of socks. Replacing her shoes, she wondered if things could get any worse. She was depressed about everything that had been happening. She wasn't with Dad. She wasn't with Mama. This was a day that people were spending with loved ones all across the country. She felt utterly alone.

These people that I'm sitting with don't know me. They don't love me. Rabbit had traveled so much searching for her happy place. Now she was sitting, surrounded by people who were thrilled about a new pair of socks. She got up and headed to People's Park for the upcoming free Christmas Dinner. *There are so many people living here on the streets. I wonder how long one could last in this manner.* The smell of the food made her nauseous. She knew she needed to eat, but she was too sick to think about it.

The days passed quickly after Christmas. Rabbit visited Dad. He gave her a check to take to the clinic. She visited

Jasper and his mother. She returned to Mama's apartment and waited for December 30th. On the day of the appointment, Will took care of little brother while Mama accompanied Rabbit to the clinic. They sat together in the waiting room without speaking.

Chapter 26

A TIME FOR PRAYERS

Rabbit was appalled to see how many other girls were coming into the clinic. The nurse lined them all up like cattle. Instead of performing each procedure separately, they were all checked in together. A nurse called her name and told her to follow. She saw Rabbit hesitate. "It's okay. They are not doing it yet. This is just the sonogram." She looked at Mama. Mother waved her hand, encouraging her daughter to follow the nurse.

Entering the exam room, Rabbit had to climb up on a table. The nurse applied a cold gooey gel to her belly. She explained, "We are going to take a look. We have to make sure there isn't anything abnormal going on before they prepare you for your procedure."

Rabbit laid on the table with her eyes shut tight. The nurse tried to calm the girl, "Try and relax. This isn't going to hurt at all...Well look at that!" her eyes stayed shut. "Come on girl, don't you want to see your babies?"

Babies?? Rabbit opened her eyes and lifted her head. *Sure enough.* Tears streamed down her face in full force now. The nurse spoke to her gently. "You know, they haven't done anything yet. It isn't too late to change your mind.

They can simply give you your check back at the front counter and you can walk right out of here."

Rabbit choked, looking at the gray screen. She could see two babies cuddled up against each other. She felt like she was going to vomit. Seeing that was too much for her. The nurse turned off the screen and handed the girl a paper towel to wipe her belly clean.

Returning to the waiting room, Rabbit sat down at her mother's feet. Laying her head in Mama's lap she cried openly and loudly. The woman petted her daughter's hair. "There are two of them!" She sobbed in Mama's lap. "There are two babies in there Mama. I feel terrible. I just saw them and I don't know what to do."

Mama spoke to her daughter softly, combing her fingernails through her hair. "Just pray honey. You pray to those babies. Tell them how much you love them. Let them know how much you love them, and that you just aren't ready yet. When you are ready to be a good mom, they will come back to you." Rabbit choked and sobbed in her mother's lap until the nurse called her name again. Shaking, she got up from the waiting room floor.

The nurse asked if she was ready and Rabbit nodded her head, wiping tears from her face. "Are you sure?"

She straightened up and responded solidly "Yes. I'm ready." She looked back at Mama. Mother assured her daughter that she would be there waiting for her when she got out. Following the nurse into another room, she passed a second waiting room full of other girls waiting in hospital gowns for their procedure.

They entered a small room. The nurse handed her a hospital gown and a bag for her to put her clothes in. She instructed Rabbit to 'get changed' and left the room. It was cold in the room and Rabbit didn't feel comfortable in the hospital gown. When the nurse returned, she explained that they would be putting an IV into her for the procedure. The nurse had a difficult time getting a vein in the girl's arm and settled for putting the IV receiver in her hand. It pinched. Rabbit winced. *I hate needles.*

Rabbit was directed to wait in a second waiting room, with the other girls. Sitting in the second waiting room, she was surrounded by girls in hospital gowns with IV receivers. *I feel sick.* They seemed to know each other. *This is almost like being in some kind of crazy social club.* The other girls chatted and exchanged stories as if there was nothing wrong with what was happening. The whole scene made her sick to her stomach. Some of the girls were talking about how many times they had been through this before.

Disgusted, Rabbit closed her eyes and prayed to her babies. *How could these girls live with themselves?* She had seen her babies and it was breaking her heart. She knew that she was making the most responsible decision. Still, it hurt terribly. *How could they possibly talk so casually about getting an abortion. This is a really serious thing.* She had absolutely no respect for these girls treating abortion like a form of birth control. She had used birth control. It had not worked. She took the whole situation very seriously and promised herself that she would never do this again.

It felt like they all sat in the little room forever, but eventually, nurses began shuffling them all onto hospital beds separated by curtains. Laying on the cold hard bed, Rabbit closed her eyes. The lights were bright above her and she prayed that it would all be over quickly. One of the nurses, told her that they would be hooking her up to the IV now. She told Rabbit that she would wake up needing to go to the bathroom, but cautioned the girl to be careful not to get up too quickly.

"Make sure to call a nurse for help. Don't try to get up by yourself." Rabbit felt a strange coldness moving into her veins and then everything went black.

I have to pee really bad! Rabbit opened her eyes. She felt a little dizzy. The IV was not in her hand anymore. She started to sit up. The room spun fiercely and she quickly put her head back down. "Hello?" she heard her own voice echoing in the cold room. A nurse moved quickly to her hospital bed.

"You have to move slowly" a voice warned her. The nurse helped her get up and get to the bathroom door. Moving into the bathroom, she tried to assure the girl, "You will be fine" and closed the door behind her.

Leaving the clinic with Mama, Rabbit felt tired and extremely depressed. *I have just done something awful.* She was sure she made the right decision, still she felt horrible about it. The compassion that her mother had shown her prior to the procedure seemed to have turned to cold indifference on the ride home. Every bump the van hit made Rabbit sick to her stomach. Mama and Will decided it was now time to give her the talk that she had expected from Dad when she had first called him for help.

The *"have you learned your lesson"* attitude they showed Rabbit, cut her deep. Didn't they understand that she was going through severe emotional pain? This had been a traumatic experience for her!

Will seemed more interested in hurrying up and getting her back to the apartment so that she could stay home with her little brother, while they went to the Dead Show.

They went back to the apartment. Rabbit spent the evening babysitting. As soon as she was able to get her brother to sleep, she left her body. *I'm done being here, in pain. I need to feel free. I need to leave my sorrow behind.*

The following evening was New Years Eve, and Rabbit returned to the parking lot at the Oakland Coliseum for the Dead show. She didn't talk to people. She tried for a little while to somehow acquire a ticket, without results. She thought perhaps she could find someone she knew to hang out with. She was depressed and alone, and feeling like she really needed a friend. She spent most of the night just walking around. She talked to herself a lot. And cried a lot.

Late in the night, people poured out of the Coliseum after the show. Rabbit wandered around trying to find Will so she could ride back to the apartment with him. She couldn't find him anywhere. Afraid she would miss him, she walked out to the street where cars were pouring out of the parking lot. She never saw his car pass her by. Cold and exhausted, she gave up trying to find him, once she realized that all the cars had left the lot.

Rabbit had missed catching anyone she knew and now she would simply have to trek across town on foot. *Walking across Oakland in the middle of the night on New Years Eve does not feel safe.* She was cold, hungry, and tired and afraid to stop anywhere. It was early morning by the time she reached her mother's apartment. She slept most of the day in the apartment.

Rabbit decided that she needed to go someplace healing. She packed up all of her gear, informing her mother that she was going up to Mendocino. "I promise, I am only going to be gone a week. I just need to spend some time in the woods." Mama didn't say much. Rabbit headed across town, catching a bus down San Pablo Avenue. Getting off in

Albany, she walked the rest of the way down to the Gilman Street on ramp and set her bag down against the railing.

Hitching up to the Mendocino, Rabbit detoured up Navarro Ridge to visit the places she had found tranquility in the past. She walked past the field that would be filled with daffodils in just two months. She returned to house they had rented. Walking quietly up the driveway, Rabbit scoped out whether anyone new had rented it. It was still empty. She found the remnants of what her mom and Will had left behind when they fled back to Oakland. She picked through stuff, looking for anything that might be useful, edible, or perhaps she could sell or trade with someone on her adventure.

Hitching down Navarro Ridge she headed into Mendocino. Rabbit walked to the bakery to see if she would know anyone there. She searched for her old friends, and found that she felt again like a stranger in this town. She went to the school to talk to her old teacher. "I have made a lot of mistakes." She asked, "Is there any way I could try again to finish school here?"

He tried to explain the complications of how she would have to have a host family and a local address. It wasn't impossible, but it would be very challenging and take a lot of commitment on her part. He questioned whether that was something she could handle. He was right to question her commitment.

———— ∞ ————

Asleep. Dreaming of fire dancing around me. Flames inside me. The spark flies. My eyes left wide. Open. To the pain of my reality. Keeps twisting, churning, filling me.

Eyelids burn. Why run? Away from the demon that catches. Miles away. Dig down below. The surface of existence lies to me. Truth to another. Face. What you are afraid to touch. Isn't there. Any other way to create validity is to spurn imagination. Destroy your weaknesses. Where is the key? In my mind. The door you cannot see. When you interpret the soul. To disillusion thy self. Destroy the reality. Delusion. Breaks down the walls of your future. And what of my past? Where can I hide? From my emotions. Follow me nowhere. I'll take you there. I know the path well.

Rabbit ran into Cole. He had his own car. They drove around and smoked and talked and listened to music on his tape deck. Eventually, he had to go to work and dropped her off. She went and visited with a couple other friends that she ran into. One in specific had also developed a considerably unhealthy drinking problem. They spent an evening drinking and talking. Rabbit tried to tell her old friend "You are a beautiful intelligent person and you will do well. You just need to take better care of herself."

Rabbit had looked for Richard and had been unable to find him. She decided to just head up to Comptche and hope for the best. Rabbit wasn't able to get in touch with him and headed to his house, praying that it would all work out okay. Eventually she landed on the doorstep of someone who had been one of her best friends in Mendocino. They had talked for hours on the phone, from their respective houses. He shared himself with her and she loved that they could talk about things for hours. She had felt attracted to him, and in competition with him. She had been glad for their friendship and was hoping that she would be welcome.

Richard's mother invited Rabbit in, assuring her, "You are always welcome here!" Richard didn't seem as thrilled with the surprise visit. She could tell right away that he felt uncomfortable, and it made her feel awkward. Thankful for a safe place in the woods to recuperate, Rabbit tried to tell him, "I don't expect you to entertain me. Just pretend like I'm not here. I just needed to be away from everything."

Rabbit spent time talking with Richard's mother. She napped and read on the couch. She offered to help in the kitchen. Eventually he came around and suggested they go downstairs and hang out. The two played pool together and talked a little. Things loosened up, and then became more awkward. After an clumsy drunken night of overstepping boundaries, Rabbit excused herself and hitched back down the hill.

The trip down to the bay area was a quick trip compared to many of the past couple years. It wasn't long before Rabbit was dropped off close enough to the Bay Area to get access to public transportation. Like a great magnet, Berkeley drew her back. The center of an ever-spinning vortex, no matter where she went, Rabbit always returned to Berkeley. This time, there was unrest among her people.

⟩(●)⟨

Rabbit heard a rumor that Mama had left town 'to escape the cops'. Concerned for her family's safety, she headed to Oakland to check it out for herself. When she arrived at the apartment, Rabbit was mortified to find it empty. There was nothing left behind. *I was only gone a week and she left town without telling me. They could be anywhere. Was I not important enough for them to stick around? What about my little brother? Is he okay?* She returned to Telegraph to look for answers and found none.

Rabbit wandered around the Bay Area in a daze. She was depressed. She felt lost wondering what happened to her family. She spent some time hanging out in front of the Old Berkeley Inn site. A few weeks dragged by while she spent the days on the streets and nights in the alleys, or in motel rooms with other heads and freaks. Her romantic interests changed from week to week, as she made new friends in passing.

Rabbit didn't see Jasper much. She started tagging along with some of the hippies that had been friends with Will. Hoping to find some kind of clue as to where Mama had disappeared, they headed to San Francisco. Hanging out on Haight Street, hustling for Will's old friends provided a temporary distraction. Things got hot and they headed back across the bay to Berkeley. After a week or so of getting no information from them, she began to feel like she was wasting her time.

People continued to ask Rabbit almost daily if she was pregnant. It struck a painful chord, and she became defensive. *I am just shaped this way! My body is hideous.* She spent a lot of time using hallucinogens to leave her body behind. Floating above the group of hippies, she wondered if they could tell that she had left her body. She began talking with other deadheads about Spring Tour. She wanted to go this time.

Perhaps I will find clues about Mama on tour? Maybe I'll run into her at a show!

In front of the Old Berkeley Inn site, Rabbit laid out her blanket and made camp during the day. Careful not to block the sidewalk too much, she organized a display of patch-work hats, bags, and wallets. She spent the morning sitting and sewing patchworks from clothes that she had dug out of the free box in People's Park. She babysat other folks' backpacks. People brought her food and intoxicants. Friends would come by and hang out for a while, and then move on. Her blanket was like a shop, a destination, a place to meet up with other people.

Rabbit spent a few days at a time with someone, and then she'd move onto hanging out with someone else for a few days. She sought out other people who had been friends with Will. Hoping they would give her some new insight on the whereabouts of her mother, she poked and prodded with little success. What she got instead was com-pany, adventures, and attention. They fed her pills and pow-ders and liquids.

Rabbit met a guy whose face was half-paralyzed. He was traveling with a group of friends in an RV. She wanted to travel with a group like that. She enjoyed talking with them, and Jack's story was intriguing. She knew she still had to find clues about her mother's whereabouts, and she wasn't going to find them traveling north with these guys. She sug-gested that perhaps they would meet again on the road somewhere.

Dad had given Rabbit a leather bomber jacket for Christmas. She traded it for a pair of leather moccasins. Someone gave her a bright orange frame pack, so she was able to consolidate a lot of her gear. Her bedroll fit nicely on the bottom of the pack. The new packing system would make traveling much more manageable.

Cat began hanging out with a cute little hippie boy from Alabama named Harold. He was sweet, and she hoped to travel with him to the South for the upcoming Spring Grateful Dead tour. One morning, she found out that Harold had left in the middle of the night with his crew. They were heading out to Georgia.

Hanging out with some other folks who were equally tired of the scene, Cat again began to plot an escape. *Berkeley is a black hole. It's fun for a little while, but seems to suck the life right out of me. No matter where I go, I always end up back in Berkeley.* Rabbit's new friends agreed to help her escape with them.

Sitting underneath an overhang the group tried to stay dry from the everlasting rains. One of the guys showed up, breathlessly announcing that he had found them a ride East. "This couple is going to Florida. They said that they could drop us off in Georgia along the way. But we have to get ready to go now!" *We are going to make it to the East coast for Spring Tour!* Rabbit was too excited to ask any questions. They packed up their gear and headed out to meet up with the potential ride.

Loading up into the car, Rabbit was surprised at how nice the car was. She hadn't known any hippies or freaks with cars this nice. *There is air conditioning, heating, and cruise control!* They piled their bags into the trunk and loaded into the back seat. A young scrawny fellow was driving and his girlfriend sat in the passenger seat up front. They made little conversation as they pulled onto the highway. Satisfied with the thought of making progress, Cat let herself fall asleep against the cold window.

Chapter 27

NO LINE DANCING

When Rabbit awoke, they were pulling into a gas station in Auburn. They all got out to stretch their legs while they got gas. The girl asked if anyone else could drive for a while. "My boyfriend has a fever and needs to rest."

Rabbit responded that she knew how to drive, but she didn't have a license. The driver responded "That's okay. Neither do I." As he climbed into the back seat, Rabbit took his place in the driver's seat.

Pulling back on the highway, Rabbit was careful to use the cruise control. She didn't want to get pulled over. Winding up the slow highway into the mountains, the other passengers slept. *I wonder how someone could buy such a nice car without a driver's license. Something isn't right.*

As the needle moved down the gas gauge toward the E, Rabbit watched for signs indicating another gas station. Pulling off the highway into a small station in the mountains, Rabbit tried to rouse the sleeping passengers. "Does anyone need to go to the bathroom?" A couple of hands raised from the half-sleeping bodies.

Parked at the gas pump, Rabbit asked their hosts if they had money for the gas tank. They responded that they didn't have any money. Between change that they dug out of the car, and a little bit from the other guys, she managed to put a few gallons into the gas tank.

Pulling back out on the highway, more questions ran through her head. Pulling over state lines into Nevada, her anxiety heightened. *Something is terribly wrong with this situation.* Everyone else in the car was asleep.

Rabbit pulled off the highway and onto a small side road. *I'm just going to leave this group. They are all asleep. I'll just pull my bag out of the trunk and sleep somewhere on the shoulder. In the morning, I will continue to hitchhike on my own.* She didn't trust the group she was with and wanted to get away from them. Pulling over onto the shoulder, she turned off the car.

"Why are we stopping?", asked a voice from the backseat.

Rabbit didn't answer. As she reached for the handle to open the door, police lights lit up behind them. "What do I do?," she panicked. So did everyone else in the car.

In the back seat, the guys were cursing. "Fuck! Fuck! What are we going to do?"

Rabbit responded that she was the one in the driver's seat. Why were they so freaked out? "Because the car is stolen!" they responded.

Oh shit. And I am the one in the driver's seat. "Thanks a lot guys! You could have told me sooner!" And the police were tapping on the window. "Get out of the car with your hands up!"

Before she knew it, Rabbit was pinned on the cold hard ground. Icy wind blew through the thin fabric of her pajama pants. The policeman was firm and loud. She was crying. She told him the same story over and over. "I was trying to hitch a ride to Georgia and these folks offered. Then when the driver got a fever, they asked me to drive." He asked her for her information. She gave it to him, crying the whole time.

Scared and cold, Rabbit rode cuffed in the police car. When she got to the juvenile detention center, she asked where the other guys were. She was informed that they were all over 18 and had gone to jail. The intake officer asked her all the same questions the policeman had and more. He wanted to know how to get in touch with her parents.

Rabbit provided no further information. She insisted that she didn't know where her parents were. She kept crying and saying she wanted to die, so they put her in solitary confinement. Rabbit was allowed to come out for food and one hour of social time per day.

They other girls in the detention center were mean. Rabbit didn't try to talk to them. She asked where the guys were and was informed that 'the boys' were kept separately on the other side of the facility. *I don't like it with the girls. They all seem a lot rougher than me. They all brag about the bad things they did to land in here. I was simply in the wrong place at the wrong time.*

During social time, all the girls had to iron. The girls ironed clothing for the girls and the boys. Rabbit had never been fond of ironing, now she hated it even more. *I am never going to iron anything again. Ever.*

After about a week, the folks at the detention center were able to track down Dad. After about another week, he appeared for the hearing. Sitting in front of the judge,

Rabbit was asked the same questions that she had been asked before. She told the same story without deviation. "I had been hitching to Georgia and these were the people that I got a ride from. I didn't know the car was stolen. I know it's wrong to drive without a license, and I understood why it's wrong. I won't make that mistake again."

The judge told her that once the owner of the car had gotten his vehicle returned he had dropped the charges and everyone else had been released on their own recognizance. There were a few things the judge didn't understand. "Why were you trying to go to Georgia? Why didn't you provide information for your parents? You couldn't possibly *like* being here?"

Rabbit looked down, fidgeting with her hands. She didn't know how to respond. *I didn't want my dad to know I was in trouble. I would have provided information for my mother, if only I knew where she is.*

Rabbit was nervous. Sitting in this small room before a judge, sitting next to Dad, she felt the overpowering strength of disapproval around her. She didn't like being there. In fact, she hated it. The Juvenile Detention facility for the Reno, Nevada area was rougher on her than being on the streets. She had spent the majority of the past two weeks, in and out of manic states of depression and rage. Locked in a small stone room, she had been cold and miserable.

It's true that the chances of running into a dire situation were much greater on the streets. But on the streets she had the freedom to stand up for herself, and the opportunity to try and run away. In here, she was locked in a room. She was forced to interact with people she didn't know, who didn't want to know her. They felt like very mean and close-minded girls. On the streets, there were poets and free-thinkers, outlaws and criminals, young and old. On the streets, Rabbit got to hang out with the guys and be part of a group. Here she had been caged in despair.

When Rabbit told the judge that she was traveling to Georgia to go to a Grateful Dead show. The judge laughed at her. Telling her to go find something else to do, she added, "Jerry Garcia is too old for you anyway." *What is that supposed to mean? Did she really just say that to me?*

Rabbit remained calm and spoke very little in the courtroom. Apprehensive of Dad, she wondered what he was going to do after this. They had notified him of her whereabouts a week prior. He had let her sit in there for another week. She shifted in her seat.

The judge announced that Rabbit would be released into the custody of her father. He would have to pay for her release. She was appalled. *The other folks in my group were not all adults. Some of them may have been, but I know at least one of guys was underage. They all lied and ended up in jail! A couple of days in and they were released. I told the truth and had to spend two weeks in here. What kind of bullshit is this? Now Dad has to pay the facility for taking care of me for two weeks! I should have just lied!* She was frustrated about her own honesty. She was positive the release bill was going to make Dad even more angry about the whole situation.

After the hearing, Rabbit was escorted to a room where she was given her belongings and the opportunity to change back into her own clothes before leaving. Of course, her bags and bedroll had been lost with the car. She would not be able to get any of her traveling gear back. *I might as well go back to California with Dad. Without my gear, I've essentially lost my house anyway!* After being left alone in the room, she went through her "bag of belongings." As she changed back into the thin pajama pants, Rabbit recalled how cold it had been the night she was arrested. She shuddered. *What is going to happen now?*

Rabbit was called from the holding room. As she was brought into the lobby, she saw Dad paying the cashier. The lady behind the window could have been selling tickets or collecting for the electric company and it would have felt the same. So clean and transactional, she felt like a commodity, or a stereo being purchased back from a pawn shop. Dad looked stern and remained quiet.

⟫⟨⟨❶⟩⟩⟪

The ride back from Reno felt much shorter than she had expected. Dad explained that she 'had to do something.' He was taking Rabbit back to Walnut Creek. He was not going to let her 'just run off and be on the streets' again. She was going to stay with him. He would not charge her anything, but she would be required to make some changes.

"You have to either enroll in school or get a job. Which you choose to do is entirely up to you. However, you have to actively do it."

Rabbit rode, quietly listening. There was no reason to argue with Dad. She was overwhelmed with the idea of trying to go back to school. *He knows that I'm going to do whatever I want to do. He just doesn't want me heading out with no money in my pocket. His point is valid. Traveling with nothing is not the most fun.* Tired and finally someplace that she knew was safe, Rabbit fell asleep. As the truck neared the house she grew up in, she began to wake up with a crunch in her neck. *Coming home.*

——————

At first Rabbit tried to follow the rules. Her father had made his point clear. She had to do something with her time. It was her choice whether she went back to school or got a job, but she had to actually do it. She was too embarrassed about going back to school so far behind her peers. Convinced that going to school in the suburbs would be a hell that she could not handle, she agreed to look for work.

Walking around during the day, Rabbit looked for help wanted signs and filled out a couple of applications. She was terrified handing them in. She was sure they would think it was a joke, like she was pulling a prank applying for the job. *I bet they just look at my application and joke about it with their co-workers while they rip it up and throw it away."Who fills an application with the name "Firecat". Is this a boy or a girl?"* She truly believed that she would never get a call back.

Walking all over one town got old fast. As the sun beat down through the cool spring wind, sadness filled her. *Wouldn't it be wonderful if someone I knew just happened to be driving by? They would pull over and holler for me to get in. Then we would hang out, talking and catching up on old times and new times. And they would see me for who I am and like me. It will never happen. I am alone in this town and the only people that would know me will only point and sneer.*

Wandering past storefronts in Walnut Creek, Rabbit looked for places that had hiring signs posted. *Wouldn't it be cool if I could get a job at the coffee shop? Maybe then I would make some friends in this town? Things might not be so bad if I had someone to talk to.* The coffee shop was not hiring. She checked a few other places. Filling out an application in front of the clothing store, she got nervous. *They aren't even going to call me. My clothes aren't nice enough, not trendy enough. I don't look enough like a girl.* Walking back into Clothestime, Rabbit was greeted a second time by the hesitant clerk. She politely accepted the application and dismissed Rabbit as if she were a customer. "Thank you. Have a good day."

⸻ ⸺◦⸻ ⸻

Once a week, Dad attended a country & western dance class at the horse club on Mt. Diablo. He decided that he would take his daughter with him, since she was there anyway. Dad's girlfriend wasn't all that interested in taking the class, and this would give his daughter something to do. He didn't really present the idea as an option, and she didn't waste energy protesting. She needed him to love her despite her failures.

At first Rabbit was apprehensive. Dancing with Dad was awkward. He led and she was supposed to follow. Instead, she kept leading. He got really frustrated, trying to show her how to follow. *I'm not doing it on purpose!*

Rabbit felt sure she was disappointing her father. Still, by the time they were heading down the hill, he seemed happy. Animated from dancing, he talked to Rabbit about different dances as he drove them home. *There are so many different kinds of dancing. He doesn't really expect me to remember all this, does he?*

Dad continued to chatter about dancing as Rabbit fell asleep against the window glass. When they arrived home,

Rabbit was quick to find her bed. Sleeping solid, she woke late in the morning the following day and lingered around the house for several hours. *This house is too spooky. I don't really want to go out job hunting, but I'm not sure I can handle being here alone.* Memories of sadness haunted her.

Dad had turned Rabbit's old bedroom into his office. Heading down the hall toward the office, convulsion of emotional pain rippled through her spine, stealing air from her chest. She paused to catch her breath, leaning her head against the wall in hall. "God make it stop." She closed her eyes and was slapped hard with memories from only a few years prior.

Standing in the hall. Banging my head against the wall. Harder. Harder. And again. I just want to pass out. I want to hit my head so hard that it kills me. Maybe if they came home and found me dead on the floor they would start to care about me. It'll never happen. Nobody cares about me. I could disappear today and no one would ever notice. I might as well be dead.

Pain shot through Rabbit's chest. She opened her eyes as they filled with tears. *God damn. That is not a memory I want to relive. Is there no place in this house that isn't haunted with depression?* Instead of going into the office, she turned into the guest room to grab her cigarettes, sunglasses, and jacket. *I am not ready to deal with people, but I've got to get out of this damn haunted house!*

Sitting on the back porch, Rabbit lit a smoke and looked for the sunniest spot she could sit. Stretching out in the sun like a cat, she listened intently to silence. Hanging out in the back yard, she allowed her thoughts to wander. So many questions and she couldn't focus on any of them. Blurry, they continued to evade clarification.

After exhausting walking routes in Walnut Creek, Rabbit began to spend time wandering around Pleasant Hill. *Maybe I can get a job at the Bowling Alley?* They were not hiring either. *The movie theater is too big and intimidating.* Fear kept her from entering several businesses. Another week passed, and Rabbit was off to the dancing class with Dad again. This time, she was looking forward to it.

Rabbit didn't want to admit to herself that she was actually enjoying a country and western dance class. She could admit that she liked being able to spend quality time with Dad. They had gotten very few chances to spend time together. *We used to go to the Baseball games.* She had lost interest in going to baseball games when hanging out in Berkeley became more interesting. Going to the games had felt like 'kid stuff' to the young teen, who had been more interested in parties.

Rabbit managed to learn the basic principles of the two step and country swing. She didn't get any better at following a lead, but Dad didn't seem any more disappointed than he had the first night. He laughed when they stumbled and smiled while they danced. She decided that swing dancing was worth learning, and vowed to stay away from line dancing at all costs in the future.

A couple weeks of wandering around Contra Costa County, looking for work had not produced any interviews or call backs. With Dad's help, Rabbit navigated her way through the forms to file income taxes. Excited to see she would be receiving a return, she started quietly making plans for the money. Internal dialogue impacted her enthusiasm. Dad was beginning to question her effort and she began to lose her desire to get a job before Summer tour. *At least I will have the money from my tax returns to take with me on tour.*

Every couple days Rabbit actually put effort into looking for a job. At least it gave her something to focus on, some kind of regular structure. Perusing the classifieds was disheartening. *I don't have retail experience and I don't want to work in fast food.* She didn't want to work anywhere that she had to pretend to be something she was not. The problem was she had no idea how to present herself, or what job would be a good fit. Another week passed and she still had not found a job.

With no faith in the possibility of actually getting a job, auto-pilot led Rabbit back to Telegraph. *Maybe I can get a job in Berkeley?* Heading up toward the Ave, she looked in windows for Help Wanted signs. *Nobody seems to be hiring around here either. That's okay because I'm gonna leave anyway.* She decided to linger and chat with vendors as she made her way toward campus.

Talking with one of the jewelers, Rabbit showed an interest in his wire work. After chatting with him a while, she had managed to talk herself into something of an internship. She agreed to come and do piecework for him, and he agreed to teach her different techniques. He said that he had worked with other young people before and he didn't mind. She was excited about it. She was remained cautious, keeping an eye on the time. Trying to be respectful of Dad's rules meant that she would have to show up back home before it got late.

Riding back on the subway train, she considered whether to tell him about the jewelry work. *He'd probably get mad that I went to Berkeley when I'm supposed to be looking for work. He might force me to go back to school.* That was the last thing she wanted to do. *School was hell and I'm never going back.* She decided to lie and simply tell him that she had walked around but she couldn't find any new hiring signs.

After a few weeks of this, Rabbit finally admitted that she was enjoying the weekly dance classes. Secretly, she was glad that nobody she knew could see her there. If anyone asked, she would tell them that Dad forced her to go with him. She had started to open up to Dad a little, but she felt uncomfortable whenever he gave her a chance to talk. It was much easier just listening to him ramble on about whatever topic was on his mind that evening. She really didn't want to disappoint him. She began to feel like she had been there too long.

⚬≪◈≫⚬

Going to Berkeley a couple of times a week had given Rabbit some time to learn jewelry techniques. She had acquired some tools and supplies. Working on little pieces of jewelry in her spare time had afforded her a small collection of trinkets that she could potentially trade.

Slowly, she began gathering all the things she thought that she would need on tour. Losing her travel bags in Reno meant that she had to start all over. *This time I am going to do it better.*

Chapter 28

SUMMER TOUR

When tax returns arrived in the mail, Rabbit was ready to leave. Packing up and heading out, she didn't even say goodbye. Sleeping in late, and leaving while Dad and his girlfriend were both at work made it easy to avoid confrontation. She knew he would be disappointed, but she wasn't going to stick around for the lecture. Waiting at the bus stop on the corner, she prayed the bus would come before anyone drove by that knew her.

The subway was the safety zone. Once she was in the gates, Rabbit could feel freedom. She could go to Berkeley, she could go to San Francisco. She could go anywhere. She was free again. Auto-pilot delivered her to the Rockridge station. Waiting at the bus stop in the windy corridor under the subway tracks, she watched all the passing people.

Everyone has a purpose. Everyone seems to know what they're doing, where they're going. I still have no idea. I mean, I know I want to travel. But at this very moment in time, I really don't know where to start.

Soon on a crowded bus, Rabbit avoided eye contact until she was moving for the exit door. Relieved to be back on the street, she wandered toward Telegraph looking for familiar faces. She made her way to the corners frequently populated by heads and freaks. *Somewhere nearby, I'm bound to find a friend.* She craved acceptance, acknowledgment. She wanted someone to hear her, see her, feel her just the way she was.

Nearing the strip, Rabbit's blood began to heat up and accelerate. Like oil pumping through her, she could feel her gears getting ready for the road. *I can't leave yet. I don't know where I am going.* Patchouli coated melodies drifted by as she approached a group of heads hanging by the old annex. Instinctively, her steps slowed to a casual rhythm. *I can do this. I've got this.* Smiling, she allowed herself to let go of anxiety and trust herself.

Shifting into her just-another-guy-in-the-crowd mode, she shuffled up to the guy at the end of the line. "Hey now brother. You got a smoke? I got a quarter." She smiled, holding the quarter between her fingers. The exchange was made. "Thanks bro." Rabbit set her bags down against the building, perched on them, and lit the smoke. She hovered for a while until conversation made its way to her end of the line.

I wonder how long it will take for them to realize I am a girl? Maybe they won't notice. Then a pretty girl walked up. The stranger was lovely. Underneath the thick layers of jacket she hid a thin gender-less frame. Her hair was short and blond. Her features delicate, with amazing eyes. Rabbit was immediately struck. *Sit down next me! Sit down next to me!* She tried to stay calm and casual as the girl approached.

As the stranger added herself to the end of the line, Rabbit got the opportunity to talk with her. "I'm Erin." She was so easygoing that Rabbit forgot to be nervous. Forgetting for a moment that gender might be a problem, she began flirting with the new person. To her surprise, Erin responded shyly with a great big smile and scooted a little closer. The day waned away as the two talked. Everyone else seemed to disappear.

Getting up and walking, Erin and Rabbit talked more. Hiking up in the hills, Rabbit shared the glorious view with her new friend while they talked even more. *Where did she come from? This lovely person likes me just the way I am!*

Erin never commented on Rabbit's gender. She simply acknowledged her as a person. Emotions danced and swayed in Rabbit's chest as they kissed. Intertwined in the roots of a great tree with the Bay Area spread out before them, she wished the moment would last forever.

The air began to get chilly and they headed back down to the civilization. They had not had their fill of each other and expressed this clearly with one another. "Just one more day," Erin said, "and then I have to get back to my itinerary." She was staying at a hostel in San Francisco for just one week, and then heading back out on the road to her next destination. "I am just not done enjoying you yet."

Giddy, Rabbit responded, "I would go anywhere with you."

Taking the subway into the city, they made their way to Chinatown. Sneaking her new friend into the hostel, Erin crept quietly down the hall to her little room. Once inside, they shed most of their layers and crawled under the blankets on her cot. Spending half the night lost in each other, and the other half lost in dreams, the two had to lay very close to fit on the cot. Waking up early, Erin smuggled Rabbit back out of the hostel before first light.

Hand in hand, Rabbit and Erin wandered the streets of San Francisco until they ran out of things to say. Almost all of a sudden, they both loosened their hands and let go. Their conversation began to shift toward parting words. Erin stopped and kissed Rabbit deeply, one last time. "Thank you for a lovely experience" they both said to each other. Then, almost as suddenly as Erin had appeared, she was gone.

Rabbit was happy. She actually felt happy. She was practically skipping. *Well, I am in San Francisco now. I might as well head up to Haight Street. Will circulated himself in this area as well. Maybe I can find clues about my mother there?* Instead, she found Jasper.

After the affirmative experience of spending two days with Erin, running into him had felt serendipitous. *Things are getting better!* He was staying in an apartment off lower Haight with a couple of other guys. It didn't take long for them to end up walking into his apartment together.

Before long, days had passed. She had felt really good when she found Jasper. Rabbit stashed away her tax money, saving it for summer tour and set her sights on convincing Jasper to go on tour with her. Acceptance was exactly what she had been craving. She needed to feel loved.

Drinking and powders and sex quickly consumed their time together. The intoxication was blurring her perception. She began to feel an urgency. While Jasper was at work, she wandered around San Francisco.

Rabbit spent hours hustling for a few dollars, some smokes, and a good buzz. A couple of hours before his shift was up, she began making her way across town toward the shop where Jasper worked. She would be there waiting outside when he closed up shop, and they could walk back to the apartment together.

Hanging out on Haight Street felt hollow and lonely. While she was able to hustle, and fit in with the guys, eventually one of them always decided to hit on her. Rabbit didn't want to flirt with them. She didn't want them to even recognize her as female. She just wanted to be one of the guys. She decided that she would try going to the gay part of town. *Maybe I'll have better luck there?*

Wandering down Castro Street, Rabbit felt intimidated by the change of scenery. These people didn't look like people she was used to talking with. There weren't groups of people that she could simply join the way that she did in Berkeley. Maybe she had come to the wrong place? Sitting on some steps, she watched people going by and tried to work up the courage to panhandle. Eventually, the day was over. With very little change in her pocket, she headed back across town to meet up with Jasper.

⸻))《◆》((⸻

Rabbit decided to perform an experiment. *I'm not going to give up on the Castro yet.* "Jasper, I need to borrow one of your shirts. Do you have any button up shirts?"

He handed her a shirt that was clearly too big for her, as she attempted to tie down her breasts with a scarf. He raised his eyebrows, shrugged his shoulders, and commented, "That doesn't look very comfortable." He had learned that Rabbit came with quirks, and there was no use in trying to understand her motives.

"Thanks! This will have to do." She grabbed the shirt from Jasper, and put it on the floor next to her. Squatting in the mirror, that was leaned up against the wall, she examined her work. *If I could just eliminate this cleavage.* He reminded her not to mess up his shirt, as he didn't have a lot of nice button ups, and proceeded to get ready for work.

"Don't worry! I won't mess up your nice shirt."

The two left the apartment together, walking toward the smoke shop. When they reached his job, Rabbit kissed Jasper and wished him a good day before continuing up Divisadero toward the Castro. *I wonder if I will do better if I pretend to be a guy. Today I am going to be 'Charlie.'*

As she walked up and over the hill, past the hospital, she tried to prepare herself for the coming challenge of talking to people. "Today is going to be great! I can do this! I've got this!"

Rabbit reached the big intersection at Embarcadero. Crossing the street, she passed the theater and peered down the sidewalk at her perching options. *Where should I sit?* She saw there were others who clearly had taken up post on certain corners already. *This is not my territory. I have to find a spot that isn't already someone else's spot.* Finally she settled on the same steps she had perched the previous day.

As Rabbit talked to people that day, she introduced herself. "I'm Charlie..." She tried talking with people but folks on the street seemed to be too busy to stand around and talk with her. They had places to go and things to do. Watching women walk by with hands clasped touched her. Rabbit wanted to feel that comfortable with herself. Watching the men walk by with hands clasped confused her.

As the day passed, Rabbit was distracted by her wandering thoughts, several times forgetting her goal for being there. She was supposed to be making money, but she was barely trying. Her thoughts raced with questions. *What if I was supposed to be a boy? What if God made a mistake?* She remembered being in Middle School and telling people that she had been born both male and female. *They said I was crazy.*

Hanging out on the street in the Castro, she found the some of the men attractive. She felt sure that none of them would give her a second glance. She found the interactions between the female couples attractive in another way. She liked watching them and tried to imagine what it would be like to have 'a real life, with a regular girlfriend.' The women who had time to talk with her seemed very nice, almost tender. They asked her name, but nobody questioned whether she was male or female.

After spending a couple of days doing this, Rabbit was revisited by an unexplainable depression. The partying at night was wearing her thin. She had too many questions going through her brain to be able to handle the static of the city. *I have to get out and get back on the road so that I can think, so I can breathe.* After spending another drunken night fucking and fighting, she packed up her stuff and left Jasper behind in San Francisco.

———————•《()》•———————

Following the ocean down the coast, Rabbit made her way south. Santa Cruz greeted her with misery at sunset. Hopelessness seemed to linger in the air, in the shadows, and in the rubble of the remnants of Loma Prieta's handiwork. Wandering up and down the boardwalk, she looked for people that felt friendly to her. Failing to find anyone with whom she felt a connection, she wandered out into the darkness of the beach.

Lying her blankets under a lifeguard tower, Rabbit fell asleep listening to echoes of people in the distance. When her bladder woke her, in the early hours, she was refreshed by the quiet sound of the ocean. She dug a hole in the sand, wrapped the blanket around her, and relieved herself discreetly. She filled the hole with dry sand and began packing up her bedding. Walking back up to the boardwalk, she predicted finding no answers in Santa Cruz and resolved to continue heading South.

Hitching down the Capitola Highway was slow. When Rabbit finally got a ride, it only took her as far as Monterey. The town did not feel friendly to her. After hustling up some food, and finding a bathroom, she headed back to the road. The afternoon was fading fast and she might as well have been an alien. When she finally got a ride, they said they were only heading as far as Big Sur. She took it, just to accomplish movement.

It was already dark when Rabbit got dropped off in Big Sur. With the exception of a couple of small businesses on the side of the highway, it seemed more like a road sign than a destination. The woods were beautiful. If she had not been so hungry and depressed, she might have actually enjoyed her surroundings.

Something spooky about the place made Rabbit nervous. Her stomach was twisted in knots. Walking slowly around the bends of the narrow winding highway, she searched for a safe place to camp out for the night.

Sleep was awkward and painful. Leaning up against her bags, Rabbit had fallen asleep with only one blanket over her. Cold dampness clung to her bones. She wanted to be warm. She wanted to eat something. She wanted to feel safe. None of that was happening here. There was little traffic and even less people. If she was going to get out of here, she would have to do so on foot.

— ‹‹(⦿)›› —

Little splashes of sunlight peeked through the trees. Walking warmed her some, but did nothing for Rabbit's stomach. It had been a couple of days since she had eaten a good meal. It was easy to avoid facing her demons when her mind was distracted by the immediate necessities of food, shelter, and movement. Her sadness provided no clarity. *If I could just find a warm place to sit inside and eat, I would feel so much better!*

Sometime in late morning, a car pulled over. The driver said he was heading inland. Rabbit took the ride, just to get back in motion. *So much for following the ocean.* He drove wildly along the back roads heading east. Rabbit's bladder beat fiercely against the inside of her groin, as she clasped the side of the seat quietly for a couple of hours. When he finally dropped her off, she thanked the goddess for protecting her as she watched his car drive away back onto the interstate.

Foggy darkness had settled over the valley as Rabbit walked along the off ramp. Ducking underneath the cloverleaf, she was able to take shelter in the shadows for the night. *I've gone far enough. The possibility of getting a safe ride at this hour is not worth the effort.* Hollow winds echoed against cement while she hid her head underneath the cover of her sleeping bag.

Morning presented a vast landscape of tall grass. Assessing her surroundings, Rabbit peered down the road and prayed for a good day. The highway cut through the fields like a river of lava, warm asphalt glistened in the early morning sun. It was going to be a hot day in the valley, with little shade offered on the road. *Please bring me a long ride in an air conditioned car. With kind people? I could really use a break. Someone with food maybe?* Packing up her bedroll and fastening it up to her bag, she prepared for the day's journey.

Rabbit made her own path down the hillside over large clumps of dirt and weeds. Approaching the on ramp, she double checked for any oncoming traffic. *No cars for miles.* She crossed the pavement and followed the shoulder about halfway down the on ramp. In the distance, the hazy image of a gas station danced like a mirage near the next exit. *Maybe walking to the exit will increase chances of getting a ride? Or maybe some food? A bathroom with a sink would be fantastic! I really need to wash my face and hands.*

It felt like an hour before she reached the gas station. The boarded up building covered in cobwebs was an immeasurable disappointment. *Coffee and a toilet? Is that so much to ask? Maybe some running water? I give up.* She walked all the way around the building to look for a safe place to squat. After finding a hidden corner and relieving herself, she returned to the front of the abandoned gas station.

Rabbit put down her traveling gear. Sitting on her backpack, she pulled an apple out of her side satchel and rubbed it against her shirt. *Saving the fruit for every now and then will only last so long. Where the hell am I going anyway?* After eating the entire apple except the seeds, she tossed the seeds into the grass at her feet. *Grow little apple seeds! Take over the world with your roots!*

Reloading herself like a pack horse, Rabbit headed back to the on ramp, and a more visible location. Sitting on her backpack, with her side satchel in her lap, she laid down her head and waited for a car to pass. Watching to make sure it wasn't a police car before sticking out her thumb, she monitored traffic and prayed for a ride.

After a couple of hours, someone pulled over. Bland and harmless, they offered an air-conditioned ride with little conversation. *Thank you Goddess!* It was over 100 degrees in Valencia when they dropped her off by the shopping center. Rabbit was done traveling for a little while. Reaching some kind of civilization meant that it was time to get more supplies.

━━━━━《《◉》》━━━━━

Making her way to the grocery store, Rabbit sat in front and hustled up enough money for a little bit of food. As she walked through the store, she felt all eyes on her. *They expect me to steal from the store. They want me to steal from the store, just so they can have an excuse to mess with me. I'm not that stupid. You can't set me up folks!*

At the register, she was courteous and friendly with the clerk. "I don't need a bag, thank you. Save a tree right?" she remarked as she gathered the groceries into her arms and walked out.

Across the parking lot, a lone tree was positioned near the entrance of the shopping center. Setting up underneath the tree in the grass, Rabbit proceeded to lay out her blanket for a picnic. She carefully placed her bags at one end, and her shoes along the outer edge of the blanket. As she ate her lunch, she pulled jewelry from her backpack and began organizing it on the blanket in front of her.

Finishing her lunch, Rabbit packed the remaining food away, and replaced it with her jewelry making supplies. Water bottle at her side, she sat in the shade making jewelry and watching cars as they drove by. A couple of people stopped by and looked at her wares. One person bought a necklace for $10. A couple of others made small talk and then moved on without buying.

The digital display at a nearby bank blinked 108 degrees and then 5:30 pm. *What am I doing? I don't really know where I am. The man in the last car said that downtown LA is right over the hill from here. But I don't know if I really want to go to Los Angeles. What am I searching for? I know I want to be happy, but right now I feel exhausted and lonely.*

A truck with a cab-over camper pulled up, covered with stickers and parked in a slot adjacent to the tree. *This is definitely a freak wagon! Maybe I will meet some cool people and find a place to crash for the night?* Excited, she jumped up from the blanket and headed toward the short man as he climbed out of the truck. She recognized Jack right away. "Oh my gosh! What are you doing here?"

"I was just about to ask you the same thing!" Jack replied as he reached out to give her a hug. He followed her over to her blanket. Hanging out in the shade, they talked for a while under the tree. She shared her road stories since San Francisco and he explained that he was originally from Valencia. After a while of talking, she was packing up her gear and climbing into his truck.

Hanging out with Jack could be fun for a little while. They parked in front of his mom's place for a couple of days, hanging out with local friends. Then they headed over the hill into the valley and spent a couple days parked in a friends driveway. Every day was a different party. No real purpose or goal, except to enjoy each moment.

The week long party came to a head with a kinky weekend somewhere outside Palm Springs. By Monday, Rabbit was pretty exhausted. Partying for a week straight had run her ragged. She got Jack to drive her to Santa Monica where they parted ways.

Santa Monica was fun before, and the weather was agreeable. *Hanging out by the boardwalk is like being on Telegraph Avenue. The big difference is here, there's a beach and girls roller skating in shorts and bathing suit tops!* In the early morning hours, the street folks creaked and grumbled. Most of the storefronts didn't open up until 10 or 11 am, so the early morning city belonged to the freaks and appeared as destitute as their empty pockets.

Sunglasses and hangover peppered the street corners like empty bottles and dirty napkins. A week of sleeping on the beach was more than enough to get the full experience. Hippies were starting to migrate away from the city and Rabbit decided to make one last trip North before heading out on Summer Tour. *One last attempt to get Jasper to join me on Summer Tour!*

——— ⋙«⦿»⋘ ———

Thumbing back to San Francisco delivered Rabbit safely back into Jasper's world and she immediately began trying to convince him to come on tour with her. "It will be an experience you will never forget," she insisted. He pointed out that he was not a hippie and didn't really get excited about the music the way she did. "You always have fun at the shows. How can you turn down an adventure? Do you have something better to do here?"

The time spent waiting for departure crawled at a snail's pace. Powders infiltrated her daily life with little hesitation. By the time they headed for the Bus Station, Rabbit was exhausted and begging for the change of pace. Convinced that traveling would help her distance herself from the temptation of the addiction, Rabbit was jumping out of her skin as they climbed aboard the bus destined for Las Vegas.

It was a long uncomfortable bus ride. After what felt like forever, the greyhound drove through downtown Vegas, making its way to the bus station. Rabbit's anticipation was renewed peering out the window. Dead heads on every street corner inspired her to daydream about the upcoming adventure. Getting off the bus, they didn't know which way to go and began wandering the streets with their gear.

Socializing with other hippies, they managed to find people willing to give them a ride to the stadium. Arriving on Dead Lot felt like returning home. *The traveling city always feels like home. I know that everything I need can be found here.* Rabbit immediately began wandering in search people she already knew.

Jasper and Rabbit went into the first show together. The desert heat would have been unbearable, had it not been for the line of sprinkler hoses strapped around the inside of the stadium. Dancing in the cool spray, hippies laughed together with dripping clothes. Wandering through the crowd in direct sun dried her clothes quickly and Rabbit returned to the refuge of the sprinklers frequently.

The next day, Rabbit ran into Jack in the parking lot. He was searching for a miracle ticket. Picking up speed as she recognized him, she called out and greeted him enthusiastically. Overjoyed, he hugged and kissed her, spinning her around clumsily. Soon they were catching up on the last few weeks of events and she was shoving a ticket into his hand.

Still exhausted from the previous day, Rabbit decided she needed some time to wander and search for a ride heading east. She had gotten into the show the night before and was satisfied with the experience. It seemed like the right thing to give her ticket away to him. Jack thanked her as he locked up his truck.

"You should probably hurry up and go. The show is starting soon!" she urged as he headed toward the stadium.

——)(●)(——

Within a couple of days, Jasper and Rabbit were heading east in a VW Van crammed full of freaks. It wasn't the most uncomfortable ride. Everything seemed to be going fine until they got pulled over and searched by state troopers in Nebraska. The travelers stood in the brisk windy twilight watching the drug dogs, and waiting with anticipation for whatever was going to happen next.

After spending over thirty minutes tearing everything out of the van, and spreading the mess on the side of the road, the troopers decided that they could not find any reason to detain the group of travelers.

The officers said, "You are free to go." Then they drove off, leaving behind the mess. It took a while to gather everything up and put it all back in the van. *Nice of them to destroy our stuff and then make us clean it up.*

It had gotten dark and very cold. The travelers complained about the fiasco as they re-packed the van. When they finally pulled back onto the highway, they were all glad to be warmer and moving. They were very nervous driving the rest of the way through Nebraska. When the van pulled over state lines into Iowa, the passengers all cheered and started breathing again.

It was raining when the van arrived in Buffalo, New York. Driving through town, they found that many locals were charging folks to park overnight on their property. Allowing camping, meant that Dead Lot was protected by the lines of private property and it could go all night. The only thing keeping the party from getting out of hand was the cold rainy weather.

The first show in Buffalo was getting ready to start by the time they were piling out of the van. Rabbit and Jasper did not make it into the show that evening. During the show, the two traveling lovers wandered away from each other.

Rabbit found Harold from Alabama. She was so excited to finally find the boy that she had wanted to catch in Georgia earlier in the year, that she forgot about keeping track of Jasper. She followed Harold around like a puppy and by the end of the night, he had made arrangements for her to ride along with him to the next show. Waking up in the morning in his tent, she quietly emerged in search of Jasper.

When the two travelers found each other, Jasper was clearly unhappy about Rabbit's disappearing act the previous evening. He had hung out and made friends with other people and made his own arrangements for traveling to the next venue. With ruffled feathers, they went their separate ways on the adventure of Spring Tour. It didn't take long for Rabbit to separate from her Alabama boy. She soon found that she was making friends and moving on much the same way she had in her previous travels.

After hitchhiking from one Dead Lot to the next, every venue seemed to have become the same city over again. It had been a novelty at first, when the experience was new. Now, it was the same people, plus a couple of new people, at every location. People came and left tour like they would any other city. It began to feel destitute, almost desperate. By the time Rabbit reached Chicago she was tired of it and ready for a change.

Rabbit ran into Jasper again in Chicago. She was traveling with a small group, and he invited them all to join him at his father's place in the city. While camping and hotel room parties had their appeal, it was getting to be exhausting. It was rejuvenating to be in a residence, eat regular food, take a regular shower, and sleep inside a home.

They all visited that evening and took off for Dead Lot the next day. The concert was great. The experience had been totally worth the effort. Still, Rabbit was ready to get back on the road. This time, she did not want to head to the next venue. Strung out and beat down, she was ready to leave tour.

———————≈((◊))≈———————

Convincing one of her new friends, Annie, to travel with her, Rabbit found a ride heading to Colorado. Several other travelers had a similar idea about leaving the tour early to go to the National Rainbow Gathering. It was pretty easy to find a ride to the gathering, right off the Lot. A couple of days later, the two girls were hiking up a hillside through a stream of hippies and naturalists.

Pitching a tent together, and piling their bags inside, Annie and Rabbit went their separate ways. Wandering together only for a little while, it felt perfectly natural to pursue their own interests. Eventually landing in the same tent, they talked a little but mostly just snuggled and went to sleep. The slow pace of the gathering was nice at first, but within a week the two girls agreed that it was again time to travel.

Hitchhiking out of Rainbow proved much more difficult than getting a ride there. The two headed to Oregon. After a few days, and a couple of rides that made Annie nervous, they were happy to arrive in Eugene. Nothing interesting was happening, so they headed back out on the road. The two girls pointed South with the traveling gear and thumbs out. They were pleased to catch a ride with a cool hippie driving a cargo van, all the way to the San Francisco Bay Area.

Chapter 29

NEW CAR, NEW JOB

Annie accompanied Rabbit to Dad's house in Walnut Creek. They arrived the day before Rabbit's eighteenth birthday and Dad accepted both of them without question. The two girls stayed in the small spare bedroom, sleeping on Rabbit's old bed together.

On her birthday Dad took them to the Alameda County Fair. They looked at everything, ate all the bad food, and went on rides. When they got back to the house they were exhausted. The two girls collapsed onto the old bed and wondered what would happen next.

After resting a little while, Rabbit got up, leaving Annie lying in bed. She went out onto the back patio for a cigarette. Dad came out there to talk with her.

"You are an adult now. What are you planning on doing next?" He inquired.

Rabbit didn't know. She rambled off a list of ideas. "You can stay here, but it will cost you $50 per week. That will include utilities. You will have to get some kind of a job."

Rabbit listened to what he had to say. He went back in the house, leaving her alone on the back porch. She finished her cigarette and went back into the bedroom. *Dad was so nice all day for my birthday. Then he had to end the day like this!* She told Annie they would stay for the evening and then leave the following day. *Thats ridiculous how much money he wants! Why should I have to pay to stay in my own fathers home?*

The next day, they headed to Berkeley. Sitting on the train, Rabbit thumbed through a newspaper. *I am an adult now. I guess I better stop fucking around and actually get a job and a place to live. I'm an adult now? I was never able to figure out what being a teenager was supposed to feel like. Now I have to figure out what it means to be an adult. This is it. No turning back now.*

She flipped through the rentals and was appalled to find how expensive apartments were. She moved onto rooms for rent. Once she started actually looking at rent prices, she quickly realized what a cheap deal that her Dad had offered. Pride kept her from going back.

It only took about a week of late night shenanigans in her old Berkeley stomping grounds and Annie had enough of Rabbit. She was falling back into a pattern of misery and substance abuse that Annie had not witnessed when they had been traveling together. Her behavior led to more than one brush with the police. Highly intoxicated, Rabbit's behavior was less than exemplary, to the point of being abusive.

Annie was done. She left Rabbit alone, returning to traveling with the same fellow who had given them a ride from Eugene. It hurt in a way Rabbit couldn't understand. She immediately repressed her feelings, pushing forward on a rocky path of self destruction. *Well, that's fine. I'm an asshole. She is better off without me anyway.*

⸻⸻•《●》•⸻⸻

Earlier that year, Rabbit had learned of a house where people got paid to do kinky stuff. It was a fantasy house, not a brothel. She had been assured there was 'no sex happening there', that it was all 'strictly legal.' Girls working there got paid to tie guys up and whip them, or dress clients like great big babies, or one of a variety of other kinky fantasies. She had decided that she wanted to try it out. The catch was she had to be 18. *I'm 18 now! Why not?*

Rabbit tracked down the right people and was able to get an interview at the fantasy house. She had an address and vague public transit directions. She had a difficult time finding the place and was surprised at how little the house stood out in the neighborhood. *If I had blinked I would have missed it.* She wondered whether that was on purpose.

Rabbit felt awkward and excited entering the house. *It looks just like a house on the inside too.* The living room had been transformed into a waiting room. She was led through the living room and kitchen, to sit at a small dining room table, on the far end of the kitchen. Occasionally a woman in little more than underwear walked into the kitchen and made short conversation with Rabbit and the manager before disappearing into somewhere else in the house.

The manager asked Rabbit why she was interested in the position. She made up answers, trying to sound grown up. *I don't really know what I'm looking for. I just need a safe place. I need an income. I need to be a grown up now. Please just give me a chance.* Her feelings of self worth were intrinsically intertwined with her sexuality. She tried to pretend to be strong and confident.

Rabbit was ashamed of herself and she didn't understand why. The other girls were beautiful and she felt ugly. She liked feeling wanted and thought it would be a great self esteem booster for her to get paid in the process.

"And you will have to choose a new name." the manager explained to Rabbit. "You can pick it. But it has to be something that nobody else knows you by." She thought about it for a little while and responded. "I like 'Myriad'." *A myriad of delights. I am sure I can do anything if I just put my mind to it!*

The manager explained the rules of the house, and that none of the girls were ever allowed to have sex with or solicit clients. She let Rabbit know that they worked hard to keep their operation strictly legal in order to maintain a safe space for everyone. *Yes. Safe space. That's what I need.* There was something exciting about the opportunity to explore fantasies with the safety of knowing that she wasn't going to be forced to have sex at the end.

All the 'girls' took turns answering the phones and setting appointments for sessions with one or more of the 'staff'. The phone was an inbound phone line only and was not to be used for personal calls. The 'receptionist' was never allowed to identify herself to the caller. Whomever was booking appointments was instructed to book sessions based on the clients' fantasy not the girl, using a matrix of boundaries to determine which 'girl' was the best person for the client. Each 'girl' was expected to be honest about their boundaries and not to sign up for anything that they were not comfortable doing. It was essential that everyone involved was comfortable with the situation or it was not appropriate.

The manager explained that it was the responsibility of the person doing the session to properly clean up a room immediately after, so that the room would be ready for the next session. Each room was equipped with a cabinet full of all the tools and toys anyone could possibly want or need for most basic sessions. Rabbit was intimidated by the sheer numbers and organization of it all. She misinterpreted her reaction as an internal challenge.

"The only other thing that you will need to change is your hair." The manager explained. "I can see that it has been dyed blue. Now it's fading to green. You will have to change your hair to a more feminine color."

When Rabbit first started working at the House, she had a tough time with transportation. It did not take long for the boss to agree to let her sleep there overnights as long as she was discreet and clean. She would stay for a few days at a time and then take off on her unscheduled days. The income enabled her to begin saving for a car.

The manager taught Rabbit how to drive, and took her to get a Driver's License. It was extraordinarily helpful. She seemed to be the type of person that helped a lot of people. The girl was very appreciative and thanked her repeatedly.

"Remember, I only help people that are making an effort to help themselves," her boss responded.

⸻ ((◦)) ⸻

Rabbit found a car in the newspaper that was cheap enough for her to afford. $800 for a 79 Toyota. She made the call and set up an appointment to go and meet the guy, and take a look at the car. It was a manual transmission. *I don't know how to drive a stick shift car, so this will give me an opportunity to learn!* It was pale yellow, the color of Mexican beer. The Toyota Corona was a sedan with a good sized trunk. *This is perfect for me!*

Rabbit explained to the guy selling the car that she was trying to buy her first car. She asked if he would be willing to take payments. He agreed and drafted up a sales agreement outlining the payments. She would get the car when she had paid seventy five percent. She would get the title when she had made the last payment. She was overjoyed and gave him the first payment.

Rabbit visited once per week with money until finally she had paid it off. *Now I have a car to live in! This is a step up!* Rabbit drove out to Walnut Creek to show Dad. She told him that she had been working, but omitted the details of her job. She thought that he would be proud of her, when he saw that she had managed to do all this without his help. He seemed skeptical, and she left feeling determined that his opinion didn't really matter anyway.

Rabbit decorated her new car with bumper stickers. She began to collect stuff with the money she was making. She bought more undergarments and high heels for work. She bought more records. Even though she didn't have a record player, these were treasures to her. *I can't wait until I have my own apartment. I will have the best stereo and I can listen to all these records! But for now, this car is my apartment, and it is better than sleeping on the streets. It's totally my space.*

Late at night, Rabbit pulled up to the curb next to the People's Park and parked in plain sight. She made sure all her doors were locked before crawling into the back seat, covering herself so completely that anyone passing by would not see her sleeping, but only see a pile of stuff in the back seat. In the morning, she emerged from the blankets and began to organize for her day. Folding all her blankets and taking inventory of her basic necessities, she prepared to leave the safety of her car.

With clean clothes in her day pack, she headed to the juice bar. *Fresh squeezed orange juice to start my day. If I don't eat much it's important to eat well.* Next stop was the Cafe' Med for breakfast. Rabbit ordered breakfast, got her coffee and headed upstairs to the restroom. Changing clothes and freshening up in the tiny bathroom was a challenge. She tried to be to be quick and discreet.

Coming out of the restroom, Rabbit searched for a seat upstairs in the smoking section. Going down the stairs to pick up her food, she read the posters for demonstrations, punk shows, raves, classified ads and random poetry that plastered the wall at the bottom of the stair well. Somewhere in the middle of all the postings, a bold print notice asked people to be responsible and manage postings in an organized manner.

Sitting along the upstairs railing, Rabbit watched the door and windows as she ate breakfast. She searched for someone she might know. She was always hoping to spot something that would bring a feeling of comfort or familiarity. Most days she didn't actually see anyone she wanted to talk to. *That's okay. I am probably better off without the distraction.*

Rabbit congratulated herself on the effort of a normal routine and began to the mentally prepare herself for going to work. She got up and placed her empty breakfast dishes in the bus bin by the restroom, making room on her small table for her notebook. *Journaling every morning is a good habit. If I ever want to do anything with my writing, I had better get in the habit early on.*

She tried to use her notebook as a tool to sort out the abstract bits of emotion that swam around in her. She didn't know what she was supposed to do, but she knew she wanted to feel in control of herself. She lit another cigarette and took a sip of her latte. *Cold already.*

A desperation tugged inside her chest. It seemed that she was missing something. Not really sure what she was supposed to be looking for, self judgment convinced her that she must be doing something wrong. Rabbit packed her things back into her day bag and headed back down the stairs. Leaving the Cafe', she paused briefly to talk with the blanket vendors across from the juice bar. They seemed mostly focused on the short term goals of a single day. She made small talk without investing much into her words or theirs. She knew it was time to aim for more than one day at a time.

The rumor mill whispered traces of stories about Rabbit's family. She didn't know whether to believe the stories that trickled through the grapevine. Glad to finally have some idea of where she might be able to find her family, she was disturbed by some of the things she heard. *Who knows what the truth really is?* She filtered bits and pieces and determined that she could find her mother in Lawton, Oklahoma. *Why the hell would Mama go to Oklahoma?*

Rabbit made her way back toward her parked car. She didn't want to hear any more stories. More people tried to talk to her, but she was ready to leave. As she opened the door to her car, another person tried to strike up conversation. Having a vehicle was a sign of wealth in this community and she was not overflowing with abundance. Another ten minutes of verbal shuffling and she was able to get her car door closed again.

=◄((◉))►=

Driving from Berkeley to San Pablo could have been a short trip if Rabbit drove a direct route. However, learning to drive a manual transmission was a slow process. Rabbit was nervous that her lack of experience would increase chances of getting pulled over. She took back roads through the neighborhoods that peppered the lower hills. Winding through small streets offering great vistas, she made her way from Berkeley to Albany, to El Sobrante, and then descended into the backyard of San Pablo.

The whole trip took about an hour. Rabbit liked the meandering routes. Driving more slowly than the main street traffic gave her the opportunity to enjoy architecture and landscaping. Pulling up to the curb a few houses down, she grabbed a day bag packed with costume garb for the day's sessions. Attempting to move silently and discreetly from car to house, she carefully closed the white picket gate behind her.

Although she didn't feel a connection to any of the other girls, Rabbit knew she was safe in the House. She took comfort in the safety, but somehow felt like she wasn't good enough to be there. Thankful for the opportunities the job was giving her, she still felt a great sadness walking into the building. There was a dread that she couldn't describe following her. Despite the illusion of safety, they still had to generate enough revenue to maintain the monthly bills or the place wouldn't survive.

For every client that arrived for their appointment, there were three who never showed up. Sometimes the phone rang often. Some days the phone was silent for hours. They all waited, hoping that another great day would sweep through the house, lifting all their spirits. Occasionally, one of the girls would get a client who liked golden showers. They'd offer to tip an extra $20 to every girl who could urinate on them. All the extra girls would sit in the kitchen gulping down big cups of water, waiting in line for their $20 turn.

Rabbit's first month working at the house was an anxious experience for her. The boss took Rabbit under her wing. She helped her to gain some self-confidence, a driver's license, a car, and a basic sense of integrity. By the second month, she was mobile. The feeling of freedom that accompanied her mobility played tricks on her. She expected her ability to move freely would loosen her heavy heart. Still, the hidden anvil in her chest grew larger and heavier.

Playing fantasy games on a daily basis was pushing buttons that Rabbit didn't know existed. She got a thrill out of some sessions. Whereas, other types of fantasies left her feeling ugly and worthless. She didn't understand the roller coaster inside herself. *This job was supposed to help me figure some things out about myself. Why am I getting more confused?*

Rabbit understood that different people processed stress in different ways. *What we are doing is a public service. I should not feel bad about it because I am helping people relax in ways that are unique and personalized.* She did not judge herself for her actions. Instead she judged herself in comparison to the other girls. *I am surrounded by strong, beautiful, amazing women. Why do they terrify me?* She wanted them to accept her into their world. Something kept her from being like them. They sensed her distance.

Some of the girls tried to include Rabbit socially. Joining a group of her coworkers one evening, Rabbit found herself in an apartment in Oakland. The girls all seemed comfortable with their bodies. Sitting around half-dressed, talking about feminism and gender equality, she felt alienated. Her reverence of the female form felt like it was rooted in an entirely different garden. The girls may have tried to include her but she didn't feel the effects of their efforts. Somehow she managed to excuse herself from the evening early on. Crying in her car as she drove up to hills, she questioned her inability to connect with her peers.

What is wrong with me? I want so much to feel accepted. All the energy she spent searching for common ground left her feeling exhausted and empty. *There is no common ground. I feel like a young man in disguise, spying on these fantastic women.* She felt dishonest. Something inside her was sure that if they found out how she felt, she would be fiercely ejected from what little sanctity she had found in her current routine.

The pain inside sent Rabbit reeling. Driving through the hills, the twinkling lights of the Bay Area shone like a solar system below her. Pulling into Inspiration Point, she turned off the motor and wiped her face. Something was wrong with her. Her sexual identity was trying to work itself out. The more she asked questions, the more confused she got. *All those people driving around the bay, shining stars below me, they are all free. They know where they are going. They all have a purpose.*

She felt like the only person in her world. *Here in my world, I am completely alone. Traveling across the country and back, up and down the coast, in and out of the cities and the hills, I have covered all this ground soul searching. Why do I feel like I have made no progress at all?*

Eventually, Rabbit decided to return to the Ave. Coming down out of the hills, she let herself head back to the center of her gravity. Parking next to People's Park, she locked up her car and wandered down to Telegraph. *The guys on the Ave recognize me as a part of their world. What details make these interactions different? Do these people know me better?* She didn't require as much courage to face guys like she did with girls. When Rabbit felt rejected by girls, it reminded her of her own internal isolation. When guys rejected Rabbit as a female, it didn't bother her as much. She didn't care about whether they thought she was an attractive woman. When the guys did pay attention to her feminine characteristics, she put them down for it. Strangely, she was more interested in them relating to her as a peer. Of course, this didn't make any sense to her. It probably made even less sense to them. Still, they weren't really paying attention to what was important to her.

Chapter 30

OLD HABITS DIE HARD

Rabbit wandered down to Miller's Outpost to see who was hanging around. This was the place she knew she could find respite from her pain. *Someone here will have something to make me feel better.* There almost always was something that made her feel better. She had been hiding from her pain with different substances for a few years now. Tonight, she needed something especially strong. The pain had become intolerable.

Powders came to visit her hiding places, numbing wounds that Rabbit couldn't see. The evening carried over into many more and before long, her boss was showing concern. She could see that Rabbit wasn't doing well, but the young woman could not see it for herself. She allowed powders to give her a false sense of control. *If I can find a way to tackle my fears, I'm sure to discover the strength I need to overcome this misery.*

A couple weeks of using powders regularly and Rabbit began to feel more disoriented than she had before. *Why is everything so confusing?* The aching in her chest grew deeper and darker. Looking in the mirror, she caught a glimpse of what her boss had been talking about. *I am forgetting self care. I have to keep an eye on that.* She attempted to push herself through another regular morning routine of juice and breakfast. She forced herself through the motions of her job. She pushed her limits every chance she got.

The powders were not providing the same numbing effect, and her pain was pushing back. She had to use more and more to hide from her misery. Rabbit felt trapped by her fears. She began making a concentrated effort to identify her fears specifically. *If I can identify and overcome each one of my fears, systematically, I can cure myself of whatever is wrong with me. Whatever that is keeping me from being happy will go away if I can extinguish my fears. So what is so big and scary that I am afraid of?*

Rabbit was terrified of needles. One of the street dealers convinced her that she would enjoy the high so much more intensely if she used a rig. Engulfed in the anger at her own inadequacies, and the determination to overcome them, Rabbit talked herself into getting fixed with assistance. Moving into the shadows of an alley, the dealer showed her how to prep the powder for the needle. As he fixed her up, she shook with fear and tension. As he pulled the needle out of her arm, her head spun faster and harder than she had expected. Her internal pain was replaced with an overwhelming feeling that she could accomplish anything.

Coming into work after being up all night did not make Rabbit any prettier. Rabbit's boss could see her sliding downhill fast. She tried to talk to Rabbit about her goals. "What is important to you? Where do you want to be going?" Nothing really got through to her. She was experiencing a strange combination of feelings after her sessions.

Rabbit started to feel really dirty. Memories of a naked man holding her down haunted her. There was something that cut through her like a rusty blade every time a client called her a 'Dirty Bitch'. *What does it mean? Why does it hurt so much? This isn't being forced on me. These sessions are completely within my control, and I am being compensated fairly. Why do I feel so worthless?*

———————◦《◎》◦———————

Rabbit had a repeat client that was paralyzed from the waist down. He spent weeks saving up to come in and spend just thirty minutes at a time with her. She understood his need for being in control. Rabbit felt great compassion for him as he put clothespins on her breasts. She could see his excitement as tears rolled down her face.

Five, ten, fifteen pins on each breast, the pain jolted through her nerves. She sat still and obedient, on her knees. She let him place clothespin after clothespin on her breasts, until there was little skin left to pinch. Each time he pinched her, tears welled up as she thanked him for his gift.

When the session was finished, he was always very kind. The man was so thankful to have this place to come and be powerful. Rabbit empathized with his feelings of powerlessness. Yet, she was always glad when he was gone. Her breasts were so sore from thirty minutes of clothes pins. It took a good hour of crying and rubbing her chest before she could force herself into another session.

By the end of the third month working at the House, Rabbit had gotten swept up in the vortex of her addiction to powders. Unlike binges of the past, she was using needles regularly now. She had separated herself from her body so violently that she felt like she was looking at a stranger in the mirror. The crash and burn of substance abuse and self inflicted emotional abuse was taking its toll. Finally, Rabbit went to visit her boss.

"I can't do it anymore. I'm so sorry for failing you. You have been so kind to me and helped me so much, but I just can't keep this up." Rabbit explained, as she sobbed, with her face in her hands.

The manager told Rabbit that she wasn't worried about the house, as much as she was concerned about her 'girls'. She could see that Rabbit was struggling and wished her the best of luck on her own personal journey.

"If you ever need to list the house as an employment reference, simply list the position as Receptionist, and I'll be happy to return any reference check calls." She assured the young woman, as they parted.

Rabbit went back to trying to make money hustling at the Outpost. This did not help her accomplish anything positive. In her state of disorientation Rabbit said things and did things that were not at all in her character. She was dishonest and untrustworthy. People who had known her for years crossed the street when they were walking by. They avoided making any kind of eye contact. She got the feeling people were ashamed of what she had become and did not want to be connected to her. *Now I really am the Dirty Bitch after all.* She was more ashamed of herself than she had ever been before. She decided that she needed someone to love her unconditionally. So she got a puppy.

Getting high had ceased being her goal. Now, Rabbit just wanted the pain of withdrawals to go away. She felt like she was going crazy. When the effects of the drugs drained from her system, she ached like she never had before. She was she sitting in alley, away from the peering eyes of foot traffic. Shaking and twitching, she still needed help shooting up. She didn't want tracks on her arms, so they aimed for her legs.

Rabbit looked away from the needle, trying not to focus on the fear inside her. She saw a used condom lying in a heap less than three feet away. The ground was filthy. Broken bottles lie open, exposed, ants crawling through the bottles, focused on their path, their surroundings did not matter. She closed her eyes. *What is my path? Can I see it? I have no idea where I am going.* Rabbit remembered the old black and white commercials from the last decade warning folks of the dangers of drug use. *I never believed it was really like this. It seemed like a big joke on television.* How could she take anything seriously when it was on TV? Now, she was seriously miserable.

Rabbit sat on her day pack in front of the Outpost. Her new puppy was a source of healthy love and attention that she relished. But he didn't fix anything for her. She was still miserable. In desperate need of a shower, and a good night's sleep indoors, she talked with friends, trying to make arrangements to stay indoors for an evening. She allowed a friend to sleep in her car for the night, since she was not going to be in the car.

When she returned the next morning with her dog and her day pack, she found the car missing. *That asshole! I was just trying to be nice and this is how he repays me!* She was livid. The car had been Rabbit's house. Her record collection was in the trunk. Her blankets had been in the car. All of her extra clothes had been in the trunk.

My entire life was in that car, and now it's gone. Everything that I have worked for in the last few months is gone! In just one night! Her depression dove deep into the pits of her misery. *This is how I am going to die. Probably soon.* Something needed to change. She was terrified.

Rabbit hunted down more powders, but she couldn't find anyone to help her with the needles. She had not overcome the fear enough to fix herself. The guy who had stolen her car was the guy who had been helping her with her needles. Now he was gone and she didn't know what to do. She shoved a fingertip covered with powder into her nose, and then licked her fingers. It didn't get her high, but it did take a little edge off her cravings.

Rabbit wandered aimlessly throughout neighborhoods with her dog. She panhandled when she got the opportunity. She meandered dumpster diving for anything that might be helpful or edible or just plain interesting. Her dog was cute, so that helped a little when she actively tried to get money. A Border Collie and Labrador mix, his all black coat and friendly bouncy attitude made everyone smile. She shared her food with him. He gave him attention and love when she could not love herself.

The wandering began including frantic ramblings as Rabbit started to experience withdrawals. She realized she was in West Oakland and decided to try and find the apartment of someone who might help her out. Aiming and overshooting, doubling back, and eventually finding the right apartment building was not the best thing for her to be doing in this part of town.

People walking eyed her. Police driving by eyed her. She looked like trouble and she didn't seem to be going anywhere in particular. To make matters worse, she was clearly ranting at great length with other people. Only the puppy accompanied her. She began to notice people looking at her and got paranoid.

When Rabbit arrived at her friend's apartment, she was

not well received.

"It's not okay to just show up without calling first!" The woman responded firmly. "You are looking pretty bad. I am not going to extend you any credit. You need to leave now."

Rabbit left quickly and headed back up through shady neighborhoods of crack dealers and poor family homes. Walking for hours, getting lost from time to time, Rabbit navigated by identifying landmarks. *Like jumping across stones in a creek. First find San Pablo Ave. Then Ashby Station. Turn toward downtown. Cut through the neighborhoods. I know I can find Telegraph again.*

Rabbit was angry. *If she was really my friend she would have helped me. I'm in so much pain. I just need something to take away the pain!* As the withdrawals progressed, she felt more and more like a zombie stumbling up the sidewalk. Spasms of emotional pain shot down her spine, from her brain to the tips of her fingers. Rabbit could feel tremors of nausea welling up like storm clouds in her eyes.

Feeling like she was going to vomit hatred out of her ears and misery out of her tear ducts, Rabbit sat in the middle of the sidewalk. Rocking and sobbing, she wrapped her arms around the little dog. He licked her face and tried to take away her pain. After a while, she was able to get up and keep moving. She repeated this process several times in different places along her trek.

Fifteen miles and seven hours after leaving People's Park, Rabbit returned in search of something or someone that was familiar to her. *I need something concrete, something real. Half-out of my body, I'm trapped on a plane just a half-dimension away.*

Reality didn't seem to have much impact on her. She felt pain and hunger but not really. She knew where she was, but nothing felt real. *Like being an extra cast member wandering the streets in Night of the Comet.* She perceived her world as deteriorating rapidly.

Passing by People's Park, there were few in the park. They weren't technically supposed to be in the park after dark, although sometimes people attempted to sleep up in The Woods. Rabbit didn't feel comfortable sleeping in the park at night. She was always nervous the police would come and harass her, or worse, that she would get jumped or robbed. Instead of stopping in the park, Rabbit walked the perimeter scanning for people or cars she might recognize.

Coming down Haste, Rabbit passed the place she had so often parked her little yellow car house. Anger welled up in her, followed by a overpowering feeling of hopelessness. Passing the new chain link fence that separated the outside world from the vacant lot on the corner, she swam through memories of the Berkeley Inn. *The Fire. Torn up mattresses in the hallways. Walking through the lobby with hot chocolate and tea for Mama. The People's Park Annex, last year.* All the time she had spent setting up shop on the edge of the property danced around with pictures of the the men who had worked behind the counter in the lobby of the resident motel.

Rabbit blinked. The empty lot groaned behind the chain link fence as she turned the corner to head to the Outpost. Rabbit looked ahead of her, for someone she could trust. Some of her friends were sitting around among their bags, bundled up to stay warm. She stopped to talk with them, and quickly sat down to join the crew. Scant foot traffic reduced the chances of anyone actually making any money at this hour. Still there was always a hustle in the making. Scheming and planning, they had to create a future in which they could look forward, a place and time where they could exist.

Moving from person to person, her puppy made sure everyone got a chance to pet him. Returning to Rabbit, he was satisfied to lay down next to her. He was probably just as exhausted as she was from walking all day. Still fighting with the edgy pain of withdrawals, she was melancholy and her friends were concerned.

"I don't want to be hooked on anything. I just need this pain to stop." Crying through her words, she was desperate for someone to help her.

———◦《◦》◦———

It took very little discussion for the guys to decide they were going to do something to help. Rabbit had helped so many people over the last couple of years and now it was her turn. She was ashamed and apologized too much. "Don't worry Rabbit. We love you. Everything is going to be okay."

The night was rough. The best they were able to come up with was a little smoke and some vodka. She passed out in the pile of backpacks, while her friends worked together to find something else to help her.

"We're gonna get you so high that you are just gonna pass out and sleep off your withdrawals." Her friends assured her, as she fell asleep in the park.

Three days in a row, Rabbit's friends took turns getting her really high on something entirely different, and then watching over her, her puppy, and her stuff while she slept it off. By the fourth day, she awoke starving and itching to get out of her skin and out of Berkeley.

"I gotta get away from this place. I gotta go somewhere that I can't slip into the same old patterns."

Her friends agreed, with some concern. "But, you are in

no condition to travel."

She insisted that she had to leave Berkeley. *I just want Mama. I want to see her one more time. I need to be able to see that she is okay.* They protested.

"If you have to travel, don't go alone. At least make sure someone is with you." A street rat that had known Rabbit for a few years chimed in. "That'll be me." She knew better than to decline an offer when it came from Gargoyle. She knew she would be safe with him on the road.

The plan was to go to Boulder, Colorado. There were good people there. Getting away from the drama of all the mess she had gotten into, would be a first step in getting healthy. Finding a safe place to land would also be necessary. Rabbit's traveling partner looked overwhelming at first glance, and it took them a little while to get rides. She was thankful for his company and his help. Despite his gruff appearance, he never tried to impose himself on her. Instead he seemed to relate to her as his friend, one of the guys.

Traveling in October was cold going through the mountains. Somewhere in Colorado, it began to snow. Standing by the side of the road, the two travelers shivered. Puppy seemed excited about the flurry of snowflakes. He barked and jumped around, trying to coax them into play. Cars passed more slowly as the snow flurries thickened.

An older couple pulled over to pick them up. *I smell talcum powder and menthol.* They drove a small white economy car. It was a chore squeezing into the back seat, two people and a puppy and all their stuff. The layers of clothing that had protected them from the outside cold quickly proved to be too much for the well heated car.

They were less than 200 miles from their destination. At first Rabbit got excited, thinking that it would be a short ride. Her excitement faded as the snow flurries thickened and the driver was forced to slow to about ten miles per hour. The people up front did not seem like the typical people to pick up hitch hikers. The old couple made a point to state, "we don't normally pick up hitchhikers, but we felt bad for you standing in the snow." Soon the car was not moving much faster than the travelers could have walked, but it was much warmer inside the car.

After several hours of inching along in the snow storm, Rabbits bladder began to ache terribly. Her legs cramped up. Her stomach cramped up and she would have been hungry except the odors in the car were making her nauseous. She prayed that the ride would come to an end. She was quiet and trapped. There weren't any options for escape.

Finally the car made it over the pass, rolled down the hill into Denver, and dropped off the travelers. Scouting the covered darkness under an overpass, they bundled up and fell asleep until sunrise. First light of morning woke the travelers and they headed back out to the highway. Catching a ride up into Boulder, they headed to Penny Lane. Hanging out at the Cafe' was warm and inviting. Folks were accepting and helpful. Despite the cold snow and icy environment, Rabbit felt like she had reached a safe place.

After spending the better part of the day hanging out, Gargoyle and Rabbit were able to track down her friend Polly. Rabbit had met Polly during her travels and had promised to return to Boulder to visit at some point. Now, here she was in the dead of winter, sick and begging for help.

Polly brought Rabbit to a safe house where she could detox, rest up, and ultimately heal in warmth and safety.

Gargoyle stayed on for only a day before heading back on the road. He had delivered her to safety and it was time for him to move on. Thanking him profusely for saving her life, Rabbit hugged Gargoyle goodbye and wished him safe travels.

Rabbit wandered Boulder a little bit during the days that week. Although she spent some time exploring, most of the week was spent inside resting. After seven days of being there, she began to feel trapped. Also, Rabbit believed that she had worn out her welcome in the safe house. Staying for a little while was acceptable, but if she was going to stay for an extended period of time, she really needed to be able to contribute somehow.

———— «◉» ————

Rabbit decided it was time for her to leave. The girls at the safe house seemed concerned about her traveling alone in winter. She was stubborn and insisted everything would be fine. *I'm determined to find my mother. I'm already this close.* Traveling east on 70 into Kansas, Rabbit questioned her own sanity for making the decision to travel. It was really cold everywhere and people here were not quick to give her rides. She felt uncomfortable with every ride she got. She felt like everyone was staring her down, judging her. She was afraid of the whole world. She kept moving forward because she really didn't know what else to do.

Heading south through Kansas on I-35 was especially long and cold. *So much wind and not enough nice people.* For a place where it was supposed to be very religious, the people here struck her as very judgmental. *Why should people look at me like a criminal? They don't know me. I'm trying my best and I don't like being here any more than they like me being here.* Rabbit was terrified she would get arrested and end up getting lost somewhere in a Kansas jail. It took her a few days, but eventually Rabbit managed to make it all the way to Lawton, Oklahoma.

She was exhausted and very cold, arriving in Lawton. She had asked her last ride to drop her off at a convenience store, instead of just on the road. She was looking for a telephone booth with a phone book. The sun had set hours ago and the wind cut through her as she rifled through the phone book. Finding the number was easy, but making the call was a challenge.

Chapter 31

KEROSENE AND CHAIN MAIL

The phone rang. Pick up, pick up, pick up! It's cold out here! "Hello?" The voice on the phone crackled.

"Mom? It's Cat. I'm at this little quickie mart. I just got dropped off here in Lawton, but I don't know where I am. Can you tell me how to get to where you are?"

The girl could hear the panic and surprise in her mother's voice on the other end, as Mama handed the phone off to Will. "Cat? Where are you?"

She told Will where she was, and he told her to stay put, indicating that he was on his way to come pick her up.

Will pulled up in a barrel of a noisy truck. Cat threw her frame pack in the back of the truck next to a dented wheelbarrow and dirty buckets. Her feet stepped up into garbage and tools scattered on the floorboard. The big metal frame rattled and moaned as she slammed the door shut. With no heater, she felt like she was riding in a big old freezer. Sheltered by the wind, and blasted by his loud stereo, she felt the full force of being someplace she knew she didn't want to stay.

Will asked Cat many questions on the way to the house. Where had she been? How did she get there? Had she traveled alone? Did anyone else know where she was? She was angry. They had left without telling her. Why did she have to answer any questions? She didn't talk much. She was tired and cold. She just needed rest from the road.

Cat walked in the door and knew that she was in the right place for now. Looking around the living room, the influence of her mother's decorating style was prevalent. Although the surroundings were not nearly as vibrant as they had been in Berkeley or Mendocino, it was still clearly packed with faeries. Little orphans, dolls, and painted toys filled in nooks and crannies on bookshelves throughout the room.

Mama greeted her daughter with a great big tear-filled hug. Then, with her hands on Cat's shoulders, she pushed her daughter back as if to examine her. "You look like hell."

"Thanks mom. That really helps. I could use a shower."

She picked through her daughter's hair. "I'll say! You have head lice, bad. Take your bags directly to the laundry room, then go straight to the shower."

Rabbit was mortified. She was exhausted. She was ashamed. They set up a cot for Cat in the laundry room across from the washer and dryer. She got cold air coming in from the back door and warm exhaust air from the appliances. Mama seemed disappointed that she had a puppy with her. Taking care of a toddler was already a challenge for Mama. The thought of having a puppy in the house was a stress that she had not expected.

Cat's laundry immediately went into the wash while she headed to the bathroom. Mama found some clothes for her daughter to put on while the traveling clothes were in the laundry. She rounded up an old shampoo bottle, and filled it halfway with shampoo. Pulling a bottle of kerosene from under the sink, Mama filled the bottle the rest of the way with the kerosene. She replaced the cap to the shampoo bottle and shook it fiercely.

"This is what my mother did when I got bugs in my hair." Cat cringed at the smell. "You gotta wash your hair with this every day until the bottle is empty." Her stomach turned. She took the bottle, and thanked Mama for helping.

Standing under the warm running water of the shower, Cat washed off the road and watched her exhaustion pour down the drain. She shampooed her hair with the foul smelling concoction. Large bugs fell out of her hair and washed down her body. Black dots followed the current of water around her feet and down the drain. She groaned. She felt so dirty. She proceeded to put another layer of the kerosene shampoo mixture on her hair, holding her breath as she scrubbed.

Cat talked with her mom and Will a little after the shower. She told them about spending a week in Boulder. She told them briefly about hitchhiking from Boulder with just her puppy for company. They were not happy with the risks she had taken.

"I wasn't happy you guys just disappeared. I spent the better part of the year worrying about you!" She was angry and they were defensive. She retired to bed before too long and sleep overcame her quickly.

⫸⫷

The beginning of November was too cold to be hitchhiking anywhere. Cat spent the next week visiting and catching up with her mom. She shared the story about traveling from Boulder to Lawton. Mama shared stories about the misery of being trapped in Oklahoma. Neither shared many details.

"Will moved us without warning." Mama explained. Things had gotten worse than he had alluded to. She had not known how badly the debts were stacking up. Will had been having trouble finding consistent work and his mother had assured him there was plenty of work in Lawton.

When they first arrived in Lawton, they had spent a few months living with Will's mother. It had taken some getting used to. While Mama and Will's mother got along okay, they did not live well together. Mama couldn't handle someone else standing there telling her how to be a parent. She had experienced the environment as negative and unhealthy. Will had more difficulty finding work in Lawton than he had hoped for.

Mama made it clear that Cat could stay for a while in the laundry room, but they could not afford to support her. "Anything that you need money for, you'll need to come up with on your own." Cat was intimidated by the prospect of looking for a job. She didn't know her way around, and she had never actually had a real job. Working at Kirkle had not required an interview or resume. The work had not required that she conduct herself in a professional manner. Working at the House in San Pablo had been a unique experience that she was cautious not to discuss in detail.

Over the course of the next few days, Cat shared some more of her road stories, carefully omitting incriminating details that might reflect errors in judgment. It didn't take long for Will to talk her into going to work with him. He promised to pay her what he could. She figured it was better than sitting around the house and it was easier than looking for another job.

Will had a workshop across town with all his tools and plenty of storage space. He was proud to show it off to Cat, giving her a grand tour when they arrived the first day. He got out and opened up the big shop doors so he could pull his truck inside. Once inside, he turned on the big lights and closed the big barn style doors. He proceeded to show her every nook and cranny, explaining what his plans were for every item and group of supplies.

Their work day usually started by getting up very early, stopping for coffee and donuts, and heading to the shop to pick up supplies and tools. It was very cold, and they generally tried to get as much done in the morning as they could. Being a stone mason, he was concerned about giving the mud enough time to set up before the evening freeze. Cat was not opposed to working short days.

Red cowboy boots poked out from the bottom of her jeans. A plaid button-up work shirt peeked out from underneath her jacket. Bulky from layering pajamas underneath her clothes, Cat looked larger than she was. Topped with a beanie, there was nothing feminine about her. She didn't spend much time thinking about her gender, and instead focused on working as hard as was necessary to complete the tasks Will gave her.

Much of her workday was spent cleaning and moving rocks, bricks, and stone. Loading and unloading the truck was quite a workout. She began to build muscle and gain weight. Her ability to lift bags of cement into the truck noticeably improved within a couple of weeks. Mixing cement by hand in a large metal tub with a shovel and hoe was especially good exercise for her upper body. She quickly found herself shedding layers when she would have otherwise been cold.

One of the gigs Will got required building a brick mailbox enclosure. The bitter cold offered Will a very small window of time to lay bricks. If they worked too late, the mud would freeze before it set properly, which could damage the quality of the completed project. Consequently, they took three or four days to do a job that could have been completed in one long day, given the right weather conditions.

Across the street from their job site, a small construction company remodeled a house. Will knew the foreman running the show across the street. They made small talk from time to time, leaving the subordinate employees without supervision for short periods. The remodeling crew was using a small electric cement mixer to mix the mud for their stone work. Will bragged about how good a worker Cat was, despite the fact that she was only an 18 year old girl.

The second day on the job, the foreman from across the street razzed his employees when he took them out to lunch. He said that they were slacking off while the "girl across the street" was kicking ass. He threatened to "fire them all and hire her instead." They reacted by stepping up their pace quite a bit. They had been shamed by the comparison.

It made Cat feel good that he was boasting about her work performance. Still, she soured a little at the comparison. "Why is it such a big deal?" He responded that nobody wants to be compared to a girl. She grit her teeth and kept working.

At first thought, the only difference that she might have with the crew across the street was related to her lack of experience. She didn't think that what was under her clothes should make a difference, especially when she looked the same on the outside. When she got hot and took layers off, her breasts gave her away.

A little over a month of working with Will, and seeing very little money to show for it, her enthusiasm began slipping. He had handed her $10 here and there. Cat knew that she should have been making more than that, with all the hours she was putting in. He explained that he had to take care of bills first, and continued to put her off. She felt like she was being used.

———————=((O))=———————

Riding around with Will gave Cat the opportunity to learn her way around Lawton. She had seen a store that intrigued her. She decided she would walk around town and see if she could find it. Traveling across town with icicles hanging off the trees, and the wind blowing, made the walk feel like it took hours. When she found Things Medieval, she was happy to be inside where it was warm.

The store had been set up in a house with a big wrap around porch. Cat noticed right away that the front porch seemed to be a place that people just hung out. The owners didn't seem to mind. She had very little money to buy anything, so she took her time perusing all they had to offer. There were herbs and crystals, books, tarot decks, runes, and trinkets. Artisan crafted items were featured, including various chain mail accouterments.

Cat told them she had just come from the west coast in October, and she wasn't sure how to find people like herself. "So I was excited to find you guys!"

She hung out for a while talking with them and then wandered back across town to her little laundry room and her puppy. She returned the next day to hang out and talk some more. This time, she asked them if they were hiring. They said that she could make chain mail. The owner explained that he paid by the pound, not by the hour and took her in the back of the shop to show her the workstations.

———◦«(◦)»◦———

Cat did not feel comfortable at her family's house. There was something unnerving about Will. *As long as I'm there, they expect me to work for one of them. I shouldn't have to choose between riding along with Will on his side jobs or taking care of my brother so Mama can 'get things done.'* She didn't want to feel taken advantage of. She preferred doing something that could potentially afford some compensation.

Cat began spending most of her afternoons hanging out at Things Medieval. She worked on chain mail and took breaks hanging out on the front porch, smoking and writing. She didn't get more than five dollars per day and often only two or three dollars. Still, they didn't seem to mind if she was chatty. She began to make friends with other regular customers. The shop seemed to be an important social reference point for a slice of Lawton's counterculture. She began to look forward to the coming days.

Talking with folks at the shop, Cat found out about a nightclub called Industrial Dreams. It seemed to be another place, like Things Medieval, that people went to hang out. She was nervous about going into a club by herself. The anxiety of being surrounded by several people she didn't know was a huge hurdle to overcome. Finally, at the end of December, she swallowed her fear and went out in search of the club. She had been saving up for a little while, so that she could afford to go out for New Years Eve. It was a long cold walk across town to find the club. When she did, she was reluctant to turn around and make the trip back anytime soon.

Cat was nervous going into the club by herself. It was an 18 and over club. They served soda for the minors and beer and wine coolers for those 21 and over. She made no attempt to purchase alcohol, and instead opted for a pop. Taking the can, she headed across the room and settled into a chair at an empty table.

Cat scanned the room, hoping to recognize someone from the limited group of people she had met at the store. She saw nobody that she already knew, but noticed that the people seemed to know each other. This place was also full of regulars. Distinctly aware of being an outsider, she felt isolated. Sitting by herself across the room certainly didn't help her blend in.

As the club filled up, people began dancing. *I want to dance. I like to dance!* Cat liked the music they played. Still, she was self conscious. She wanted to be noticed. She wanted people to talk to her, and yet she was terrified of standing out. She had dressed up and put on makeup. She felt like she was wearing a costume, and hoped that it would attract people who would like her.

Over the course of the evening, Cat managed to make conversation with a guy who bought her drinks. He kept buying her drinks until, at closing time, he offered to drive her home. She had no desire to walk home in the freezing dark, and certainly liked the attention. Of course, he was probably way too drunk to drive, but she couldn't see straight, and really liked his Jimmy 4x4. *I want a car like this!*

In front of her family's house, they made out for a while before she poured herself out of his sexy SUV. Stumbling into the house, Cat headed directly for the bathroom. She emptied out her stomach in the toilet. Attempting to be quiet, she stumbled through the living room and kitchen on her way to the laundry room. She prayed for sleep as the room spun. Soon, she was unconscious on the little cot in the laundry room.

A couple days later, SUV guy caught up with her at Things Medieval. They made plans for a date. Cat was excited. *I haven't actually been on very many real dates.* Most of her romantic experiences had been social or simply a matter of intoxication. *This is chance to get to know someone without intoxication.* They went out to see The Last of the Mohicans.

Afterwards, they spent a long time making out in his car. Eventually, they ended up having sex in the SUV. She wasn't terribly impressed by the experience. They never had a follow up date. He never even called and she was only a little upset when it occurred to her that she had been used. At least I don't have to make up an excuse not to go on another date with him.

⸺⸺)((◉))(⸺⸺

Cat began to develop friendships with people that she met hanging out at the store, gradually bleeding into the evening times. She returned to the club only a couple of times before she worked up the nerve to start talking with the gal working behind the bar. As Cat got to know the bartender, she learned that her husband was the DJ and the two of them were the owners of the club. Developing a friendship with the owners led to getting a night job at the club.

By the end of January, Cat was working five nights a week at Industrial Dreams as a server. She began to get attached to the both of the owners. Spending several nights at their place, she developed an emotional relationship with both of them independently. Each relationship was unique and had a strong draw despite their differences. Cat

was physically attracted to the woman, while she was intel-
lectually attracted to her husband.

They both seemed delighted to have Cat there, but
things got complicated pretty quickly. Cat preferred avoiding having to go back to the cot in the laundry room, and
was thankful when other new friendships provided a variety
of couches to crash on.

Working at the club, folks got to know Cat as 'the new
server' relatively quickly. People were nice to her. She began talking with the customers about how much she really
needed new glasses. She complained of headaches. She
hated her old glasses, in bad shape and no longer effective,
she wore them infrequently.

A group of the regulars all got together and pitched in
enough to pay for her glasses. She was so surprised! *It was
$250 for the exam and glasses. I would never have been
able to pay for that myself!* When she got the new glasses,
she made a point to show everyone and thank them all for
their help.

Cat learned of a Cafe' on the outskirts of town. Without
a car, she had to coordinate with friends that were mobile.
They began going out to the Cafe' regularly in the afternoons, before going to open the club. It was a fun little hole
in the wall with red and white checkerboard plastic coated
tablecloths.

The owner offered a very short the menu of hot dogs,
hamburgers, fries, and soda. He also had a limited menu of
coffee choices. He didn't seem to mind when his place was
full of young people. Cat loved going there, and wished that
it was close enough to the middle of town that she could
walk there herself.

Cat made friends ranging from 18 years old to folks in
their late twenties. Her social life exploded as she began

partying with her new group of friends. She went back to the laundry room less and less frequently. Her puppy was left behind and became a burden on Mama. Cat's family was not appreciative.

"You are going to have to get rid of the dog." Will announced one afternoon.

Her family made it clear that they could not afford to care for him. "You are not taking proper care of the dog."

She was briefly angry with them, but could not argue because they were right. Talking with her friends, they located a good home for him, where he would get lots of love and care. *Now I have one less reason to go home.*

Every week Cat was moonlighting with a new couple of friends. The social group that she had been introduced to was a very large community. In February, she met a gal who drove all the way to Lawton from Wichita Falls, Texas. She was in the navy and a very masculine woman. Cat was impressed that Navy girl did not try to get her drunk, instead offering to buy her Dr Pepper.

Cat brought the Navy girl home to the laundry room after closing. They tried very hard to be quiet making love. Navy girl came back every Saturday for the next few of weeks. She seemed to enjoy spending time with Cat. Very few people wanted to be sober and intimate. It felt good being treated with respect for a change.

Chapter 32

NOTES FROM COFFEE

It was common practice for the club employees and some of the regular customers to get together for breakfast after closing time. The bouncer would walk from the back end of the club, making a clean sweep towards the front door.

"If you don't work here, and you ain't fuckin' someone who works here, get the fuck out!" He'd announce with outstretched arms, as he made his sweep.

Two thirds of the people would leave. The close knit group of regulars who were friends of the owners and employees would hang out, sitting in the middle of the dance floor. As the employees worked on cleaning and closing up shop, the social crew stayed out of the way, attempting to sober up before driving.

After locking up, five to ten of them, depending on the night, would pile into cars and head over to IHOP for coffee and breakfast. Taking over a booth, they'd all squeeze in loudly. Sometimes there would be other customers, other times they'd have the place to themselves. Drinking coffee and gossiping about anything and everything, they were a loud profane group. In the middle of all the conversations, Cat would sit and write.

Cat wrote down what she heard with no editing to make it logical. Occasionally she would tell everyone to stop talking, and she would read what she had written so far. Everyone laughed at how crazy the different conversations sounded when they were mixed up together. Notes from Coffee became just as regular a practice as breakfast at four in the morning. The writing inspired her to continue abstract free-writing on her own time.

Weekday evenings at the club were not as busy as the weekends. Cat continued to make new friends with regulars who were not as closely knit with the owners. A beautiful woman with whom she had been flirting with regularly, came in one night talking about photographs. She invited Cat to go with her and some other folks after closing time to go 'play with a camera.'

Cat found the woman attractive and jumped at the prospect of taking dirty photos with her. When closing time came, Cat refrained from going to breakfast and opted for leaving with Camera Girl and a group of relative strangers. Reconvening at Rick's house, one of the club regulars, the group continued partying in their living room.

Cat realized soon thereafter that the evening was not going to play at as she had hoped. Camera Girl was wasted and already having sex in the kitchen with the host of the house. Cat was uncomfortable. She didn't know any of the other people in the house. She had really just come along to hang out with Camera Girl but had no intention of interrupting anyone. Nor was she going to leave and wander across town at four in the morning. She settled on conversing and eventually making out with Rick's best friend, Jim.

The unlikely couple ended up having fun despite their awkward introduction. They seemed to get along okay. He was apparently also a regular at the club. She began spending more time with him, including sober time. The nights were never sober though. She often accompanied Jim to Rick's house after closing time after that first evening together.

———⸱«(❋)»⸱———

Cat was enjoying spending time with Jim, but tried not to be around his best friend alone. She had discovered soon after her first night there, that the host was married. His wife, Mary, was not terribly happy with the way he conducted himself. Still, she put up with the ruckus because several of the people in the social group were also her friends.

When things began to get serious with Jim, Cat felt obligated to break things off with Navy Girl. She did so unscrupulously with a telephone message. Afterwards she felt bad, that perhaps she should have handled it differently.

She informed Jim of her decision. "You had better take good care of me. I broke up with a beautiful woman for you." Then she brought him to meet her mother.

Jim was in the Army, stationed at Ft. Sill, and was the last person Mama expected Cat to bring home. Mama got along with Jim well and seemed impressed by the respect he showed her daughter.

Jim was entirely too big to fit on her laundry room cot. Cat certainly wasn't going back to the barracks with him. So they ended up spending a couple nights a week sleeping together on Rick and Mary's couch. Despite the apparently exclusive relationship that she was building with Jim, Rick continued to hit on her. She was appalled that he would do that. *Dude! What's wrong with you? You have a beautiful wife!*

Cat kept herself very busy with social activities. She spent a lot of time writing. She was intoxicated every night, miserable and running from her misery. She didn't know what she supposed to do next. As an adult, she was expected to 'make something of herself.' Sitting on the front porch at Things Medieval, she hung out smoking cigarettes and writing. Trying to work through whatever had been nagging at her brain, didn't seem to show results. She continued to drink every night, numbing what little feelings she had for herself.

Starting to get worn out by the drama that seemed to engulf the scene at the club, Cat began to hate her job. She only made two dollars per hour, and the tips were terrible. She was lucky to get five dollars per night in tips. Meanwhile, the head waitress seemed to make a whole lot of tips. *She's flirty. I'm flirty. What am I doing wrong? What is she doing differently than I am, to make such a big difference in tips?*

———⊰⟨⟨◉⟩⟩⊱———

A rumor began spreading that the bartender was having sex with some of the regulars, and that was where her "tips" were coming from. Cat was disgusted. *I'm not going to promise favors just to get my tips up. I'm certainly never going to make much money when I'm competing with her!* The club was failing miserably, and her husband was frantically trying to save it. Cat was no longer impressed by the situation and began to wish she could quit. She felt bad about the idea of quitting, so instead, she decided she would just put herself in a position where they would have to fire her.

It was Saturday and Jim did not have to work. The Chainsaw Kittens were scheduled to perform at the club.

I just don't have the motivation to deal with the insane crowds tonight. It's going to be packed! She would have to go in and deal with customers pinching her ass, calling her sweetheart, and tipping her nothing. She didn't have the patience. *Today is as good a day as any to get fired!* They prepared for the evening by spending the afternoon at Rick and Mary's place drinking Vodka and Blue Curacao.

Cat arrived in a large group at Industrial Dreams. Just as she had predicted, the place was packed. A loud line of people waited at the door to get in and pay the cover charge. When Cat stumbled in two hours late for her shift, it was apparent that she was too drunk to work, and had no intention of doing so. The evening was a blur. The next day she tried to remember. *I can't remember them actually firing me. But I'm sure that I don't have a job there anymore.* She didn't end up returning to the club more than a couple times before they shut down for good.

Cat began to revisit Things Medieval and spend more time there again. She also began to actively look for an actual job. She spent most evenings with Jim. In the midst of their drunken activities, the two of them began to joke about eloping. They got the bright idea that if they got married, he would get a pay increase that would enable them to rent a house.

"If I'm married, I'm allowed to live off-post!" He reasoned. "And you will get out of your mother's place."

It's the perfect plan! Over the next couple of weeks, they spent some afternoons when he was off duty, driving around looking for a place to rent. Toward the end of March, Jim managed to apply and get approved for, a week of leave. Just before his leave, they took the necessary steps to secure a big three bedroom house with a wrap around porch.

Cat loved the house. It was only $350 per month. Without warning folks exactly what they were up to, Jim and Cat packed up his little truck and took off on a road trip. Cat convinced him that they should get married in Boulder, Colorado. They pulled into town on March 30th. She directed Jim to Penny Lane, where she was able to track down her friend Polly.

Polly was happy to see Cat again, and agreed to be the witness for the marriage ceremony. Unfortunately, she wasn't able to help them find a couch to sleep on for the night. She offered them her car to sleep in, which had more room than the cab of Jim's truck. In an effort to save money for gas and other costs, they opted for sleeping in the car. It was terribly cold. They woke up early and shivering.

The next day they went to the courthouse and got married. Cat explained that it was 'essential that they get married on the 31st and not wait another day.' She didn't want their wedding anniversary to be April 1st. *People will think our marriage is just a joke.*

Polly stood as their witness. Cat and Jim exchanged vows, signed the papers and then they were married. *What to do next?* The newlyweds started driving west. Making their way across the country, the newlyweds drove towards the sunset. Following a path that she had traveled so many times before without direction, she was now moving with purpose and intention.

Cat was on her way to see her Dad once again. This time, she would show him that she was truly an adult. She had grown up. She had gotten married. She would no longer be moving aimlessly through life. They were on their honeymoon. They would return to Oklahoma in a week and move into their new house. It would be their home together. He would take care of her and she would take care of him.

Cat put her feet up on the dash and lit a cigarette. She looked over at Jim and smiled. *Now my father will be proud of me.* With his left hand on the wheel, Jim stretched his right arm out, and squeezed his new wife closer while he drove. She kissed his cheek and turned up the radio. *This is going to be a great life!*

CPSIA information can be obtained
at www.ICGtesting.com
Printed in the USA
LVHW091608140520
655625LV00001B/60

9 781977 223630